BEAUTY
AND THE
BILLIONAIRE BOSS

by

SERENITY WOODS

ISBN: 9798862124507

CONTENTS

Chapter One

Belle

"Sorry, Belle, I'm not going to be able to pick you up this afternoon," my brother says. His voice through the phone sounds regretful, but that doesn't help my predicament.

"Alex!" My jaw drops with disappointment. "You promised!"

"I've been asked to do a presentation to the Prime Minister and the Health Committee at two, and it'll probably go on for a couple of hours, so I'll miss the ferry."

"Name dropper," I grumble. "Ordinary people just say they've got a dental appointment."

"James was supposed to do it." He's referring to his friend and colleague. "But he's flying to Australia because his dad's sick, so I've had to take over at the last minute."

I huff a big sigh. "It's okay, I understand. I'll have to see if there are any flights available, although it's a bit late notice."

It's the fourteenth of March, and it's only four days until our sister Gaby's wedding on Saturday, which has luckily coincided with the Easter break at university. Gaby and Alex live in Christchurch, which is eight hours from Wellington—half by ferry, half by car. Ordinarily I'd have flown, but I have several big boxes I want to take home for the holiday, and I didn't want to have to struggle across the airport with them. I could hire a car, but I'd have to pay through the nose for it because I'm under twenty-five.

"Keep your knickers on," he says. "I've organized for someone else to drive you down."

"Who?"

"Damon."

My heart skips a beat. Ooh. Damon Chevalier. Alex's best mate. Twenty-six years old. Six-foot-two. The spitting image of the Norse god Thor, or the movie actor who plays him, anyway. Rumor has it that Damon has a huge magical hammer, too—not that I'll ever get to see it.

"He's far too busy to worry about driving me down," I scoff.

"I've already asked him, and he's agreed."

Damon was obviously too polite to say he didn't have the time to escort his friend's kid sister on a journey that should only take an hour by plane but would take eight by road. "Why's he going down so early? I would've thought he'd fly down on Saturday." I know his family own a private jet.

"He's spending a few days at Kia Kaha, helping me with our latest project. He's staying down here till after the wedding."

Kia Kaha—Māori for 'stay strong'—is the company my brother runs with James and his other friend, Henry, in the field of robot-assisted physiotherapy. They help rehabilitate people with impairments using a mobility-aid exoskeleton they invented called MAX. Damon's a software engineer too, and he occasionally works at Kia Kaha.

"What's the latest project?" I ask.

"We've nicknamed it The Hands-On Robot or THOR for short."

"Well, isn't that ironic?"

"Why?"

It's probably best I don't explain. Alex doesn't like it when I drool over his mates. Instead, I say, "What does it do?"

"It's a new, smaller exoskeleton for children. If they have a disability like Spina Bifida or Cerebral Palsy, or if they've had a spinal cord injury, it can help strengthen their lower limbs and give them the confidence to practice walking."

"That's so cool, Alex." I love that my brother has such vision. He's the brains behind MAX, and he's helped so many adults already. He is a grumpy bastard, which I'd like to be able to pin down to a particular event, but actually he's always been cranky—he was just born that way.

He has a heart of gold, though, and I'm not surprised he's turned his attention to helping children.

"Damon will be at your place at three," he informs me, as uncomfortable with praise as ever. "Ready for the 3:45 ferry. I've changed the ticket name."

"Alex!" I'm nervous now. "Come on, he's not going to want to babysit me. What on earth are we going to talk about?"

"I dunno. Regale him with your talents. Pull a rabbit out of a hat or something. Gotta go. See you tomorrow."

"But—"

It's too late—he's ended the call.

"Gah!" I stomp into the kitchen where my flatmate, Jo, is eating breakfast. She took over a vacant room in the house we share with two other girls at the start of the university year in February. She's great fun, and we've already become firm friends.

She glances at me and obviously spots my pout. "What's going on?"

"Alex can't pick me up," I say sulkily. "He's sending his best mate to drive me down."

"Who is it?"

"His name's Damon Chevalier. He's a software engineer. Oh God, it's four hours on the ferry and four by car."

"So what's the problem? Don't you get on?"

"Oh yeah. We get on fine." I wrinkle my nose. "I have a huge crush on him, though."

"Ooh." She picks up her dish in one hand and her coffee in the other. "You totally need to tell me more about this. Come on."

Grumbling under my breath, I collect a bottle of water from the fridge and follow her into the living room.

"So how long have you known him?" she asks.

I unscrew the bottle and have a swig. "Oh, years. Before Mum and Dad divorced, we lived in Wellington. Alex met Damon on the first day of high school. I was six when he first came to our house. Alex said, 'This is my youngest sister, Michelle,' and Damon sang the Beatles' song, you know the one." I sing the first line, and she nods. "I said, 'What does ma belle mean?' and he said, 'It's French for beautiful,' and he winked at me. Winked! He was only twelve, for Christ's sake. He called me 'ma belle' all weekend, and for some reason it stuck."

"Seriously, that's why everyone calls you Belle?"

"Yeah."

"Oh my God, that's so romantic."

"It's really not. I wish it was. He treats me like his kid sister. He'd still pull my braids, if I had any."

She grins. "Does Alex know you like him?"

I sigh. "I'm hoping he's forgotten. When I was about fourteen, my family had a big beach party. I got there late, and Damon was coming out of the sea in his swim shorts. I hadn't even been kissed—and he was twenty, and he worked out."

My eyes glaze over at the memory. "He was like Tangaroa, the god of the sea, all tanned and muscled, and his wet shorts clung to his…" My lips twist.

"Was he…?"

"Oh yes. Very. I stared at him with my mouth open. And Alex caught me."

"What did he say?"

I adopt my brother's deep voice. "'Michelle Winters! Avert your eyes!'"

She chuckles. "He didn't like you looking at his friends?"

"Not one bit. He locked me in the car for half an hour as a punishment. When he let me out, he said, 'I don't want to see you looking at any of my mates like that again.'"

"And have you?"

"Of course I have. I just make sure Alex isn't watching." We both chuckle.

"I can't wait to meet Damon," she says. She flicks her eyebrows up. "Maybe it's a good thing you're single now…"

I push away the twist I feel inside at the thought of my recent breakup. "Nah. Even if he was interested—and he's not—Alex would have warned him off. He's always told his mates not to go near his sisters and vice versa."

"Didn't work with Gaby and Tyson," she says. In five days, my sister will be marrying another of Alex's friends.

"That's true, but she's braver than I am. Damon would never be interested in me, anyway. He's had loads of girlfriends, and they're always really tall, sexy, skinny blondes. And I'm…" I gesture at myself. I'm five-two, and my hair's chestnut brown and prone to static, so I always wear it in a ponytail. I'm nowhere near as sophisticated as his usual girls.

"Belle," Jo scolds. "I never know if you're being serious when you say things like that. You must know how beautiful you are."

"Eye of the beholder and all that," I mumble, uncomfortable with the compliment.

She purses her lips. Then she says, "You have to admit your boobs are nice though."

"They're okay," I say with a short laugh. They don't seem anything special to me, but she's bi and polyamorous, so I trust her opinion.

"Wear a low-cut top tomorrow," she states.

"Jo… he'd eat me alive."

"Wow. Then you should definitely show some cleavage."

I giggle. "No, I mean he's far too… grrr."

"Wouldn't that be cool, though? To go with an older guy who knew his way around the bedroom? Someone who was chocolate chip cookie dough ice cream and not plain old vanilla?"

"Mmm."

We fall silent as we both think about that. Then our eyes meet.

"Are you thinking about sex or ice cream?" she asks.

"Both," I reply, and we laugh again.

"I'll have to suggest that to Ian," she says, naming one of the guys she's currently seeing. He's a lot older than us, in his thirties, I think.

"Suggest what?"

"Buying some chocolate chip cookie dough ice cream so they can cover me in it."

"Yeah, but you'd just lick it off yourself."

That makes us both dissolve into giggles.

Eventually, I sigh. "I'm so envious of you and your adventurous sex life."

"I've told you, you can always join in," she replies mischievously.

I give her a wry look. "I'm very flattered, but you know that's not my thing."

"Shame. We'd have a lot of fun."

"I'd rather start with something other than missionary before I progress to three in a bed."

Her brows draw together. "I can't believe what an arsehole Cole was. I'm so glad he's not on the scene anymore."

"Yeah, me too." My gaze drifts out of the window, though, as I think about my ex. I ended it, but it's only been a few weeks since we parted, so the wound is still very raw. I don't regret breaking up with him because, by the end, ninety percent of the relationship was toxic. He was disrespectful, dishonest, and although he spoke as if he was God's gift, I didn't enjoy sex with him any more than I did the other two guys I've been with. But I'd be lying if I said I didn't miss that other ten percent of the relationship—having someone to cuddle up to in bed at night, to watch movies and go to parties with.

"Don't," Jo says sharply.

I look back at her, startled. "What?"

"Don't you dare start regretting leaving him."

"I'm not. But it wasn't all bad."

"Have you forgotten how many times I found you crying in the bathroom?"

"No," I admit sadly.

"He was like a Pavlova dessert—he looked great, but when you broke through the surface there was nothing but air inside. There wasn't even any interesting fruit. I saw him in his boxer-briefs, and his banana wasn't anything to write home about."

"You're so wicked."

"You'll find someone better," she assures me. "You're too sweet to be single for long."

"I don't want to be sweet," I grumble. Even though I'm nearly twenty-two and about to qualify as a lawyer, because I'm on the small side I look younger than my age, and most people treat me like I'm a kid. Even Cole often spoke to me condescendingly, in words of one syllable, as if he thought I was too young or simple to understand. I hate that more than anything.

"There are worse things than being called a good girl," Jo says smugly.

I have no real idea what she means. "Don't tell me any more about your sex life. There's not enough foundation in the world to cover up my green complexion."

She grins. "Have you packed yet? You want to borrow any of my clothes?" She's a couple of inches taller than me, but we're of similar build, and we often swap clothes.

"I dunno. Maybe. Let's go and have a look." We head off to her bedroom to check out her wardrobe.

"Obviously you've got your bridesmaid's dress for the wedding," she says. "What about the rehearsal dinner? What are you wearing to that?"

I go and get the outfit I'd planned—a short white top with my flare leg black trousers and nude-colored stilettos.

"Not bad," she says, "but it's not really going to make you stand out from the crowd."

"I don't want to stand out."

"Belle… Come on. You want something like this." She pulls a dress out of her wardrobe.

I hold it against myself and look in the mirror. The hemline rises to mid-thigh at the front and drops almost to the calf at the back. The band at the top runs from one arm across the bodice to the other arm, revealing the shoulders and neck. The dress is a deep plum color, and it's absolutely gorgeous.

My eyes meet hers in the mirror. "I couldn't wear this in a million years."

"Why not?"

"It's so… sophisticated. And I'm… not."

"Fake it till you make it, girl. You're sophisticated inside. You just need to stifle the country chick and let that urbane girl out. Go on, try it on."

Tempted, I slip off my jeans and tee and pull the dress on. It fits me perfectly. I turn from side to side, staring at my reflection.

"It fits you better than me," Jo says, coming up to straighten the band at the top. "You look a million dollars—you totally have to wear it."

"I feel so bare at the top."

"You should wear your hair down. That'll help."

"Only if I want to look as if I've been pulled through a hedge backwards."

"I keep telling you to use a better conditioner." She takes out the elastic from my hair and lets the strands tumble over my shoulders. "See? It'll make you feel less naked, and you don't look like a schoolgirl anymore. Although some guys like that…"

I laugh and turn, swishing the skirt around. "It is gorgeous. Are you sure you don't mind if I borrow it?"

"Of course not. I bought it for my nephew's christening, but I haven't worn it since. I've got a clutch to go with it. It's in here somewhere."

While she ferrets around in her chest of drawers, I continue to study myself in the mirror. It suddenly occurs to me that maybe one reason

SERENITY WOODS

people treat me like I'm eighteen is because I still act the same way I did when I was that age. What was it Jo said? Fake it till you make it? Maybe if I wore something like this, my friends and family would look at me differently. Perhaps I'd see myself differently.

I'm not sure I'll have the courage to wear it. I have the horrid fear that everyone will burst out laughing when they see me, like when a toddler walks into the room in her mother's high heels and pearls and with lipstick all over her face. But I'll take it with me. Who knows, maybe I'll feel braver when I'm down there.

*

At 2:45 p.m. I'm almost ready, touching up my makeup in the bathroom, when there's a knock at our door.

"Shit." He's early. I stuff my makeup into the bag, yelling, "Can you get it?"

As I go into my bedroom to pack the makeup bag into my case, I hear her open the door and then say sharply, "What are you doing here?"

Frowning, I straighten and listen.

"Where's Belle?" A man's voice asks. Oh fuck. It's Cole.

"She's out," Jo replies.

"Where?" he demands.

"That's none of your business."

"Come on, I just want to talk to her."

"Well, she doesn't want to talk to you."

"Why are you looking over at the door? She's here, isn't she?"

"Hey!" Jo sounds alarmed. "You can't just walk in. Hey!"

It's not fair to ask her to deal with him. I walk out and discover him striding through the living room, obviously with the intention of coming into my bedroom to find me.

"What are you doing here?" I snap.

He stops and studies me, sliding his hands into the pockets of his jeans. I haven't yet put my boots on, unfortunately, as their two-inch heel would have given me a bit of height. Cole is only five ten, but it still feels as if he's towering over me in my socks.

He's the same age as me, and a good-looking guy, with longish dark-blonde hair and unusual light-blue eyes that still give me goosebumps.

I take a step back, and he follows me. "I want you to leave," I state.

"I just want to talk." He gestures to the bedroom. "Can we go in there?"

"Absolutely not."

"If you're happy with Jo hearing everything I have to say, then fine."

I hesitate. Jo is wonderful, and I love having her support, but she's outspoken and a tad judgmental. It's going to be difficult for us to talk in front of her. "Come on," I say grudgingly.

"Belle," she snaps.

"It's okay." I hold up a hand to her and lead him through to my room.

He closes the door. "Thank you. She's so mouthy."

"She cares about me, that's all. What do you want? Why are you here?"

He tips his head to the side. "You look nice."

I look down at myself. I also borrowed half a dozen items from Jo that I hoped would make me look more sophisticated than my usual baggy tees. Today I'm wearing my normal bootcut jeans, but I've topped them with a cream cashmere V-necked sweater and pearl earrings that give me a touch of the sophistication I feel I've been missing.

His gaze slides to my breasts in a very obvious eye-dip before returning to mine.

"What do you want?" I repeat. He still makes my heart race, but I wish it didn't.

"Just to talk."

"There's nothing left to say."

"Come on, don't be like that. You said we needed some time apart to think, and I've given you a couple of weeks."

I bite my lip. "I said that because you wouldn't accept that we were over. I don't want to get back with you, Cole. We're done."

"You don't mean that."

"I do."

"No, you don't. Come on. I agree that things got heated, and we needed a bit of time to ourselves. And I thought about stuff, and I know I can get a bit heavy sometimes. I'm sorry about that, and I'll be different, I promise."

"Don't," I say desperately, because I'm not strong, and I don't want him to talk me into going out with him again. "Please, Cole."

"I miss you." He looks at my mouth. "Have you missed me?"

I swallow. "No."

His jaw tightens. "Don't lie to me."

Irritation flares inside me. "I'm not lying. I haven't missed the way you always try to tell me what I'm thinking. Or the way you put me down all the time."

"I didn't put you down."

"You did! You're so patronizing. Always telling me what to do."

"That's because you're so fucking useless," he says with some amusement.

My face heats, because he's right. I'm clumsy, I constantly lose things—my phone, my watch, my purse, my sunglasses. I get panicky when I need to phone people or organize things. I'm always getting lost. I forget appointments and phone numbers and names. I'm hopeless in so many areas of my life. But it stings to have it pointed out.

"I know," I snap, "but somehow I'm still managing to cope without you."

"Aw, you don't mean that. You know we were good together."

I glare at him. "No, we really weren't."

"Sweetie, come on…" He moves closer to me and slides an arm around my waist. I brace my hands on his chest, resisting, but not pushing, not yet.

"Stop it," I say as firmly as I can.

"Don't say you haven't missed me," he murmurs.

I stiffen as I smell alcohol on his breath. "Jesus. It's three o'clock. Are you drunk?"

"I've had one drink."

"One quadruple."

He just laughs.

Suddenly, I'm tired of this. Of the arguments, the mind games, of the way he made me feel unworthy, of the constant disappointment. I'm lonely, but that doesn't mean we should get back together. I can do better than him.

I push him. "I want you to leave."

"Aw, Belle. I've missed you. Your soft body. Your beautiful breasts. Come on. Let's go to bed, and let me remind you how good it was."

"It wasn't good! It was shit. You treated me like a sex doll— something you could use when you needed relief." I'm beginning to get upset now. Jesus, why did I agree to let him in? Jo was right. I should have listened to her.

He pulls me toward him again and murmurs, "Come on, Belle. I've taken my punishment."

I push him, but this time he doesn't let me go.

"I want you to leave," I say once more.

Instead, he bends his head to kiss me.

I turn my head to the side, banging on his chest. "Cole! What the fuck! Get off me."

In response, he takes both my hands and pins them against the wall with one of his, then grabs my chin with the other and holds it, crushing his lips to mine. He presses up against me—oh jeez, he has a hard on.

Any affection I had for him rapidly dissipates. I don't want to hurt him, but I'm going to have to if he doesn't cease. "No!" I say firmly. "Stop!"

Chapter Two

Damon

Karori is one of New Zealand's largest suburbs and often gets congested, even when it's not rush hour. I set off at 2:15 to get to Belle's place and end up arriving at 2:50.

Checking the GPS, I pull up near the address Alex gave me and turn off the engine. It's a pleasant enough neighborhood, well-kept, the large houses containing decent-sized gardens. The owner of Belle's house has obviously decided to rent it out to students, and I know she's sharing it with three other girls. Belle's mother is mega-rich, and Belle could undoubtedly afford her own flat closer to town, but I guess she enjoys living with her friends.

Although I fly to Christchurch about once a month to work with Alex, Belle only goes home during the holidays, and I haven't seen her for over a year. I saw quite a bit of her when I was younger, though, and we've always got on well, so when Alex asked if I'd consider driving her down for the wedding, I was happy to agree, even though it's a long journey.

It's quiet and oddly misty, and I turn up the collar on my jacket as I cross the road and go up to the front door, knock, and wait.

Just a few seconds later, it opens to reveal a young woman with short black hair and attractive green eyes.

"Hey," I say, "is Belle there? I'm Damon."

Her brows draw together, and she glances over her shoulder before looking back at me. "Come in. I'm Jo." She moves back and closes the door behind me as I pass her.

I walk forward a few steps, find the living room empty, and turn to face her. "Is she here?"

She nods. "I'm a bit worried—her ex turned up."

My eyebrows rise. Alex told me Belle had broken up with him a couple of weeks ago. "About fucking time," were his actual words to me, along with, "The guy's an arsehole. I didn't like the way he treated her."

"They're in her room," Jo adds. "He wanted to talk to her alone. I told her not to go, but she wouldn't listen."

I frown. "What's the problem? She knows we're leaving at three, right?"

"Yeah, but I heard raised voices. He's a bastard, Damon, and he treated her like shit. And I'm sure I smelled alcohol on him when he walked past." She gestures with her head for me to follow her and crosses the living room.

I hesitate, not wanting to stick my nose in. I'm sure the last thing Belle wants is someone interfering in her relationship. But Jo stops and beckons to me, so I follow her into the corridor to the bedrooms.

We pause there, a few feet down from a closed door. I can hear a guy talking now in a low voice, "Aw, Belle. I've missed you. Your soft body. Your beautiful breasts. Come on. Let's go to bed, and let me remind you how good it was." Jesus, what an idiot.

"It wasn't good!" Belle snaps, her voice clear through the thin wall. "It was shit. You treated me like a sex doll—something you could use when you needed relief."

My eyes meet Jo's, and she winces.

Cole murmurs something in a low voice. Belle replies, clearly, "I want you to leave." Then, after another few seconds, "Cole! What the fuck! Get off me."

Okay, so this is turning from an argument into abuse.

"You want me to go in?" I ask Jo softly. She swallows and nods.

There's a thump, then Belle yells, "No! Stop!"

Immediately, I open the door and go in. Cole has her up against the wall, her hands pinned above her head, and he's kissing her, even though she's squirming and trying to break free.

I grab a handful of the back of his T-shirt and haul him off her. Then I put an arm across his throat and propel him back until he meets the opposite wall with a crash. I'm about four inches taller than him and much heavier, and I hold him there easily.

"Stop it," I snap as he struggles, banging him against the wall, and he exhales with an 'oof' and goes limp.

I look over at Belle. She's standing there, visibly quivering, both upset and furious, judging by her expression. "You okay?" I demand.

She meets my eyes, then nods. I let Cole go and take a step back, but when he attempts to move, I put a hand on his chest and push him back up against the wall.

Jo tries to put an arm around Belle, but she pushes her away and walks up to stand by my side.

"Sweetie," Cole says. His surfer-dude hair is lank and greasy, and he's obviously been drinking. Jesus, what did she see in him? "I just want you back, that's all."

She takes a step forward. Then, just as he begins to smile, she brings her knee up sharply, right into his nuts. He groans and bends forward, hands clutching his groin. "Fuuuuck," he moans.

I laugh and look at her with admiration. "Want me to get rid of him?"

Eyes flashing, she nods, so I take a handful of his tee again and half-guide, half-drag him out through the house to the front door. I open the door, then pause with him on the threshold.

"If she tells me you've come within ten feet of her without her permission," I tell him, "I'll cut your bollocks off and ram them down your fucking throat, you hear me?" I shake him until he groans and nods, and then I push him out and close the door behind him.

Moving to the window, I make sure he's wandering off down the road—in the opposite direction to my car—before I turn and see the two girls coming into the room. Judging by the look on their faces, they both heard what I said to him.

"Wanker," I say, and Jo laughs.

Belle's not smiling, though. Her cheeks bear twin spots of red. I go up to her, fighting the urge to give her a hug, as I'm sure the last thing she needs is yet more unwelcome physical contact.

"Are you okay?" I murmur. "You're sure he didn't hurt you?"

She shakes her head and looks up at me with her huge blue eyes. The fact that she's only around five-two and the way she always wears her hair in a ponytail makes her look younger, but she is—and has always been, ever since she was a kid—incredibly beautiful, small but in proportion, with lips that naturally curve up, although now her bottom lip is trembling.

"Belle…" My brow furrows.

14

"I'm not upset," she insists, "I'm fucking furious." But she presses her fingers to her lips, and her eyes turn glassy.

"Aw." I hold out my arms. She closes the distance between us and rests her forehead on my shoulder. I bring my arms up around her and give her a hug, then kiss the top of her head. She feels tiny and fragile, and protectiveness surges through me. "You're okay, sweetheart," I tell her, rubbing her back. "He's history."

"Fucking arsehole," Jo says, crossing her arms.

Belle huffs a shivery sigh, then moves back, and I lower my arms. She clears her throat. "I should have listened to you," she admits to her friend. "I was stupid to go in there with him."

Jo frowns. "Hey, you didn't know he was going to do that."

Belle looks at me. "Thank you for rescuing me."

"Didn't look as if you needed much rescuing," I reply, amused, thinking of how she kneed him.

She meets my eyes, her lips curving up a little. Then she takes a deep breath and blows it out before saying, "I suppose we need to get a move on."

"You're sure you still want to go?"

She nods vigorously. "I'll just freshen up and get my case." She disappears back into her room and closes the door.

"Thanks," Jo says to me. "I'm glad you were here." She glances over her shoulder, then indicates for me to follow her into the living room. Once we're there, she looks back at me and says, somewhat mischievously, "So… she's single now."

I lift an eyebrow.

"She likes you," she whispers.

"The last thing she needs is a guy like me," I reply wryly.

"Because you're such a bad boy." Jo flares her eyes.

"Some would say I am. Plus she's my best mate's little sis. She's out of bounds."

She sighs. "Shame. She needs a bad boy, and I don't mean like that twat, Cole. He was shit in bed, by the sound of it. I think all her partners have been. I keep suggesting she get herself a girlfriend. At least most girls know where the clitoris is."

I give a short laugh. "You're interested in her?"

"Oh, I love her to bits, but she's only interested in guys, unfortunately." She leans forward conspiratorially and whispers, "The other day she was grouchy about something, and I cracked a joke about her needing to get laid. She said no thanks and that she didn't enjoy sex. I don't think her previous partners have been great in bed. She needs someone who knows what he's doing to show her how good it can be, you know? You'd be doing her a favor."

"Stop meddling," I scold, with only a little firmness, because she's obviously looking out for her friend.

She shrugs and winks at me as Belle comes out.

"I'm all ready," Belle says, pulling her suitcase behind her. She's put her boots on and donned a jacket, and she looks as if she's gathered herself together.

"Come on then. Nice to meet you, Jo."

She grins. "Likewise." She gives her friend a big hug. "You go and have a wonderful time, you hear me? Don't give that tosser a single thought."

"I won't." Belle hugs her back, then follows me to the front door. "Did Alex mention that I need to take these?" She gestures at the two large cardboard boxes by the front door.

"Yep. He said you didn't want to take them on the plane. What's in them?"

"Stuff."

"Glad we cleared that up."

"It's not drugs or radioactive material," she adds.

"Okay…"

"I'll tell you later," she states. "But it's not illegal. Is that all right?"

I shrug, intrigued, but not wanting to pry. "Sure."

"I'll take one," Jo says, but I bend and pick them both up. They're heavy, but I'm easily able to carry them.

"Wow," they both say together.

I give a short laugh and head out of the door. "Come on, or we'll miss the ferry."

I lead the way to the car and unlock it with the key fob.

"Damon!" she says. "Oh my God! I thought you had a Bentley."

"I do. Just got this beauty." It's an F-type Jag, in a gorgeous Ligurian Black. It's sitting on the roadside like the big cat it's named after, looking as if it's ready to pounce on a wounded antelope. "I knew you'd appreciate it."

She's always been into cars. As a kid, when other girls were drawing princesses and unicorns, Belle was sketching Porsches and Ferraris.

When she was younger, I took her out a couple of times in my E-type, and she spent the whole time looking as if I was flying her to the moon.

"I thought you might like to take it for a spin through the South Island," I tell her.

She stares at me, her baby-blue eyes widening and her mouth forming an O. "You're kidding me?"

"I put you on the insurance."

"Damon, are you serious?"

"Sure." I slide the boxes onto the back seat, then lift her case into the boot. "Thought we might as well make the most of the journey."

"Oh my God, thank you."

I chuckle. "In you get."

We slide onto the Ebony Windsor leather seats and buckle ourselves in. "It smells amazing," she says. "All leather and new carpet. When did you get it?"

"Monday."

"Jesus, Damon!"

"You're the first person I've taken out in it." I start the engine, and the car gives a throaty purr. I reverse back a few feet, then slide the car out, heading north toward the ferry. "She's looking forward to stretching her legs on the coast road."

She explores the dash, opening compartments and running her fingers across the leather. "She's beautiful. I'd love a car like this."

"Why don't you have one? I would've thought you, of all people, would want to drive, and it's not as if you can't afford it." Alex and Gaby have an Audi R8 and a BMW M4 respectively. Her mother is a famous actress, one of the most famous in Hollywood, so Belle and her siblings must have plenty of cash to go around.

"Parking is such a nightmare," Belle says. "It's easier to Uber everywhere in the city. And anyway, I don't like flashing money around. People change when they know my family's rich."

I give a short laugh. "Tell me about it."

"You too?"

"Yeah. My ex and I were having a party, and a friend came up and told me he'd heard her boasting that she'd hooked a billionaire and was about to land me. Five minutes later, she proposed to me in front of everyone."

"Seriously?"

"She went down on one knee and everything."

"Oh my God! What did you do?"

"I walked out."

"I'm guessing she didn't react well to that."

"She cut up all my suits and keyed my fucking E-type."

She inhales sharply. "What a bitch!"

"Yeah."

"Do you miss her?"

"Nope."

She laughs. "Are you dating anyone else at the moment?"

"Nope. Playing the field."

"Sowing your wild oats?"

"Planting as many cereal grains as I can."

She giggles. "Still the rebel playboy. You haven't changed."

I thought I had, for a while. When I met Rachel, I was working hard, and I was tired of the dating scene. The notion of having someone of my own, of being special to someone, maybe even of settling down, appealed to me. It was a huge mistake. We weren't compatible at all, and she drove me nuts. It was the third time I'd had a committed relationship fail, and I haven't dated anyone seriously since—haven't even been close. When I need to scratch the physical itch, I just go on Tinder. Who needs the hassle of a full-time relationship anyway?

"Nah," I confirm. "Old dogs and new tricks, and all that."

"Old dogs," she scoffs. "You're only, what, twenty-six?"

"I'll be twenty-seven in a few weeks. I'm moving into a retirement home next month." She laughs, and I smile. "I'm glad you're not upset anymore. He's not worth it."

"No," she says firmly, "you're right. He isn't." She hesitates and tucks a stray strand of hair behind her ear. "I know it's ridiculous, but I was starting to miss him. I'm kind of glad this happened. I'm definitely not getting back with him now."

"I'm pleased to hear it. I didn't want to have to handcuff you to the steering wheel."

She's quiet for a second, and when I glance at her, her eyebrows have risen, and her face is alight with humor. "Damon Chevalier," she taunts, "I never knew you were so kinky."

"I meant to stop you going back to him," I scold. "Only you would get turned on at the thought of being handcuffed to a car."

An image of her naked, chained to the steering wheel and sitting astride me, springs into my mind. Uh-oh, best not to think about Belle Winters and sex in the same sentence.

"So how's your course going?" I ask, trying to distract myself. "You're doing law, right?"

"Yeah. I hate it with the intensity of a thousand suns," she says cheerfully.

I look at her in surprise. "Seriously?"

"Yep. But Mum said she'd only pay for my degree if I did something 'worthwhile.'" She puts air quotes around the word. "And I hate the idea of being a doctor even more than being a lawyer."

"Couldn't you talk her around?"

"You know what Mum's like," she says, and looks away, out of the window.

Kaitlyn Cross—she never took her husband's surname of Winters—made a name for herself in romcom movies, and I'm sure she's a multi-millionaire, if not a billionaire, by now. She's also a right piece of work. Why she ever married the quiet, rather ordinary Mason Winters, I'll never know. They divorced when Alex was in his final year of high school, so Belle would have been around twelve. Kaitlyn moved to L.A., and Mason, who was originally from Christchurch, went back south with his girls. Alex stayed in Wellington and went to Victoria University with me, although he's since moved back to Christchurch. Mason has now met and married a lovely woman called Sherry, and he seems much happier than he was with the prickly, selfish Kaitlyn.

Gaby has learned to handle her mother, and to say what Kaitlyn wants to hear, even though she often does the opposite behind her back. But Belle's too soft to confront her mother head on, and too honest to lie to her, and she's sensitive enough that Kaitlyn's criticism regularly hurts her feelings. I've seen her face fall several times when her mother has been harsh with her, so I can see why she's not been able to stand up to her in this instance.

It's a cheek though that Kaitlyn insisted Belle do law or medicine, as if she herself is a rocket scientist. I'd have thought that because she was involved in the arts, she'd have encouraged her children to follow their dreams, but I know she told Alex and Gaby the same about only paying for their degrees if they did certain subjects. Luckily, Alex has only ever been interested in computers, and that met with Kaitlyn's approval. Likewise, Gaby wanted to be a teacher, so she didn't run into any opposition. It's obviously only Belle who's struggled.

It would be easy to criticize her for not choosing a major she felt passionate about and paying for it herself like most people do, but I know the majority of students in New Zealand graduate upwards of fifty thousand dollars in debt, and I can't blame anyone for wanting to avoid starting adult life without huge loans. Mason's not really in a position to help her financially, either. As far as I know, when he walked out of the marriage, he refused to take a cent of Kaitlyn's vast wealth, and only accepted child support from her. He's a teacher at the local high school, so I don't imagine he has the money to give Belle the freedom to study whatever she wants.

"Sometimes I wish I'd been braver and done something different," Belle admits. "When I'm sitting there trying to learn the development of social policy and its importance in court decisions and law reform, I think I'd much rather be thousands in debt but doing something fun."

"I get that. What would you have studied, if you'd been able to choose?"

"Actually, I probably wouldn't have gone to uni at all. I'd rather have gotten a job, but Mum would never have agreed to that."

"What kind of job would you have liked?"

"Well, I am working now doing something I enjoy, so I'd probably do that full time."

"Oh, what do you do?"

"It's a secret. I might tell you later. I'll see how I feel."

"Is it connected with the boxes on the back seat?"

"Yeah," she admits mysteriously.

There's no time to press her more, though, because we've arrived at the ferry, and the line of cars is already boarding. We check in, then slot the Jag into its space on the boat. Leaving her case and boxes in the car, we lock it and head up to the premium lounge.

We both had lunch before we left, but we go over to the buffet and help ourselves to a Danish pastry and order a couple of lattes, then take them back to two seats by the window and make ourselves comfortable. The ferry is already pulling out of the harbor, heading for the Cook Strait that separates the North and South Islands and connects the Tasman Sea to the northwest and the South Pacific Ocean to the southeast.

Belle curls up in her seat, pulls pieces off her Danish, and pops them in her mouth. I can smell her perfume—something light and flowery, making me think of lying in bed on a lazy summer afternoon, half-covered by a sheet, the warm breeze from the open doors blowing across our skin.

I blink. Steady on, Damon.

I've been very careful to do my best to avoid thinking about Belle in that way. It was easier when she was a kid, but it got tougher once she became a teenager. I can remember going to stay with Alex and his family in Christchurch one summer when we were at university. She must have been about fourteen. I hadn't seen her for a year. She arrived late, and I can still remember the shock I felt, sharp and sudden as a bee sting, when I came out of the water and saw her standing on the sand. She was wearing a fuchsia-pink bikini, and she had curves where she'd never had any before. She was staring at me, too, eyes wide.

Alex said, "Jesus," glared at me, and then strode up to her, grabbed her arm, and dragged her off. When I saw her again about half an hour later, she was wearing a sundress and looked sulky, so I had a feeling he'd told her off.

Since then, she's only grown more beautiful, like a rosebud gradually opening in the summer sun, and it's become tougher to remember she's Alex's kid sis, and to tease her like a brother rather than do what I really want, which is to pin her against the wall and crush my lips to hers. It's a shame, especially now I know she likes me, but she's so young, and she needs someone a lot more suitable than me. Having any kind of relationship with her is out of the question.

I have a sip of my coffee and clear my throat. "So, come on then, spill the beans. What's in the boxes?"

Chapter Three

Belle

"I'm not ready to tell you yet," I inform him.

I'm saying it more to tease him, because he's already been nicer to me in the past ten minutes than Cole was in the whole time we were together.

The fact that he's put me on the insurance for the car warmed me through. When I add to that the way he took Cole by the scruff of the neck and practically threw him through the door, and then came and gave me a hug…

It's been a while since I saw Damon, and although in my head I compared him to Thor, I'd forgotten just how gorgeous he is. He's tall, maybe six-two, and big, his gray T-shirt stretched across his broad shoulders and wide chest. The denim of his jeans clings to his solid thighs. He has a lazy, sexy smile, and whenever I've seen him, he always looks as if he hasn't shaved for three or four days. By far the most attractive thing about him, though, are his light-brown eyes, the color of gingerbread, that always look as if he's thinking about something raunchy.

He has a mouthful of coffee. "You know the more you refuse to tell me, the more intrigued it makes me."

"Yeah, I know."

He laughs and has a mouthful of his Danish, eating it in three large bites. He's manspreading, sitting with his knees wide apart so one of them is resting against mine, but I don't want to correct him, because I like him touching me, even if it is only our patellas. I can smell his cologne, something expensive with woody tones and a touch of vanilla—it makes my mouth water. He's so… earthy. I bet there's nothing he wouldn't do with or to a woman in bed.

Jesus, I have to stop thinking about him and sex in the same sentence. I've got eight hours with him. I'll be melting into a puddle if I don't rein my brain in right now.

"So are you looking forward to the wedding?" he asks.

Actually, I was wrong—the most attractive thing about him is his voice. Low and gravelly, not quite Vin Diesel, but not far from it. It makes me weak at the knees.

Relieved to be distracted, I nod enthusiastically. "Gaby's so happy. I can't wait to see them tie the knot."

My sister, who's three years older than me, started dating Tyson at high school. They stayed together even though she moved to Christchurch, flying to see each other as often as they could, and at twenty-two were talking about getting married. And then he was involved in a terrible car accident. It broke both his legs, damaged his spine, and put him in a wheelchair, and doctors told him he'd never walk again. But his best friends at university—Alex, James, and Henry, and Damon—were determined to help him. Tyson was the reason they created MAX, and with the aid of the exoskeleton they've been able to help him exercise to strengthen his limbs. After four years, he's now able to stand for a short while on crutches. Gaby has supported him all this time, never wavering.

"Alex was telling me you've been helping him with THOR," I say.

"Yeah, that's right. Has he told you about his plan to integrate it with gaming software?"

"No! Is that where you come in?"

"Yeah. I thought it was a great idea. Kids are much more likely to want to do their physio if it involves levelling up every time they take a step."

"That's so cool. How close is it to completion?"

"A few months yet. That's partially why I'm coming down this week—to iron out a few kinks."

Kinks. And now I'm back to sex.

I bet he's really kinky. He has that look in his eye. I have no idea what being kinky entails, but whatever it is, Damon Chevalier is definitely it.

Damon has a mouthful of coffee, his lips curving up as I continue to stare at him. "What?"

I clear my throat. "Nothing. So how are things at Kingpinz?" He owns the company with his two brothers. They started off making prosthetics, and have also been working on an augmentative and alternative communication device, the kind that Stephen Hawking used, with a voice synthesizer. "How's MOTHER coming along?"

"Good. Kip's hoping to get it up and running by August."

"Saxon's twins are due soon, right?"

"Yeah, Catie's something like thirty-seven weeks but twins usually come early, so it could be any moment. Saxon said this morning that yesterday she spent all day cleaning, which is apparently a sign it's not far away."

"Nesting, right?"

"Yeah."

"Is she terrified? I think I would be, especially with twins."

"No, she's surprisingly calm. She told me she's excited and determined to make the most of the experience. Not that I think it'll be her last pregnancy. Saxon seems determined to form a full rugby team."

I chuckle. "I can't imagine him as a dad. He's so irreverent and boyish. I thought Kip would be the first to have kids out of you three."

"I have a feeling he won't be far behind. He's been seeing this girl up in Gisborne."

"Oh, really?"

"Yeah. He flies up and sees her, and she's coming down over the Easter weekend."

"What about you?" I ask, curious. "Do you want kids?"

"Gotta get a wife first."

"How very traditional of you," I say, and he gives a short laugh. "So you do see yourself settling down at some point?" I ask.

He slides down in his seat a little, stretching out his long legs and crossing them at the ankle. "Nah. Don't think it's in the stars for me."

"Why? You'd make a great dad."

He gives me an amused look. "Clearly, you don't know me very well."

"Aw, Damon, I've known you for fifteen years! You act as if you're a bad boy, but I don't think you are, deep down. I think you're a pussy cat."

He meets my eyes, still amused. "Meow," he says lazily, and something about the way he says it makes my heart bangs on my ribs.

"A very naughty, kinky pussy cat," I add, and he laughs. I smile. "Seriously, though. I don't think you're half as mean as you make yourself out to be."

His smile fades, and he shrugs. "I'm cursed where relationships are concerned. Any decent girl should run a mile when they see me coming."

My mouth opens to reply, but his words ring in my head, *when they see me coming*, and suddenly all I can think of is how he'd look in those final moments of passion. Oh God…

His eyebrows lift, and his lips curve up a fraction. "Belle…"

I clear my throat and hastily change the subject. "Thank you for coming to my rescue today."

"Oh, I don't think you needed me at all. If I hadn't come in, I think you'd have soon sent him away with his tail—or some other part of his anatomy—between his legs."

"I don't know." I shiver. "I tried to get free, and I couldn't. I don't want to think what might have happened if you hadn't pulled him off me."

He frowns, and for a moment I think he's about to scold me for inviting Cole into my bedroom, which is what Alex would have done had he been the one who'd turned up. But he doesn't. His voice is a bit bossy though when he says, "Well, if he ever turns up again, for God's sake just ring the police."

"Yes, sir," I reply before I can stop myself.

His eyebrows rise slowly. I hold his gaze, and we study each other for a long moment.

"Are you going to be trouble on this journey?" he asks.

"Of course not." I nudge him with my elbow. "I'm just teasing."

"Hmm." He narrows his eyes at me, but he doesn't push it, and changes the subject instead. "Alex said you went to the Foo Fighters concert in January?"

"I did! Did you go?"

"Yeah. I didn't see you."

"There were a lot of people there, weren't there? I think the Foos are the GOAT. It's the second time I've seen them."

"Me too, I saw them in Auckland. I went to see Crowded House as well."

"Oh, I love Neil Finn. What were they like?"

"Amazing. So many great songs. I came out hoarse."

I laugh. "Yeah, I know what you mean. I saw the ABBA tribute band and I didn't stop singing once. Oh, and I saw Kendrick Lamar just before Christmas. He was fantastic, too."

I thought that after an initial polite conversation he'd turn to his phone or laptop and hardly talk to me again, but he shows no indication of being bored. We talk for a while about other concerts we've been to, both here in New Zealand and in Australia, and after that we chat for a bit about movies and TV series we've seen. I discover that our tastes are similar—we both enjoy good TV, and we've seen a lot of the same shows. We both adore *The Grand Tour*, and we discuss our favorite episodes, and what cars we've seen on there that we'd love to drive.

We get ourselves another cup of coffee, and then, as it's nearly six p.m., we both choose a chicken burger with fries. While we eat and talk, the ferry heads slowly through the Strait toward the South Island. It's still an hour from sunset, but the sun is heading toward the horizon, and the sea is a deep purple, with the peaks of the waves brushed with copper. I know it's only twenty-two kilometers or fourteen miles wide at its narrowest point, but it always surprises me that it takes three and a half hours to traverse. It has strong, unpredictable currents, and the sea is growing choppy in the brisk breeze. People around us are beginning to feel the swell. Some are gravitating to the windows where they can watch the horizon, while others disappear to the cabins.

"You feeling okay?" Damon asks me when yet another person stumbles past us, clutching hold of chairs and tables as they totter from side to side.

"Yeah, I don't tend to get seasick. You?"

"Nah. Son of a sailor's son." He grins. "Okay, come on then. You said you were working when you're not studying. What job are you doing?" His eyes are filled with curiosity.

"Do you promise not to laugh?"

"I can promise to try."

"I guess that'll have to do. Okay. Here goes. I'm a street magician."

His brows rise again, this time with astonishment. "Seriously?"

"Mm-hmm."

His lips curve up into a smile. "I remember you doing magic tricks as a kid. You did a show in front of everyone when you were eight."

"Yeah, I've always been into it. I've improved since then, though."

"I do seem to remember cards falling out of your sleeves," he says, and I grin. "So you actually go out into Wellington and do tricks on the street?" he asks.

"Yep."

"Whereabouts?"

"Everywhere. Usually Cuba Street, but also Courtenay Place, the train station... anywhere lots of people congregate."

"Is it legal? Do you ever get moved on?"

"Yes, it's legal—I've got a busking license. You're allowed to busk for up to ninety minutes per location, per day. I don't usually get asked to move. I suppose I draw business in, more than anything."

"It's amazing. It must have taken a lot of courage to perform that first time. Cool that you can fit it around your studies, though. So what's your routine like? What kind of tricks do you do?"

I flush, thrilled that he's not mocking me, and that he seems interested. I usually make light of it if I do happen to tell people, almost as if I'm trying to preempt their disdain, but privately I love what I do, and I'd do it all the time given half the chance.

"I do mostly card tricks on the street," I reply, "all the basic ones: the Two-card Monte, Here Then There, Ambitious Card, the Biddle trick, Twisting the Aces, that sort of thing. They're all kinda basic, and you can do them without a table. I also do children's parties."

"Seriously?"

"Yeah, and at those I tend to have a few more props. I'm always sending away for new stuff. I'm a member of the Wellington and the Christchurch Magic Society, and the Magic Circle in London."

"Wow." He looks really impressed.

I wasn't sure whether I was going to do this, but Alex's comment about entertaining Damon by pulling a rabbit out of a hat prompted me to prepare something just in case. He's been so supportive, and because I really like him and I'm feeling mischievous, I take the plunge.

"Want to see my new trick?"

"Absolutely."

I open my purse and take out a pack of cards and a permanent marker. "It's called the French Kiss," I say.

His lips curve up, but I can see how curious he is.

Sitting on the edge of my seat and turning so I'm facing him, I take the cards out of the pack. My nails are currently painted alternate red and black, and as I play with the cards, I know it looks as if the hearts and spades are leaping off the cards and fluttering around.

"Just an ordinary deck," I tell Damon. I've spent years familiarizing myself with the feel of cards. In the evenings, while I'm watching a movie, I'll slide them through my fingers, turn them over, do false cuts and double lifts and one-hand cuts, and now they slip gracefully from one hand to the other. His gaze is drawn to them, and he seems captivated by the fluid movements.

Outside, the horizon rises and dips with each swell of the waves, the movement making my stomach flip. Or is it just that I'm sitting so close to him? He glances up at me at that point, and the look in his eyes makes me inhale.

"A French Kiss is the most intimate exchange," I tell him, still moving the cards, even though our gazes have locked. He has the most beautiful brown eyes. "It's adventurous and visceral, a meeting of the mind as well as of the mouth." I drop my gaze to his lips for a moment before looking back at his eyes, intentionally provocative, because it's part of the trick. I keep my voice low. His eyes have turned very intense.

"Choose your card," I say softly, "and reveal it to me." My words are chosen carefully to encourage the sensation of privacy and secrecy. He takes one and turns it over to show me the Ten of Hearts. I pass him the marker. "I'd like you to sign it, so it's obvious it belongs to you, and only you."

He's intrigued now. He signs right across the card with big, bold writing—not a signature, but his name, Damon, bold, possessive. I can imagine him writing it on a woman's back in the darkness like a brand. I stifle a shiver.

Accepting the card from him, I place it face up on top of the deck, turn it over, then pick it up. I fold it in half, and in half again. Then I take it between my thumb and forefinger and move it close to his mouth.

"Open," I murmur. Obediently, smiling, he opens his mouth. Heart hammering, I slide the card between his teeth and gently use my other hand to close his jaw.

"My turn," I tell him. I turn the cards face up and fan them, select one—the Six of Diamonds—and place it face up on the top of the pack. I sign it with my name, or rather the name he gave me: Belle.

Trying to concentrate, I draw a heart next to my name. Next, I put down the pen and fold the card the same way, in quarters. Damon watches my hands all the time. Like most people, he's waiting for me to slip up, to spot where the switch happens. He doesn't know I've already made it.

"Now for the magic," I whisper.

Slowly, so he can see every movement, I place the folded card between my teeth. Then, keeping my eyes on his, I move forward in my seat and lean closer to him. I let my gaze drop to his lips. He doesn't move, but I can see his chest rising and falling faster than usual.

Normally, when I'm doing this trick with a stranger on the street, I stop a foot away and just look them in the eyes. But as I lean closer, Damon takes the card further into his mouth, moving it back behind his teeth. Why has he done that? Anyone would think he wants me to kiss him…

I stop, look into his amused eyes, then mirror him and take the card further into my mouth, too. Now there's nothing to stop me brushing my lips against his. Leaning closer, I give him a soft kiss, feeling the answering whisper of his breath across my mouth.

Ooh, that's given me a funny feeling in the pit of my stomach, and my pulse is racing. I pause for a moment, my lips on his. Then, reluctantly, I move back. His eyes gleam.

Keeping my hands where he can see them, I delicately remove the card from my mouth and unfold it once, then a second time. Then I flip it over and show him his name in the middle, written in his own handwriting.

His eyes widen, and he laughs and removes the folded card from between his teeth. "Open it," I instruct, and he unfolds it to reveal my name with the heart next to it.

"Holy shit," he says. "How the fuck did you do that?"

"Sleight of tongue," I reply, and smile. My lips are still tingling where they touched his. That was a naughty thing to do, but I don't regret it.

"Seriously, Belle, that was amazing. I don't suppose you can reveal how you did it?"

"The cards switched. It's magic."

He chuckles. I grin as I collect the cards and pen and put them back in my purse.

"I love the way you handle them," he says. "It's hypnotic."

"I'm glad—it's supposed to be."

"You're very graceful."

"Thank you. I practice a lot."

"Yeah, you'd have to. I bet the kids love it."

"They're much more gullible than adults, so it makes it easier. Grownups are always watching to see how it's done. Children are willing to believe in magic. Kinda like dressing up as Santa, I guess."

"How often do people catch you?"

"Almost never. They sometimes think they know how it's done, but you distract them with another trick, or make a joke."

"Misdirection?"

"Exactly. It's an art form in itself."

He shakes his head in wonder. "I'm stunned. Alex never told me."

I shrug. "I'm sure he thinks it's dumb. Most people do. Cole laughed out loud when I told him."

"I said he was a wanker."

"And you were right. He used to make fun of me if anyone mentioned it, so I stopped talking about it."

He frowns, his eyelids lowering to half mast, as if he's imagining springing an attack on Cole on a dark night. But in the end, he just says, "So the boxes in the car are full of props?"

"Yeah, and, you know, outfits and stuff. It's all about the performance, making people laugh and enjoy themselves."

"I bet you're amazing at it." His eyes are full of admiration. Mmm. I like the way he's looking at me. "Have you heard of the Marilyn Monroe effect?" he asks.

"No."

"It's where people transform from the ordinary into the extraordinary. She used to enjoy walking around New York City in ordinary clothes because nobody would notice her. One day she was out with a friend, and nobody was looking in her direction. And then she said, 'Do you want to see me become *her*?' And apparently she just flipped some kind of inner switch, and cars began to slow, and people were turning their heads to look at her. I don't know if you're aware, but when you were doing the trick just then, it was as if you flipped that switch. You exuded this kind of... I don't know what to call it— radiance, I suppose. You mesmerized me."

BEAUTY AND THE BILLIONAIRE BOSS

Chapter Four

Damon

Belle's jaw drops, and her cheeks flush. "Nobody's ever said anything like that to me before," she whispers.

I shouldn't be talking to her like this, and I certainly shouldn't have encouraged her to kiss me. She's just broken up with her boyfriend, so she's a tad vulnerable, and Jo told me she likes me, but her youth and her relationship to Alex mean she's strictly out of bounds. He's always been very protective of her, especially since his parents separated. I'm not quite sure why—he's never told me exactly what happened—but something tells me it's not as simple as him being worried about her because her mother moved away.

But the thought that no man has ever told her how special she is makes anger flare inside me. Like all women, she deserves to be worshiped and placed on a pedestal.

"Not that I thought you were ordinary before," I add. "I've never thought that."

The redness in her cheeks darkens. "Stop it," she scolds. "Now I know you're mocking me."

"No, I'm not. I never lie. I'm glad you broke up with Cole. He doesn't deserve you. Why did you date him, anyway? Surely men must be falling over themselves to get to you."

"Hardly. I don't… you know… put myself out there much. I'm not a confident person."

"You're kidding me? You've just told me you're a street magician. You have to have some measure of self-confidence, surely?"

"That's different. Like you said, I become someone else when I'm doing magic. When I'm myself, I'm not great with people, especially guys. I get tongue-tied and embarrassed."

"You're not like that with me," I say, puzzled.

She shrugs. "I've known you for a long time, and it's not the same anyway."

"What do you mean?"

"Well, you've just given me a lovely compliment, but I know you'd never be interested in me."

"What makes you say that?"

She laughs. "I'm hardly your type. I'm not a D cup, for a start." Her eyes dance.

"Aw. I'm not that shallow."

"I've seen photos online of you with some of the women you've dated. They're all tall and blonde with big boobs. You're telling me you really chose them for their conversation?"

My lips twist. "Sometimes."

"Oh, come on. And look at me." She brushes a hand down herself. "You have to accept I'm not model material."

She speaks quite frankly, without self-pity. She really doesn't think she's attractive.

Pushing aside the warning voice in my head, I say, "You might not be tall, and you're not blonde, but you're stunning, Belle, and you're *sexy as*."

She pushes me. "No, I'm not."

"Yes, you are. You think I can't see the longing in your eyes when you look at me, but I can. You'd be a firecracker in bed, given half the chance."

Her jaw drops again, but this time she laughs. "Damon!"

"Ah, come on. You think I've never noticed what you looked like in your bikini whenever we had beach parties? You've got a fantastic figure. You're smart. Funny. Interesting. Beautiful. Why'd you think I called you ma belle? I'd date you in seconds, if you weren't Alex's kid sister."

She stares at me. Her eyes are filled with wonder. Enjoying that, I hold her gaze.

"You're kidding me," she whispers.

I shake my head. "But you *are* Alex's little sis. And I'm older than you. You need someone your own age, so you can discover things together, a step at a time."

Her gaze drops to my mouth. "What if I don't want someone my own age?"

I should stop this now. We're getting far too intimate. But the sun is setting, and the lounge is almost deserted. The movement of the boat is enough to make my stomach flip with each dip and swell of the waves, adding to the unsettled feeling she's giving me.

"You don't want me," I tell her firmly.

"Don't tell me what I want," she says, a little sharply. "Cole did that all the time."

"I'm sorry," I say gently. "But I'm not suitable for you."

"I thought you were single."

"I am. But like I said, you're too young."

She snorts. "You're only six years older than me."

"At this age, that's a vast gulf." I shift to the edge of my seat, waiting for the boat to pitch down before I get up, and give a short laugh at the look on her face. "Don't pout."

"I'm not pouting."

"Yes, you are. Don't tell me, you have a brat kink?"

Her eyes widen. "What's that?"

"Google it," I tell her, amused. "I'm going to the Gents."

*

Belle

I watch him walk off, admiring his tall frame and his bold, confident stride, even though the boat is pitching. Then I pull out my phone and type in Brat Kink.

I'm still reading, open-mouthed, when I glance up and see him walking back. I watch him stop to let a woman pass him, smiling when she says thank you. He's such a gentleman. I like that.

He returns to his seat and lowers down beside me.

"I'm not a brat!" I exclaim, trying not to sound like one.

"You're the baby of the family. I distinctly remember you having a tantrum and stamping your feet."

"Oh my God, I was, like, six years old!"

He chuckles and stretches out his legs, smiling. "Any idea what the weather's going to be like at the weekend?"

"Oh no, mister, you don't get to change the subject after forcing me to Google BDSM terms. You totally need to elaborate on the brat kink thing."

He gives me a wry look. "I shouldn't talk to you about that."

I give an exasperated huff. "You started it. Anyway, I'm not six, I'm twenty-one. I want to know about this stuff, but I don't know who else to ask."

"I have a feeling Jo might be able to help."

I try to get the top off my bottle of water, but it's on really tight. He holds out his hand, and when I pass the bottle to him, he twists it easily and gives it back.

"I loosened it," I say sulkily, having a swig as he grins. "I haven't known Jo that long, and she's so confident…" I screw the lid back on slowly. "I'm embarrassed to admit how little I know."

He frowns. "What about your boyfriends?"

"I haven't had that many."

"You never spoke to Cole about anything like this?" he asks.

"No. So I'm totally clueless. Please, please enlighten me."

He gives a short laugh. "I really shouldn't."

"Damon, come on, I know you'd never make a move on me in a million years. I feel safe with you. And I don't have anyone else to ask."

"Hmm." He runs his tongue over his top teeth, and for a moment I feel as if I've opened a Labrador's cage and discovered there's a lion inside.

I'm convinced he's going to refuse to talk about anything intimate and change the subject again, but instead he says, "I… uh… overheard you say to Cole that he treated you like a sex doll. So he wasn't great in bed?"

I'm embarrassed he overheard me say that. "Not really, not that I have much to compare him to. I've only had a couple of other partners. I… uh… I've never liked sex that much, actually. I've never quite got what all the fuss is about."

He looks up at the ceiling for a long moment. He purses his lips, as if he's considering something, and gives a short huff. Then he sits up a little in his chair and turns to face me.

"Did Cole give you orgasms during sex?" he asks.

I shake my head.

"Your other partners?"

Another shake.

He runs a hand over his face. "Jesus. Surely you had one during oral?" When I don't answer, his eyes widen. "You're kidding me? None of the guys you've been with have gone down on you?"

"No." Even though I'm embarrassed, I have to stifle a laugh at his incredulous look.

"Why not?" he asks, obviously baffled.

"I don't know. They never offered. I assumed guys didn't like doing it."

"Well, I guess some don't, but…" He seems at a loss for words.

I nibble my bottom lip. "Do you like doing it?"

His eyes take on a sultry look. "Yeah." He tips his head to the side and says in a lazy voice, "You taste nice."

I know he means girls in general, but the implication that I would taste nice if he went down on me fills me with heat.

"Most girls say it's the easiest way to achieve an orgasm," he adds.

My gaze slides to his mouth as I imagine him kissing down my body, parting my legs, and then kissing me down *there*. Holy shit. The thought makes my head spin. How would it feel?

"Any guy worth his salt will give his partner oral," Damon says. He looks bemused, almost as if he thinks I'm making it up. "A guy should never take it without giving it. Did you get any foreplay at all?"

I'm getting more and more embarrassed now. I'd assumed my experience was normal, but his indignation suggests I've been naïve.

"Be honest," he adds.

It's too late to stop now. And besides, even though I'm starting to feel resentful toward the guys I've been with, I'm learning so much that I don't want him to stop talking.

"Honestly?" I say. "I think the men I've been with thought of foreplay as a hurdle they had to overcome before they got to the good stuff. There was a bit of kissing and groping, and then they went at it for about two minutes before they… you know. And that's it. I assumed it was the same for everyone."

"It's not," he says. "You really think Jo would be happy with that?"

I blink at his sharp tone. "What am I supposed to do? Demand a guy go down on me? Insist that he give me an orgasm?"

"Well, yeah. Maybe not insist, but request? Tell him how you like to be touched and pleasured."

I don't reply. I can't tell a man how I like to be touched because I don't know.

He frowns. "Belle, can I ask you a question? A personal one?"

I shrug. "Sure."

"Have you ever given yourself an orgasm? When you're on your own, I mean?"

My face burns. "Um... no. I don't think I've ever had one."

He looks horrified. I'd find it funny if I didn't feel so sad.

"You don't touch yourself?" he asks, confused and curious.

"Um... no. I thought it was... I don't know... wrong somehow."

"Belle," he says. "Jesus Christ."

"What?"

"It's not wrong! It's perfectly normal."

I blink. "How do you know?"

"I just do."

"Do you do it?"

"Yeah. Every guy does it. And most girls, I would think."

My jaw drops. I honestly didn't know.

"Masturbation isn't wrong," he says softly. "It's natural. Orgasms release endorphins, and they feel good. Jesus. How do you cope when you feel..."

"Feel what?"

"Horny?" he asks, with a touch of amusement.

"I go for a run," I reply.

He gives me a pained look. "I don't know whether to laugh or cry."

I bite my lip, but I'm unable to stop the laughter rising. He joins in, and it takes a whole thirty seconds before we're finally able to stop.

"It's not funny," he admits. "I'm so sorry."

I shrug, my smile fading. "Like you said, if I didn't laugh, I'd cry."

"You've never watched porn?" he asks.

"No."

"Your parents never talked to you about this kind of thing?"

"Mum told me girls shouldn't think about sex."

"Fuck me. That explains a lot."

"She moved away when I was twelve. Dad explained how babies were made and about periods. But not about sex."

"And Gaby? She's never discussed it with you?"

"God, no. I love her dearly, but we've never had that kind of relationship."

I can see he's not considered that not all siblings are close like he is with his brothers. "And don't ask me if I've ever spoken to Alex about it," I add. "Because I think you know the answer to that."

"What about your friends? I thought girls talked about sex and exchanged experiences."

"Not my friends. Not in detail, anyway."

He seems completely flummoxed. "You've never been interested in reading about sex?" he asks. "Finding out about it?"

"Honestly? I've not thought about it much. When I was younger, I thought it would just… happen. And when I did start having sex, I assumed my experience was the same as everyone else's. It's only since I met Jo that I've begun to realize that's not true."

"I honestly don't know what to say," he admits. "Sex is a big part of my life, and I can't imagine it being any other way."

"Well, maybe you can understand why I was so shocked at your Brat Kink comment."

"I'm sorry about that. I feel as if I've gone into a Year Seven classroom and started reading *Fifty Shades* to the kids."

I inhale with indignation. "I'm twenty-one," I remind him hotly. "I'm not a kid."

"I know."

"Do you? Would you like to take a look at my boobs as evidence?"

His lips curve up, but to his credit he doesn't eye-dip me. "I know you're not a kid," he says softly. "I didn't mean to sound patronizing."

"I'm naïve. Unsophisticated. Unworldly. I know that. And I find it embarrassing and a tad humiliating to admit to the sexiest guy in the world just how clueless I am." I don't miss the way his smile broadens at my compliment. "But despite that," I continue, "this has been the most open conversation about sex I've ever had." How can I make him understand? "For so long I've felt powerless where sex is concerned, and what you've told me is starting to make me feel… liberated. In control. Does that make sense?"

His eyes hold affection as he says, "Yes, I can see why you might feel like that."

"So enough about me," I say. "It's your turn to talk now." I look at my phone. "It says that in BDSM a Brat is a consensual role that the submissive takes on, being disobedient to provoke attention and punishment from their dominant." I look back up at him. "I don't think I'm a brat," I say doubtfully. "Six-year-old tantrums aside, I hate confrontation."

"Yeah, but it's not real in the bedroom. It's about acting out fantasies. Pushing a guy's buttons until he snaps. I'm sure you'd enjoy doing that."

Would I? I try to picture being sassy with him, and purposefully not doing what I'm told in order to provoke him. What would he do?

"I don't know anything about BDSM," I admit.

"You know what it stands for?"

"I had to look it up. Bondage and discipline. Domination and submission. Sadism, and… something."

"Masochism. You know what each of those means?"

"Sort of. So the brat kink thing is to do with the domination part of it?"

"Mostly. What do you know about that?"

"Practically nothing. I think it's where the guy is a Dom—dominant—and the girl is a Submissive, right?"

"Yeah. It's not always that way around though. Sometimes the woman can be the dominant one. She's said to be a dominatrix."

"Oh, okay. One of the girls at uni mentioned something about it the other day. She was wearing a T-shirt that had a string of letters on it, and when I asked what it meant, she just laughed and said to ask her Dom. I was going to Google it, but I couldn't remember what it was when I got home."

"I bet I know. Type this into your phone. STFU."

"I know that bit."

"Keep going. ATTD."

I type the letters in.

"LAGG," he says.

"Yeah, that was it." Once all the twelve letters are in, I press search. The definition is right at the top.

Shut The Fuck Up And Take This Dick Like A Good Girl.

My jaw drops. "Whoa, Damon!"

His lips curve up.

"Oh my God. What… when… how…"

He chuckles. "It's the kind of thing a Dom says to a Brat. It's all in fun. Power play, you know."

"I really don't."

His brow furrows.

"Are you… are you into it?" I ask. "BDSM, I mean?"

He tips his head from side to side, eyes sparkling. "Some elements can be fun."

I study him with new eyes, barely able to breathe. "You're a… Dom?" The thought of him saying that acronym to a girl… to me… oh my. It gives me a funny feeling deep inside. Would I like it? I'm not sure.

But he says, "Not in so many words. I'm not part of the BDSM world, and I don't go to sex clubs or anything. I just find the dynamic interesting."

The dynamic. Does he mean he likes his women to be submissive to him?

Jo said, *There are worse things than being called a good girl,* and I've heard her call Ian daddy before. Does that mean they're into the Dom/Sub thing? Wow. I'm so ignorant.

"Do your girls call you Daddy?" I ask Damon.

"Jesus…" He rolls his eyes.

"I'm curious. Seriously, Damon. Who else can I ask? Alex?"

"Yeah, all right. No, I'm not into the Daddy Dom thing. And I'm not into restraints or impact play."

More words I haven't heard of, in this context anyway. "Restraints—you mean like handcuffs?"

"Yeah."

"You did mention handcuffing me to the steering wheel."

"It was a joke, Belle. Or at least I'd use silk scarves, not handcuffs." He smirks.

I daren't think about him doing that to me. "What's impact play? It sounds like when Jerry hits Tom with a saucepan."

That makes him laugh. "It's when you use something to strike the other person."

"You mean whips?"

"Yeah. Or paddles or canes."

"Holy shit." My eyes are so wide I think my eyeballs are close to falling out and bouncing on the carpet. "You like whips and stuff?" I whisper.

"Definitely no whips and stuff," he says firmly.

"So you're not into punishment?"

"Depends how bad you've been. The occasional smack with a hand might be needed if you've been really naughty." Once again, he talks as if he's about to take me to bed. His lips curve up, and then he gives a short laugh. "The look on your face…"

"You're enjoying shocking me, aren't you?"

"Kinda."

I glance around, unable to believe I'm having this conversation with Damon Chevalier, of all people. But there's nobody around—the lounge is practically deserted now. I look back at him, a shiver running down my back as I discover him watching me, his eyes slightly hooded. I know he wouldn't make a move on me, but is this turning him on, too?

I clear my throat. "When I asked if you were a Dom, you said 'not in so many words.' So you are sort of one?"

He rests his head on his hand again. "I'm not really into labels. I like what I like. I guess if I had to label myself, the closest would be Soft Dom, but again, it's a loose term."

"What does that mean?"

"Google it."

I type it in and then read out the definition. "A Soft Dom isn't into sadism or humiliation. They like to use praise and encouragement to give their submissives pleasure. They don't punish submissives and are patient and nurturing. They like to encourage their submissives to be the best version of themselves, and they enjoy caring for, pleasing, and protecting their submissives. They are the gentlemen of the BDSM realm."

I lift my gaze to him. He smiles. "Like I said, I'm not into the whole BDSM thing, but I like the dynamic."

Warmth fills me. "You mean you're bossy in bed?"

"Yeah, that about sums me up. And I have a bit of a praise kink."

"A praise kink?"

"It's also called affirmation play. Most people find it difficult to take compliments in everyday life. So it's about being told you're valued and valuable, and being praised for your skills, behavior, or body parts."

"Do you like the girl to praise you? Or do you praise the girl?"

"I like doing the praising, although I'm not averse to a compliment or two."

Wow, I can think of a billion compliments I could give this guy.

"So it turns you on to do this?" I ask, breathless.

He seems to find my fascination amusing. "Yeah. It makes me feel good. It's not uncommon for men. Those who take it to the extreme are called Pleasure Doms."

"Welcome to the Pleasure Dom?"

He laughs. "Yeah. They enjoy praising their partners and giving them as many intense orgasms as possible as a reward."

A tingle runs down my spine. "A man who wants to give his girl multiple orgasms? I'd be happy with just one."

He brushes his hand over his face. "Jesus. Don't say that. I should have broken both of Cole's legs."

I give a short laugh, studying him curiously. "But when you say multiple... you really have the patience for that?"

"It doesn't take hours, Belle. It can take some women longer than others, but apparently the average is fourteen minutes. In my experience, it doesn't normally take that long."

"Seriously?"

"Yeah. Anyway, I don't care how long it takes. I'm rarely in a rush."

I shake my head in bewilderment. "Are you a Pleasure Dom?"

"Nah. I'm not into the whole control thing that Doms need, where the Sub has to ask permission to come, and the Dom punishes by withholding orgasms. That's never sounded like fun to me. Sex should be about pleasure. Not just quantity of orgasms, but quality. Drawing out pleasure can make them more intense. Anything that involves making the other person feel good, I'm into. I like giving pleasure. And I love women. I'm not ashamed to admit it."

I stare at him with an open mouth. He's so frank and unembarrassed—it's such an eye opener for me. And he keeps talking about orgasm*s*, *plural*. I didn't know men like this really existed. I didn't know about anything like this.

He opens his bottle of water and has a drink, puts the top back on, then smiles. "Don't look at me like that. I'm not that unusual."

It's an easy thing for him to say, but I've listened to other girls talk, and I have my own experience to compare. "I think you are," I whisper. "Not every woman is lucky enough to meet someone like you."

"You need to have some one-night stands," he jokes. "Try before you buy."

"Oh my God, I couldn't. I'd die a thousand deaths if I slept with someone I didn't know. You obviously have, though."

He just grins.

"How many one-night stands have you had?" I ask curiously.

"Guys don't really put notches on their bedpost, you know."

"Come on, give me a ballpark. Five? Ten? Twenty? Fifty? Oh my God, over a hundred?"

He rolls his eyes. "I don't kiss and tell."

"Who was the best you've ever had?"

"Belle…"

"Aw, come on. I'm interested. You're educating me, remember? What makes a girl good for you in bed? Is it if she gives good head?" I know men like blow jobs, if nothing else.

"It's not about whether someone does A, B, or C. It's about enthusiasm and connection."

"Are you serious?"

He looks puzzled at my incredulity. "Yeah."

"I would have thought a guy like you would get impatient with someone who didn't know how to do stuff."

He gives me a hurt look. "I don't expect a girl to know anything. As long as she's willing and keen, I'm happy to do all the work."

I shake my head in wonder. "I've learned so much today."

"Glad I could help," he says, his brows drawing together. "I think."

"I know people joke about sex being like flavors of ice cream, but it really is like knowing there are a hundred different flavors in the shop, and only ever having tried vanilla." I think about everything he's told me and feel a surge of envy. "I suppose you'd be chocolate chip cookie dough."

"Nah. Neapolitan."

Puzzled, I say, "Why so?"

His lips curve up. "Think about it."

"Um… it's vanilla, chocolate, and strawberry."

"I like all three," he says. "Especially the chocolate and strawberry. The colors, I mean."

"Pink and brown?" Oh shit, I think he's talking about vaginal and anal sex. My face burns at how clueless I am. "Oh my God."

He sees my blush, laughs, and says, "Aw…" Putting his arm around me, he pulls me toward him, and I rest my forehead on his shoulder. "I'm so sorry," he says, and kisses the top of my head. "I didn't mean to embarrass you."

"It's okay, I'm just so fucking naïve."

"You're very sweet."

"Yeah, that's the word every girl wants to hear."

He chuckles. "You're an intriguing combination of sweet and sexy. It's not a bad thing. I'm envious of the guy who gets to teach you everything."

I look up at him. His arm is still around me, and he's smiling.

"I can't imagine going to bed with a guy like you," I whisper. "Do you really give a girl an orgasm every time you sleep with them?"

"Yes, sweetheart. Every time."

"How do you know they're not faking?"

"Well… I guess I don't." He blinks. "That's a thought that's gonna fester."

I giggle. Then I nibble my bottom lip. "How do you do it?"

"Belle…" He gives me a pained look.

"Please, Damon." I'm burning with curiosity.

He sighs. "I make sure there's plenty of foreplay, so she's well lubricated. I use my fingers and tongue as many times as I have the stamina for. And then make her come during penetration."

"That's possible?"

"Sure, if you're in the right position. If not, adding fingers or a toy should get you there."

"I'm assuming you don't mean a Barbie doll."

He reaches out his hand and tucks a stray strand of my hair behind my ear. "I'm guessing you've never owned a vibrator?"

I shake my head.

He sighs again, drawing another strand slowly through his fingers.

"I wish you weren't Alex's friend," I say wistfully.

His gaze drops to my lips. "Me, too."

I remember how we kissed while I did the magic trick. His lips were firm and warm. I want to kiss him again, but I'm not brave enough to be the one to close the distance. He's so experienced and sexy, and I'm just a clueless kid in his eyes. I don't want him to reject me.

Instead, I look up into his eyes, unable to hide my longing as I imagine going to bed with him. Having him tell me I'm beautiful and amazing as he moves inside me. Being cheeky to him, taunting him until he holds me down and… does stuff I can't even imagine. What would it feel like to have an orgasm? I have no idea.

He holds my gaze for a long moment, then looks at my mouth. He lowers his head—I don't know if he's doing it consciously—but his mouth is now tantalizingly close to mine. We sit like that for what feels like an eternity, an inch apart, our breaths mingling. I can almost hear his desire fighting with his conscience. Will he kiss me? There's nobody around to see. No way that anyone would ever know.

Finally, though, he gives a little huff and moves away, leaning back in his chair. Then he reaches across to his other side, picks up his jacket, and brings it back to rest on his lap. Why's he done that? He gives me a wry look. Ohhh… he must have an erection…

Holy heck, Damon Chevalier has a hard-on for me.

"Don't say a word," he instructs moodily, moving his hand so his arm is resting along the back of my chair rather than around me. We're still sitting close, though, and I can smell his cologne, and feel the warmth of his body through his top.

"Didn't realize you had principles," I say sulkily.

He gives a short, grouchy laugh.

"Just for that," I tell him, "I'm going to ask you questions about sex all the way to Christchurch."

"Jesus."

"Serves you right."

He turns his head to look at me. "I'm sorry."

I poke him in the ribs.

He brings up a hand, slides it to the back of my head, and pulls me toward him. For a second, I think he's going to kiss me this time… but he just touches his lips to my forehead.

"You'll find someone," he promises, lowering his hand. "Next time, just don't settle, and don't sit back and wait for him to get it right. To be fair to Cole, we're not born knowing how to please a girl in bed, although most of us watch porn so we usually pick up stuff from there. But there's nothing wrong with you explaining what you want."

"I tried," I reply, "but he saw it as a threat, I think."

He gives a long sigh. "Well, hopefully the next one won't."

A heaviness settles in my stomach, and I turn in the chair, drawing up my legs, feeling embarrassed. What the hell am I doing, flirting with my brother's best mate like this? Damon works with Alex—he's not going to jeopardize that relationship for a fling, especially with an inexperienced girl like me who doesn't know the first thing about pleasing a guy in bed.

"Not far now," he says, and I look up to see the lights of Picton glimmering in the distance. The sun is almost below the horizon, and the sky is the color of a fresh bruise—purple and orange and yellow.

"I'm sorry," I say.

He looks back at me. "You've got nothing to feel sorry for. I'm the one who should apologize. I'm older. I'm the guy. I shouldn't have said all that."

"I'm so glad you did, though. I've learned so much. I just wish…"

He sighs and looks back out at the sea. "Yeah, me too."

I rest my chin on my knees, and we sit there silently until it's time to return to the car.

Chapter Five

Damon

We make our way back to the Jag, and it's not long before I'm easing the car out of the ferry and through the small town of Picton, heading south. The sun has set now, and the Jag purrs as it slides through the twilight.

Once we're on State Highway One, I pull over at a petrol station, fill the Jag up, and treat us both to a latte. Then, as we head back to the car, I hold the keys out to her.

She stares at me, eyebrows rising. "Seriously?"

"You passed your defensive driving course, didn't you? I told you, I put you on the insurance so you could drive it."

"Even though it's dark?"

"Belle, as you rightly reminded me, you're twenty-one. You're one of the best drivers I know. Go on."

Eagerly, she takes the keys and gets in. We buckle ourselves in, she starts the engine, then eases the car out onto the highway.

"Ohhh… she's beautiful," she murmurs, increasing the speed to the national limit once she's on the straight, the Jag stretching her legs without a beat.

I smile and pull out my phone. "Want some music on?"

"Yeah, sure."

"Anything in particular?"

"No, anything."

I choose one of my playlists from Spotify and start it playing. Neil Finn starts singing *Pineapple Head*, and Belle begins humming along.

I check my emails, then, surreptitiously, I bring up the search engine and browse for a site with orgasm statistics. I scan it, my forehead creasing into a frown as I read.

I'd thought that Belle's sexual journey was unusual. My brother, Kip, told me that his girl, Alice, was a virgin when he first slept with her, but that was because she'd been unable to date due to looking after her mother. From the few hints he's dropped, she wasn't completely innocent, and she knew what to expect in bed. Most of the women I know are confident and sexually liberated, and they all joke about orgasms and sexual positions, and make it clear that they expect satisfaction in bed, the same way guys do.

I wasn't totally surprised that Belle said she'd never come with a partner. But I'd assumed that the majority of women indulged in self-care, and so I was puzzled when she told me she's never touched herself, and she's never had an orgasm on her own.

However, the Internet gives me some shocking statistics.

Some I would have been able to predict. On average, men take five-point-four minutes to orgasm, but women take fourteen minutes with a partner, eight minutes during masturbation. No surprises there. Women who receive oral are twenty-three percent more likely to orgasm during sex. That's become very obvious to me. And 81.6 percent of women don't orgasm from intercourse alone and need clitoral stimulation to come. Again, no real surprise.

But the next set of stats surprises me. Ninety-five percent of heterosexual men usually or always orgasm with a partner, compared to sixty-five percent of heterosexual women. Fifty-nine percent of women have faked an orgasm. And a stunning five to ten percent of women have *never* had an orgasm. That's a much higher statistic than I would have imagined.

It does add that many of those women are pre-orgasmic—they haven't had an orgasm yet, but will later—rather than anorgasmic, meaning they are unable to orgasm. That suggests to me the reason they haven't had an orgasm is less a medical issue and more a psychological issue, or maybe even just down to technique.

I turn off my phone, looking out into the rapidly fading twilight landscape as we head through Mount Richmond Forest Park toward the eastern coast of the South Island. I don't remember my parents ever sitting me down and talking about sex, but they've always been happy to answer questions in a way that didn't embarrass me or make me feel stupid. Both Saxon and Kip, who are two years older than me, have always joked about sex and been open about it, as have my mates.

I can't imagine being in Belle's position, clueless and without any support. The fact that her mother moved to L.A. when Belle was twelve must have had a significant impact on her, although from what she said, it doesn't sound as if Kaitlyn would have been helpful anyway. Fancy telling your daughter that girls shouldn't think about sex. Jesus. Shame is such a damaging emotion. If you don't explore your own body and find out what you enjoy, how can you communicate that to a partner?

Equally, I don't understand the guys she's been with. Sex is great, and orgasms are fantastic, but I can't imagine ever going at it, finishing, then rolling over and leaving the girl unsatisfied. As a youth, like many guys, I imagine, I watched porn and knew the basics of how to make a girl come, and I was eager to try it out when I started having sex. I like giving a woman an orgasm. It makes me feel good. How fucking selfish do you have to be not to be interested in doing that?

"Penny for them," Belle says.

I glance across at her. I told her I shouldn't have had that conversation with her, but the truth is that I was pleased it made her feel liberated. It makes my heart ache to hear her say she felt powerless. If nothing else, I hope I've made her feel it's okay to explore her sexuality. Still, I shouldn't discuss it with her any further. I managed to resist kissing her. I'm proud of myself for doing that. It would make my life a lot easier if I lied now and said I was thinking about food or rugby.

But I've never been one for an easy life.

"I was thinking about orgasms," I say.

She laughs, her face lighting up. "Is it true that men think about sex every seven seconds?"

"Oh, I would think that's a severe underestimation."

She giggles, and I smile.

"So what were you thinking about?" she teases.

"Ah, just about the things you said on the ferry. It makes me angry."

"I make you angry?"

"No, I said 'it', not 'you'. The thought that you haven't been able to talk to anyone about this, and that you were made to feel it was shameful. I just hate that."

She doesn't reply. She just watches the headlights illuminating the road that's snaking into the dark night.

"Promise me something," I say. She glances at me but doesn't speak. "Promise me you'll think about exploring what makes you feel good. You know, on your own."

Her lips curve up a little, but she just turns her gaze back to the road.

For a while, we don't speak, and just listen to the music.

She's been driving about an hour, and we're not far from where the road hits the coast when she indicates and pulls over in a layby.

"You okay?" I ask, surprised.

"Yeah." She puts the handbrake on and unbuckles herself. "Are you okay to take over?"

"Sure. What's up?"

She reaches over to the back seat, collects her purse, retrieves a pack of Panadol from it, and pops two of the white pills out. She meets my gaze and hesitates before opening the bottle of water and swallowing them. Then she wipes her mouth with the back of her hand. "Just my time of the month. I'm cramping a bit."

"Aw, Belle. You should have said."

"I'll be okay. I've loved driving her, though, thank you so much. I just need to change position."

"Of course. Come on, let's swap."

We get out of the car, and both walk toward the back. When we meet, I take her hand, pull her against me, and wrap my arms around her.

"Poor thing," I murmur, rubbing her back. "Is there anything I can do?"

She buries her face in my chest, inhales, then blows the breath out slowly. "You smell nice."

I smile and kiss the top of her head.

"I've got a microwavable heat pack for when I get home," she says. "That normally helps. It's day three of my period, and it normally only lasts four or five days, but for some reason I'm really achy this month."

Frowning, I release her, and we get back in the car.

Less than five minutes later, though, I pull into a petrol station and, as the tank is still nearly full, park to one side.

"Come and get your heat pack out of your case," I tell her, picking up our empty coffee cups.

Her eyebrows rise, but she doesn't question me. We get out of the car and go around to the boot. She unzips her case and ferrets around until she finds the heat pack. I take it from her and say, "You want anything else?"

She shakes her head.

"Okay, get back in the car. I won't be long." I go into the petrol station, dump the empty cups, and take the heat pack up to the guy on the till. "Is there any chance you could put this in the microwave? My friend isn't feeling well and we're heading down to Christchurch. I'm happy to pay."

He waves a hand. "Nah, it's okay. Give it here." He takes it from me and starts it heating.

While I wait, I look around the shop and pick up a couple of bits, then return to the till and pay. "Thanks," I say, taking hot pack from him, "I appreciate it."

I head back to the car, get in, and hand her the pack.

"Aw," she says. "Thank you." She places it over her tummy, then brings up her legs and curls up in the seat. I slot two bottles of cold water into the cup holders and hand her a paper bag. She opens it and chuckles.

"Naughty boy," she scolds, taking out the extra-large packet of Maltesers and the pack of mini Twixes.

"Cure for all ailments," I tell her. "Especially girly ones."

"True." She opens the Maltesers, and soon we're on the road again, passing the bag to each other and crunching on the malty chocolates.

The Pacific Ocean to our left is inky black, topped with silver from the rising moon. The sand is also black, invisible in the darkness. I'm glad it's not raining. This coastal road can feel a bit dicey in wet weather. At the moment, though, I'm enjoying the night drive, listening to music, the Jag purring away as it eats up the miles.

"Cole would never have done that," Belle says out of the blue, after about ten minutes.

"Done what?"

"Stopped and heated the pack for me. It wouldn't even have entered his head. Is that part of your gentlemanly Soft Dom thing?"

I shrug. "Don't know. You're my friend. You're in pain. Why wouldn't I do what I can to help?"

"Damon, I've just said, even my boyfriend wouldn't have done that. Don't you think that makes you unusual?"

"I think it makes him a twat."

She giggles. "Yeah, you could be right."

I take the Malteser bag from her and help myself to a couple. As I crunch them, I glance at her. She's watching me with a small smile.

"What?" I ask.

She shakes her head and pops a Malteser in her mouth.

I give her the bag back and turn my attention to the road as I unscrew my water bottle and take a swig.

"Tell me more about what you do in bed," she says.

I cough into the bottle. "That nearly came out of my nose. Don't say things like that."

"I'm curious."

"It killed the cat, you know."

"Then I'm intrigued."

"That's just another word for curious."

"Damon, come on!" she pleads. "I need to know more. How bossy are you in bed?"

"Jesus."

"I bet you're really bossy."

My lips curve up, but I don't answer.

"I'm intrigued about the brat thing," she says. "What do you do if the girl misbehaves, if you don't like punishment?"

I send her an amused look. "I didn't say I didn't like it."

"You said you're not into impact play."

"Not all the time."

"But you might… you know… spank? Sometimes?"

"Sometimes. If a partner enjoys it."

"And you use silk scarves?"

"I have done."

"I don't know if I'd like that. I'd be too worried the guy would do something like… you know… inserting his… you know… somewhere I didn't want." She pulls an 'eek' face.

I frown. "Sweetheart, that shouldn't be what it's about. If you want to try out this kind of thing with a partner, it's best to talk about it beforehand. There are even questionnaires you can download on the Internet where you indicate what you're prepared to do and what you're not."

"Are they called limits?"

"Yeah. Deciding limits is about setting boundaries. Nobody—and I mean nobody, Belle—has the right to do anything to you that you don't want done. You don't tie someone up so you can violate their boundaries. Absolutely not." My voice is hard, partly because I'm beginning to suspect someone—probably Cole—has done things to her without her permission.

"Okay," she says. "I get it."

"But you can set hard and soft limits."

"What's the difference?"

"Sometimes you might be... intrigued, as you put it, about something, so you might say that's a soft limit—that you haven't tried it before, but you might be interested in giving it a go with the right guy, providing he's careful and gentle and backs away if you tell him to stop. Hard limits are absolutes—things you don't want to do under any circumstances. If someone does them when you've made it clear you don't want them to, that's violating consent. A big part of pleasure is about finding someone you trust."

"Hmm." Her gaze flicks over me. "Okay. I'm sure it'd be difficult for me to fill in half the questions though. I don't know what stuff is or whether I'd like it!"

I reach out and hold her hand for a moment. "Honey, you shouldn't be worrying about this. It can sound scary and weird if you've not done much of it. You just need to find yourself a nice young guy who's prepared to help you take time to explore sex. Someone patient and caring. Don't think too much about it now."

But she shakes her head and says, "I'm not worried, and I don't find it scary. I wish I knew more about it all. I like the idea of talking with a partner about limits. I think it would give me a sense of control."

It's an interesting phrase to use, and it makes me think of her comment about feeling powerless where sex is concerned, and that our discussion helped her feel liberated.

I'm beginning to wonder if there's something she's not telling me. Either about her relationship with Cole, or about something else that's influenced how she feels about sex. Her mother's attitude might be something to do with it, of course.

I don't want to ask, because if I'm right, then it's private, and I'm sure she'd share if she wanted me to know. But it does make me more willing to talk. If knowing more about sex helps her feel better and more prepared for her next relationship, how can I turn her away? We're not born knowing these things, and not everyone is lucky enough to have supportive friends or family to educate us.

Ah, hell, she probably won't agree anyway.

"Okay," I say. "Get out your phone and find a questionnaire, and we'll see what kinds of things it suggests."

Chapter Six

Belle

I stare at Damon, surprised at his answer. "Seriously?"

"Yeah," he says. "Should be fun." His eyes sparkle.

My lips curve up. He's so wicked.

Can I really do it? Ask Damon Chevalier intimate questions about sex?

Oh my God, absolutely I have to do this. I know I'm going to get embarrassed, but it's such a great opportunity. Who better to satisfy my curiosity about sex than someone who's obviously an expert in the field?

"Okay." I take out my phone.

He laughs. "I didn't think you'd go through with it."

"I've called your bluff. Have you changed your mind?"

"Nope."

"You don't find talking about sex with me embarrassing?"

"Nope."

Well, I'm not going to flinch first. "What should I Google?"

"Something like… sex questionnaire?"

I type it in and click on one of the links. "Okay. Wow, there are lots of questions. You really want to do this?"

"Do you?"

"Absolutely." I grin at him, and he laughs. "I'm not doing it on my own, though," I warn him. "You've got to answer the questions too."

"Yeah, all right. So the answer can be yes, soft limit, or hard limit, right?"

"Sounds good. Let's start with an easy section. Stripping. So, strip for your partner, and have your partner strip for you. That's a yes from me. You?"

"Definitely."

"You'd strip for the girl?"

"Of course, if she wanted me too. I wouldn't expect her to do anything I wouldn't be prepared to do." He purses his lips. "Well, maybe one or two things. We'll get to that section in a minute."

Not sure what he means, I blink at the thought of him slowly removing his clothes to reveal his taut, muscular body.

He starts laughing. "We've got a lot of topics to cover," he points out. "You can't stare at me like that on question one or we'll never get anywhere."

I blink, trying to erase the fantasy of him. This isn't about picturing Damon as my partner every time I read out a question. That's not what this is leading to.

Oh God. It's going to be impossible not to imagine him in every single scenario. This is going to backfire on me big time.

I clear my throat and look back at my phone. "Go to a strip show and get a lap dance from a stripper while your partner watches, and vice versa. Hmm. I'm not sure if I could do that. I think I'd be too embarrassed. You?"

"Yeah, soft limit, I guess, meaning if she really wanted to go, I'd go, but it's not really my thing. I'm a private kind of guy."

"Okay, the next section is about multiple partners. Wow. When you click on 'add one person into the mix' there are a gazillion sub-questions."

"Like?"

"'All of you give oral to each other,' 'Have him fuck the other person while you make out with him...' I... um... I'm not sure about that."

"No, hard limit from me, too. Not interested in crossing swords."

"What does that mean?"

"Touching another guy. Each to their own, not a problem if you like it, but not my thing."

"What about another girl?"

"I'd rather concentrate on just one. I'm not really interested in having other people joining in."

"Oh," I say, relieved, "I'm glad."

"Why?" he says, amused.

"I don't want to seem like a prude."

"It's not prudish to want to keep your partner to yourself, honey. No answer you can give is prudish, okay? You don't have to do anything just to please someone else."

"Okay," I say softly. I love how he makes me feel better.

"Go on," he prompts.

"Have you ever been to an orgy?"

He winces. "God, no. Hard limit."

"Yeah, me too."

"Fun to watch on porn," he says. "Not so much fun to take part in, I'd imagine."

"Oh. You've watched it?"

"Uh… Might have."

I chuckle, still reading. "What's *bukkake*?"

"It's where lots of guys ejaculate over one person."

"Oh! Right. Wow, I'm learning a lot." He's so matter of fact, as if discussing what you like is nothing to be ashamed about. It's kinda sexy. "Hard limit," I add.

"I'd have something to say if it wasn't," he says.

I give a short laugh. "All right, let's move on to sexy clothing. There's a list of fabrics: cotton, fishnet, lace, Lycra, satin, see through, and silk. Yes, I guess?"

"Definitely yes. Especially the silky stuff. And lace. I like lace."

"On you or the girl?"

"The girl. Can you imagine me in lace underwear? No, don't answer that."

I smile. "There's a list of clothing and underwear. I'm not really averse to anything."

"Nah, me neither. Although too much PVC might be a soft limit."

"I can't imagine you in PVC somehow."

"It gets stuck to the hairs."

"Are you very hairy?"

"No, just the regular amount. But covering yourself in talcum powder just to get the damn stuff on doesn't seem very sexy to me."

"You know far too much about that."

He just grins.

"There's a section on outfits," I say. "Nurse, schoolgirl, that kind of thing." I glance at him. "Do you like anything like that?"

His lips curve up, so I know he does.

"Let me guess," I say. "Schoolgirl."

He laughs. "What makes you say that?"

"Intelligent guess. I have a feeling you like 'em young."

"You make me sound like a pedophile."

"Jeez, I don't mean kids. I've seen photos of you with other girls. They're all pretty young."

"They've all been older than you, Belle."

"But you like a girl to be younger than you, right?"

"Yeah. I'm not unusual in that."

"I guess. But you like the idea of showing a girl what to do, right? That's where the Dom thing comes out in you."

He just gives a short laugh.

"Mr. Bossy," I add, and he grins.

I click the next section. "Positions. Wow! There are so many! Easy, intermediate, and difficult. They've all got names."

"Like?"

"The Backwards Slide." I click on an information link. "Oh. Right. The guy sits on a chair. The girl squats astride him and leans back, hands on the floor. It says it works better with a partner who has a well-proportioned penis." My gaze slides to his. "You'd be all right, then."

His eyebrows rise. "Belle Winters!"

"What? You're the stuff of legend in Wellington."

"No, I'm not."

"You're a national treasure. A *taonga*."

"Jesus."

"There's talk about the Tourism Board putting you on their list of things to see. Maybe even adding you to the Seven Wonders of the World."

"Will you stop? I'll be the biggest disappointment since everyone realized London's Big Ben was only a bell."

I have a fit of the giggles, and soon we're both laughing.

I click on another link. "What about the Standing Wheelbarrow?"

He glances at my phone to see the picture. The guy's standing, and the girl is upside down, her hands on the floor, with her legs up around his waist.

"It looks a bit uncomfortable," I say doubtfully.

"I'm not really into positions that could give either of you a coronary."

We both start laughing again.

"I wouldn't say no to any position if she really wanted to try it," he says.

"What's your favorite?"

He shrugs. "Girl on top. It's easier for her to achieve an orgasm that way."

Heat rushes through me as if I've drunk a cup of lava. He says it so casually. My gaze lingers on him. The sleeves of his gray tee cling to impressive biceps. I can still smell his cologne, along with the car leather—subtle, masculine scents.

"Although," he says, and I realize he's still considering his favorite position, "from behind is awesome—it makes the guy more dominant, which I like. But missionary takes some beating. Nice to look into a girl's eyes as you... make love to her."

"You were going to say 'as you fuck her.'"

"Yeah," he admits. "Sorry."

"No, keep going. You're teaching me a lot."

"I'm not sure if that's a compliment." He gives me an amused look. "What's your favorite position?"

I look back at my phone. "I don't know, really. I haven't tried that many. I... wasn't super keen on all fours. Is it silly to say I didn't find it very romantic?"

"No, not at all. It is... ah... mechanical, shall we say. Not everyone enjoys sex hard and fast. There's nothing wrong with liking it gentle, Belle. Just make sure you tell the guy."

I nod and look at the next section. "This is about porn. Watching it together or making your own. Um... well, I've never watched any, so I don't really know. I guess you, ah, think it's okay?"

"I'd be lying if I said I hadn't watched any."

"You like watching it with a partner?"

"Yeah, if she wants to. It's not everyone's cup of tea, though, and that's okay. Would you like to try watching some?"

"Maybe. I'm not sure." My heart picks up speed. "I don't know how I feel about it. What's it like? Is it very matter of fact? I can't imagine it being sexy. It seems a bit... cold—people doing it for money, you know?"

"Well, there's a very wide range. You do get some that's more romantic, and of course nowadays a lot of couples upload their own, so it's not all acted. The thing is, if your partner makes you feel loved and respected, sex can be a place where you explore the more… earthy side of your relationship. Does that make sense?"

"Um… not really."

"If you were with a guy you adored, and sex with him was fantastic, then maybe you'd enjoy exploring different things with him gradually, one at a time. On their own, some sex stuff can seem cold, as you say, or even scary, but with someone you love, you might find yourself turned on by all sorts of things you can't imagine right now."

"I can't imagine ever getting turned on by a butt plug." The words come out before I can vet them, and my face heats again.

He doesn't laugh, though. He sends me a glance before returning his gaze to the road. "You can tell me to mind my own business," he says eventually, "but did Cole do something to you that you didn't want done?"

I chew my bottom lip. I haven't told anyone this, not even Jo. But there's something about Damon and this night that loosens the padlock I'd placed on my mouth. In the car, it feels dark and warm and secret and intimate, and I feel safe with him. And I'm never going to get this opportunity to talk about things so frankly again.

"He wanted us to do anal," I admit. "I wasn't keen, but he kept pushing me. He said the best way was to start with a toy, and so he bought one, and one night he just started using it on me. I didn't like it, so he held me down and…" I stop at the look on his face. "I told him to stop, and eventually he did, and he got angry and said I was being prudish. We had a huge row. That's when I walked out."

Damon's mouth is in a thin line. "Please, please tell me he used lube or oil or something."

"A bit of… um… spit. Do you think that's why it hurt so much?"

"That motherfucker. I'm going to smash his fucking teeth down his fucking throat."

I stare at him, taken aback by his vitriolic reaction.

"Are you all right?" he asks. "Now, I mean. He didn't do any serious damage?"

I smile. "No, I'm okay. It stung for a few days, but it's fine now."

"Jesus Christ."

"Damon, I'm all right."

He huffs a big breath. "Listen, if any guy goes even remotely near that area again, you make sure he uses a whole fucking tube of lube first."

"I will."

"Don't laugh, it's not funny."

"No, it's not, but you're very sweet." I look at my phone. "How about being filmed while having sex?"

"I'm not sure we should keep going with this."

I lower my phone, feeling a twinge of guilt. "I'm sorry. I shouldn't have said anything."

"It's not that, Belle. I'm going to pop a blood vessel if you tell me anything else like that."

"It's all right, there's nothing worse than that." I hesitate. "The thing is, this is really helping."

He glances at me.

"I mean it," I murmur. "You're so open. I think it's wonderful. I don't want to be prudish in bed. I want to do fun things, but it's as if I've been in a sort of cage, and you've found the key. And I feel that if I understand more, I'll have the ability to make an informed decision. Does that make sense?"

His expression softens. "Yeah."

"So can we keep going?"

"All right."

Happily, I look back at my phone. "So what about being filmed having sex? I'm not sure. Soft limit? I'd have to be talked into it, but… maybe, if the guy was interested."

"Yeah, that's fair enough. It's a tougher question for girls than guys, I think, as it's usually the guys doing the filming, so they're often not in shot. Remember, it's about trust. You don't want to find yourself splashed all over the Internet."

"Oh, I didn't think of that. Yeah. Imagine if I'd let Cole film me." I shudder. I absolutely know he'd have posted it online to punish me for breaking up with him.

"With a long-term partner, it can be fun," Damon says.

"You've done it, obviously."

He just smiles.

I chuckle. "Okay."

"What's next?"

"Places. There's a list. Oh my God! It's got things like in a library."

"As long as you keep the noise down," he says, and laughs.

"Would you?"

"I'm not keen on exhibitionism or being discovered. I don't find that sexy. I want it quiet and private. Just me and… her."

I nod happily. "I agree. Okay, next. Massage. Giving and receiving. Yes to both from me."

"Likewise. Massage is hot."

"I imagine it is."

"Don't tell me, The Twat wasn't interested?"

I just look at him. He mutters something and waves a hand to move on.

"Kissing and licking. It lists all the body parts." I give him a mischievous look. "Anything you wouldn't like kissed or licked?"

"Nope. It should be a major part of sex before you even get to the good stuff."

"You sound as if you put the girl's pleasure before your own," I say curiously.

"Hey, whatever she's feeling amplifies what I'm feeling a hundredfold. Turning her on turns me on. Giving her an orgasm makes me feel a million dollars. So yeah. I definitely put my partner's pleasure first."

Imagine going to bed with someone who thought like that! It makes my head spin.

I clear my throat so my voice doesn't come out as a squeak. "Next is dirty talking. Hmm. You first."

"Imagine I'm saying this in Meg Ryan's voice. Yes, yes, yes!" he says, and we both laugh.

"You like it?" I ask.

"I do. I think it's hot. You?"

"I don't know. I haven't really tried it. Do you prefer that you do it, or both of you?"

"Both, if she's willing," he says. "But I get that it can feel awkward at first. You need to feel relaxed and comfortable with a partner. Have a few drinks, maybe. And I'm not into degradation or humiliation or anything like that."

"You like praise, right?"

"I do. Very much. Do you think you'd like that?"

"Um… I don't know. Maybe. I don't really know what it would involve. I'm thinking of the acronym now." Shut the fuck up and take this dick like a good girl. I shiver. "Do you say that to your girls?"

"No. I'd never tell a girl to shut the fuck up."

"So what would you say?"

"Belle…"

"I'm curious. What would you say instead of that phrase?" I give him a pleading look. I really want to know.

His gaze caresses my face for a moment. Then he looks back at the road and says, "Something like: you look so beautiful going down on me. You have the most amazing mouth, and I love what you're doing with your tongue. You know exactly how to turn me on." His voice has taken on a lazy tone. "I might still call you a good girl," he adds. His lips curve up.

Ohhh… fuck. That's so hot. And so lovely. It makes my eyes prick with tears. Why can't I find someone like this?

I look back at my phone. Best if I move on, I think. "Masturbation. Oh, well, no idea about that. It says watch your partner or have them watch you. Is that, you know, normal?"

"Oh yeah."

"So a yes from you?"

"Definitely." He speaks very firmly. Then he glances at me. "Soft limit for you?"

"Um… sort of. It's hard to say when I haven't done it."

"No, that's true. Did our previous conversation about it help? Are you thinking about it?"

I scratch at a mark on my phone. "I'm not sure. Maybe."

He falls quiet, and for a moment I think he's going to question me further, but eventually he just says, "All right, honey. Next section?"

I scroll down. "Well, things start getting a bit spicy now."

"Ooh. Read on."

My lips curve up. "There's a list of non-penetrative sex. Different places to put your… ah… bits and pieces. What the hell does bagpipe mean?"

He snorts. "I think that involves the armpit."

"Jesus, really? What about *sumata*?"

"It's a Japanese term, it's a bit like dry humping or frottage?"

"Frottage?" I giggle.

"That's the proper term," he protests.

"I don't want to know what frottage cheese is."

That makes him laugh. "So what do you think?"

"Oh God, I don't know. I mean, armpits? It doesn't sound very sexy."

"I agree."

"Soft limits I guess. I'd need to be persuaded."

"Likewise."

"Okay, next is oral sex. Again, no experience receiving."

"Are you trying to make me cry?"

I chuckle. "What's a 69?"

"The girl lies on top, but the other way around, so you can both give oral."

"Seriously?"

"Yeah."

"Whoa. My head's spinning."

"Soft limit?"

"Mm, no, not necessarily." I meet his eyes. He gives an impish smile. I can't even come close to thinking about doing that with him.

"What's next?" he asks softly.

"Anal sex." I look at the sub-headings. "What's 'tossing the salad'?"

"It means anilingus. Eating ass, or rimming."

"Oh. I didn't realize they were all the same thing. Right. Hmm. There are lots of options with various toys and fingers and bits of your anatomy in different places."

"Hard limit for you, I'm guessing."

I look out of the window, thinking. My experience with Cole certainly didn't warm me to the idea.

"It's a hard limit on anything being inserted into any of my orifices," Damon tells me. "Just so you know you're not alone."

"Oh. Okay." That comforts me a little. "But you don't mind doing the inserting?"

"Only if the girl's into it, and not everyone is, and that's okay. If it did happen, there would be tons of lube and fingers first and it would be very gentle and pleasurable for you. Her, I mean."

I blink. That was obviously a slip of the tongue. How does he manage to make it sound so hot?

"There are plenty of fun things you can do the normal way," he says, mistaking my silence for fear, I think. "It's about pleasure. And it can be fun to push boundaries and try something new. But you have to be able to trust your partner."

I trust you. I think it, but I don't say it.

"There's a big section on toys," I tell him.

"What do you think? Would you be interested?"

"I don't know," I say shyly. "Maybe. Some of them sound a bit scary. Electrostimulation? Nipple clamps? Ow! Not my thing."

"Aw, Belle. Don't jump straight to nipple clamps, for God's sake. You'd start with something small and simple, like a bullet vibrator. They're the same size as a tube of lipstick. And you wouldn't have to insert them if you didn't want to. You just use them on…" He glances at me. "Sensitive areas. The buzzy feeling is nice."

"Oh. Okay. You've… um… tried a few?"

"Yeah. You don't need them. But they can be fun. One step at a time, eh?"

I nod. "Okay, the last section is fetishes. Wow. That's a long list. What's *Tamakeri?*"

"Jesus, no, no, no!"

"Why, what is it?"

"Cock and ball torture. Don't click on that link! Fucking hell. My balls just shrunk to the size of walnuts."

I giggle. "Shall I show you some pictures?"

"A whole universe of no."

"All right. Yeah, probably a hard limit on a lot of this. Jesus… what? Do people really do that?"

He glances at the diagram. "Apparently. I think it's illegal in some countries."

"Hard limit."

"Ditto."

"And that. And that! Oh my God. Seriously?"

He looks and gives a short laugh. "Not for me, thanks."

"You're not into any of this?" I ask. "Fire, or wax, or needles, or knives?"

"Nope. Hard limit."

I feel oddly relieved. "People like some weird stuff."

"They really do. But that's okay, you know? What is it they say, 'Don't yuck someone else's yum?'"

I laugh. "I haven't heard that."

"I think it's very important. I have no doubt I like stuff that would turn some people off. Each to their own. It's about finding someone else who likes what you like, that's all."

I think about that. It makes sense. I like that angle.

"There's a whole section here on food you can tick," I tell him. "Does it mean putting the food on your partner?"

"I guess."

"Baked beans! Cheese! Oatmeal! Really?"

"Not keen on the savory options. Chocolate's cool. Or that squirty cream."

"Jo said she'd like to cover herself in chocolate fudge brownie ice cream, then lick it off."

He laughs. "I can imagine her saying that."

"I guess that could be fun."

"Mm." He glances at me, then returns his gaze to the road.

"I'm not sure about most of this stuff though," I admit, returning to the list.

"That's okay," he says. "Me neither."

"What's *shibari?*"

"Some kind of rope bondage. Belle, stop reading."

"I'm enjoying myself. What's a golden shower?"

"Oh my God, please stop."

"I'm guessing it doesn't involve Mountain Dew."

"Are you teasing me?"

I giggle. "A bit. What's bootblacking?"

"Polishing someone's boots."

"No, come on, really."

He laughs. "It is. It's a submissive thing. There's a lot of leather used in BDSM. Belle, put your phone down."

"Why?"

"You don't need to know all this stuff. Please, please, start at the beginning and don't worry about all this."

I put the phone down. "I didn't even know half of it existed. God, I'm so incredibly naïve."

"And I like you like that."

"Damon! I'm not a kid!"

"Maybe not. But you don't need to dive right into the deep end. You shouldn't be thinking about knives and whips. First you need to find a decent guy you trust who'll help you find what you like, and who'll give you some good oral first. Then you can worry about the rest of it. Now, pass me a Twix. I'm starving."

Amused at how he manages to talk about oral and Twixes in one breath without embarrassment, I open one and hand it to him, then do the same for myself.

While I eat, I look out of the window, at the dark, somewhat menacing sea. I wouldn't like to do this journey on my own at night, but I realize I don't mind at all being in the car with Damon. I feel safe with him, which is odd when I know that he has a reputation with women. If we lived in the eighteenth century, he'd be one of Jane Austen's rakes, but I trust him implicitly. I guess it's because I've known him for so long.

It gives me goosebumps to think that he's probably ticked off a good percentage of the items on the list I've just been reading.

First you need to find a decent guy you trust who'll help you find what you like, and who'll give you some good oral first.

It's such a shame he's Alex's best mate. He'd be perfect to fill that role.

"We're at Kaikoura," he says. "About halfway. I'll stop for five minutes, okay?"

"Yes, sure."

He comes off the state highway, parks in a deserted area by the beach, and switches off the engine. "How are you feeling now?"

"Better. The Panadol has kicked in."

"Come on, then. Let's stretch our legs."

Chapter Seven

Damon

We put on our jackets, get out of the car, and walk a few feet to the edge of the beach. Kaikoura is a big whale-watching center, with lots of boats leaving daily to see the magnificent sperm whales, or to take people to swim with the dolphins. The place is deserted now, though, the moonlight turning the scene black and white.

"Apparently, the bay rose up over six feet in the 2016 earthquake," I comment as we look down at the ocean.

"I didn't know that," she says.

I look down at her. She's gazing out to sea, lost in thought.

I'm no hero. I have a reputation, mainly because I've been with more than my share of women, especially since I broke up with Rachel. Some of them have wanted more, and I've broken a few hearts when I've walked away. But I always make it clear I'm only interested in something short term, so I figure it's not my fault if they end up wanting more. And when I do sleep with a girl, I like to think I'm always considerate in bed. I'd never do anything to a girl without careful consultation, and I'd never push someone to do something they weren't keen on. Where's the fun in that?

So I'm still struggling with what Belle told me about her ex. To think he tried to use a butt plug on her without her permission, without lube, and probably without even some foreplay first... Fucking hell. I get angry every time I think about it. Fucking moron.

Poor Belle. No wonder she's so confused about sex. Even if there is nothing else going on—and I'm still not sure she's told me everything—it would be enough to make any girl reluctant to try something new.

"Penny for them," I say softly, the same way she did to me in the car.

"I was thinking how sometimes they compare an orgasm to waves," she says, looking at the water as it rolls up the sand. She looks up at me. "Is that how it feels?"

"It's more like a good sneeze," I reply, and she starts laughing. My lips curve up. "I'm serious. You know how when you've got a heavy cold, and you get one of those sneezes that starts in your boots and takes forever to come and then whoosh—it shakes your whole body?"

"Kinda."

"It's a bit like that."

"So not like waves, then?"

"Well... I think it's described like that because it comes in pulses."

"Oh? I didn't realize that."

"Same as with guys. Like, when a guy comes, it doesn't all happen in one go, right? It takes five or six... you know... surges. Jets."

She's looking at me with a kind of wonder. "And it feels good?" she asks.

"Yeah. It feels great. It's as if you're trying to get through a locked door, and you're pushing up against it, and it won't open, and then suddenly it gives way, and you burst through."

She sighs. "It sounds nice."

Ah, shit.

I reach out a hand and cup her face. I'm not sure if it's because the moonlight has bleached all the color away, but she looks very pale. I brush a thumb across her cheek. "Are you feeling okay?"

"Yeah. Just a few cramps."

"Aw, Belle." I pull her into my arms. She buries her face in my T-shirt, and I wrap my arms around her.

We stand like that for a while. She's slim and tiny, although I can feel her breasts against my chest. I feel a flare of protectiveness, and something else knotted up inside it. A very, very strong, dangerous surge of desire.

No, no, no, no, no. Absolutely not. Damon Chevalier, it isn't your mission in life to make sure every woman experiences pleasure in the sack. Take off the fucking cape and tights. You're not a superhero.

But I've never been good at doing what I'm told.

"Orgasms are great for cramps," I say.

She gives a short laugh. "Don't torture me."

I close my eyes and screw up my face. I can't believe I'm about to say it. Alex would castrate me.

Good job he's not here, then.

I rest my lips on the top of her head. Her hair smells of mint. "I'm just saying. Maybe I can help."

She goes still. Then, slowly, she lifts her head and looks at me. "What?"

"I dunno. You're breaking my heart. I'm just saying, if you want me to show you…" I shrug and give her a helpless look. Jesus. I must be fucking crazy, but the thought is so hot I can't stop myself.

Her jaw drops. "W-what are you saying?"

I try not to laugh at her wide eyes, and fail. "I'm saying I'll give you an orgasm, if you want one."

She stares at me. "What? When?"

"Now."

"Here?"

"Well, probably the car would be best. It's a bit breezy outside."

Her expression turns wry. "You're teasing me. Damon… you almost had me then."

I lift my hands to cup her face and look into her eyes. "I'm not joking."

Her smile fades. We study each other for a long moment.

She moistens her lips with the tip of her tongue. "But… what about Alex?"

"He's not here."

"No… but… I thought…"

"I'm not offering a relationship, Belle. Alex is very protective of you, and his friendship is important to me both personally and in a business sense. You have to understand that. Plus, you're a lot younger than me. But… I like you a lot, and you're very sexy, and I'm gutted that no guy has ever made you come. It's a fucking crime. And apparently they do help with cramps. So I'm saying, if you want to go back to the car, and make out for a bit, I'll show you what to do, and what it feels like."

"Oh my God. You're serious."

"Yeah. If you don't want to, no worries. We'll just carry on our way and forget I said anything."

*

Belle

My heart is thundering. I really think he's serious.

Holy shit. I can't think what to say. I can't make out with sex god and billionaire Damon Chevalier in the back of the car and let him slide his hand into my underwear and touch the most intimate place on my body.

Can I?

OMG.

He's waiting patiently for me to answer. He looks amused by my confusion. Wow, he's so incredibly gorgeous. And he's looking at me the way a tiger looks at a piece of prime steak. It's turning me to caramel inside.

He's offering me an orgasm. Oh jeez, I want one so badly.

"What do you want in return?" I ask.

"I don't want anything. I want to help you, Belle."

"Out of the kindness of your heart," I say incredulously.

"Out of the kindness of my heart. Plus, it's hot."

"So you don't want sex?"

He hesitates, just for a second, then says, "No."

"So what? A BJ? I'm not averse to it, I'd just rather you be up front about it."

He shakes his head. "This isn't about me. It's about you. All I want is to make you come." His voice is so sultry that it fills my entire body with heat.

I blink, then swallow hard. "What if I can't?"

"That won't happen."

"You don't know that. There must be some women who can't."

He tips his head from side to side. "I'm fairly confident I can get you there."

"How?"

"You're not the only one who can do magic." He lifts his right hand, waggles his fingers, and gives a mischievous smile.

Oh Jesus.

"But…" I whisper, "we've still got a couple of hours' drive. And you said it can take some women a long time."

"I'm not in any hurry. Are you?"

I push him. "Damon!"

He laughs. "What?"

"I can't believe you!"

He grabs my hand and pulls me toward him. "Don't you want to know what it feels like?" he murmurs, lowering his head until his lips are close to mine. "I want to show you, just once. I want you to know what to do, so you can tell your guy how to please you. And so you can please yourself."

I think he's being genuine. He really wants to help.

I would be crazy to say no. Right?

"Okay," I whisper.

His face lights up, and I know then that he expected me to say no. "That's my girl," he says, lips curving up.

He moves a bit closer to me, looking down into my eyes. His gingerbread-brown ones are *hot as*, and I know that despite his assurance that this is all about me, it's not totally a selfless act. He told me, *Anything that involves making the other person feel good, I'm into*. This turns him on, too.

He waits a second, and then he lowers his head the final inch and touches his lips to mine.

His mouth is firm and warm, and he gives me a few kisses before I feel his tongue touch my bottom lip, requesting access. Shyly, I open my mouth, and he brushes his tongue inside, against mine.

Oh man. I'm kissing Damon Chevalier. My childhood crush, my teenage fantasies, and the very adult desire I now feel, all combine to make heat rush through me, firing all my nerve endings. Lifting up onto my tiptoes, I raise my arms around his neck, sink my hands into his hair, and thrust my tongue against his.

I feel him inhale and go still for a few seconds, and I move back, embarrassed that I've somehow overstepped the mark. I know this isn't a romantic thing for him.

"Sorry," I whisper. "Did you want me to… you know… just let you do everything?"

He gives a short laugh, his eyelids dropping to half-mast. "No." Turning me, his hands on my hips, he moves me back until I meet the side of the car with a bump hard enough to jolt the breath out of me. He doesn't apologize, though. He just moves closer, pressing me up against the car. His lips hovering above mine, he waits for a second. "I should have guessed," he says with some amusement.

"Should have guessed w—"

Before I can finish, he crushes his lips to mine.

Oh shit. If I thought the first kiss was explosive, this is thermonuclear. He plunges his tongue into my mouth, and I groan, returning the kiss, which is so hot I feel like a chocolate truffle subjected to a blowtorch. Ooh, he kisses like a god. Why am I surprised? This guy is obviously an expert. He must have practiced a lot. Well, I'm going to pretend he's mine, just for tonight.

Damon strokes his hands down my arms, takes my hands in his, and laces his fingers through mine while we continue to kiss. He slows the kiss down, and his lips move across mine with tender pressure, his tongue sliding gently against mine. Mmm… that's nice. The hairs rise all over my body. I didn't expect this. I thought he was going to bundle me in the car, unbutton my jeans, and shove his hand down them.

I sigh, and he lifts his head and looks at me. "All right?" he murmurs.

"Mmm." I don't know how to say that I've never kissed anyone like this. God, I'm such a fool. I've watched movies where this happens, but I've always assumed it was highly romanticized, and that nobody did it like that in real life. Cole wasn't interested in making out. Sex with him was like leaping into a Formula One car when it was already doing over a hundred miles an hour and only fifty meters from the finishing line.

Damon looks up as a car comes down the state highway and continues south past us. It's gone ten now, so the road is quiet, and there are no other cars parked by the beach. But he still watches it go, then looks back at me, eyes alight with mischief.

"Come on," he says, "I want some privacy."

He opens the front passenger door and moves the seats forward, then does the same to the driver's side. "I feel like I'm sixteen again," he says, laughing, as we move the boxes from the back seats onto the front ones. Then he gestures for me to climb in the left passenger door. He shuts it behind me, goes around the other side, gets in the right side, and closes the door.

"Keep your jacket on," he says as I curl up on the seat. "I don't want you to get cold." But he takes his jacket off, draws it over us, then pulls me into his arms and gives me a big hug. Surprised, I nestle against him, loving the way his body heat warms me through beneath the jacket.

"You're sure about this?" he murmurs, lifting my chin to look into my eyes.

I nod, heart racing. "You?"

"Oh yeah. But I just want to say, if you want me to stop at any point, just say so, okay? I won't be upset or angry."

"Damon, I seriously think if you stop, I might die."

He gives a short laugh and cups my face. "I'm not getting out of the car until I make you come," he murmurs, brushing his lips across mine. "Okay? I don't care how long it takes. I want to do this for you."

I nod, breathless with longing and excitement.

He strokes a thumb across my bottom lip. "You have the most amazing mouth. It's so soft, and this bottom lip…" He sighs. "You're unraveling me."

I'm not sure what he means by that, but it sounds like a good thing.

"Hopefully we can ease some of those cramps," he says.

"Oh yeah. This is purely medicinal."

He chuckles. "Yeah."

"I… um… I'm wearing a tampon, just so you know." My face heats.

He shrugs. "Okay. Wouldn't have bothered me if you weren't."

"Damon!"

He looks amused. "What? It's perfectly natural. I've earned my red wings." He smirks.

My face burns at the thought of what that means. "Oh my God." Cole wouldn't come within a mile of me at that time of the month.

He just laughs and kisses me. Ooh, this is nice, all cuddled up to him in the back of the car. It's warm beneath our jackets, and he smells good, and I love the way he kisses me, as if he has all the time in the world. My lips feel hyper-sensitive, and when he nibbles my bottom lip and then brushes his tongue across it, I tingle all over. Is this really happening?

We kiss for ages, slow and unhurried. For a long time, the road is quiet, people locked in their houses, the road free of traffic. Eventually, a car passes behind us on the state highway, its headlights briefly filling the Jag with light, and then it's gone, and it's just us in the inky darkness, with a brush of silver starlight to illuminate us.

"Turn around," he says, shifting on the seat so his back is against the side door. I move so I'm leaning back against his chest, half on his lap. "Good girl," he murmurs, his breath whispering across my ear.

I shiver. Ooh. That's hot.

He finds the bottom of my sweater and slips his hands beneath it, resting them on my abdomen. "Poor baby," he says softly, stroking his hands there. "I want to make you feel better. Let's see if we can relax those tight muscles."

I don't say anything, my chest rising and falling fast as my heart races. He traces his fingers lightly over my stomach, then higher, across my lower ribs, beneath my bra. "Can I undo this?" he whispers.

I swallow, nod, and lean forward a little so he can find the catch. He flicks it with two fingers, and it pings undone.

"Jesus," I say, leaning back against him again and closing my eyes. "That was smooth."

"We aim to please." He slides his fingers beneath the wires of the cups and lifts them up. "Do you like your breasts being touched?"

I don't answer, remembering how Cole sometimes grabbed them while we were having sex, squeezing them so hard it hurt.

"Open your eyes," Damon says. "Look at me." His voice is low and growly. When I look up into his gingerbread-brown eyes, he instructs, "Don't think about him." Then he cups my breasts with his warm hands.

I flush at the heat in his eyes as he lowers his mouth to mine. While he kisses me, he strokes his thumbs over my nipples. My breath leaves me in a rush.

"Do you like that?" he asks, teasing the tips with the pads of his thumbs. I swallow and nod. "Good," he says. "Because I'm going to play with them for a while."

My answering sigh turns into a soft moan, and he kisses me again. "Your breasts are amazing," he tells me in between presses of his lips to mine. "The perfect size and shape."

"I think they're my best feature," I reply, my voice little more than a squeak.

"I dunno, the rest of you is pretty good. You've got a nice ass. But yeah, these are superb." He takes the tips between his thumbs and forefingers and tugs them, ever so gently. "When you're on your own, you should start by doing this."

I close my eyes. Holy shit. Nobody's ever touched me like this. Does he really think I could do it to myself? Do other women do that? Without feeling guilty or shameful? I don't think Damon has an ounce of shame in him.

How fucking wonderful.

He does as he promised, and plays with my breasts for ages. At one point, he lifts his fingers to his mouth, licks them, then returns them to my nipples, spreading the moisture across the sensitive skin, and I shudder as he continues to tug and squeeze them, so gently it makes my throat tighten with emotion.

The windows are starting to steam up now, and I'm finding it hard to sit still in his lap. I can feel his erection against my butt—he's definitely turned on, too. I'm not sure whether I should touch him. He said he's not expecting anything, but it seems wrong to just sit here and let him do all the work.

Turning a little to face him, I slide a hand down his front, over his belt, intending to stroke him. He catches my hand, though, and moves it away.

"No," he says firmly. Mr. Soft Dom.

"Damon…"

He turns me again, pulling me back against his chest, then pops the button at the top of my jeans. "I told you," he scolds. "This is all about you tonight."

"But—"

"Belle. I want you to sit still. Close your eyes. And just concentrate on how you're feeling. Because I'm going to ask you to describe it to me." He slips his right hand beneath the elastic of my underwear. I suppose I could take my jeans off, but he doesn't ask me to. Instead, while his left hand moves back beneath my sweater to my breast, he eases the fingers of his right hand down beneath the tight denim. I feel him stroke my mound, and then he carefully slips his middle finger down into my folds.

"Ah, fuck," he says. He laughs then and shifts on the seat, pulling me tighter to him, making himself comfortable. "This is going to be easy as," he says.

"Why?" I ask, breathless, as he strokes me.

"Because you're wet and swollen, Belle. You're halfway there already." To my surprise, he slides his hand out, then picks up mine. "Look." He starts moving my hand into my underwear.

I resist, eyes widening. "Damon!"

He stops and chuckles, kissing my neck. "I want you to feel how turned on you are," he murmurs. "It's important to know your own body, Belle. You're so beautiful. You feel so good. Don't you want to know how to pleasure yourself?"

"I… um…"

"Come here." He puts his hand over mine, and slowly eases them both beneath the denim. My fingers glide over my smooth skin, and then he pushes them down, so they slide into my folds. The skin there is swollen and slick with moisture, and I shiver at the sensation of my own fingers touching myself. Oh... wow...

"Here," he murmurs, taking my middle finger and pressing it right at the top. "You know about the clitoris?"

"Um... yeah. It's like the Holy Grail, right?"

He sighs. "You've really never done this?"

"No." My face is burning. It feels so wicked, and yet he talks as if it's perfectly normal.

"Lesson one," he says. Holding my hand, he circles my finger. "Can you feel it? It's like a small button."

I close my eyes. "Yeah..."

"Everything else down there is sensitive, and you need to explore to see what feels good, but this little button is the key. Most women can't have an orgasm unless this is being touched."

"Oh. I didn't know that." I feel so stupid.

"Even during penetration, you need to pay it some attention, with fingers or a toy, if you want to have an orgasm. And what we're going to do now is tease it until you come, okay?"

"Oh jeez..."

"Do you want to do it? Or do you want me to do it?"

I swallow hard. "You do it."

"Okay, sweetheart. That's all right." He lets me remove my hand. But before I can tuck it beneath his jacket, he covers my fingers with his mouth and sucks.

"Jesus, Damon!"

"Seems a shame to waste it." He slips his hand back into my underwear. "What?" he asks as I stare at him, mouth open. "You taste amazing."

"Oh my God."

He chuckles and starts arousing me, his fingers moving slowly and gently through my folds. Then he lowers his head and kisses me.

I feel dizzy, as if the Earth is slowly tilting off its axis. While he kisses me, he teases my left nipple with his fingers, and at the same time he strokes between my legs. Oh God, that feels amazing. I feel him dip his fingers a little lower, not into me, but I realize he's collecting the moisture there and bringing it up to coat my folds, so his fingers can slide easily through them.

I feel like such an idiot. I never realized that's what happened when I was turned on—that the moisture is a natural lubricant. Cole was always inside me in less than a minute, and sometimes it was uncomfortable and difficult for him to get all the way in. Did he not know, either, then? At school they told us how babies were made, and about contraception, and gender roles and stuff like that, but I don't remember anything about how to make sex pleasurable. My parents never told me, and maybe they never told him. How are we supposed to know?

"Ah, baby girl," Damon murmurs, "you feel so good. You have such an amazing body. So soft, and you smell fantastic." He nuzzles my hair. "I wish I could go down on you, taste you properly."

I close my eyes and a little moan escapes my mouth. "Are you trying to sex me to death?" I whisper.

"The French call the orgasm *La Petite Mort*." He nibbles my ear. "The little death. So yeah, maybe." He nuzzles behind my ear. "How do you feel?"

"As if you're melting me. I'm turning into a puddle."

"That's all your muscles relaxing, and all the hormones and chemicals shooting through you right now—endorphins and dopamine and oxytocin."

"Really?"

"Yeah. Sex is supposed to make you feel good. If it doesn't, you're not doing it right."

"I don't feel as if I'm relaxing. I feel as if I'm being tightened with an Allen key."

"That's good. Your body is getting ready to come. You're doing amazing, baby. I knew you'd have no trouble. You were made for sex. The only trouble is going to be stopping you when you get going." His sexy chuckle rumbles deep in his chest.

"Ahhh… Damon…"

"Don't fight it. Try to relax."

"Don't stop."

"I won't. I promise."

His fingers are slick and sure, pressing lightly as they swirl over my clit and down through my folds. The world has faded away, and all there is in the universe is this car, this seat, this man, and the sensations spiraling through me.

"You're so wet," he whispers, sucking my earlobe. "That means you're almost there, baby girl. Can you feel it coming?"

"I… don't know…"

"Tell me what you're feeling."

"It's hard to describe…"

"Is it warm? Tight? Is it in one place or lots of places?"

"It's… all through me. I feel… mmm, warm, and loose, and tight at the same time." Every time he tugs on my nipple, I feel an answering clench deep inside. He's so gentle, but it's driving me crazy. Oh God, I've never felt like this before…

"That's it. You're moving your hips now, showing me what you want. That's good. Oh, we're so close."

"Damon…"

"Yeah, come on, baby. You're so fucking sexy. Slowly, now. Take your time. This is going to be amazing."

He sounds so confident, so sure. Oh God, what's he doing to me… this is so strange and intense… I've never felt this sensation of leaving myself behind before…

He shifts beneath me then, moving me more onto his lap, and with his knees he nudges my legs so they fall either side of his. He then parts his knees as far as the car will let him, opening me up in a way that makes me gasp because it feels so abandoned. His fingers slide down, collecting more moisture, and then swirl once again over my clit.

I let my head drop back on his shoulder. His touch is unrelenting, and although all along I've doubted him, suddenly I realize that he's not going to stop until it happens, whatever it is. A bubble of panic rises inside me. This is so intense, so unlike anything I've felt before. It feels incredible… and terrifying… I feel as if I'm hanging onto a ledge, but it's a long way down, and I'm afraid to let go.

"I've got you," he murmurs. "I'll catch you. Let yourself fall."

I want to… so much…

"Close your eyes," he whispers.

I let them fall shut. Now, in the darkness, beneath his jacket, in the quiet and warmth, I'm all alone, private and safe, with just his sure, determined fingers. *I trust you.* I don't know whether I say it or just think it.

I feel a sensation begin deep inside me, spreading out like ripples from a stone dropped in the sea. I hold my breath, and without thinking about it I arch my back, pushing my breast into his hand, tilting my hips up.

He obviously senses it because his fingers slow and he says, "Ah, baby…"

The feeling intensifies, swift and sharp, as if the ripples have reversed and are moving back toward the center. My lower muscles contract in a tight squeeze, and then all of a sudden these strong pulses hit, oh my God, so deep inside, hard clenches—one, two, three—and he's holding me so tightly, and his fingers aren't stopping, and it keeps going—four, five, six—and I jerk between each one, and I can't describe how it feels, but it's exquisite and ecstatic, he's right, like a huge, satisfying sneeze, like the taste of swallowing the finest chocolate or a mouthful of the coldest best champagne, like being on a rollercoaster when it suddenly goes down and you get that lurch in your stomach—seven, eight… I cry out, saying his name, almost sobbing with pleasure…

And then, like a wave, it recedes. My muscles loosen, leaving me trembling, and my breath comes in deep gasps.

That's what it feels like? He makes women feel like this every time he has sex? Multiple times? This is how all women feel when they have an orgasm? No wonder sex is talked about so much. I feel incredibly naïve and stupid and ignorant and oh, so angry.

Then I look up into his warm brown eyes, and all I can think is how crazy I am about this guy.

Carefully, he withdraws his hand and wraps his arms around me.

"The first of many," he says, and kisses my temple.

And that's when I burst into tears.

Chapter Eight

Damon

Ah, shit. "Aw, Belle." I let her turn on my lap and bury her face in my shoulder, and I hold her tightly.

She's trembling, overcome, I think, with the intensity of her first ever orgasm. I kiss the top of her head and rub her back, making myself comfortable so I can give her time to recover.

She stops crying fairly quickly, but continues to tremble for a while, little shivers that I find awkwardly erotic. I will my erection to go down, but every time she shudders, it seems to think it's going to get some action, and hangs around.

After a while, she lifts her head and turns in my lap to face me. The elastic of her ponytail has loosened, and her hair is mussed, strands escaping to frame her face. Her eyes look huge. Fuck me, she's beautiful. The innocent air she's always exuded—the childlike naivety—has been replaced by a kind of sultry wonder as she studies me.

I let her look, tucking a few of the strands of hair behind her ear. Eventually, though, my lips curve up and I say, "You okay?"

She moves her hips, rubbing against The Erection That Will Never Die. "Can I do something about that?" she asks.

I shift her a few inches to the left so her beautiful soft bottom isn't squeezing me. "No, I'm okay. It'll go down on its own. In a year or two."

She gives a short laugh. "You're sure?"

"I'm sure."

"I don't mind."

"Well, thank you, but that's not what this was about."

"It would be nice to return the gesture, that's all." She licks her lips.

Jesus. I summon the last dregs of willpower I possess and shake my head. "I'm good."

She sighs and shifts off me, zips up her jeans, then curls up on the seat, and we sit facing each other.

"How's the stomach?" I ask.

She rests her hand on it. "It does feel better, actually."

"Told you."

"Don't be smug."

I chuckle.

"I can't believe you did that," she says.

"I told you. Magic fingers." I waggle them. Then I give them a sniff.

She thumps me, laughing. "Damon!"

"I'm never going to wash again."

"Oh my God. You're an animal."

"You've only just realized?"

She meets my eyes. "Thank you."

I smile. "You're welcome."

"I don't just mean for the orgasm. I mean for everything. I don't think you'll ever truly understand what you've just done for me."

I'm not quite sure what she means. "It was hardly an onerous task. And anyway, I enjoy a challenge."

She doesn't smile, though. "Just talking to me like that, about sex… I feel… empowered. Is that crazy?"

I shake my head, secretly touched. "Happy to oblige."

"God, you're so fucking casual about it. How did you get to be so laid back about sex?"

"I dunno. Practice?"

"Are your brothers the same?"

"Yeah, pretty much."

A car goes past, the lights sweeping over us, then leaving again so we descend into semi-darkness once more. I think about my family, and how different it might have been if we hadn't been able to talk.

"My folks were always open about everything," I tell her. "We were all in the living room one evening watching TV. You know that Saxon and Kip are twins, and they're a couple of years older than me? They'd just started high school, and they thought they were all grown up and cocky. Well, a character on the TV made a joke about a condom. So I said, 'What's a condom?' Saxon said, 'No glove, no love,' and Kip said, 'Wrap it before you tap it,' and they both laughed. Dad glared at them and said, 'Guys, you're not helping,' and Mum said, 'Answer your brother, please, when he asks questions like that. You weren't born knowing either.' So they both apologized, and then Saxon said, 'You know the gloves the doctor wore when he stitched up your knee? A condom's like one of the fingers cut off.' And Kip said, 'You put it on your knob, so you don't make a girl pregnant when you have sex.' And I was like, oh, okay, and we all went back to watching the movie."

Her jaw drops for a moment. "Oh wow. I can't imagine being like that with my family."

"I've always thought Alex seemed pretty open."

"Yeah, well, he's always taken it upon himself to protect me. He'd never talk about anything like that in front of me."

I frown. "Why? I mean, I get that guys are protective of their little sisters, but he seems a bit over the top."

She shrugs, playing with a button on her jacket.

"Can't you talk to me?" I ask gently. "You can trust me."

"I know."

"Is it to do with your parents?"

"I don't really want to talk about it, Damon."

I'm disappointed, because I thought we forged a bond this evening, but I can't force her to talk. "That's okay. Well, you know where I am if you ever want to discuss it with anyone."

She nods and clears her throat. "I suppose we should get going."

"Belle," I say gently. "Come here." I hold up my arms. Her lips curve up a little, and she moves into them.

I hug her, smiling as she nestles against me, nuzzling my neck. She sighs, and the whisper of her breath over my skin stirs something deep inside me. I look down, seeing the cute curve of her Cupid's bow, and remembering the softness of her mouth. The way she parted her lips and let me slide my tongue against hers. I want to kiss her again.

I go to lower my head, but at the same time she sighs again and moves back. "Come on then," she says. "It's getting late, and I don't want you to get too tired on the road."

Reluctantly, I get out, and we move the boxes from the front seats to the back. We scoot the chairs back, and then we get in, and I start the car. Soon we're back on the state highway, heading south toward Christchurch.

We don't say anything for a while. I concentrate on the road, lost in thought.

When I finally glance across at her, I find her curled up in the seat, head pillowed on her bent arm as she rests it against the window. She's asleep.

Reaching behind me, I pick up my jacket, bring it forward, lay it over her, and tuck it around her, then turn up the heater a little, as the temperature is dropping. Then I look back at the road, pressing the accelerator, the Jag springing into life and taking the increased speed in her stride.

I drive for over an hour while Belle sleeps beside me, barely stirring. I'm glad she's getting some sleep. I hope that when she wakes, she'll feel less achy. From what I understand, orgasms are beneficial for period pain, and I don't want to boast, but I think the one she had was quite a whopper, so hopefully it'll help.

My lips curve up at the memory of her crying out my name as she came. I could feel her panic, the fear of the unknown, as her muscles tightened. How must it have felt, not knowing what was going to happen? I can't remember my first orgasm, but I was pretty young, early teens, I guess. I knew what was going to happen because I'd heard Kip and Saxon joke about it several times, but I still remember it being a surprise—exquisite and blissful, and also slightly alarming to have all that fluid erupting and having no control over it. It's different for girls, obviously, less messy, easier to hide. But clearly still as shocking, so much so that it made her cry.

I feel a twinge of remorse deep inside and give her a guilty glance. I don't regret it *per se*. It was a crime that she'd never had an orgasm, and also that she thought it was wrong to touch herself. I'm disgusted with her mother for making her feel that sex is dirty. Why do people say things like that? So I wanted to help her, to show her how it works, and what it feels like. Kind of like how I once taught Kennedy how to play golf.

Except, of course, it's nothing like that, and I'm kidding myself if I think I acted out of the goodness of my heart, like a kind of perverted big brother. Making Belle come with my fingers was fifty percent generosity and fifty percent pure selfishness, or maybe even twenty-five, seventy-five, because even though I didn't come myself, it turned me on to do it, and I know I'll be jerking off to the memory of it at some point in the near future.

Ah, fuck. I brush my hand over my face. Damon, you selfish bastard. You can't just go shoving your hand down the knickers of every young girl you meet and making them come in the back of your car just because it makes you feel good. She's young, impressionable, recently single, she likes you, and you've just given her the first orgasm of her life. Do you really think the seeds of disaster haven't been sown?

I think of Alex and wince. When I was a kid, my dad told me that the best way to judge whether my behavior was on track was to ask myself whether I would tell my mother what I was doing. If the answer was no, the likelihood was that I shouldn't be doing it. Obviously, there are caveats to that, but I think it's a good rule for judging whether or not an action you're considering would offend someone close to you. And the fact that I would never tell Alex in a million years that I've just fingered his baby sister tells me that what I've done could not even remotely be classed as good behavior.

Still, it's done, and I'm not the type of guy to beat himself up over something that's too late to rectify. Whether or not it could be classed as 'right', the fact is that I did mean well, and I am pleased that she said she felt empowered.

The Southern Alps to my right are just darker patches against the night sky, their snowy tops glimmering as more stars spring out against the black velvet. Wow, it's a clear night. It reminds me of camping as a kid. Our family sometimes went with my aunt and uncle and their kids, Christian and Kennedy. I have blissful memories of those days. Until Christian died, anyway. Life wasn't so much fun after that.

I haven't spoken to Kennedy in a few days. I'll have to give her a call when I get back to Wellington, meet up for coffee or something. She's married now, with a beautiful baby boy, and she doesn't need me keeping an eye on her anymore, but I still like to check in on her and let her know I'm there for her if she ever needs me.

My mood darkens, and I lose myself in my memories, just me and the Jag, watching the road pass under her wheels.

*

Belle

I open my eyes slowly. I'm facing Damon, and for a moment I don't move. His elbow rests on the window ledge, his fingers brushing his lips, and he's lost in thought.

Oh man, he's so handsome. I must have dreamed what happened in the back seat, right? He can't possibly have hugged me, kissed me, slid his hands beneath my jeans, and made me come. Just the thought makes my head spin.

I'm still filled with wonder. The physical sensation was one thing. I never realized that's what an orgasm would feel like. I didn't know my own body could do that. Why did it feel so good? I'm nervous about exploring myself, but I definitely want to feel that again.

However, the notion that it was Damon who got me there is a whole other matter. I didn't think beyond the fact that he offered, and I couldn't have said no for all the tea in China, or any other Asian country for that matter. I didn't think at all about what happened next.

I'm not offering a relationship, he told me. So do we just go back to normal? To him being my brother's best mate? Oh my God, how do I do that? How can I act normal during the wedding with the memory of the way he murmured in my ear while he touched me? His deep voice softly saying, *Ah, baby girl, you feel so good. You have such an amazing body. So soft, and you smell fantastic…I wish I could go down on you, taste you properly…*

I swallow hard. I have to be sensible about this, or I'm going to get my heart broken. Take it for what it was, Belle, a brief encounter to introduce you to what will hopefully be a lifetime of sexual adventure.

He gives a soft sigh. He's frowning, lost in thought.

"Penny for them," I say.

He glances over, starlight glinting in his eyes. "Hey," he murmurs. "How are you doing?"

"I'm okay." I look ahead, at the endless road. We've left the coast, and to either side I can see only the dark shapes of trees atop rolling hills. "How long have I been asleep?"

"About an hour. We've just gone over the Hurunui River. We've got about an hour left."

"I'm so sorry. I zonked out."

"It's cool. You obviously needed it. How are you feeling?"

"Okay." I feel suddenly shy.

He smiles, then looks back at the road.

"What were you thinking about?" I ask. "You looked sad."

He sighs. "The stars remind me of being young and camping with my cousins. My dad's a twin, and our two families used to go together.

Sometimes we'd go up into the mountains. Usually somewhere by a beach."

"Why'd it make you sad?"

"You don't know about Christian?"

I shake my head. I've not heard the name before.

"It happened before I met Alex," he says. "Christian was my cousin, and his sister's called Kennedy. Christian was the same age as Saxon and Kip."

I know they're a couple of years older than him. I met them at the twenty-first birthday party that Damon and Alex held together at Damon's parents' house. It was a huge do, with hundreds of friends and family, and it went on long into the night, long after Dad and Sherry had taken me back to the hotel we were staying at.

I don't miss that he's speaking about Christian in the past tense, and my pulse picks up speed.

"We'd gone camping to the beach," he continues, "and the guys decided they wanted to swim out to a cave on the headland. Kennedy and I were only ten, but we weren't going to be left behind. So we all swam out, and we spent an hour in this cave, fucking around. In the middle was a large rock pool, only about three feet deep. Behind it, rocks were piled up against the back wall of the cave. Christian was like a monkey, always climbing. He decided he wanted to get to the top of the rocks and began climbing up them. He'd almost gotten to the top when he slipped, and all the rocks came tumbling down."

My mouth forms an O. "Oh no."

"He came crashing down to the bottom, and half the rocks fell on top of him, and on Kennedy, who was sitting on the edge of the rock pool. He went under the water, beneath the rocks. We tried to get him free, but the rocks were too big and heavy. Saxon went under to try and blow air in his lungs, but eventually he came back up and just said, 'He's gone.' Kip swam out to get the adults, and Saxon and I started moving the rocks off Kennedy. They'd crushed her arm—she was crying, and there was blood everywhere. It was fucking awful."

"I didn't know," I say softly, my heart breaking for him. "I'm so sorry. So Christian..."

"Died, yeah. He was gone long before the paramedics turned up."

"What happened to Kennedy?"

"She lost her arm. She has a prosthetic one now."

"Oh! Is that why you and the guys got into designing them?"

"Yes. We wanted to help her. She's fine now. You'd love her, she's bright and bubbly and funny."

I smile at his obvious affection for her. "You're fond of her."

"Yeah, she's one of my favorite people in the whole world. She's married to Jackson, he's great, and they have a baby, Eddie. We catch up most weeks."

"That's nice."

"Least I can do."

I survey him for a moment. "That's a strange thing to say."

"What do you mean?"

"The least you could do? Why did you say that?"

He shrugs.

I frown. "Damon? Do you mean the least you could do because of what happened to her and Christian? Because you couldn't save him or stop her losing her arm?"

"Yeah, I dunno, maybe."

"You know it wasn't your fault, right?"

"Fifteen years of therapy have tried to convince me of that."

"But they haven't succeeded?"

He hesitates. "I know it wasn't my fault. Of course it wasn't. I was ten years old, and so was Kennedy. Christian was twelve and thought he knew everything—he and my brothers would never have listened to me, even if I'd said I didn't think we should go to the cave, which I didn't. I couldn't have stopped him climbing the rocks. And I couldn't have saved him—the rocks were so heavy they had to call the fire brigade to come in and get them off him."

"But it still haunts you." It's a statement, not a question.

"Yeah. I have nightmares about it. Not so much about Christian—I didn't go under the water, and I didn't see him drown. Saxon's the one who has to deal with that. But I dream about Kennedy crying. I sat there holding her, and she just kept sobbing and saying, 'It hurts, Damon.'"

He stops and swallows, his brow darkening. Even now, all these years later, the memory still has the power to make emotions rise inside him.

"So that's why you've made it your life's work to look after girls," I say.

He glances at me, and I smile.

"Hardly," I say wryly. "I'm not a good guy, Belle."

"Oh, bullshit."

"You don't know me as well as you think you do. I'm cursed where relationships are concerned. I've had three long-term ones that have all ended badly. And I've broken more than my share of hearts."

"You're not cursed," I scoff. "You just haven't found the right girl."

He doesn't smile. "Do you want me to tell you how many one-night stands I've had? How many times a girl has asked me to call her the next day? And how many times I've walked away with no intention of doing so?"

"Are you trying to convince me, or yourself? Are you seriously trying to persuade me that you're uncaring only an hour after you give me a mind-blowing orgasm?"

"Don't make out like I was being altruistic. You felt my hard-on, right?"

I blush. "Yeah."

"It turned me on, too."

"It'd be pretty weird if it didn't."

"Belle…"

"You can't convince me you did it only because you got off on it. But don't worry, I won't tell anyone how sweet you were. Probably."

"Don't you dare tell Alex."

"I promise I won't—if you call me baby girl one more time."

"Don't," he scolds, trying not to laugh.

"I think I am a brat," I reply. "Go on. Once more."

"Belle, stop it."

"Make me."

"Jesus." He runs his hand through his hair. "This was a mistake."

I feel a pang inside. "Aw, don't say that. I'm sorry. I'm only teasing."

He grunts. "Don't make me wish I hadn't done it."

I don't reply, because I don't want him to regret it. I want him to think about it. To remember how it felt. Because I know I'm never going to be able to forget him.

Chapter Nine

Belle

We don't talk about it for the rest of the journey. He puts the music back on, and I try to sing to The Weeknd and Post Malone and Kendrick Lamar without thinking of the moment that Damon slid his hand beneath the elastic of my underwear and swirled his finger over my clit. Oh my God. How can I think about anything else?

But I'm a good girl, and I don't mention it again. Not until we enter the Christchurch suburbs, anyway. At which point I've been biting my lip for an hour, and the torture of sitting next to him and not talking about what happened has finally gotten to me.

"Where are you staying?" I ask as he slows the Jag and takes the turning for Riccarton, where my father and stepmother live.

"In The Garden House."

"Oh, of course." It's a beautiful boutique hotel on the edge of the Avon, overlooking Hagley Park, and it's where Gaby and Tyson are holding the wedding, so most of the guests are staying there.

I clear my throat. "Are you working at Kia Kaha tomorrow?"

He nods. "Alex is on the six-a.m. flight back."

"I'm so glad he had to do that presentation at the last minute."

He glances at me and gives a small smile. "Me too."

"Clearly, God does exist."

He chuckles.

I study his face, lit by the streetlights as he navigates the suburbs. He's so handsome. All his talk about one-night stands and being cursed with relationships doesn't frighten me, because I've known him a long time, and I can see that what happened with his cousins has affected him deeply.

I want to slip beneath the façade he presents to everyone else and cuddle up to the vulnerable guy I know lies beneath. I want him to whisper endearments in my ear again, and to have him touch me the way he did in the darkness and the silence of the car. But I also want more than that. I'm so intrigued now by our discussion of sex. I want to taste him, and for him to taste me. If he can make me feel like that with his fingers, what would it feel like if he gave me an orgasm with his mouth? How would it feel to come with him inside me? Oh my God. I think I'll die if I don't go all the way with him now.

"If you have any free time, we could always catch up again for a coffee," I say mildly.

He glances at me again, then returns his gaze to the road, slowing as he approaches the street to my father's house. "I don't think that's a good idea."

"Why?"

He just purses his lips.

"Afraid you won't be able to resist me?" I tease. That earns me another wry look. "Aw," I say, "we're both single consenting adults. Where's the harm?"

He cruises past the neat line of houses with their well-tended gardens, then slows and stops outside my father's. He turns off the engine, sits there for a moment, then unbuckles his belt and turns to me in the seat.

My heart races. I think he's going to tell me off, but instead he just studies me. His eyes are almost black in the semi-darkness.

"I told you," he states, "I'm not offering a relationship."

"Who said anything about a relationship?" I look at his mouth, remembering how it felt to kiss him, his tongue sliding against mine. "I'm talking about sex."

He runs his tongue over his teeth and looks away, out of the window.

"Don't you want to teach me?" I say. "I need someone to show me the things we talked about. You said I need a man I trust. I trust you, Damon."

"Jesus. Don't say that."

"Why? I do trust you. I've known you for fifteen years. You're my brother's best mate. You're a good guy."

"No, I'm not."

"Don't give me that. I know you."

"Belle," he says, his voice hard, "you really don't. Don't spoil this. I did what I did because I felt sorry for you, and I wanted to help. But like I said, it wasn't all altruistic. Tonight, when I go back to the hotel, I'll think about what I did and probably jerk off because it was so fucking hot. How do you think that makes me feel? You're my best mate's little sis. He'd kill me if he found out what I did."

"So don't tell him." My heart is racing at the thought of him touching himself while he thinks of me. The way he's so frank about it... oh God that's so sexy.

"That's not the point," he snaps.

"So what is the point? I know it turns you on to think about me. And I know you like to pleasure women because you told me. So why don't we have a bit of fun?"

"No."

Silence falls between us.

Eventually, he rolls his eyes. "For God's sake, don't sulk."

"I'm not sulking."

"Yes, you are."

"Can you blame me?"

He huffs a sigh and gets out of the car.

Grumbling to myself, I unbuckle my belt and get out. I retrieve my case from the boot, he gets the boxes from the back seat, and we take them up to the front door.

The door is flanked by two panels of frosted glass and surrounded by a brick porch. I stand the case up, and he bends and puts the boxes on the floor, then straightens.

"Damon..."

"No," he says.

Wow, he's so much taller and bigger than me. I know he likes that. All the girls I've seen him with in photos have been small. And he prefers them to be younger than him. I have a feeling he likes that I'm inexperienced, too. He loved giving me my first orgasm. And I'm pretty sure he'd enjoy showing me the ropes in bed.

I've never done anything like this before. Do I have the courage? If I don't, I know he'll walk away, and that'll be it. Tonight he gave in to his desire, but he won't make the same mistake again.

I move closer to him and place my hands on his chest, then lean against him. "You'd be doing me a favor," I murmur in the sultriest voice I can summon. "Come on, gorgeous, help a girl out. You've teased me with one orgasm, don't you want to give me more? And let me reciprocate? Don't you want to make love to me?"

His eyes blaze. Without warning, he walks forward, forcing me to move back against the brick wall of the porch. He only stops when he's right up against me, forcing me to look up at him with wide eyes.

"Stop it," he snaps, leaning on the wall above my right shoulder. "Just because I'm Alex's mate, and you've known me for a long time, it doesn't mean you know me."

"But—"

"I don't date nice girls, Belle. In fact, I don't date at all anymore. And I don't make love. I fuck, okay? I go on Tinder, and I meet girls who state they're looking for a one-night stand, and I take them to a hotel, and I fuck them. Then I get up, and I leave. I don't spend the night, and I don't call them the next morning."

I blink, taken aback by his harsh words.

"I like sex," he continues, "and I like hot girls, and yeah, I've known you a long time, and I felt sorry for you. Nobody should be afraid or ashamed to touch their own body, and I wanted to show you how good it felt. But that's as far as it goes. You need to find someone of your own age who'll be sweet and gentle, because I'm neither of those things."

"What if I don't want someone sweet and gentle?" I ask, breathless.

"That's your prerogative, but I'm not your answer. My friendship and business relationship with Alex is too important to me, and I'm not going to blow it on you, Belle, no matter how much you bat those pretty little eyelashes at me."

I don't reply, not knowing how to handle him. He seems angry, but I think it's all for show. His words are at odds with his admission that he likes to give a girl pleasure, and his actions in the car—he was sweet and tender in both what he said and what he did. He's trying to put me off, because he thinks I deserve better.

"I helped out my friend's baby sis," he says firmly. "That's all. A good girl like you doesn't want a bad guy like me."

I can't help it—my lips curve up at his use of 'good girl'.

He glares at me, and I press my lips together, dropping my gaze to his chest.

We're silent for a moment, and then I slowly lift my gaze to his. He looks a mixture of amused and exasperated.

"Please don't pout," he murmurs. "I can't cope with that."

His deep voice sends a shiver all the way down my spine. I stick my bottom lip out further, keeping my sulky gaze on him. He studies it, his eyelids dropping to half-mast.

"Would a good guy do this?" he whispers. Then he lowers his head and presses his lips to mine.

I hold my breath as he kisses my bottom lip, then lightly brushes his tongue across it. Oh… I close my eyes, a soft moan escaping my lips as my nipples harden in my bra and I clench deep inside.

He lifts his head a fraction, and I feel his breath across my lips.

"You're unraveling me again," he says, a tad resentfully, grudgingly. His big body is pressed up against mine, and when he speaks, it's like holding a tuning fork up to my ear, sending vibrations through my bones, making my body hum.

I swallow and moisten my lips with the tip of my tongue. "I'm sorry," I say, even though I'm not. I can smell his cologne, and the way he's teasing me with his mouth just inches from mine is making me dizzy.

"You're a bad girl," he says.

I lift my gaze to his. "Wanna spank me?"

He stares at me, and then we both laugh.

"Jesus," he says, moving back, "Will you please go inside?"

"Yeah, all right." I take out my key, slide it in the lock, and open the door. Dad and Sherry will both be in bed by now, so I need to be quiet. "Well, have a good day tomorrow."

"You too." He steps back out. I lean against the door jamb as he turns to face me and slides his hands into the pockets of his jeans. I'm almost level with his eyes now. I love that he's a big guy. Imagine having him on top of you, pressing you into the mattress. Ooh.

"Thank you," I say as graciously as I can. "For so many things. For saving me from Cole. For driving me all this way. For letting me drive the Jag. For talking to me about everything. And for…" My voice trails off as I look into his eyes.

"You're welcome." He gives me a boyish smile. Despite his talk about being older than me, he's still very young, only twenty-six.

"When's your birthday?" I ask, knowing it's in April.

"Next month," he confirms. "The nineteenth." He gestures at my midriff. "How are you feeling now?"

"Not too bad."

"You take care of yourself, okay?" There's a glimmer in his eyes. Is he suggesting I take care of myself? My face flushes, and his lips curve up. He was totally suggesting that.

"'Night," he says, and he turns and walks back up the path to his car. I watch him go, see him get into the Jag, and he waves as he pulls away.

Leaving the boxes and my case by the door, I go through to the kitchen, grab a bottle of water from the fridge, then head to my room. Even though I'm at uni now, Sherry hasn't touched my room, and it still bears the dark colors, black and purple, that I liked back then, the books I read in my teens, and the clothes I didn't take with me.

Quietly, I visit the bathroom, then get into bed and stare up at the ceiling thinking about how Damon was so insistent that he wouldn't risk Alex's friendship for me, only to follow it up with that sexy kiss. *A good girl like you doesn't want a bad guy like me.* I sigh in the darkness and turn onto my side. Did he really do what he did in the car? It feels like a dream. I'd never have believed an orgasm could feel that good. I close my eyes, remembering his husky whispers in my ear, the way he teased my nipple with his other hand. How he said, *This is going to be easy as… You're halfway there already.* So confident. So fucking sexy.

I slide into sleep, my dreams filled with his gingerbread-brown eyes.

*

Exhausted from all the emotion and the journey, I sleep right through until eight a.m. I pull on an old pair of PJs from the drawer, visit the bathroom, then go out to the kitchen to discover my father and Sherry getting ready to leave for work—Dad at the local boys' high school, Sherry at a primary school.

"It's Rip Van Belle," Dad says as I walk in. He's around fifty-four and five-foot-eleven, with hair that's still brown and thick, although his short beard is almost completely gray.

"Hey you," I say, going up to him for a big hug.

"Hello, sweetheart." He squeezes me and plants a kiss on my temple, then releases me so I can go over to Sherry. She's a few years younger than him, a little curvy, with fluffy blonde hair that bounces around her shoulders and attractive laughter lines at the edges of her eyes. She's been good for him, and they're happy together.

"Hey, Belle." She hugs me too. She's been like a second mother to me—a better mother than my own, in fact. "Good to see you," she says.

"It's great to be here." I take a bit of toast that's still in the rack on the kitchen counter and get some jam out of the fridge. "Only four days to go until the big day! How's Gaby doing?"

"Running around like a chicken without a head," Dad says cheerfully. Then his smile fades and he exchanges a look with Sherry before saying, "Your mother gets in this morning, by the way."

I concentrate on spreading the jam over the toast. "Where's she staying?"

"At The Garden."

"Oh, of course." Poor Damon. Hopefully he won't bump into her.

"She wants to see you," Dad says, gathering his wallet and keys. "I told her to text you once she's here, and maybe you can meet her at the hotel or something."

"Sure." I take a bite of the toast and crunch it. I have no intention of seeing my mother alone, but I won't tell him that. "So, are you two off?"

"Yep. Sherry finishes at midday today so she'll be home then."

"We've got a family dinner tonight," she tells me.

"Oh, okay."

"Did you have a good journey down?" Dad asks.

"Yeah. Damon brought his new F-type Jag and let me drive it."

Dad's eyes widen. "Wow. That was brave."

"He said I'm the best driver he knows," I say wryly. "I don't think he'd have let me otherwise."

"He's a sweetie," Sherry says. "So good of him to drive you. He called in about half an hour ago, by the way. He dropped something off for you."

"Oh?"

She gestures at the dining room table. I look over and see a square pink box with a ribbon and a small envelope stuck to it. Puzzled, I go over to it, remove the envelope, and take out the small card. It bears a short message in his large, bold handwriting.

Belle,
Hope you're feeling okay!
Open this care package when you're on your own.
D x

I look back at Sherry. She raises her eyebrows. "What is it?"

"I joked yesterday that I hadn't had any Jaffa Cakes for months," I tell her, thinking on my feet. "He's bought some for me."

"Aw, what a love." She picks up her purse and laptop bag. "Come on, Mace, or we'll be late."

"I'm coming." He waves goodbye to me. "You having a rest today, honey?"

"Yeah, taking it easy."

"All right, see you later."

"See you around one," Sherry says, and follows him out. The front door opens and closes, and then I hear them getting in the car and the engine starting.

I look back at the box on the table and pry the lid off. Slowly, my lips curve up. I was on the right lines with my joke about Jaffa Cakes. The box contains a pack of Maltesers, and a small box of expensive truffles in various flavors. There's also a jar of relaxing bath salts, and a paperback, a fantasy romance I've heard a lot about but haven't read yet. How thoughtful—I can eat the chocolate and read the book while I'm having a bath!

I lift the book out, then realize there's something underneath it. Another box, about six inches long and four inches wide. I take it out, my eyes widening as I see the picture on the front. Jaw dropping, I open the box and take out the item inside. It's a bullet vibrator, the sort he described to me in the car. It looks exactly like a tube of lipstick, about four inches long, red and shiny. There's also a small tube of lubrication.

As I tip up the box, another note flutters out. It's a little longer than the others.

I charged it up. It's ready to go. And it's waterproof. Try using it in the bath. Might help your stomach! The girl in the shop assured me that the novel has some of the best sexy scenes, too. Thought it might help to get you started. Let me know how you get on :-) I want a report!

My face fills with lava. The cheeky bastard!

I turn the vibrator around in my fingers, then press the button at the bottom. It leaps to life in my hands, buzzing against my skin, making my heart pound. Wow. It has seven speeds, and I cycle through them, my eyes widening again at the feel of the topmost one.

I turn it off, put it back in the box, and replace the lid. I go over to the coffee machine and start making myself a coffee, my heart racing.

I couldn't possibly use it. It was one thing to let Damon arouse me with his fingers in the quiet darkness of the car, but it's another to do it to myself. I wasn't even comfortable when he moved my hand down with his. I mean, yeah, it was sexy to see how turned on I was. But to do it myself, when I'm alone, purely for pleasure? It's so decadent. Isn't it? Damon would say it's perfectly natural, but even the thought of it feels wicked.

After pouring the steamed milk over the espresso, I go back to the box, retrieve the paperback, and take it and the coffee out onto the deck with a couple of the truffles.

I'll have to think about the other item in the box for a while.

Chapter Ten

Damon

After a solid five hours' sleep, I arrive at Kia Kaha at eight a.m. and slot the Jag into the visitor's parking spot at the front of the building.

Alex and I were part of a close group of friends at university that included James Rutherford, Henry West, and Tyson Palmer, all of us computer engineers in one form or another. From the beginning, Alex talked about the idea of us all forming our own company, but it was only when Tyson had his accident and ended up in a wheelchair that the decision was made to focus on robot-assisted physiotherapy.

When we graduated, I thought long and hard about moving to Christchurch and going in with Alex and the others in the creation of the firm. But at that point, Saxon and Kip were in the process of forming Kingpinz. They were keen for me to be one of the directors of the company, and once they explained that their vision was to create improved myoelectric prosthetics for Kennedy, I didn't need further convincing. I've never regretted my decision, because Kennedy will always come first for me, but I visit Christchurch often to spend time with Alex and the others, and help out with MAX, and now THOR, where I can.

The succession of earthquakes in 2010 and 2011, including the devastating 6.3 earthquake on 22 February 2011 that killed 185 people, also caused major damage to the land, buildings, and infrastructure. Over fifteen hundred buildings were demolished, and the city entered a period of complex rebuilding and restructuring.

Kia Kaha is based in the center of the city, in a brand-new building overlooking the Avon River. In Māori culture, *kaitiaki* or guardians are chosen to advocate for elements of nature, and Henry, who is a member of the South Island iwi or tribe, Ngāi Tahu, worked with the local *kaitiaki* to plan and design the new office.

The design is biophilic—which is about finding a way to connect people with nature, culture, and place. Raw materials such as punga logs, reclaimed Kauri timber, and river stones are visible throughout the offices, while the many native plants give the impression that the building and nature are working together to provide the best environment possible. Māori symbols and storytelling are interwoven throughout the building.

It's a beautiful, sustainable workplace that celebrates the company's connections to Māori culture and values. Recycled and salvaged materials were used in its construction, and the office is resource and energy efficient, designed to use thirty-five percent less energy and thirty percent less water than a typical office. I love it here, and always enjoy coming to visit.

I enter the lobby, which is large and open plan, and filled with sunshine from the many windows. A crescent-moon-shaped reception desk curves around the seating area, the front created from a carved light wood that tells the story of Tāne-mahuta, god of the forest. Green ferns in white pots on either side increase the feeling of being surrounded by nature.

I glance at the painting on one wall of Rangi and Papatūānuku, the primal couple in Māori mythology, and smile.

"Hey, Rebecca." I go up to the receptionist, who beams at me.

"Good morning, Mr. Chevalier."

"Damon," I scold, signing the register. "I keep telling you. My dad is Mr. Chevalier."

She sticks her tongue out at me, and I laugh. She's worked here from the beginning, and I'm pretty sure she likes me. I'd never ask her out, though. *Don't shit on your own doorstep*, my dad once told Saxon when he dated and then promptly broke up with a girl who worked in Dad's office, making it very awkward for our father when she sat sobbing at her desk. It's a rule I've always stuck to, and I've never gotten involved with anyone I work with or who's related to someone I know.

I think about Belle, and try not to wince. Until now.

We're not involved though. I think I escaped before any damage was done.

"Go through," Rebecca says, offering me a visitor badge. "They're expecting you."

I take the badge, clip it onto the lapel of my suit jacket, give her a smile, then head left to the boardroom in the corner of the building.

The room overlooks a large, terraced bank that leads down to the Avon. Even though it's still early, a punt sails gracefully through the slow-moving water, the punter dressed in Edwardian costume, while a coxed four shell overtakes them, the rowers pulling hard on the oars.

The boardroom includes a large, square table that seats fourteen, although only four places are taken at the moment. Relieved to see the table laden with pastries and muffins as I didn't have time for breakfast, I approach the glass door, which slides open. All the doors in the office are automatic to make it easier for Tyson in his wheelchair.

I grin at them. "Morning!"

"Hey." The guy on the left raises a hand, then returns to typing on his laptop. Alexander Winters is the same height as me but a tad slimmer, with jet-black hair. His nickname of Oscar the Grouch has been well earned over the years, but it doesn't change the fact that he's smart, hardworking, and loyal to a fault. He's my best mate, after my brothers,

Everyone in this room has money, and we all consider ourselves sophisticated, to a certain degree. We all wear smart suits and expensive aftershave, we all have expensive watches and top-of-the-range phones. But James is the guy for whom the word brio was invented. He wears Italian suits, even to work, he always looks as if he had his hair cut five minutes ago, and women have assured me he's the best-looking guy in the whole of the country. A descendant of the New Zealand physicist Ernest Rutherford, James is as smart as his ancestor but manages to combine that with also being a mischievous playboy. He was the one who always fell in the pool at parties, who's broken practically every bone in his body, and who seduces nearly every woman he meets. Alex says James's ancestor must be turning in his grave, but even though he looks like a rebel on the surface, James is fiercely loyal to his friends, and I like him a lot.

Henry West also got his name from a famous Kiwi: George Henry West. George—whose Māori name was Kāi Te Rakiāmoa—was the first pilot of Māori descent to join the Royal New Zealand Air Force in 1936, and Henry is immensely proud of his heritage. He's enormous, at least six-four, and built like a brick shithouse. Like a lot of Māori guys, he tends to be reticent in company, only speaking when he has something important to say, but he's a great guy. He's the only one of us currently married, to his long-time girlfriend, Shaz, although Tyson is obviously going to join the ranks of hitched soon.

The last director of Kia Kaha is Juliette Kumar. She's a physiotherapist who Alex met at uni when he pulled a hamstring playing rugby. She once said her inclusion in the company was necessary as a civilizing influence, to stop the guys making fart jokes all the time. Alex replied that nothing would stop us making fart jokes. But it's true that her presence makes us all behave better. She's of Māori-Indian descent, tall and slender, with long dark hair, light-brown skin, and attractive dark eyes. She's very much a modern Kiwi woman, independent and spirited, and sporty. But her mixed heritage is very important to her. She has a Māori tattoo and a traditional bone comb in her hair, and although she wears business suits to work, socially she sometimes wears a traditional sari, and she often paints a bindi on her forehead. She's wearing one today. I know it's a representation of the third eye chakra and it can be a religious symbol or used to indicate the wearer is married, but it's also used as a beauty mark. Juliette once told me that for her it's a way to embrace her Indian culture, and for her it represents honor, love, and prosperity, which I thought was great. I wink at her, and her lips curve up.

"Morning," she says, about to get up. "Do you want a coffee?"

"No, it's fine, I'll get it. Would you like one?"

"Well, if you're offering…"

I smile, go over to the coffee machine on the table to the side, and start making two espressos.

"What time did you get here?" James asks.

"Around 12:30 a.m."

"Long journey," Henry says. "Did you bring the Jag?"

"Yeah." I turn the machine off and bring the cups over to the table. I take the seat next to Juliette and pass her one of the cups. "She drove like a dream. Belle loved her."

"You let Belle get behind the wheel?" Juliette teases.

"I did. She's a better driver than the rest of us put together." I glance at Alex, my heart giving a little bang as I see him sitting back, studying me. He doesn't say anything, and for a moment I think Belle must have told him what happened on the journey, and I wait for him to leap across the table, grab me by the lapels, and punch my teeth down my throat.

Instead, he says, "I'd love an espresso, Damon, thank you."

I just chuckle, and he rolls his eyes. "Did Belle tell you that Kaitlyn's arriving today?" He never calls his mother Mum, which tells you a lot about their relationship.

My eyebrows rise. "No. I don't think she knew." I'm sure she would have mentioned it if she had.

"Is Ryan Webster coming with her?" James asks. She met the famous movie star on the set of one of her action flicks, and they've been glued to each other's sides on social media for over two years now.

But Alex shakes his head and says, "They broke up, apparently."

"There was a photo on Insta of her at the airport, crying," Juliette advises us.

"Staged or genuine?" James asks.

Juliette shrugs. "It looked genuine. She wasn't wearing any makeup, and she was trying to hide her face behind her collar. I'll show you." She taps on her phone.

I exchange a glance with Alex. His relationship with his mother is complicated. They both have hot tempers, and it's rare for them to have an exchange without it devolving into a shouting match. I once heard him call her a pretentious, heartless witch. She responded with, "And you're a grumpy, soulless bastard. I guess you really are my son, right?" It's mostly superficial—he obviously loves her to bits, because he wouldn't get so angry if he didn't. But I'm aware of an undercurrent, presumably something to do with his father and the reason they broke up. He doesn't like to talk about it, though, so I remain in the dark.

"Here," Juliette says, turning her phone to show us. It reveals a photo of a woman almost unrecognizable as Kaitlyn Cross—her hair hangs loose and untamed around her shoulders, her face is free of makeup, and she looks fragile in the jacket she's pulled tightly around her as she tries to hide her face from the cameras, something she rarely does.

"We always knew that Gaby and Tyson were never going to be the stars at their own wedding," Alex says sarcastically. "This has only cemented that."

"She looks vulnerable," I comment mildly. "Maybe don't go in with guns blazing straight away."

He mutters under his breath and glares at his laptop, but he doesn't disagree, so hopefully I've dissuaded him from yelling at her as soon as she walks in the door.

"Where's Tyson?" I ask.

"He's gone with Gaby to pick Kaitlyn up," Juliette advises. "He'll be in later."

"We ready to start?" Henry asks. "I've got a Zoom call at ten and I wanted to go over THOR's specifications."

"Yep." Alex nods. "Let's start."

We spend the next couple of hours working. Just before ten, Alex says, "Okay, Henry's got his Zoom call and I've got a meeting. Shall we meet back here at eleven?"

We all nod. "All right if I work in here?" I ask the others.

"Of course," Juliette says. "You need anything?"

"No, I'm good. I might take a walk down to the river to stretch my legs, and then I'll get stuck in." They're having a problem integrating the gaming software that James has written with THOR's base program, and I've offered to help troubleshoot, as I've had some experience with connecting Kip's MOTHER software with the voice synthesizer we created.

While the others head back to their offices, I make myself another coffee in a takeaway cup, leave my laptop on the table, and open the sliding doors that lead out onto the deck. I walk down the steps of the company's private terrace, and sit on the bench at the bottom, overlooking the river.

Willow trees arch gracefully like ballerinas on the opposite bank, and a flock of ducks waddle through the reeds before launching themselves into the water. It's often cooler down here in the South Island than it is in the North Island, but today the March sun is warm on my face. I can smell donuts, sweet and caramel. Where's that coming from? Must be the café around the corner.

Pulling out my phone, I bring up the text message I received from Belle about an hour ago.

Just wanted to say thank you for the care package. She ends with a <flushed face> emoji.

As I was mid-conversation, I only had time to respond with: *Glad you liked it! Don't forget, I want a report.* I added a <devil face with horns> emoji.

She didn't reply.

I shouldn't continue with this, really. I shouldn't have given her the vibrator, either. But I was driving back from dropping her off early this morning when I passed a late-night adult shop, and I couldn't resist going in and treating her. I'm only trying to help, right? It's an absolute crime that she's never touched herself.

I type in a text and send it.

Me: *So, how are you getting on? Any luck?*

Belle: *I've eaten the truffles, yes.* She adds the <face with stuck-out tongue> emoji.

Me: *Come on. Own up. Have you tried it?*

Belle: *You're a very naughty boy.*

Me: *Is that a yes?*

Belle: *Not yet.*

I frown, a little disappointed.

Me: *Aw. I thought you'd be running into your bedroom to try it!*

Belle: *I haven't plucked up the courage yet.*

I blow out a breath.

Me: *What are you doing right now?*

Belle: *Sitting on the deck, reading the book you bought me.*

I think of her curled up on the outdoor sofa that sits on her father's deck, surrounded by colorful cushions.

Me: *What are you wearing?*

Belle: *LOL, I'm still in my PJs. Being lazy today.*

Me: *What color are they?*

Belle: *Light blue and silky.* She sends me an <angel> emoji.

Oh Jesus. That's it. My attempt to behave myself immediately flows down the river and disappears around the corner.

Me: <Exploding head>

Belle: *LOL. You had your chance last night.* <lips> <eggplant> <fireworks>

I huff a sigh. I'm already beginning to regret turning her down.

Me: *Are you trying to make me* <rocket> <fist> <water droplets>

Belle: *Hahahaha! Maybe!*

Me: *Already did that last night.*

Belle: *Seriously?*

Me: *I told you I would. Now it's your turn to* <wave hand> <cat>

Belle: *Damon!*

My lips curving up, I dial her number and press the phone to my ear.

*

Belle

The buzz of the phone in my hand makes me jump. My heart racing, I answer it. "Hello?"

"Bonjour, ma belle." His deep, sexy voice sends a shiver straight down my spine.

"You're such a naughty boy," I scold.

He chuckles. "I'm only trying to help your cramps."

"Yeah, yeah." I smile. "Thanks for the care package."

"You're very welcome."

"The book's good."

"The girl in the shop recommended it. I know you like fantasy stuff."

"It's quite saucy."

"That's mainly why I got it. Want to read some to me?"

"Absolutely not."

"Oh, now you're embarrassed? After making me answer that questionnaire?"

I grin; he has a point.

"So why haven't you tried the vibrator?" he asks.

I glance at the box that's now sitting on the deck table. I got as far as bringing it out here.

"I need to work up to it," I reply.

"Why don't you have a look at it?" he asks. "Describe it to me."

"Seriously?"

"Are you alone?"

"Yeah. Dad and Sherry have gone to work."

"Go on, then," he says.

I reach over to the box and take the vibrator out.

"So how big is it?" he asks.

"About four inches. It's a dinky little thing. It looks like a tube of lipstick without the lid."

"Have you turned it on yet?"

"Only briefly."

"Go on. Let me hear it."

Feeling mischievous, I press the button. The bullet leaps into life, humming in my fingers.

"I can hear it," he murmurs.

"It has seven speeds," I tell him. "Seven! Jeez." I turn it over in my fingers, enjoying the silky smoothness of it, and the feel of it buzzing on my skin.

"Okay," he says, "so here's what we're going to do. I'm going to give you instructions, and you're going to do as I say."

My eyes widen. "What?"

"Lie back on the sofa."

"Damon!"

"Your garden's private, isn't it?"

He's right—the large lawn is surrounded by a high fence. "Yeah…"

"And you're alone?"

"Yeah…"

"You can go into your bedroom if you'd rather, but I bet it's nice out there in the garden, in the sun."

I sigh. "It's lovely."

"So lie down on the cushions and get comfortable."

I can't do this. Can I? It feels so wicked… and yet there's something about Damon that makes it all seem so normal.

My heart in my mouth, I pull the cushions into a pile, turn and lie back on them, and draw the blanket that was over my legs up to my chest. Now I feel warm and safe, and even if someone was watching, they wouldn't be able to see what I was doing.

"Okay," I whisper.

"Good girl," he murmurs.

"Oh jeez…"

He chuckles.

"Where are you?" I ask.

"Sitting on the bench out the back of Kia Kaha. So I can't get up to anything, unfortunately. Now, first of all, I want you to stroke it over yourself. Start with your hands and arms. Just get used to the sensation against your skin."

"I'm going to put you on speakerphone," I tell him.

"Okay."

I prop the phone on a cushion close to my ear so I can leave both hands free, then start doing as he told me.

"Tell me what you're doing," he says.

"I'm holding it in my right hand and moving it across my left."

"How does it feel?"

"It's nice. It makes me tingle."

"They say a quarter of your total body surface can be involved in sexual pleasure. I think it's more than that. Stroke it across the pads of your fingers, your palm, and then your inner wrist."

"Mmm."

"Does it feel good?"

"Mmm, yeah."

"Now carry on down your inner arm. As you move down, lift your arm above your head so you can stroke the bullet all the way down underneath your arm."

I do as he says, stretching out on the sofa. The overhang ensures I'm in the shade, but the dappled sunlight coming through the nearby tree falls across the deck, moving as the leaves rustle in the light breeze, and it's lovely and warm. I feel relaxed and almost sleepy, but the buzz of the bullet across my skin ensures my pulse is continuing to pick up the pace.

"Now move it around your neck," he instructs. "Lightly, where it touches bone. Up your throat, around your jaw, over your ears. Don't forget your hair and scalp, and the nape of your neck."

I follow his instructions, sucking my bottom lip as I brush it beneath my hair, over my neck.

"What feels the nicest?" he asks.

"Mmm... my ears... and the nape of my neck... ooh, and my hair... I didn't expect that."

"The scalp is full of nerve endings. It's why hair pulling is a thing. Gentle tugging can be sexy."

I don't answer, conscious of my face warming at his sexy directions.

"Now, I want you to slip it inside your bra," he says.

"I'm not wearing one. PJs, remember?"

"Jesus." He mutters something. "All right. Move it over your upper body, over your top," he instructs.

I draw it down over my collarbone and then across my breasts.

"How does that feel?" he asks.

"Good..."

"Tell me what you're doing."

"Um... moving it over my breasts."

"Close your eyes."

I do, and it makes me focus on the movement of the bullet, and the sensations that are spiraling through me.

"Circle the tip around your nipple," he says.

I do as he says, biting my lip as my muscles clench deep inside. "Mmm."

"That feel good?"

"Mmm. Yeah. Very good."

"Do it to the other one. Nice and slow. Around the outside, the areola. Then on the end."

I'm having trouble lying still now. I leave the bullet resting on the tip of my nipple, and answering shivers ripple all the way through me.

"Mmm... Damon..."

"Good," he says, his voice low and sultry. "Now bring it up to your mouth. I want you to carefully brush it over your lips."

I do as he says, unable to stop a sigh escaping them.

"Now place it in your mouth," he says, "mind your teeth, but make it nice and wet."

I can't believe I'm doing this. It's so wicked. I do what he tells me, though, sucking it until the surface is coated, feeling the buzzing on my tongue.

"Now move it under your top and touch it to your nipples," he instructs.

I slip the bullet beneath the hem of my top and move it up. As it touches my left nipple, it transfers the wetness to the already sensitive skin, and I moan.

"Ah," he says, "that's good. Keep it there. Find which part feels most sensitive."

"Mmm... the tips..."

"Yeah. Hold it there."

"Ah, Damon. It's making me squirm."

"That's good, that means you're getting ready for sex, baby girl."

His endearment makes me inhale, because it takes me back to the car, when his murmurs in my ear were almost enough to make me come.

"Now, open the lube, and squeeze a little onto your middle finger."

Biting my lip, my face warming, I do it.

"I want you to move your hand beneath the elastic of your PJs," he says. "Slide it down, the way I showed you in the car. Tell me how it feels."

I slip my hand under the elastic of my PJ trousers and the underwear I'm wearing, and slide my middle finger down into my folds, transferring the lube there.

"Oh," I whisper.

"Are you nice and wet now?"

I scrunch up my nose, embarrassed and turned on at the same time. "Yes."

"That's great, baby girl. Are you wearing knickers?"

"Yeah." I wonder if he's going to ask me to take them off.

Instead, though, he says, "Good. Slide the bullet down into them."

I do it, lifting the elastic with my left hand, and guiding the vibrator down. It buzzes across my mound, making me shiver.

"Stroke it down the outside," he says.

Slowly, I move it across my outer labia. "Mmm... that feels good..."

"Touch yourself with your other hand," he instructs. "Open yourself up. Use your fingers first. Can you feel your clit?"

Shyly, I slide my finger down. It's easy to find the little button nestling in the folds, and I sigh as I rub my finger over it. "Yes."

"Okay, make sure the bullet is coated with lube, and so is all your skin."

"Mmm... okay..."

"Now slide the tip of the bullet down."

A moan leaves my lips. "Ohhh..."

"Good girl. Move it around and explore what feels good. No inserting, because that's not what it's for. Just stroke it through your skin. Enjoy the way it makes you feel. And when you're ready, move it to your clit and hold it there."

Feeling decadent and wicked, and yet also oddly emotional, I do as he says, exploring myself, discovering which parts of me are most sensitive, and what feels nice. Eventually, as he instructed, I bring the tip of the bullet to my clit and hold it there.

"Tell me how it feels," he says, his voice low and husky.

"It's amazing," I admit, sucking my bottom lip, because somehow it heightens the sensitivity all over my body.

"You can use the tip, or lie the bullet down so it's touching your clit and the area beneath it."

I try it, sighing as I find he's right. "That feels so good."

"Hold it there, baby. And now I want you to bring your other hand up to your breast."

I follow his directions, sliding my left hand beneath my pajama top to touch my right breast.

"I want you to play with the nipple," he says. "Tease it while the bullet does the rest."

Eyes closed, I arch back into the pillows as I arouse myself, lost in the blissful feelings rising in me like bubbles in champagne. "I wish you were here," I whisper, imagining his mouth on mine, and that it were his fingers moving between my legs.

"Me too, baby girl. I'd be kissing you right now. I'd kiss your sweet mouth, and then I'd kiss down your neck to your breasts and suck each of your nipples until they're wet and hard."

Oh Jesus, he's really trying to kill me with sex. I groan, flicking my nipple, tilting my hips up so I can angle the bullet further down into my folds.

"Then I'd kiss down over your stomach," he continues, his voice even huskier, "and move between your legs so I could go down on you."

"Ah, Damon..."

"I want to taste you, Belle. I want to slide my tongue into you and suck that nectar right out of you. I want to slip my fingers inside you and stroke you there while I tease your clit with my tongue, until you cover my hand with your moisture, until you're so fucking wet that we're both drowning in it. I'd tongue you until you were filling the room with your moans and crying out my name, clutching the covers, and arching your back. And then I'd suck your clit, and as you come I'd feel it pulsing on my tongue."

"Oh God..." His words, my fingers, and the sweet buzzing of the bullet are driving me to the edge. I'm so wet... I never thought that would happen. And this time I recognize it—I can feel it building inside me the way it did in the car. Tension beginning deep within me as my muscles start to tighten, an oh-so-wonderful sensation that makes me breathe with deep, ragged gasps as the world around me fades to nothing, and all that exists is Damon's deep voice in my ear teasing the orgasm out of me.

"Are you going to come for me, baby girl?"

"Ohhh... yes..." I bite my lip as it hits, intense and overwhelming. My muscles inside clench in exquisite pulses, five, six, seven times, and it's so beautiful and blissful that a sob escapes me.

"Ah," I hear him say, "sweetheart..."

The pulses die away, and I lift the bullet and turn it off. I blink as tears fill my eyes, and lie there, boneless and exhausted, while the autumn breeze brushes across my hot face.

"Good girl," he says, and I'm pretty sure he's smiling.

Chapter Eleven

Damon

The others arrive in the boardroom one by one, James first, then Juliette, then Henry when he finishes his call, and finally Alex, muttering something about his meeting overrunning.

He glances at me, and even though I know my face is carefully blank, he still says, "All right?"

"Yep." I drop my gaze to my laptop and pretend to read the screen. *I totally didn't just talk your little sister into having an orgasm on the phone.*

We work solidly for an hour. We've just helped ourselves to a coffee and a donut and are settling down for the next phase when my phone buzzes in my trouser pocket. I slide it out and rest it on my thigh. It's a text from Belle that's just a line of emojis: <telephone>, <lip bite>, <pointing finger>, <cat>, <hot pepper>, <water droplets>, <smirk face>. It ends with <halo face>—I'm a good girl. Literally our whole telephone conversation in one pictorial text.

I stifle a laugh and text her back. *Naughty girl* <heart>

Belle sends me two emojis: <Peach> and <hand>.

Jesus? Did she really just ask me to slap her ass?

I laugh out loud, smothering it as everyone looks over at me.

"Something funny?" Juliette asks, amused.

"Sorry." I wipe the smile away.

"You're texting a girl," she says, her eyes gleaming.

I meet her gaze, lips curving up, but I don't reply.

"Anyone we know?" she asks.

I just lean forward for one of the muffins that have magically appeared on the table.

"Whoever she is, she won't be around for long," Alex says wryly, turning his attention back to his notes.

Ouch. Thanks, dude.

"I know it's early, and THOR won't be ready for a few months, but I want to talk about the first trials," Henry says. "Juliette, have you got the list of applicants?"

She starts going through the list. I listen for a few minutes, but I'm not involved in the patient selection process, and I drop my gaze back to my phone. As surreptitiously as I can, I message Belle back.

Me: *Don't send me texts like that when I'm talking to your brother.*

Belle: *LOL. Serves you right for what you did this morning.*

Me: *I was just trying to help.*

Belle: *Yeah, RIGHT. Tell me it didn't turn you on.*

Me: *Okay, it might have had some effect...*

Belle: *You're so wicked.*

Me: *I did try and tell you.*

Belle: *You realized you've created a monster?*

Me: *LOL what do you mean?*

Belle: *I can't stop thinking about <water droplets> now.*

Me: *My work here is done <devil>*

Belle: *In fact, I think I'm going to have another go.*

My eyebrows rise a fraction. I glance around the table, but everyone's studying the list on the laptop, listening to Juliette, and nobody's looking at me.

Me: *Seriously?*

Belle: *Yep. I'm walking into my bedroom right now. Closing the door. Lying down. I have my new best friend with me.*

I picture her on her bed, the bullet vibrator in her fingers, and stifle a sigh.

Me: *I'm trying to work.*

Belle: *I'm not stopping you. You don't have to read my texts.*

Well, she's right. For a few minutes, I listen to James explaining which case he thinks we should use as a trial.

Then I drop my gaze to my phone again. Belle has sent a handful of texts.

I'm turning it on now. Ooh! Little buzzy bee.

I found a list of erogenous zones online. I'm going to try them all out.

Mm! Back of knees feels good.

I've discovered I like my hair being touched. I wonder how it feels to have it tugged?

Somewhat dazed, I look back at the others. Juliette has a bee in her bonnet about a particular boy who she says would benefit from the trial, but James says the kid's father isn't on the scene, and he's wary of the emotional stress it might put on a single mum if the results are unimpressive. The two of them are arguing. I'm keeping well out of that discussion.

I return my gaze to my phone. My lack of response hasn't stopped Belle.

I'm now <pointing finger> <melon> <melon>

I stifle a laugh. The minx.

Mmm, Damon…

I'm getting <hot pepper>

Now I'm <pointing finger> <cat>

Oh my God I'm so <water droplets>

I stifle a groan and blow out a breath. Jeez, this girl…

"Maybe we should bring the mum in for a discussion," Henry suggests. "We should be able to tell pretty quickly if we think she'll be able to cope."

"There are plenty of other applicants," James states.

"We should choose based on which patient would benefit from the trial the most," Juliette states hotly.

"To be fair," Henry says, "I think James is right. There are wider implications here. The child has to have support at home."

"So you're saying a single mum can't provide the same support as two parents?" Juliette asks mildly.

He meets her gaze. "You know that's not what I'm saying."

"Do I?"

"Juliette," James snaps, "come on. None of us is implying a single mum can't bring up a perfectly well-adjusted child. But we know how much emotional strain there is on parents of children who are in the position of needing treatment. I'd rather have a kid whose mum has support at home from her partner, that's all."

"Bullshit," she says. "The kid doesn't deserve to be passed over just because you don't think the mother could cope on her own. Alex, what do you think?"

He turns his pen in his fingers. "I think we should bring her in, if you think the kid is a good candidate."

The conversation continues, somewhat heated. I'm not worried; the five of us and Tyson have always worked through problems like this, and none of us takes offense if voices get raised or tempers fray, because we all want the best for the business.

I look back at my phone. At first I thought Belle was just texting to wind me up, but I'm beginning to suspect she really is doing this. More texts are appearing.

Do you want to know what I'm thinking about while I <pointing finger><cat>?

I'm thinking about that questionnaire…

Would you like to <scarf> *me to the* <bed>?

I stare at the phone. Is she saying she'd like to be tied up?

I'm thinking about you <tongue><cat><water droplets>

And about me <tongue><eggplant><water droplets>

And you and me <pointing finger><okay hand>

This girl is driving me insane.

Another text pops up.

God help me, but I'm even thinking about <pointing finger><peach><donut>

I rest my elbow on the arm of the chair so I can cover my mouth with my hand.

Ahhh… Damon… this feels so good…

Me: *Belle, Jesus.*

Belle: *Ha, I knew you were still there!*

Me: *I'm in a meeting.*

Belle: *You opened the cage, Damon. You let me out. You can't put me back in now.*

I try to concentrate on James as he talks, but there's no way the dude can hold my attention when I'm being sent such hot messages, and my gaze soon dips back to the phone.

I'm so <fire>

<Overheated face>

I'm thinking about you, Damon.

<eggplant><eggplant><eggplant>

<Biting lip>

Oh God, I'm going to <water droplets>

There's a brief pause during which I can't take my eyes off the phone.

Then a single emoji comes through.

<firework>

I close my eyes and wince as I try to calm myself down.

When I open my eyes again, everyone around the table is staring at me.

"Are you having a coronary?" James asks.

"Kinda." I run a hand through my hair. "Sorry. Did you ask me something?"

"You've got to tell us who she is," Juliette says.

"Just a friend."

Her eyebrows lift. "Friends first? Ooh, Damon, that's not like you."

"Will you stop? So did you come to a decision?"

Alex sighs. "All right, let's bring Finn Macbeth in for the trial."

Juliette's face lights up.

"The single mum?" I ask.

Alex nods.

"Thank you," Juliette murmurs.

James looks at his laptop. "Is her name really Mistletoe?"

"She goes by Missie."

"To be fair," Henry says, "it's not her fault her parents gave her a weird name."

Alex rolls his eyes. "I'm sure I'm going to regret this."

"You'll love her," Juliette says. "She's spunky."

"Just what I need," he replies, "a feisty brat on the trial—and I'm not talking about the kid."

"Actually, I think that's exactly what you need," she says with a grin.

My phone buzzes. I look down automatically.

Belle: <woozy face>

Me: *Stop it. They've just asked if I'm having a heart attack.*

Belle: <laughing face>

Me: *I'm going back to work now. Behave.*

Belle: <woman kneeling>

Fuck me.

Me: *That's a submissive pose.*

Belle: <tick><book>

She's been reading about it. She's telling me she's a good girl. I huff a sigh, feeling a bit faint.

Me: *Jesus. Leave me alone, woman.*

I finish with a <heart> emoji so she knows I mean it in the nicest possible way.

I turn the screen off and slide the phone back into my trousers.

She sends me a couple more messages over the next hour. I don't read them right then, but every time my phone buzzes in my pocket, it makes me smile.

*

After a while, the door swishes open, and Tyson comes in.

"Damon!" He steers his electric wheelchair up to me and high fives me. He's a good-looking guy, heavyset, with dark, slightly curly hair. His spinal cord injury five years ago was incomplete, meaning that he retained some motor and sensory function below the waist, but for a long time his bowels, bladder, and sexual functions were impaired, and doctors told him he'd never walk again. He was in a lot of pain, and suffered from severe depression.

Gradually, though, over time, despite the doctors' dark prognosis, he's improved tremendously. Gaby's constant and unwavering support has given him the determination to get better, and with the help of MAX, he's regained a high percentage of the functions he lost.

"Hey, dude." I grin at him. "How's the groom feeling?"

"Like an over-tightened nut," he says, turning the chair so he can slot into the empty space beside me.

"You want a coffee?" Juliette asks.

"Ah, yes please." When he's with strangers, he doesn't like to be assisted, but he doesn't mind us offering to help out.

"I've never seen you stressed," I say, amused. "Not like this." Obviously he was upset and angry after his accident, but he's a placid guy who rarely gets wound up about things.

"I guess if anything's going to ramp up the anxiety, it's getting hitched," James states.

"Gaby giving you headaches?" I ask.

Tyson lifts his briefcase onto the table, then leans forward and helps himself to a muffin. "Not at all. Getting hitched to her is the only reason I'm going through with it. It's everyone else."

"Don't tell me," Alex says, "is this to do with picking Kaitlyn up from the airport?"

Tyson glances at him. "Partly."

"Has she cast herself in the role of abandoned woman?" Alex asks.

"No," Tyson says. "She was actually very quiet and sad."

I look at Alex and lift my eyebrows. He frowns and looks down at his laptop.

"Gaby's a bit worried about her," Tyson says.

"Well, Kait wouldn't be our mother if she wasn't trying to hog the limelight in some fashion," Alex says, tapping on the keys. "I guess she thought weeping and wailing might be a bit over the top, so she's going for wistful and depressed."

"Or maybe she's genuinely upset," Juliette suggests, bringing over Tyson's coffee.

"Not buying it," Alex states.

"You're very harsh on her," Henry says.

"I have my reasons." Alex gestures at Tyson's laptop. "We're thinking of Finn Macbeth for THOR's first trial."

Tyson nods. "I'm happy with that decision. At least I was twenty-one when I ended up in this." He taps his wheelchair. "I was able to play sports and enjoy myself at school. The poor kid's only eight."

"The mum must be real bitter about that," I say.

"Not at all. She told me she does her best to remain positive for Finn. She's like a ray of sunshine. She'll be great to have around."

The guys all give a look that suggests they're impressed at the woman's attitude. All except Alex, whose expression remains skeptical. He finds it difficult to trust women. His mother really did a number on him.

I hope Kaitlyn isn't going to cause too much trouble while she's here. Gaby and Tyson deserve their day in the sun.

*

We work for a couple of hours, then break for lunch. I check my emails, and discover one from Helen, the head of HR at Kingpinz.

Damon,

When you're available, would you mind giving me a call? I have something I'd like to discuss with you.

Helen.

While the caterers begin bringing in platters of sandwiches and hot savories, I take my phone out through the sliding doors onto the terrace, bring up Helen's number, and press call.

She answers after a few rings. "Hello?"

"Hey, Helen, it's Damon."

"Hello, thanks for coming back to me."

"No worries. What can I do for you?"

"Yeah, sorry about this, but I want to have a quick chat about a sexual harassment issue."

Holy fuck. Even though there's a stiff breeze blowing across the terrace, I break into a sweat. "Oh." I swallow hard. "Right." My brain works furiously as I try to work out who it could be. I'm always super careful not to get involved with anyone at work. I never touch women inappropriately. And I always make sure I know the woman very well before I say anything remotely risqué. At Christmas, for example, I gave Kip's PA a kiss under the mistletoe, but only because she's in her forties and happily married. I've known her for five years, and she's more than able to handle the three Chevalier brothers when they make near-the-knuckle quips.

Surely it wasn't she who complained? I can't think of anything else I might have done that would have offended someone. But who knows in the current climate?

"What have I done?" I ask.

"What? No, it wasn't you, Damon."

Relief rushes through me. "Jesus. You gave me a heart attack."

She chuckles. "I'm so sorry, I didn't mean to imply that."

"It's okay. I just need to lie down for five minutes."

"Aw. I really am sorry."

I blow out a long breath. "It's okay."

"I wouldn't have bothered you while you're in Christchurch, but Saxon's in Auckland, and Kip's obviously got Craig to sort out." We're having trouble with one of the members of our Senior Leadership Team, and Kip's dealing with that, so I'm not surprised she wants to keep this off his desk. All three of us—Saxon, Kip, and I—have had management training in dealing with issues including sexual harassment, so she was right to come to me.

"So what's happened?" I ask.

"I was talking informally to one of the office juniors, and she said that Lewis Chaplain has been coming on a bit strong."

"Ah." Lewis Chaplain is the deputy head of accounting, the same age as me, incredibly good looking, and the one guy I thought every young woman in Kingpinz—and possibly several of the older ones—would give her left arm to go out with. I'd have been less surprised if

Lewis was the one making the complaint against some overzealous admirer.

"Who's the junior?"

"Jessica."

Jessica Lambert is only eighteen, and also works in accounts as a junior. She's small, chatty, and bubbly.

"She doesn't want to make a formal complaint," Helen says. "She tried to laugh it off. But I could see she was bothered by it."

"What's he done, exactly?"

"She says he flirts all the time and makes suggestive comments. She tried to tell him she wasn't interested, but he wouldn't take no for an answer. Then on Monday, when she was alone in the break room, he came in, closed the door, and tried it on again."

I go cold. "Did he touch her inappropriately?"

"I don't think so. I think he sort of leaned over her, intimidated her a bit."

"What did she do?"

"Tried to laugh it off. She told me not to worry about it. He's her superior, and I think she's worried about creating an unpleasant working atmosphere, or even losing her job. He's well liked at the company, as you know, and he's been here a lot longer than she has."

"Stupid question, maybe, but why's she not interested? He's young, good looking…"

"Just because he's good looking doesn't mean she should drop her knickers as soon as he walks into the room." Her voice is sharp.

I'm quiet for a moment. Then I say softly, "Of course not. I apologize if I offended you."

She clears her throat. "No, it's okay. It… it happened to me, too, that's all."

"Jesus, really?"

"Yeah, years ago, when I was a junior in my first job. One of the senior managers there was very handsome, a real ladies' man. I was in the stationery cupboard one day, and he came in, shut the door, and told me he'd had his eye on me for a while. Said he'd get me promotion if I treated him right. Then he told me to go down on him."

I blink. "What the fuck?"

"It happens, Damon."

"Jesus Christ. What did you do?" She hesitates, and immediately I say, "I'm sorry. Don't answer that. It's none of my business."

"It was a long time ago. Things were different back then. Nowadays we have policies and procedures, and employers are a lot more supportive than they were. I mean, officially that kind of thing wasn't tolerated, but it happened a lot. If you complained, you were ostracized and moved on, or even sacked for a minor grievance."

I run a hand through my hair. "I'm so sorry."

"Don't worry about it," she says, more gently. "I don't think this is the same situation. Lewis is just a young guy trying it on. It's mixed messages. Between you and me, though, she's gay."

"Oh. Fuck."

"Yeah. I told her that's irrelevant. A woman doesn't have to be gay to not be interested in a guy."

"No, of course."

"She hasn't told anyone and doesn't want him or the other girls to know."

"Sure. I'll talk to him."

"You don't have to do that. She doesn't want to put in a formal complaint. I just wanted to let you know, that's all."

"Helen, I want to talk to him. Can you set up a meeting, please?" My voice brooks no argument. "I'm back on Monday."

She sighs. "Okay. I'll book the two of you into the meeting room for eleven a.m. and send him the appointment."

"No problem. See you Monday."

"Yeah, see you."

I end the call and go back inside. The caterers have left, and everyone's helping themselves to the food. We've got a lot to get through, so we'll work through lunch, but as usual we're all ravenous, so we'll take five to pile our plates up.

"Everything all right?" Henry asks as I take my seat again.

I tip my head from side to side. "It was Helen. She's had a complaint of sexual harassment."

"Have you been chatting up the interns again?" James asks.

I send him a wry look as the others chuckle. "Not me, thank God, although I did panic at first."

"Aw, Damon," Juliette says, "you'd never do that. But I can see why you'd be worried. There must always be a fear that you've said something without thinking."

Alex shakes his head as he takes a club sandwich. "It's surprisingly easy not to sexually harass women when you put your mind to it. Guys who say otherwise need a lesson in respect."

"You're right," I reply. I look at the food, suddenly not hungry. "But even though most employers try to discourage it, we know that twenty-two percent of relationships begin in the workplace. And anyway, I think it may be a bigger picture thing. Mixed signals, you know? My head of HR said the guy got the girl alone and came on to her, and she tried to laugh it off because she was embarrassed and worried about losing her job. I guess he thought she was just teasing him. It's tough to tell, sometimes."

Alex's brows draw together, although he doesn't say anything, but James admits, "That's true."

I look at Juliette. "I'm sure you've had to deal with it more than we have. What would you do if a guy came on to you and you weren't keen?"

"I'd take him to one side and explain politely that I wasn't interested, and I'd like him to stop."

"And if he didn't?"

"I'd tell him to fuck off and keep his hands to himself."

I give a short laugh. She's always been able to handle herself.

"All joking aside though," she continues, "if she's young, she won't have developed coping mechanisms yet. If he's above her in the chain of command, and if he's attractive, she'll feel intimidated. A guy doesn't have to physically restrain a woman to intimidate her. You're all taller, broader, and bigger than most women, and not every woman is a feisty badass, especially at a young age, before we learn to handle men."

I think about what happened between Belle and Cole. It makes my stomach churn to think that women as confident as Belle and Juliette seem to be could still feel intimidated by men today.

"When I picked Belle up, she was having an argument with her ex," I tell them. "He had her up against the wall, and—"

"What?" Alex says.

Shit, she hasn't told him. "It's all right," I say quickly, "I dragged him off her, threw him out, and told him if he came in fifty leagues of her, I'd cut his bollocks off and ram them down his throat."

Alex frowns. "Is she okay?"

"Yeah, it shook her up a bit, but she's fine. But what you said made me think," I say to Juliette. "She must have felt vulnerable. What would you have done in that situation?"

"Yell for one of you to come rescue me," she says with a grin.

"I'd save you," James tells her.

"Yeah, by talking him to death. If I wanted someone to beat him up, I'd call for Henry."

James looks pained, while Henry grins and tucks into a sausage roll.

I don't smile though, and Juliette tips her head. "Why is this bothering you so much?"

I'm genuinely upset to think that Cole probably scared Belle. I knew she was frustrated, but I didn't consider how he might have made her feel vulnerable and even terrified.

I can't say that though, not in front of Alex. "This is my first sexual harassment case," I opt for, "and I don't want to screw it up. What if Lewis says he thought Jessica was interested in him? If he had no idea he came across as threatening? I find that terrifying. How do I know I've never gotten the signals wrong?" The expressions of the other guys reflect my own concern.

"Because you're respectful toward women." She glances around the room, a mixture of puzzled and amused. "Guys, come on. You're all sweethearts. I've seen you all treat girls like princesses. You don't have anything to worry about."

James scratches at a mark on his phone. "The thing I find difficult is that some women like guys to be..." He glances around, embarrassed. "You know," he finishes lamely.

"You mean during sex?" Juliette asks, frank as ever. He shrugs. Her eyes hold a touch of pity. "There's a big difference between real life and the bedroom," she continues. "In real life we want respect and equality. You're stronger than us—we can't argue with that. But it's the twenty-first century, and we expect you to be civilized and not use your strength and height and weight to intimidate us. In the bedroom, though, some of us like to explore those differences. But I can see how it might be tough for guys to know when to hold back and when to give in to the animal inside you." She says it in a teasing tone, and we all give small smiles.

"It's about communication," she continues. "Just talk to her about what your girl wants and what she considers acceptable. And look, fellas, for Christ's sake, have a safe word. Pineapple is a popular one.

That way, providing you always stop whenever she says it, you never have to worry."

"Pineapple?" James repeats.

"Don't ask me why. It needs to be something that you wouldn't use in that context. So don't have 'stop' as a safe word, for example, because if you're having fun, the girl might say it in play and not mean it."

"Can it be any fruit?" Alex asks. "Or does it have to be tropical?"

Juliette pokes her tongue out at him. "Moving on," he says wryly, "let's talk about what we've got coming up this week."

The conversation continues, and we spend the rest of the afternoon working on THOR. But Juliette's words continue to linger in my mind.

Chapter Twelve

Belle

Sherry comes home around one p.m., and the two of us spend the rest of the afternoon in the kitchen, cooking together. Gaby, Tyson, and Alex are coming around for dinner tonight, so Gaby can go over any last-minute worries about the wedding, and also because we haven't had a family dinner for a long time.

Together we make a big steak pie and a truckload of mashed potatoes, then we chop some carrots and add frozen green beans to a big pot. Sherry then makes her famous Pavlova while I sit at the breakfast bar, chatting to her as I run a deck of cards through my fingers.

My mother texts me a few times while I'm sitting there. The irony that I'd rather talk to Sherry than text her back doesn't escape my attention. Sherry was much more of a mother figure to me during my teenage years than my birth mum. Sherry was the one who washed my gym kit and helped me make my packed lunches, who put her arm around me when I cried over boys, and who talked me through friendship hiccups. She was the one who knew the bands I liked and that I preferred to wear black when I wasn't in school uniform, when my own mother was still sending me pink frills and sequins. Mum might have provided for me financially, but Sherry was there for me physically and emotionally, which I value more than money. Easy to say when you have it, I suppose, but no expensive jacket or purse from L.A. can replace the time I shared with Sherry, when we'd get back from a netball match and spend the afternoon baking cakes in the kitchen while Dad mowed the lawn.

The third time Mum texts, though, I sigh and decide I should respond.

"That your mum?" Sherry asks as she places the freshly cut Kiwi fruit onto the baked meringue.

"Yeah. She wants to see me."

"That's fair enough. When?"

"Tomorrow. But in the morning I wanted to go shopping, in the afternoon I've got the kids' party, and then it's the hen night."

"You should make time for her," Sherry says. "She doesn't come to New Zealand often."

"Exactly. And she expects me to drop everything and see her, without a thought to what I'm doing."

"That's fair, but maybe she needs to see her daughter, sweetheart? It sounds as if she's been having a tough time."

"She's got plenty of therapists if she needs to talk to someone," I say with a scowl.

"Belle," Sherry scolds.

I pout, but that makes me think of Damon saying, *Don't tell me, you have a brat kink*, and that makes my lips curve up.

"What are you smiling at?" Sherry asks.

"Nothing." I pinch a bit of Kiwi fruit, trying not to think about the text conversation we had this morning. Well, conversation is pushing it. I know I shouldn't have done what I did. I couldn't help it though. His words, *My work here is done*, and that damn devil emoji, got me all hot and bothered.

Dad comes home around four thirty, and we sit at the kitchen table and talk while Sherry puts the finishing touches to the dinner. She keeps me busy over the next hour, laying the table, folding serviettes, cleaning wine glasses, and sorting out some music to play while we eat. It's close to six when she finally comes into the dining room and looks over my handiwork.

"Looks great!" She grins. "Well done." As she walks out, she glances over her shoulder and says, "You're one place short, though."

I frown. I've laid out six settings: me, Alex, Sherry, Dad, Gaby, and Tyson. "Who else is coming?" I ask.

She doesn't answer, and I go into the hall as I hear the front door open.

Oh. Of course.

"Hello," Damon says, stepping to the side to let Alex enter.

"What are you doing here?" I ask, startled.

"Sorry," Sherry says, joining me in the hall, "I forgot to tell you that I invited Damon. Hello, sweetheart." She goes up to him and kisses him on the cheek. "Glad you decided to come."

"I'd never pass on the chance for a piece of your steak pie," he says. He's holding a beautiful bunch of autumn flowers in cellophane, and my heart skips a beat as I think that he's brought them for me, but even as the thought passes through my head, he holds them out to Sherry and says, "Thank you for inviting me."

"Oh Damon, they're lovely, thank you."

Of course they weren't for me. I'm not his girlfriend. I feel a bit sad, then remember what he bought for me this morning, and I don't feel so bad.

He's holding an oblong-shaped box under his arm, and he hands it to my dad as he comes out to greet them.

"Aw," Dad says, "you shouldn't have," but his eyes light up as he spots what it is: A Macallan Oscuro Single Malt. "Ooh, Damon. This must have cost you a fortune." He reads out the note on the back of the box while Damon and Alex take off their jackets. "'Picture yourself in a room with dark oak paneling, and mahogany and leather furniture. The oak gives way to flavors of toffee, cigar smoke, dried fruit, intense sherry, citrus rind, cracked black pepper, nutmeg, cloves and cinnamon, finished with slightly herbaceous and tannin sherry note. Wow.'"

"I ordered us an Uber as soon as I saw what he'd bought," Alex states. "No way am I driving when there's whisky like that to be had."

"Is it too early to start?" Dad asks, taking the bottle into the kitchen.

"Never," Alex replies, and Sherry laughs as she follows them out.

I take Damon's jacket from him, hang it on the peg, and turn to face him. Then I catch my breath as he moves up close to me. For a second I think he's going to kiss me, but even though he stays close, just an inch away, and he studies my mouth, I realize he's retrieving something from the pocket of his jacket. I have a blissful few seconds as the smell of his cologne washes over me, and then he moves back.

He holds the object he's retrieved out to me. "Did you think I'd forgotten you?" he murmurs.

I take the small oblong box, my heart racing. "Can I open it in public?" I ask suspiciously, as it looks as if it could contain a similar object to the one he bought me this morning.

He chuckles. "Yeah."

It's covered in olive-green paper with gold flowers, almost too pretty to open. I peel it off carefully and remove the lid. It contains eight gorgeous truffles in beautiful paper cases. The inside of the box states they're white-chocolate champagne truffles topped with edible gold leaf.

"Ooh," I say. "Damon, you naughty boy."

"Devil emoji," he says. He bends and kisses my cheek. "Ma belle."

My face warms, and he smiles as he spots the blush.

Oh, jeez. I'm going to have to sit through a whole family dinner without letting it slip that Alex's best mate gave me an orgasm in the back of his Jag on the way down here. Thank you, God.

I feel a flutter of nerves at the thought of Damon attending our informal dinner. I know his family are super rich. Alex, Gaby, and I aren't short of money either, but my dad and Sherry are the kind of ordinary working folk who have to save up for a vacation. They don't have a personal chef, and they're not used to eating at fancy restaurants.

But equally he's known us a long time, and even though his folks are well off, he stayed with us a lot while we were all growing up. He treats Sherry like a second mother, just like I do, and anyway he's like any other guy and has a huge appetite, so I'm sure he's going to enjoy the home fare.

We head to the kitchen, and the guys busy themselves with pouring a whisky and debating whether to have a splash of water with it. While they're savoring their first mouthful, Gaby and Tyson arrive. I go to the door to greet them, bending to give Tyson a big hug as he steers his wheelchair up the ramp and into the hall.

"Hello, gorgeous," he says. "Good to see you."

"Likewise." I let him pass, then smile at my sister. "Hey, you."

"Hey, pumpkin." She grins and envelops me in a big hug. She's maybe an inch taller than me, but she looks very similar, with the same blue eyes and long brown hair, although hers always looks less fluffy than mine. She's twenty-four, and we've always gotten on well, although we've tended to have our own circle of friends, and we're not super close. But I admire her, and I love her for the way she's stuck by Tyson. And I know I'm going to cry buckets tomorrow when they get married.

"Damon!" she says as we follow Tyson into the kitchen. "Didn't know you were going to be here." She reaches up and kisses his cheek.

"Sherry took pity on me," he says.

"Alex told me Damon won't be bringing a plus-one to the wedding," Sherry states, "and I didn't like to think of him sitting in a restaurant on his own this evening while we're all having a family dinner."

"Belle will have to be your plus-one," Gaby says. "She doesn't have a date either."

"Gabs!" I glare at her.

"What?" She grins. "You've always had a crush on him, admit it."

Horrified, I blush scarlet. Damon studies his shoes, trying to hide a smile and failing, and everyone else chuckles.

"Gaby," Sherry scolds, "don't embarrass her." She passes me the huge dish of mashed potatoes. "Take this into the dining room and just ignore her."

"Aw." Gaby grabs me on the way past and kisses my cheek. "Sorry, sweetie. That was a bit mean."

"Just remember it's your hen night tomorrow," I warn her. "I'm totally making you wear a veil the whole evening."

"Don't worry," Damon says, "I know I'm irresistible." I poke my tongue out at him, and he smiles. "You want a whisky as well?" he asks me.

"No, thank you. I'm not a fan."

"Can I get you something else, then?"

"I brought some champagne," Gaby says, placing a bottle on the counter.

I nod. "Sounds good."

"I'll open it." He proceeds to take the wrapping and metal cage off the top. As I take the dish of mashed potatoes into the dining room, I hear the cork pop.

Gradually everyone brings out the glasses and food, and within ten minutes we're all seated and tucking into our dinner.

The table seats eight, and I end up next to the empty seat at one end, while Damon sits next to my father at the other end. I suppose it's for the best, although I'm disappointed. It would have been nice to sit next to him, brushing elbows from time to time.

The steak pie is wonderful, as always, and the conversation flows with the champagne. The guys are on good form. They talk for a while about what's going on at Kia Kaha, and I eat my dinner while I listen to Damon's deep voice as he explains how he's helping to integrate the gaming software with THOR's exoskeleton.

The talk moves on to rugby and cricket, but I find my gaze drifting away, out through the sliding glass doors to the garden. The sun hasn't quite set yet, but dusk is setting in, and the shadows are lengthening.

For some reason I think of my mother, and I wonder what she's doing right now. Eating on her own in her room? As far as I know, she doesn't have any friends in the city. I feel a tad guilty for not getting back to her. Maybe I'll text her later, after dinner.

As if on cue, my phone buzzes in my jeans' pocket. I take it out and rest it on my thigh, assuming it's her. To my surprise, though, it's a message from Damon.

Penny for them?

I look across at him in surprise. He's not looking at me—he's listening to my father talking about the upcoming All Blacks' game, but he must have seen me staring out of the window.

Feeling mischievous, I text back a few emojis.

Me: <tongue><eggplant><water droplets>

I press send and lift my gaze. I watch him glance down, and I stifle a laugh as his lips curve up.

He tries to wipe the smile away and texts back an emoji: <devil>

Me: *Moi? I'm a* <angel>

Him: *A good girl? Hmm. I think you need a* <hand><peach>

Me: *More like* <hand><lettuce leaf><tomato>

I watch his brow furrow. He looks up as Alex asks him a question and answers him, then drops his gaze back to where his phone is resting in his lap.

Him: <shrug?>

Me: *Tossing the salad* <tongue><peach><donut>

He laughs out loud, and everyone looks over.

"Sorry," he says, slotting his phone back into his trouser pocket. He very carefully doesn't look at me. I bite my lip so I don't smile.

"Who are you texting?" Gaby asks curiously.

"No one."

"He was doing it this morning as well," Alex informs her. "He said it was a friend."

"Oh…" Sherry grins. "Come on, Damon, spill the beans."

He just smiles and has a sip of whisky.

"Aw," Gaby says, "give us a clue. Does she live in Wellington?"

"Yeah," he says, helping himself to another spoonful of mashed potatoes.

"Have you been seeing her long?" she asks.

"Nah." He digs his fork in and has a mouthful.

"Is it a long-term thing?" Sherry wants to know.

"No." He stabs a carrot with his fork and studies it for a moment before eating it. "Probably not."

My heart, which had sunk a little, lifts at his words. Oohhh…

"Do you luuuurv her?" Gaby teases.

His lips curve up. "I'm very fond of her."

"Is she pretty?" Sherry asks.

"Of course she's pretty," Gaby scoffs. "He only dates tens."

My smile fades. I push a green bean around my plate before lowering my fork. I'm not exactly ugly, but I'm not a ten, either. I'd forgotten that he's a successful, gorgeous billionaire who could have any woman he wanted. It's ridiculous to think he'd ever be interested in me seriously.

"I'm bored with this conversation," Alex states, and he starts talking about Gaby and Tyson's honeymoon, asking them about their trip across Australia by train.

My phone buzzes. I glance at it.

Damon: *You know you're an eleven, right?*

I can't stop my lips curving up, just a little.

Me: *I know I'm not, but thank you.*

Damon: *Best believe me, baby girl. I never lie.* <heart>

His endearment warms me all the way through. I glance over at him, and this time I catch him looking at me. Our eyes meet, and a tingle runs down my spine as our gazes lock for just a few seconds before I look away.

*

After dinner, we all help clear the table, and then Gaby, Alex, and I banish Sherry to the living room while we tidy up. Gaby finishes wiping down the kitchen counter, then disappears to join her fiancé. Alex stacks the dishwasher, badly as usual, and I end up banishing him as well so I can stack it properly.

I'm halfway through the restack when I hear footsteps behind me. I'm bending over the dishwasher, but I catch a glimpse of a pair of bare feet as the person pauses behind me. I don't have a foot fetish in particular, but these feet are attractive: bare, large, strong, and tanned, with neat nails. He's wearing jeans again this evening with a tight All Blacks rugby top, and he left his Converses at the front door.

I straighten and catch him looking at my butt. "Enjoying the view?"

"Yep," he says, unrepentant. "Hand emoji."

I give a short laugh, and he grins.

"I don't think you believed me," he states.

My eyebrows rise. "What do you mean?"

"That you're an eleven."

I give him a wry look as I slot the plates into the rack. "It's very sweet of you to say so, but I know I'm not. I'm a six or seven on a good day, I think."

He rolls his eyes. "You're an eleven. I'm a guy, I know these things."

"Damon, I'm quite happy with being a seven."

He folds his arms and leans a hip on the worktop. "You think because you have your hair in a ponytail and you wear tees and shorts and not designer dresses that it makes you a seven? It's not clothes or makeup that define whether you're a ten, Belle. It's not even how gorgeous you are, although you are gorgeous, and saying you're an eleven on the beauty scale is underplaying it. It's what's inside you. You have the soul of a beautiful woman, and always have had, right from when I first met you. Why do you think I called you ma belle? You were six. It wasn't because of your figure or your face, although both those things are top notch. It's because you were kind, and generous, and funny, and warm, even when you were a kid. You were pretty, as kids go, but your present physical beauty is a late edition. It's just the cherry on top of the cake, though. You're beautiful inside, Belle. That's what I love about you."

I stare at him. No man has ever crammed so many compliments into one sentence.

"What?" he asks, lips curving up.

"You love me?" I tease.

"Like a baby sister," he says without missing a beat.

I glance over my shoulder to make sure nobody's standing behind me, then look back at him. "A baby sister you like making come with your fingers?"

He purses his lips. "Um, yeah."

We both laugh.

"Is this your praise kink coming out?" I ask softly.

He shrugs, his gaze caressing my face. "I just tell it how it is." His eyes meet mine for a moment. Then he slides a hand to the back of my neck, and for a moment I think he's going to kiss me, but he just presses his lips to my forehead.

"Aw," I say. His hand is warm on my nape. I lean forward and rest my forehead on his chest.

His fingers linger a few seconds longer, stroking my neck, and when I shiver, he sighs.

"Come on," he says. "Let me help you clean up. Then we can have another drink."

I finish stacking the dishwasher while he tidies up, and then when we're done, we go into the living room. There's one armchair left, and a beanbag. He pushes me toward the armchair and lowers himself into the beanbag at my feet.

Dad gets us both a drink, and we all sit chatting for a while.

"Dad said you have a kids' party tomorrow," Gaby says to me.

I nod. "I thought I'd do a few while I was down here, so I got Sherry to put the word around at her school, and she managed to get me a few gigs. I brought my stuff with me."

"She did a trick for me on the ferry," Damon says. "It was brilliant. I think you should do one now."

I laugh. "Aw, don't mock me."

"I'm not. Have you seen her do any lately?" he asks the others. They all shake their heads, because I haven't done magic in front of any of them for years. "Go on," he says to me.

"Yes, come on," Sherry says. "I'd love to see you."

The others join in, encouraging me. I glare at Damon. "See what you've started?"

He just winks at me.

I get to my feet. "All right, but if I've got to perform, you're going to help me. Up you get."

Laughing, he gets to his feet. I take his hand and move him in front of the others. "Distinguished guests," I say, turning to face the rest of them, "I'm Belle Winters, and welcome to Winters' Wonderland. Today I have the amazing Damon Chevalier helping me out, so please, give him a round of applause!"

Everyone chuckles and claps as he takes a bow.

"You should be wearing one of those magician's assistant's outfits," Alex points out. "You know, the leotard and high heels." Damon just gives him the finger, and the others laugh.

"Dad," I say, "do you have a coin I could use, please?"

"Sure." He digs his hands into his pockets, pulls a couple out, and offers them to me. I pick the largest—a two-dollar coin.

"Thank you." I turn to Damon, giving him a mischievous smile. "Mr. Chevalier, you see this coin?" I hold it up before me with my right hand.

"I do," he says.

"Look at it," I instruct. As his gaze drops to it, I turn it around in my fingers. "You really, really want this coin," I tell him, making my voice low and seductive. "See how bright it is? You want this coin more than anything in the world."

His gaze lifts to mine, amused, then drops back to the coin.

I run it across my knuckles, from the thumb to my little finger, then back again. It's a move I practice all the time, whenever I have a spare moment, so the movement is fluid and smooth. He gives a short laugh.

"Isn't it beautiful?" I whisper.

He watches it, then lifts his gaze to mine. "*Très belle*," he murmurs.

I smile. "If you can catch it, you can keep it." I stop moving the coin, letting it rest on the top of my knuckles.

He looks at it, then reaches out a hand to take it. Just before his fingers touch it, I let it slip through mine, catch it, whisk it away, then hold it up in front of him between my finger and thumb.

Lifting his hand, he goes to take it again, but I pass my left hand across it and spirit it away. He follows my left hand, but then I unfurl my fingers and reveal there's nothing there. "That's called the classic French Drop Coin Vanish," I inform him.

Everyone whoops, and Damon laughs and gives me a wry look.

"Come on," I tease, "it's really easy." I hold it up again.

I proceed to run through my repertoire of sleight of hand coin tricks: the Finger Palm, the Thumb Palm, the Back Clip, the Shuttle Pass, the Retention Vanish… simple but impressive techniques that look great when done smoothly. Damon plays along, always going where I lead him, even though he probably guesses that most of the time the coin isn't where it appears to be. Because it goes well, and the others are enjoying the show, I end with two more complicated tricks:

SERENITY WOODS

the Harbottle Steal and the Hanging Coin, both of which make Damon's eyebrows rise in surprise.

"Thank you for playing along," I say at the end, producing the coin a final time, tantalizingly out of his reach.

To my shock, he leans forward and kisses me full on the mouth. I'm so surprised that I just stand there, and while I'm frozen, he leans across and grabs the coin.

"Ta da!" he says, smirking, and everyone cheers, even Alex.

"You always end with a jade's trick," I scold him. "I know you of old."

"You quoting Shakespeare at me now?" he teases.

"The two of you are a bit like Benedick and Beatrice," Gaby says, clapping her hands as we take our seats. "That was great, Belle. Masterfully done."

"Thank you." I sit back in the armchair, and Damon lowers himself into the beanbag, picking up his whisky. He leans an elbow on my knee while he sips from the glass. It's an innocent gesture, something he might do to his best mate's little sis that he's known for a long time. But my body burns where he touches it. And I know that tonight, in bed, I'm going to think about his lips touching mine, and the way he said, *You're beautiful inside, Belle. That's what I love about you.*

Chapter Thirteen

Damon

On Thursday, I spend the morning at Kia Kaha, going over the adjustments I've made to the software, while Alex and James work with THOR to make sure the exoskeleton is working smoothly. It goes well, and we're all thrilled with the progress we're making.

We stop for lunch around one, and sit out on the steps of the terrace, overlooking the Avon, while we eat noodles with chopsticks from paper cartons. Juliette, Henry, and Tyson join us, and for a moment it feels like our university days again, the six of us excited about being let out into the big wide world.

"Funny to think you're getting married on Saturday," Juliette says to Tyson, leaning over to steal a piece of sweet and sour pork from his carton.

He lets her, munching on a mini spring roll. "Yeah. Didn't think I'd be the one to fall after Henry."

"I thought you were going to be next," Juliette says to me. "First with Emmi, then Bridget, then Rachel. Every time, I've thought that was it, you were hooked."

"I'm a great escape artist," I reply, trying to pick a prawn up with my chopsticks.

"You guys," she says. "You're all sweethearts, even though you pretend not to be. You should all be married with two kids by now."

We snort and shovel noodles in our mouths.

"Are you bringing anyone to the wedding?" I ask Alex.

"Nope." He has a swig from his bottle of Coke Zero. "I'm hoping to hook up with one of the bridesmaids. The youngest one."

We all chuckle. The youngest bridesmaid is Tyson's half-sister, and she's nine.

"What about you two?" I ask James and Henry.

"I'm bringing Cassie," James says.

"Is she the brunette with the beauty spot above her lip?"

"That was Ruth. Cassie's blonde with big…" He glances at Juliette. "Eyes," he finishes lamely. She just gives a short laugh and stretches out her legs in the sun.

I grin and look at Henry. "Is Shaz coming?" I ask, referring to his wife.

He fishes out a piece of chicken from his box. "Nah. We broke up."

We all look at him, shocked. He and Shaz—Sharon—have been together since university, and they married a couple of years ago. I hadn't even known they were having issues and, judging by their surprise, neither had anyone else.

"She's filed for divorce," he says. "Should be all over by Christmas."

"Fuck." Tyson says what we're all thinking.

"What happened?" Juliette asks gently.

Henry shrugs. "Difference of opinion."

"Meaning what?"

"She wants kids."

"And you don't?"

He puts down his carton, unscrews his bottle of Sprite Zero, then sighs. "I can't have them."

Once again, we all stare at him, mouths open.

"Shit," James says. "Sorry, man."

"How do you know?" Alex asks.

"We've been trying since we got married," Henry replies. "But nothing happened. So we had tests, and it turns out my swimmers aren't up to it." He studies his bottle, then has a swig.

The rest of us exchange glances, shocked at his admission. He's only twenty-seven. It's so young to be writing yourself off.

"What about IVF?" I ask. "Titus's research has led to big leaps in the success rate." My cousin, with Saxon's help, has been using Artificial Intelligence to improve embryo selection.

"Or adoption?" James suggests. He's adopted, so he's a big proponent of it.

Henry screws the top back on the bottle. "We didn't get that far. Infertility puts a lot of pressure on a relationship, and it turned out ours wasn't strong enough to survive that. She started seeing someone else."

"Jesus," Juliette says, "why didn't you tell us?"

He shrugs, but I know why. It doesn't come easy to men to discuss their failures, and that's how he'll view it. And Henry is the most reticent of any of us.

"I'm so sorry," she whispers.

He leans back on his hands, tilts his face up to the sun with his eyes closed, and sighs.

"That's a reason to get drunk tonight if I've ever heard one," James states, in an obvious attempt to change the subject. Tonight is Tyson's stag night and Gaby's hen night. They decided to hold them a couple of days before the wedding to give everyone an extra day to get over their hangovers.

"Definitely," Tyson agrees.

"What about you?" I ask Juliette. "Are you bringing Cam to the wedding?" She's been dating Cameron for a couple of years now. I used to think she and Henry were going to have a thing, but she was dating someone else when she started uni, and then Henry met Shaz, and I guess the timing just wasn't right.

"Yeah," she says. She glances at Henry, not volunteering any more information.

Alex clears his throat. "Well, we'd better be getting back."

We all get to our feet and return to the boardroom, and things seem to return to normal as we get stuck back into the code. But I'm sure that the others, like me, are thinking about Henry's revelation. I feel oddly upset by it. Only a few years ago we seemed so young and full of hope for the future, with the whole world at our fingertips. But even though we're hardly old, we've all left broken relationships, disappointments, and failures in our wake, and we're all different people from what we were back then.

I'm twenty-seven in a few weeks' time. Again, hardly old, but not that young either.

It's funny how sometimes you're aware of the wheel of time turning. Days, months, years go by without you noticing, and then something shoves a stick in the spokes, and you come tumbling to the ground. It happened to me when Christian died. I was only ten, and I'd had a blissful childhood up to that point, surrounded by friends and family. I knew bad things happened to other people—accidents, illness, death—but that day in the sea cave was the first time I realized they could happen to me.

Oddly, maybe, it wasn't the moment that Christian died that has haunted me ever since, maybe because I wasn't the one who was looking into his eyes when it happened. My memory is of holding Kennedy in my arms, cradling her crushed arm. When the paramedics came, apparently I was covered in her blood, although I don't remember that. I remember refusing to let her go, and in the end they let me go with her to the hospital, although Dad had to drag me away when they took her into surgery.

For those first few months, she was the first thought in my head when I awoke, and the last before I fell asleep at night. Mum and Dad were worried about all three of us—Saxon, Kip, and me—but I know that for a while they were especially concerned about me. I moved through the days like a ghost, and even when Kennedy came home and was clearly recovering, the memory of that day continued to haunt me.

It still does. It got better, of course, because the phrase 'time heals' is a cliché for a reason. Kennedy is fine now, and sometimes days go by without us talking. I'm not consumed by shock and grief the way I was when it happened.

But when something like this happens—learning that Henry's marriage has broken up, and that he can't have kids—the first thing I think of is that day in the sea cave, and the hot, raw grief I felt for so long afterward.

For the first time in a while, I miss being at home, in my studio. I bought the house because I fell in love with it. It's huge with high ceilings, and the previous owner used it as a dance studio. There are mirrors on one wall, and the north-facing wall is all glass, so it's full of sunlight. I use it for painting, and have several easels set up with various pieces of work on the go, and a large architect's table that Kip bought me for Christmas one year that I adore. It's what Kennedy would call my happy place, where I put on music or a podcast and then immerse myself in the application of the paints onto the canvas. I don't think while I'm painting, and sometimes that lack of thought is just what I need.

But I've work to do, and a few days to go, so I get stuck into the coding, and decide that tonight I'm going to get drunk with the guys, and hopefully that will help me forget myself.

*

Belle

The kids' party finishes at five p.m. Today the birthday girl was six years old, and she'd requested a fairy party. I provided a fairy outfit for the girl to wear, told fairy stories while I did lots of fairy-inspired magic to illustrate the tale, got them singing and dancing with ribbons and bubbles, and gave them sparkly handmade necklaces I'd made out of polymer clay beads that I baked in the oven and painted. They all told me they'd had an amazing time, and I left with a big tip from the mum who'd enjoyed handing over control of the eight girls for an hour and a half, and her promise to recommend me to all her friends.

Buzzing from the event, I drive the short distance across town to Kia Kaha, park out the front, and go inside. The building is one of my favorite places to be—I love the light and airy atmosphere, and the way the pale wood furniture complements the rich green plants throughout the offices. The painting of Ranginui and Papatūānuku that hangs on one wall is absolutely beautiful. Papatūānuku lies on her back, her hair and breasts and body forming the country's hills and valleys. Rangi hovers above her, forming the blue sky and the heavens, his hair and beard filled with stars. I keep meaning to ask Alex who painted it—some local artist, I'm guessing.

"Hey, Rebecca," I say to the young woman at reception. "I'm here to pick up Juliette."

"She's in the boardroom with the others," she says.

I sign the register and press my visitor's sticker to my tee. "Thanks!" Giving her a smile, I head through the building to the large boardroom that overlooks the River Avon.

As I approach, my heart skips a beat at the sight of someone standing looking out at the river. It's Damon, and I slow, then stop walking, staring at his profile for a moment. He's wearing a suit, which isn't surprising considering he's at work, but I haven't seen him in one for a long time. It's navy blue and I think it has a thin pinstripe, and it's British cut: tight, stiff, and formal, almost military-like, with a crisp white shirt and a light-blue tie. Like most of the guys I know, his hair is cut in a neat taper fade, but whereas the last few times I've seen him the longer hair on top has been ruffled 'bed hair', today he's combed it back neatly, making him look smart and professional.

Wow, he looks hot.

As I study his face, though, I think that he also looks sad. Hmm.

I approach the boardroom, and as the door automatically opens to admit me, he looks around, and everyone else at the table looks up.

"Evening all," I say, going into the room. "Up the workers!"

"Hey." Alex lifts a hand in greeting. "What are you doing here?"

"She's picking me up," Juliette states, closing her laptop.

"Oh, of course," he says. "You're all off to dance around your handbags and get wasted on Cosmos at Limitless, right?" He names the nightclub we're heading to tonight.

"Yeah, because you're all going to be sipping tea and reading poetry," I reply sarcastically.

"Damn straight," Alex says. He holds up a hand as he recites, "'Love will find a way through paths where wolves fear to prey.'"

"Fuck me, I love Byron," Damon replies in a passable impression of Hugh Grant from Bridget Jones, and the others laugh.

I poke my tongue out at them. "Everyone's a comedian."

Juliette gets up and collects her things. As she turns, her laptop threatens to slide out of her grip. Damon crosses quickly to her side to help her, holding it as she gets a grip on her briefcase. "Thank you," she says graciously, then looks at me. "I'll just be a few minutes." She heads to her office.

I walk over to the open sliding doors and go onto the terrace. It's a beautiful afternoon, with people walking along the path on the other side of the river, and ducks gliding peacefully on the water.

"Nice day." Damon comes to stand beside me, as I hoped he would.

I look up at him and smile. "I didn't realize you and Alex knew any poetry."

"We took a module on it in our first year. We only did it to impress the girls." He winks at me. "Did it work?"

"A little bit."

He laughs. "Then it was worth it."

I bump his arm with mine. "You looked sad standing there, looking out of the window. What were you thinking about?"

He hesitates, glances over his shoulder, and then gestures at me to follow him down the terrace. He lowers himself onto one of the steps, and I sit beside him. "Henry told us he's broken up with Shaz."

My jaw drops. "No! When?"

"I'm not sure, but a while ago. She's filed for divorce, and he says it'll be all done by Christmas."

"Oh, that's so sad. What happened, did he say?"

"He said they were trying for a family, but it turns out he can't have kids."

I study him, puzzled. "She didn't leave him because of that, though, surely?"

He looks at me, the corner of his lips curving up. "I'm not sure. He said their relationship wasn't strong enough to survive the stresses of infertility."

"That's so sad."

"Yeah, I thought so, too." He sighs and looks out at the river, then glances at his Apple watch as a message pops up. He taps it, and I watch him smile.

"Someone's cheered you up, anyway," I observe, hoping it's not a girl.

"It's from Kennedy," he says. "I texted her earlier to say I was feeling a bit flat. She wants to meet up when I get back to Wellington."

The autumn breeze makes dried red and gold leaves dance across the steps in front of us and ruffles the feathers on the ducks.

"Do you have feelings for her?" I ask gently. I know she's married and has a baby, but he seems very fond of her.

He shakes his head though. "Not in that way. She's more like a sister. And now she doesn't have a brother, so I guess I feel kinda protective of her."

I watch the mallards as they hop out of the water and waddle along the bottom of the terrace. I've read that ducks tend to be monogamous, but the one male, who stands out with his green head and the white band around his neck, fusses around four females with their brown-speckled plumage, keeping them close to him.

And I realize then that Damon's like the male mallard. When he was young, his cousin was badly hurt, and he felt powerless to help her. So he's making up for it now, protecting the women around him, even if he's not romantically involved with them. I think of how he heated the pack for me in the car, and how part of the reason he gave me an orgasm was to help me with my cramps. How he bought Sherry flowers and me chocolates, and he bought me the 'care package,' as he so beautifully called it. How he just helped Juliette with her laptop. Even how 'Soft Doms' are 'the gentlemen of the BDSM realm.' No doubt it's one reason for what he calls his praise kink. He wants to keep them safe, to make them feel loved and protected, and to give them pleasure.

I feel guilty when he says or does nice things, as if I've somehow forced him into them by looking pathetic, but I realize then that he enjoys making me feel good.

"Tell me another line of poetry," I say softly.

He studies my face for a moment, thoughtful, his eyes filled with an emotion I can't quite fathom.

"'When you depart from me, sorrow abides and happiness takes his leave,'" he says, and smiles.

My heart skips a beat. "Who said that?"

"Shakespeare. It's from *Much Ado*."

"Seems appropriate," I reply, because I quoted Beatrice yesterday. "Although your quote was more romantic than mine."

He just chuckles, but I'm reminded of his text yesterday, *Best believe me, baby girl. I never lie*, and it sends a shiver down my back.

"Ready when you are!" Juliette calls from the doorway, and the two of us get to our feet and head back into the room.

"I hope you all have a great evening," I tell the guys. "Don't do anything I wouldn't do."

"We're heading toward thirty," Alex says. "We'll have two whiskies and a bowl of fries, complain the music's too loud, and be in bed by eleven."

I giggle. "See you all tomorrow at the rehearsal dinner."

They wave, and Juliette and I head out of the door.

She links arms with me as we walk through the building. "Ready for a fantastic night?"

"I am, actually." I feel a bubble of excitement deep inside, but it's not just because I'm looking forward to the evening.

I know Damon's my brother's mate, and he said he'd never do anything to jeopardize that relationship. But something's brewing between us. I can feel it in the autumn air. It's like the glow you get inside when you know winter's coming, and you crunch through red and gold leaves everywhere you go, and you dig out your sweaters and start cooking, and everything smells of hearty stews and baked apples and cinnamon. It's warm and comforting and exciting.

The only question is whether I can convince him to put aside his principles for long enough to let the spark of attraction flare into something that might just set us alight.

Chapter Fourteen

Belle

Gaby's hen night turns out to be a huge success. A dozen of us have a fabulous time at a bar and then a nightclub, drinking, dancing, and laughing. Gaby wears the veil I made her all evening, and it's around one a.m. before we finally call it a day.

Most of the girls head home, but Gaby persuades her old school friend, Aroha, to stay the night with us at Dad's place, where she's staying now until the wedding. And when we find out that Juliette's partner, Cam, is in Australia at the moment and not coming back until the morning of the wedding, we talk her into staying, too.

The four of us arrive and creep as quietly as we can into the house, which is to say not quietly at all, and make our way into the kitchen to discover that Sherry has left a plate of tiny quiches and another with small muffins, and a note to inform us there's a bottle of wine in the fridge.

"She knows us a little too well," Gaby says. "I'll take the food in. Juliette, you get the glasses. Aroha, find us some plates. And Belle, you open the wine."

"Yes, boss." I do as she says and then bring it into the living room. Gaby and Aroha sit on the sofa, and Juliette and I sit on the carpet on the other side of the coffee table. I pour us all a glass of the sparkling wine, and we dig into the quiches and muffins.

"Oh, what a fantastic evening." Gaby lies back, resting her feet on Aroha's lap. "I should get married every day."

"To the same person or to someone different?" Juliette wants to know.

Gaby pretends to think about it, and we all giggle. "There's only one man for me," she says eventually.

"But he's not available," Aroha adds, "so you're stuck with Tyson."

We all giggle again and have a mouthful of wine.

"Seriously, though," Juliette says, "I love you from the bottom of my heart for what you've done for the guy. Not every woman would have stood by him the way you've done."

"It's been tough at times," Gaby admits, in a rare moment of honesty. She's not normally one to share her innermost thoughts, and keeps her feelings close to her chest. I guess the alcohol we've imbibed this evening has loosened her lips a little, or maybe it's just the thought that she's going to promise to love him forever that's made her feel able to confess. "I mean, I've never had doubts, but he felt guilty that I stayed, and he tried to push me away for a long time."

"I didn't know that," I murmur, my heart going out to her. She was only nineteen when Tyson had his accident, and they'd only been dating for a year. It would have been so easy for her to declare she had the rest of her life ahead of her and break off with him, but she never faltered once.

She leans her head on her hand, her eyes half-lidded with sleepiness and alcohol. "I'd just started uni, so I was living in Wellington by then, and you and I didn't see much of each other."

I was sixteen, so I only saw her when she came to Christchurch. "I wish I'd been there more for you, though," I admit.

"You were so young," she says, "I didn't like to worry you. You had enough on your plate." Her eyes meet mine for a moment. I can see the guilt in them. There are a lot of things we haven't talked about that we probably should have. It's too late now, though. Too much water under the bridge.

"Besides," she continues, "I had all the guys. They were so supportive. There was always one of them to run me to the hospital or pick me up. I don't know what I'd have done without them."

"Here's a question for you," Aroha says. Because she's known Gaby since high school, she's met the guys many times. "Out of them all: Tyson, Henry, James, Damon, and Alex—if you had to have dinner with one, kiss one, have sex with one, marry one, and murder one, which would you choose for which purpose?"

"I'd murder Alex," I say without missing a beat, and we all giggle.

Gaby rolls her eyes. "Well it wouldn't be fair if I didn't say Tyson for all of them except murder, would it?"

Aroha blows a raspberry. "This is fantasy. We won't tell anyone." She grins at Juliette. "You go first."

"I'd have dinner with Alex," she says. "Kiss Damon. Have sex with Henry. Marry Tyson. And murder James."

We all burst into laughter. "Sex with Henry?" Gaby teases. "Really?"

"He's gorgeous," she says with a shrug. "I like that he's big." She lifts her eyebrows, and we all snort.

"And murder James?" I ask, puzzled. "Over Alex? Seriously?"

"Alex can cook. James can't make toast without setting something alight."

"Not really a cause for murder," I say, "but I get your point," and we all laugh again.

"What about you?" I ask Gaby.

"Hmm... I'd also have dinner with Alex because yes, he can cook, kiss Henry because, well, why not, have sex with Tyson, marry Damon, and oh God, I'd probably murder James too. Poor James."

"I'm giving you the opportunity to have sex with any of them, and you'd get off with your fiancé," Aroha comments. "I don't know if that's romantic or just sad."

"He's got a great tongue," Gaby says with a smirk, then dissolves into giggles as our eyebrows rise. "Besides," she says, "we have to keep working on his rehab. Years ago we were told that his sexual function would improve with regular use. At least that was his reason for wanting a daily workout. I never considered he might have been lying."

We all laugh again, because we're meant to. I have nothing but admiration for her, though. Although she's never gone into details, I know the accident severely affected Tyson below the waist. Clearly, though, they've managed to maintain and even improve their sexual relationship, which makes me a tad tearful when I think of how much they've been through.

"What about you?" Juliette asks Aroha. "Who would you choose?"

"Hmm..." Aroha thinks about it. She's a beautiful Māori girl, slim and stunning, with light-brown skin, dark wavy hair, and a long tattoo curving up her right forearm, each curl and line detailing her *whakapapa* or genealogy. "Let's work backwards. I'd murder Henry."

"Aw, why?" Juliette asks.

"Because he's so quiet! I love a guy who talks."

"That's true," Juliette admits. "But he says so much with his eyes."

I glance at Gaby, who winks at me. It's clear that Henry's her favorite. It's a shame she's spoken for now he's finally single.

"I'd marry Alex," Aroha continues, "because although he comes across as gruff and grumpy, he's quite the gentleman, and I think he'd treat his girl well."

I look at Gaby. She crosses her eyes, and we both chuckle.

"I'd have sex with James," Aroha continues. "Because he's so gorgeous I'm convinced my tongue's going to roll out of my mouth like a cartoon character's when he walks by."

That makes us all giggle.

"I'd kiss Damon, and have dinner with Tyson," she says, "because I'm too polite to say otherwise when I'm sitting with the bride-to-be."

"Aw," Gaby says, and pokes her with her toe.

"Your turn," Aroha tells me.

"I'd happily murder Alex," I tell them. "And then I'd have dinner, kiss, marry, and absolutely, one hundred percent, have mad monkey sex with Damon Chevalier, not necessarily in that order."

It occurs to me as the words leave my mouth that I might be a little drunk, but it's too late now, and they all burst out laughing.

"Michelle Winters," Gaby scolds. "He's far too old for you."

"Six years?" Aroha says. "Jeez, that's nothing."

"I didn't know you liked him," Juliette says to me, amused. "How long's this been going on?"

"She's always liked him," Gaby says, "I knew that."

"Does he know?" Juliette asks.

"Yeah," I say. If he doesn't know by now, then there's something seriously wrong with him.

Her lips curve up. "You've told him?"

"Ah... let's just say that on the way here in the car, something happened that gave him a good idea..."

They all sit up with a squeal. "You had sex with Damon Chevalier in the back of his Jag?" Gaby asks, jaw dropping.

"Mmm, not sex exactly..."

"Details!" Aroha demands. "We need details."

"He... ah... gave me an orgasm."

The look on their faces is so funny that I dissolve into giggles.

"What?" Gaby says. "How? Why?"

"Because I said I'd never had one."

Slowly, their smiles fade.

"Sorry," I add. "I didn't mean to kill the mood."

Aroha stares at me. "You mean you'd never..."

I shake my head.

"Not even on your own?" Juliette adds, frowning.

Another shake.

Gaby bites her lip. "Oh, baby," she says, and she pulls me toward her for a big hug. "I'm so sorry," she whispers. I think she can guess why I have issues.

"It's okay," I tell her, not wanting to spoil her hen night. "Damon sorted me out."

She moves back. Her eyes are shining, but she sniffs and just gives a short laugh. "Really?"

"He had magic fingers," I say mischievously.

"Oh my God," Juliette says, "I'll never look at him the same way again."

"Is he interested in you?" Aroha asks.

"I think so. But he says he values Alex's friendship and their business partnership too much to make a move."

"You were the one he was texting at dinner last night?" Gaby asks.

"Might be."

Juliette laughs. "Were you texting him yesterday morning, too? He was staring at his phone as if someone had hit him with a spade."

"I was sending him rude texts."

"What kind of things?" Aroha wants to know.

"Messages with eggplant emojis and water droplets," I reply, and they all whoop.

"We've totally got to get the two of you together," Aroha says.

But Juliette frowns. "His reputation with women isn't great."

"He'd eat you for breakfast," Gaby says to me, amused.

"One can only hope."

They all giggle. "Seriously, though," Gaby says, "Juliette's right. He's not got a great rep."

I draw my knees up and wrap my arms around them. "I think he's been hurt several times, and it's made him very wary about letting anyone close."

"That's true," Juliette admits.

"Are you talking about Rachel?" Aroha asks.

"That's one of them," Juliette replies. "His first girlfriend that I knew was called Emmi. He dated her for a couple of years at university."

"What happened?" I ask.

"He called in at her flat one evening out of the blue and found her in bed with another guy."

"Jesus," Gaby says, "I didn't know that."

"Oh, poor Damon," I whisper.

"What did he do?" Aroha asks.

"Just turned around and walked out. Refused to talk to her. Got drunk for, like, two weeks straight. Then he went a bit crazy for six months and slept with anything that moved. Eventually he met Bridget."

"Didn't she play badminton?" I ask.

Gaby nods. "Really well. She won the top tournament in New Zealand, and then announced she wanted to take part in the Olympics, and maybe even go professional. It meant traveling a lot. She asked him to go with her, but he was about to graduate, and Saxon and Kip were encouraging him to join Kingpinz, so I think they just parted ways. He was pretty cut up about it, though."

"And we all know about what happened with Rachel," Juliette says. "Fucking bitch. I could have strangled her."

"Were you there when she proposed?" I ask her and Gaby curiously.

They both nod. "James overheard her talking to a friend about how she'd hooked a billionaire and was about to land him. He thought Damon should know, and went and told him. Five minutes later, she went down on one knee."

"What happened?"

"He just turned around and walked out," Juliette says. "None of us knew why at the time. Rachel got up and went the color of beetroot. She was absolutely furious, and started calling Damon all the names under the sun. James, bless him, told her in front of everyone that she shouldn't have announced she wanted Damon for his money. Everyone was shocked. We all left pretty fast, I can tell you."

"He said she cut up his suits and keyed his E-type."

Juliette tries not to laugh. "Yeah. He was angrier about that than he was about her, I think. It wasn't funny at the time, though. He was pretty upset. He said he was done letting women get close to him. And he hasn't really dated anyone since, not long-term. I think he might have worked through all the girls on Tinder though." She sends me an apologetic look.

"I know he's not an angel," I reply, thinking of the devil emoji he sent me. "He told me he wasn't a good guy, and that he's cursed where relationships are concerned. He's tried to warn me off. I know he's had a lot of one-night stands, and that he likes to think he's a bad boy. But I don't believe it. You all know about Christian and Kennedy, right?" They nod. "That affected him deeply," I say. "I think he's very mixed up."

"You know he paints, don't you?" Juliette says.

All our eyebrows rise. "What do you mean?" Gaby asks. "Walls or canvases?"

"Canvases. I didn't find out until our third year at uni. He was sharing a house with the guys, and I called in one day to pick James and Alex up for a class, and they'd already left. Damon came out of his room, and he was covered in paint, and said he was in the middle of a piece of artwork. Alex told me later that Damon's parents suggested he take a degree in art, but he wanted to do something practical that would help people, and he says his art is just a hobby."

"Is he any good?" Gaby asks.

"You know the painting of Ranginui and Papatūānuku at Kia Kaha?" Juliette replies.

"The one in the lobby?" I ask. "Aw, I love that." She just smiles, and my jaw drops. "You're kidding me? Damon painted that?"

"Yep."

"Oh my God." I'm filled with wonder. "I never knew." The painting is beautiful, and sensual too, with Rangi's lips hovering just above Papa's, one arm draped over her body as if they're making love.

"He's got several hanging in his office at Kingpinz," Juliette adds. "He usually paints goddesses—Greek, Celtic, Māori—or angels, in white robes with flowing hair."

"I wonder why?"

"He says his studio is the only place that God exists for him now," she says. "Something to do with the death of his cousin, I think. The family used to go to church, but he lost his faith after that."

"Did you know he's the president of the Wellington branch of the Women's Refuge?" Gaby says.

Once again, my jaw drops. "No."

"Tyson told me last year. Damon did a parachute jump to raise money and awareness for them. I think he made a considerable amount of money, and he drew on some of his contacts and got them a lot of publicity."

I love women. I'm not ashamed to admit it. He told me that himself. I assumed he was talking about sex, but it obviously goes deeper than that. I think that deep inside the man is the little boy who couldn't help his cousin when she was in pain, and he's spent the rest of his life trying to make it up to her by looking after women in one way or another. And all he's received for his efforts is three failed relationships. No wonder the poor guy's determined not to get his heart broken again.

Gaby's eyes meet mine, and her lips slowly curve up. "You really like him, don't you?"

"I do," I admit. "I really do. But he's made it clear he's not going to date me, so there's not much I can do about it."

"Bullshit," Juliette says with feeling. "Have you never heard of seduction, girl?"

"It's not really my thing," I reply doubtfully. "I'm not really the seducing type."

"You're a woman, aren't you?"

"Kinda."

"Belle," Aroha scolds, "Juliette's right, you need to do your womanly thing on him."

My heart's racing. "What about Alex?"

"Fuck Alex," Gaby says. "It's none of his business. You're not fourteen. He's been protective of you, but you're old enough to know what—or who—you want now, right?"

"I guess."

"You need to up your game, girl," Aroha states.

"I don't know how. I'm hopeless."

"You're a law student," Juliette scolds, "so you're hardly hopeless. Fake it till you make it, right?"

It's exactly what Jo told me, and I remember thinking that maybe people treated me as if I was eighteen because I act like it. Juliette's right. I'm soon to be a lawyer, so I'm hardly an idiot. I'm nearly twenty-two. I can seduce a guy, surely?

"Juliette," Gaby says, "grab that pad of paper, will you? And there's a pencil underneath. Thanks." She opens the pad up and turns it to a blank sheet. "We're going to make a list."

"Of what?"

"Ways to seduce a man," Gaby says. "We'll get you the guy, don't worry."

"Oh jeez."

Aroha waves her glass, and I top them all up with the bottle, splashing a bit over the side. "I wonder how the guys are doing?" she asks as I mop it up with a piece of kitchen towel.

"I asked Damon about half an hour ago," I reply. "He sent me a drunk emoji. I asked him if he missed me, and this is what he texted back." I pull the message up and show them.

"Are you being an angel?" Gaby translates.

"No, he meant: Are you being a good girl? I sent him the devil emoji, and he sent back a hand and a peach."

They all squeal. "We've totally got to make this work," Juliette says, laughing.

"Come on then," Gaby says. "Let's brainstorm. Ways to seduce a man."

"Go commando," Aroha replies. "Never fails."

We all giggle. Then Gaby says, "No, you're thinking too far ahead. You're on step seven. We need to come up with things Belle can do to get him interested."

"Clothing's important, though," Aroha persists.

"If you're going to tell me to prance around in a mini skirt and boob tube, you can forget it," I tell them.

"Actually, it's not about showing skin," Juliette says. "Seducing a guy is all about the mystery. I mean, yeah, your physical appearance captures his attention, but it's your personality that captures their heart and seduces their mind."

"I like that," I say softly, and she smiles.

"You always wear jeans and tees or baggy sweatshirts," Gaby states. "You need something that flatters your figure. What are you wearing tomorrow to the rehearsal dinner?"

"Actually, I borrowed a dress from my friend," I inform her. "It's really nice and it clings in all the right places."

"Well, that's a good start," Juliette says. "And your hair? Men love it when you let your hair down."

"Mine's really fluffy."

"You can borrow my conditioner," Gaby says. "And I'll bring my curler that gives you all these boho waves."

"If you like, I'll come over and help you with your makeup," Aroha suggests. She's a beautician, and her makeup is always immaculate and beautifully done.

"Really?" I feel the first swell of hope that they might actually be able to make me look presentable.

"What else can we add to the list?" Gaby asks, nibbling the end of the pencil.

We all have a sip of champagne. "One of the most important things is not to look desperate," Juliette says. "Men like the chase. So it's not about hanging on his every word. You want to play it cool but not too cool."

"How do I do that?" I ask.

"Dance with other guys," Aroha says. "Have lots of fun. But glance over at him occasionally. Make it clear you'd rather be having fun with him."

"It's about eye contact, I think," Gaby says.

"Yes," Juliette agrees, "and occasionally you need to do that thing where you lock eyes and he can't look away." They all nod their agreement. "Guaranteed to give them a hard on," Juliette states, waggling her eyebrows.

"When you talk to him, ask lots of questions," Aroha says, "about himself, I mean, and look interested in his answers."

"That bit's easy," I reply, thinking about the questionnaire we took in the car.

"Smile and touch him a lot," Juliette says.

"Where?"

"Not his knob," Gaby says. "Not right away, anyway."

Juliette giggles. "Lean toward him and brush his arm. Smile. Look into his eyes. Moisten your lips."

"Don't dribble, though," Aroha says. "That's not sexy."

"Depends where you're dribbling." Gaby waggles her eyebrows, and we all snort.

"I've got one more tip," Juliette says. "Don't be afraid of awkward pauses."

"What do you mean?"

"If you're talking, and there's a gap in the conversation, you don't have to rush to fill it. Keep eye contact with him, smile a little, and just wait. Let your bodies do the talking."

I nod. "Okay. I'll try!"

"So that's six things," Gaby states, putting down the pencil. "Wear flattering clothes, let him see you having fun with other guys, hold eye contact, ask questions, touch him often, and don't be afraid of awkward pauses." She passes me the list. "I want to see you doing all those things at the rehearsal and at the wedding!"

I take the list, heart racing. Is it possible I could really seduce him? I've never gone for a guy like this. I'm usually far too shy, and I've always waited for guys to approach me. But I know Damon. I feel safe with him, and comfortable, too.

He's been badly hurt, though, and I know he's reluctant to share himself with anyone other than on a purely physical level. If the girls' seduction plan works, and he can overcome his principles, I'd be happy with physical contact for now. If I want more than that, though, I'm going to have to get him to trust me, and whether I can do that remains to be seen.

Chapter Fifteen

Damon

The day after Tyson's stag night, the wedding rehearsal evening is due to start at 5:30 p.m. I spend the day at Kia Kaha, return to the hotel after 4 p.m. for a brief rest and to change, then leave my room at 5:15 and walk down to reception. I'm directed by Tyson's younger brother, Freddie, who's the main usher, through the Savoy Ballroom and out into the garden.

The event planners have laid out the garden ready for the big day tomorrow, and tonight we're running through the ceremony so everyone knows what to do and where to stand. White seats in rows face the altar that's been woven with pale-pink roses and ribbons, which appears to be the color scheme Gaby's chosen, as balloons in the same color are tied to pillars at the back, and pink and white garlands loop between the aisles.

Gaby and Tyson are standing by the doorway, and they both greet me as I walk in. Gaby throws her arms around my neck and gives me a hug, and Tyson shakes my hand.

"How are you feeling?" she asks mischievously. Tyson has obviously told her about the copious amounts of whisky that were downed last night.

"Delicate." I give a wry smile as she giggles. "You?"

"Yeah, a bit fragile."

"You had a good time, though?"

"Yeah, fantastic. Such fun. We didn't get back to the house until one a.m., and then Juliette and Aroha decided to stay, and we didn't go to bed until two."

"I bet you're tired now."

"I'm on a high," she says, "although I'll probably crash early tonight. Belle said she's going to bed early too because she's so tired. Not that you can tell. Look at her." She glances to her left.

I follow her gaze and spot her sister standing at the beginning of the aisle, talking to Freddie. My heart gives an uncharacteristic jump as I inhale. Jesus, she looks amazing. I've rarely seen her in anything but jeans or shorts and tees. Her dress is a deep plum color, and the hemline reveals her knees at the front and drops to mid-calf at the back, and she's wearing sexy, black, high heeled sandals. For once she has her hair down, and it bounces around her bare shoulders in attractive waves. For once she looks her age, the sophisticated, gorgeous young woman she is.

"Wow," I say before I can think better of it. I blink and look back at Gaby.

Her lips have curved up a little. "Like what you see?" she teases.

I glance at Tyson, who chuckles. "Quite the swan, isn't she?" he says. "She looks beautiful tonight."

"She always looks beautiful," I reply, returning my gaze to her. "But yeah, tonight she's… sublime."

I watch her talking to Freddie. He's the same age as her, and I can tell by the way he can't take his eyes off her that he's attracted to her. He says something that makes her laugh, and the way she does it tells me she likes him. Well, why wouldn't she? She's young, single, and gorgeous. She could have any guy she wants.

"Don't glower," Gaby says.

I give her a wry look. "Hope you have a nice evening." Leaving them chuckling, I walk over to Belle.

She glances at me as I approach, and I have the pleasure of seeing her eyes widen. I've taken care over my appearance this evening—I'm wearing a new dark-gray Italian suit that fits really well, and I've tamed my somewhat unruly hair with product. I've even shaved, which I haven't done for a while, getting rid of the stubble I've been sporting.

"Excuse me," Freddie says, "I should be checking on the guests."

"See you later," Belle replies, and she gives him a parting smile before turning her attention to me. "Well, don't you look the bee's knees," she says, her gaze brushing down me, feather light.

"You look absolutely stunning," I return, glowing a little at her compliment.

"Thank you." She blushes and touches her hair self-consciously. "Gaby tried to de-frizz it. It's already fighting back."

I chuckle. I'm tempted to slide my hand into the brown waves and see if they're as soft as they look. Up close, I can see she's wearing makeup. It's subtle but elegant—black winged eyeliner, smoky gray shadow, and long, fluttery eyelashes. It suits her. I feel as if I opened an animal trap expecting to find a kitten and I've discovered a vixen inside.

She lifts a hand to cup my face and brushes my jaw with her thumb, light enough to make me shiver. "So smooth," she murmurs, before lowering her hand.

She holds my gaze, and the moments tick by. I realize too much time is passing without us saying anything, but I'm momentarily lost for words, captured by her startling blue eyes. Her lips curve up, and her eyes are warm. They transport me right back to the Jag, and the way they glittered in the light from the passing cars, while I slid my hand beneath her jeans, into her underwear, and down into the heart of her.

Up to this point, because I've known her a long time, and maybe because she dresses and acts young, I've thought of her as a girl, Alex's little sis who I came close to corrupting, and not, I'm ashamed to say, as an equal. But suddenly, even though I know there are six years between us, and although she might not be as experienced as me in bed, I see her as what she is—a mature, beautiful, sexy woman.

"Michelle!"

We both turn, and Belle's smile fades at the sight of Kaitlyn Cross coming into the garden.

"Fuck," Belle mumbles.

In the past I've always thought Kaitlyn looked like her daughters, but tonight she looks quite different. She's the same height as them, but she's lost a lot of weight, and she's wearing a black pantsuit that's surprisingly plain, with a white shirt that emphasizes the lack of color in her face. Her long brown hair is scooped up in a tight bun, and although she's wearing makeup, it's minimal and in neutral shades. The only concession to her wealth is the pair of diamond earrings she's sporting that sparkle in the evening light. If she was hoping to go unnoticed, though, it hasn't worked, because she's still stunning, and the stark outfit only serves to make her stand out more in a room that's filled with women who look like flowers in their colorful outfits.

"Well, look at you," Kaitlyn whispers, her eyes wide as she studies her daughter. Her accent is an odd mixture of Kiwi and Californian. She glances at me, then, and smiles. "Quite the butterfly emerging from the chrysalis, isn't she?"

I happen to agree, but it sounds patronizing to say so, so I just give a polite smile.

"What's a mother got to do to get her daughter to come and see her?" Kaitlyn says. Her tone is teasing rather than sharp, but Belle still bristles.

"It helps to be in the country," she replies. "And I've been busy. I'm not going to drop everything and come running just because you snap your fingers."

Without looking at me, she turns and walks away, over to Gaby, who's still standing by the door, greeting her guests.

Kaitlyn stares at her, then looks at me. She blinks, then forces a smile on her face. "I suppose I should introduce myself. I'm Michelle and Gaby's mother, Kaitlyn Cross."

"We have actually met before," I reply, taking her hand as she offers it. "I'm Damon Chevalier, Alex's friend." I spent a fair amount of time at their house in Wellington when I was younger, before she and Mason divorced, and Mason moved to Christchurch. She was often off filming, but when she was home I was often there, as Alex and I were inseparable as teenagers. I haven't seen her for years, though, so I'm not surprised she doesn't recognize me.

"Damon!" She looks at me with new eyes. "Yes, of course! Goodness, you've grown into such a big boy!"

I give her an amused look. "Well, I haven't been called a boy for about ten years, but yeah, I guess."

She smiles. "I'm showing my age. It's just that my memories are of the two of you tearing around the garden on bikes and then lounging in front of the TV on the PlayStation eating chips."

"We still do that. It usually involves the latest Call of Duty and a family pack of Doritos."

She chuckles. "Alex keeps me updated on what you're all up to, so I know that's not true. He told me you're helping him out with THOR."

I'm surprised that Alex has told her—I didn't think they spoke much, and the comments he made about her at the office were quite scathing. She's still his mother, though, so I guess he'd rather talk about

159

SERENITY WOODS

his work when he does have to speak to her than about his personal life.

"Yeah, I came down a few days before the wedding." I cock my head at her. She's very pale, and it's not only because of her carefully applied foundation. "I'm very sorry to hear about Ryan."

She meets my eyes, her brows drawing together. "Do you know, you're the first person to say that?"

I shrug. "Breakups are tough."

"They are. It's been very hard."

"And even harder having to go through it with a spotlight on you, I'd imagine."

She nods, then gives a bright smile. "Enough about me. Tell me about my daughter. Alex said you drove her down—that was nice of you."

"It was a pleasure," I reply, trying not to blush. "Belle's lovely, and a great credit to you."

"Not so much to me. Sherry's the one who should get all the credit."

"You're her mother, Kaitlyn. You were with Belle for her formative years. That has to count for something."

She bites her lip. "Belle," she says softly, "I remember the day you called her that. She was all of six. Such a gorgeous little girl." She looks across at her daughter. "She's turned into a beautiful young woman. I miss her so much." She stops talking and swallows hard. I frown. I don't know what happened with the divorce proceedings, but it was her decision to leave, surely? Why did she go if she wanted to watch her kids grow up?

I follow her gaze to Belle, and watch as Freddie goes by her with two guests, giving her a wink as he passes. I look back at Kaitlyn to discover her watching me with a twist to her lips.

"Are you two having a thing?" she asks.

"Me and Freddie?"

She laughs. "You and Michelle. Actually, I should call her Belle, shouldn't I? Well, are you?"

"No."

"But you want to?"

I hesitate, and it's my undoing—her eyebrows rise, and her eyes fill with delight.

"Oh, how wonderful," she says. "Does she know?"

"I'm not her type," I reply.

"Really? Who is her type?"

"Someone like that." I gesture at Freddie, who's delivered his guests and has now returned to talk to Belle. He looks young and cocky, just the sort of guy that might attract a girl of Belle's age. My suit has a timeless, fitted cut that I love, but he's wearing the tight pants that are trendy now, and although my haircut isn't exactly old fashioned, Freddie has a high-top fade with a shaved line, and an earring. I'm only twenty-six, but I feel like his grandad.

Kaitlyn snorts, though. "He's just a baby. Belle would walk all over him. She needs a man who'll stand up to her and keep her in line." She winks at me.

I'm saved by Alex, who walks up at that moment. "Keep who in line?" he asks.

"Gaby," Kaitlyn says without a beat. "I was just saying that Tyson's perfect for her. Now we need to find you a girl who can keep you under control."

I give a short laugh, and Alex smiles wryly. "Ain't no girl been born who can do that," he announces. "Come on," he says to her, "you can sit at the front with me."

She gives him a grateful look, and it's only then that I realize she's nervous. Is it because she's famous, and she's conscious of people casting her looks? Or because Mason's here? Their relationship has remained acrimonious, and I know Tyson was wary about having the two of them within close proximity of one another.

I watch Alex guide her over to the chairs, glad that he's obviously decided to take it upon himself to make sure she's okay. Maybe when he saw her, he realized what an effect her recent breakup has had on her, and took pity on her.

"Hey." It's James. "You ready to take your seat? I think we're going to start soon."

James is Tyson's best man. The two of them and Henry decided some years ago that if any of them got married, James would be Tyson's best man, Tyson would be Henry's, and Henry would be James's. It was an unspoken agreement that Alex and I would be each other's one day.

"Sure." I follow him to one of the rows and sit beside Henry. Next to him is Juliette with her partner, Cam. I nod at him and say hello.

He's a nice guy, an accountant, tall with dark-blond hair, intelligent and hardworking.

The wedding organizer, Pam, a rather scary woman in her early thirties with dark hair in a bun who's so organized she could have planned D-Day, calls for everyone to take a seat. Belle remains standing behind the chairs with the other bridesmaids: Aroha and Tyson's two younger half-sisters.

This rehearsal is just for close friends and family, about thirty of us in total. After we've run through the ceremony, we'll have dinner, which is a chance for Gaby and Tyson to spend some time with the people they're closest to, giving them more time to mingle with their other guests tomorrow who might be coming from further away, or who they don't see as much.

Pam runs through the timeline for the big day, and then the ceremony itself. She explains where everyone needs to be, and tells Gaby to walk down the aisle with Mason as the music starts. I turn my head to watch Belle following her. She bends to whisper something to Tyson's youngest sister, who has obviously asked her a question. I don't know what the bridesmaids' dresses look like, but if tonight is anything to go by, I'm sure Belle's going to look stunning tomorrow, too.

Pam shows the bride and groom where to place themselves. Gaby has a special chair to sit beside Tyson in so they're on the same level. As she sits, and Tyson moves his wheelchair beside her, Alex looks over his shoulder and winks at me and Henry. I wink back, excited to see Gaby's reaction tomorrow when we reveal our big secret.

Next is a young couple, Cillian and Tori, who are going to perform a duet on the violin and cello. They're apparently famous in the UK and play for the London Philharmonic Orchestra. When Gaby found out the two of them had come to New Zealand to visit and that they were available for hire, she was quick to book them for the big day.

Both Henry and Alex are going to do short readings. Henry will read a traditional Māori love poem. I'm not sure what Alex is doing. He told Gaby that he's going to read something rude. She threatened to saw his legs off at the knees if he did that. He's refused to tell her what poem he's picked, so I guess we'll all be entertained tomorrow when we find out.

Pam then goes through the vows, explaining how Susan, the marriage celebrant, will ask them both to say their vows before they exchange their rings. As I listen to her going through each step, with Gaby and Tyson listening intently, I'm aware of the turning of the wheel of time once again. The last wedding I went to was Kennedy's, when she married Jackson. That event provoked a mix of emotions in all of us, especially when she gave a speech at the reception saying how much she missed her brother. Maybe it's because these are important life events, and it just brings into focus how the absent person isn't here to experience them. Christian will never fall in love, have sex, get engaged and married, or have children. It makes me unutterably sad.

"That concludes the ceremony," Pam announces. "After this, the bride and groom will pass back along the aisle, and then move over to the trees where they'll have their photos. When they're complete, James will signal for everyone to form two lines through which the happy couple will pass on the way to the ballroom, and you can all throw your confetti."

She finishes with a little speech about the beauty of marriage and how she hopes the two of them have many years of happiness ahead of them, and then suggests we move into the restaurant for the evening meal. We all clap, and then everyone starts making their way inside.

Belle joins me as we walk in, and touches my arm. "Are you okay?" she murmurs. "Were you thinking about Christian?"

Surprised at her perceptiveness, I say, "Yeah."

"These rites of passage are supposed to be happy events, but they trigger all sorts of memories and emotions, don't they?" She slides her hand down to mine, holding it briefly and giving it a squeeze before releasing it.

I don't get a chance to reply because as we enter the restaurant, Freddie grabs her other hand and says, "You're next to me, over here."

She throws me an apologetic look but doesn't argue, and lets him take her to one of the round tables where the other bridesmaids and ushers are sitting.

I sit at a table with Alex and the others. It's a great meal, with a variety of choices from filet steak to braised lamb shanks to salmon, as well as two vegetarian options. Everyone at the table is on good form, too, so it's a pleasant evening. But it's marred for me by having to watch Freddie slavering over Belle for the entire evening. Jesus, could he make it any more obvious that he's interested in her? He's slung his arm across the back of the chair so it's almost—but not quite—around her, and he leans toward her to murmur in her ear any opportunity he gets. While eating his steak, he cuts off a piece and offers it to her on his fork like a lover would do. To her credit, Belle takes the fork from him rather than letting him feed her, and I notice that she doesn't touch him the way she touched me, but I'm still annoyed more than I should be. She's not my wife or my girlfriend. She doesn't wear my ring, and I have no claim on her at all.

"You could just go and pee all around her," Juliette murmurs.

I look at her, startled by her comment.

"You've spent most of the evening glaring at Freddie," Juliette says. "It's pretty obvious."

Alarmed, I look at Alex, but he's talking to his mother and doesn't appear to have noticed.

"Freddie is more her age," I say to Juliette. "I'm sure they'll make a lovely couple."

She gives me a wry look. "So you're not currently thinking about taking him out the back and beating the shit out of him?"

"Not at all." I have a sip of champagne. "I thought I'd ask Henry to do it."

We both laugh. "Why don't you just ask her out?" she says.

"Because Alex would make me into a eunuch."

"That's bullshit. He wouldn't care as long as you treated her right."

"Therein lies the problem."

"Yeah, because you're such a bad boy. I know you've cultivated your lady-killer reputation because you think it'll keep your heart safe. But you can't keep it padlocked away for the rest of your life."

"Just watch me," I mumble, trying not to watch as Freddie offers Belle a spoonful of Tiramisu. This time, she shakes her head and says no thank you, although she tempers it with a smile. Thank God. If she'd accepted, I would've had to leap over the tables and strangle the guy with my bare hands. Or get Henry to do it.

When she's finished her dessert, Belle rises, and I watch her make her way out of the restaurant, where she disappears along the corridor, presumably to the Ladies. As casually as I can, I finish my chocolate profiterole, wipe my mouth, then excuse myself, and follow her out.

I walk along the corridor and lean on the wall in the small lobby opposite the bathrooms. I only have to wait a few minutes before she comes out. She sees me immediately, and her eyes widen.

I gesture with my head for her to follow me, and take her around the corner, finding a quiet spot between the reception desk and the elevators, in a nook partially hidden behind a rubber plant.

She leans back against the wall, looking up at me, and I stand in front of her, flicking back the sides of my jacket and sliding my hands into the pockets of my trousers.

"Enjoying yourself?" I ask.

Her lips twitch. "He has a motorbike," she says.

"Great."

"He's asked me if I'd like to go with him to see Paua of One next week." It's a famous Kiwi band.

I move closer to her, looking at the beautiful curve of her Cupid's bow. She's not mine. I have no right to these feelings. But I'm consumed by jealousy at the thought of him touching her.

"Are you going to let him make you come with his fingers?" I ask, my voice little more than a growl.

I wait for her to say what Rachel or most other girls would have said: *I can do what I like*, or *I don't belong to you*, or *mind your own business*.

Instead, Belle looks into my eyes and says, "You know that's your prerogative, Damon." She tips her head to the side, looking at my mouth. She's thinking of kissing me. "You gave me my name. You claimed me, all those years ago. I've always belonged to you." She lifts her gaze to mine again and smiles.

"What are you doing?" I murmur clumsily, conscious of her mesmerizing voice and eyes, turning on the magic.

"Seducing you. Is it working?"

The space between us seems to sparkle with electricity. "A little bit," I mumble.

"You sound reluctant," she whispers. "Don't you want me, Damon?" She moistens her lips with the tip of her tongue. "Don't you want to see what I look like naked?" She takes my lapels in her hands. "Don't you want to know what I taste like? To make me come with your tongue?" She closes the gap between us, her mouth inches from mine. "To feel me clench around you while you're inside me?"

I have no words, only actions to show her how I feel. So I lift my hands and slide them into her hair, which is as soft as I knew it would be. My fingers slipping through her silky locks, I crush my lips to hers.

She moans against my mouth, which is so sexy that I'm hard instantly, and I press her up against the wall so she can feel it, while I plunge my tongue into her mouth. I didn't mean to do this; I do my best not to be forceful with women, but it's impossible to rein in my passion as it flares from a spark into a forest fire, sweeping over us and igniting us both.

Her hands slide beneath my jacket and around my waist, and I feel her nails score my back lightly over the thin cotton of my shirt. I shudder, and she sighs against my lips, her breath whispering over them.

I lift my head, and we stand there like that for a moment, our lips a fraction of an inch apart, our bodies touching, locked in an embrace neither of us wants to break.

"After the meal," I tell her, my voice gruff with desire, "I want you to come to my room."

She nods, her eyes alight with pleasure. "What number?"

"Forty-two."

"The secret to life, the universe, and everything?" she teases. She's quoting from *The Hitchhiker's Guide to the Galaxy*.

"Damn straight."

She laughs. "I'm guessing we're not going to watch TV though."

I touch my lips to hers again. "No. I'm going to give you so many orgasms, it'll make you dizzy."

"Oh God."

"You wanted to seduce me, Belle, so you have to deal with the aftereffects. I'm so hot for you, I'm about to self-combust. So I hope you're ready to get swept up in the flames, because I'm not going to hold back."

Chapter Sixteen

Belle

I return to the table on shaky legs. "You were a long time," Freddie comments. "You feeling okay?"

"A little bit wobbly," I admit truthfully. "Too many glasses of champagne, I guess."

He chuckles. "Can't say I'm keen on it. I'd rather have a beer." He finishes off his glass anyway. "You want some more?" he asks, picking up a bottle.

I shake my head and, disappointed, he tops up his own glass. He's been trying to get me drunk tonight, maybe hoping I'd go back to his room with him. He doesn't know that someone else has already claimed that privilege.

I shiver at the memory of Damon pressed up against me, murmuring against my mouth that he's going to give me so many orgasms, it'll make me dizzy. The guy looks amazing tonight. Freddie's fun, but he looks like a boy with his too-tight trousers, his earring, and his shaved head. Damon's suit fits him like a dream, tailored to his broad shoulders and narrow waist, and you can tell it's bespoke. Knowing him, he probably flew to Naples to buy it. Freddie's tie looks as if his mum has tied it for him. Damon's has an elegant Windsor knot. Freddie's cufflinks are fun rugby balls and look as if they've come out of the two-dollar shop. Damon's are Louis Vuitton and match his tie pin. Freddie's wearing Lynx body spray. Damon's cologne is spicy and smoky, and it wouldn't surprise me if it was Clive Christian, probably over seven hundred dollars a bottle.

I'm not putting Freddie down for not having money. I know it's a helluva lot easier to look suave when you're not buying off the peg. But Damon's sophistication goes much deeper than what he's wearing. I admire that he can talk about rugby and gaming with the guys, but that he's also a genius when it comes to computer programming. I love the fact that he drinks beer and eats chips out of the packet with Alex and the others, but that he also knows the difference between a twelve-year-old and a twenty-one-year-old Glenlivet.

And as for being a selfless god in the bedroom… I adore him for that.

I look across to the other table and discover him watching me, a small smile on his face. *I'm so hot for you, I'm about to self-combust…* Oh God. This man's going to eat me alive. If I'm very, very lucky.

It takes a while for the evening to wind down, though. Everyone's having a fun time, and nobody seems to want it to end. Tomorrow is when there'll be music and dancing, but tonight is all about catching up with friends and family. Leaving Freddie sulking, I move between the tables, and even though I'm excited to be with Damon, I enjoy stopping to chat with people I haven't seen in a long time.

At one point, I glance over and see Freddie deep in conversation with one of Tyson's cousins, leaning toward her as he brushes her arm. Not exactly heartbroken that I've moved on, then. I glance across at Damon, and my body warms as I see him watching me, a small smile on his lips. He can't take his eyes off me.

"Belle."

I turn at the sound of the man's voice and discover my brother standing behind me. Eek. Irritation flows through me. I'm an adult; I can date whomever I choose now. Why does he always make me feel as if I'm fourteen again?

But he doesn't look cross with me. Instead, he nods across the room and says, "You want to give me a hand? I don't want them to spoil the weekend."

I follow his gaze and see Mum and Dad standing talking together. "Jesus," I mumble, observing their stiff postures and the way they're glaring at each other. "What do we do?"

"Diffuse the tension," Alex says, leading the way across the room. "How?"

"I dunno. I'm making this up as I go along." He approaches the two of them and pins a smile on his face. "Hey. How's it going?"

"She's drunk," Dad says, not removing his gaze from Mum's face. "She finally graces her kids with a visit, and she can't even remain sober for a few hours."

Mum's face flushes. "I'm not drunk," she snaps. "I've had as much champagne as everyone else."

"Yeah, and your tolerance of alcohol has always been crap," Dad replies. His voice holds the bitterness that appears only when he's speaking to her. He's usually such a calm, placid man, and it always twists me up inside to hear him like this.

"Guys," Alex says, "not here, and not today."

They both ignore him. Mum's trembling. Dad's eyes are flashing with anger.

If they were two guys, I know that Alex would frog march one of them out of the room, but he can hardly do that with his parents, although he's glowering, so I think it's a possibility. It'll draw attention, and I don't want them to spoil Gaby's evening.

I slide a hand into the pocket of Alex's trousers. He looks down. "What the…"

Finding a coin, I extract it and bring it up between Mum and Dad in my left hand, running it across my knuckles so it glints in the light. The movement distracts them, and they both drop their gazes to it. I bring up my right hand and take the coin from the left, then open my fingers and reveal my empty palm.

Mum blinks, and then her lips curve up a little. Dad gives me a wry look.

"Why don't you take Mum up to her room?" Alex says softly. "She's been wanting to catch up with you."

I don't want to, but I can see that Mum's upset, and even though she's not blind drunk, she's obviously on the way. "Come on," I say grudgingly. "Let's go. Don't make a scene."

I collect my clutch bag, and she lets me lead her across the room. I glance at Damon, who's frowning, but I can't explain, and I'm too upset to stop and talk to him. I take Mum out and across the elevators. "What floor are you on?"

"Twenty-eight."

It's the top floor. Of course she'd have the penthouse.

The fight has gone out of her. She looks around the lobby and, seeing two women staring at her by the front desk, turns her back, sliding her hands into the pockets of her trousers and hunching her shoulders.

We wait for the doors to open, then go inside. The two women rush to join us, but I put out a hand, and they stop, disappointed, and let the doors close.

"Thank you," Mum says gratefully. She touches her key card to the panel and presses the button for the top floor, and the car rises.

She smiles, stretches out a hand, and strokes my cheek. "My beautiful baby girl. I've missed you so much."

I move out of her reach. "It's a bit late for that."

"Michelle…"

"Nobody calls me that anymore, Mum."

"No. I'm sorry. Belle. I said to Damon earlier that I remember when he gave you that name."

I scowl. I don't want to talk to her about Damon.

"Don't be angry with me," she whispers. She's very pale, and for the first time I notice how much weight she's lost. As always, her makeup is immaculate, but it can't hide the fact that she looks tired and miserable.

"I'm sorry about Ryan," I say awkwardly. I haven't spoken to her since the news broke that they'd split.

"Thank you."

"What happened?" The media hasn't been able to fathom a cause for their breakup.

"I found him in bed with someone else." Her expression darkens. "Again. It seems I'm cursed in that regard."

I stare at her. "What do you mean?"

The lift slows and pings, and the doors open. She looks at me, blinks slowly, then says, "I don't know. I am pretty drunk. Forget I said anything." She walks out, down the corridor.

I stand there for a moment, then run to catch her up. She stops outside a door, touches her key card to it, and goes inside. I enter behind her, letting it close.

The penthouse is a suite, far too large for one person, but Mum would never stay in anything less than the best. She goes through to the kitchen, opens the cupboard, and pulls out a bottle of gin. "Want a G&T?" she asks.

I nod, having a feeling I'm going to need it. "What did you mean when you said 'again'? Had Ryan cheated on you before?"

"No." She takes some ice from the freezer and tosses it into two tumblers, adds a splash of gin to each, then opens a bottle of tonic and pours a little over the gin. Pushing mine across to me, she picks up hers and then goes into the living room.

"So who did?" She's had a number of relationships over the years, mainly famous faces that have flitted across my social media. I've only ever met one of her lovers. "Not... Tom?" My stomach turns to water as I say his name.

But she just says, "No." She sits on the sofa and flops back, looking exhausted, and I remember that she must have jet lag.

"So who then?" I persist.

Her brow furrows. She has a big mouthful of her gin, then another.

"Mum..."

"It was your father," she says tiredly.

I stare at her. I feel as if she's told me that the sun rises in the west. "What?" I say dumbly.

"He'd been having an affair with Sherry for six months when I found out. It's why I slept with Tom at first, as retaliation."

I was twelve years old, and we were living in Wellington. Gaby was fifteen. Alex was eighteen, in his last year of secondary school. The atmosphere at home had been bad for a while. Mum's acting career was flourishing, and she was away a lot, filming. I know she was struggling with depression, and when she was home, I can remember some days where she couldn't even get out of bed. I guess Dad resented having to bring up three kids practically on his own, as he didn't like having a nanny in the house. My main memory of that horrible year was of the two of them screaming at each other, throwing insults like hand grenades. Alex or Gaby always took me out of the room when they started, though, so I didn't get to hear everything they said. I remember him saying she was selfish, that all she thought of was her career, and that her kids should come first.

And then one day, I got up in the morning to discover that Mum had left during the night, and Dad told me tersely that she'd moved in with her 'lover', Tom. All these years, I've believed she had an affair first, and that Dad met Sherry after she'd left.

"Why have you always let me blame you?" I whisper.

"I've never been an easy person to live with," she admits. "I'd been severely depressed, and I've always suffered with self-image issues, which of course are made worse by working in Hollywood. Your dad and I hadn't slept together for over a year. Sorry, love, TMI, I'm sure, but you're old enough now to know the truth. I drove him into Sherry's arms. I can't blame him for what he did. It still hurt, of course. Tom had already made a pass at me a few months before. I turned him down because I was married. I'm not saying that to sound superior—it's the truth. I loved your father. But when I found out about Sherry, I went straight to Tom, and we slept together that night. It was good, for a while. I fell in love with him. I was going to marry him. I thought everything was going to be all right. And then…" Her eyes fill with tears. Neither of us wants to talk about that.

"Why didn't you tell me everything?" I say, my own eyes prickling. "After Tom, why did you just leave?"

"Because your father asked me to."

My jaw drops as it all becomes clear. "He blamed you."

"Of course he did, and he was right to."

"Mum," I say, horrified, "it wasn't your fault."

"Don't forgive me," she says, starting to cry. "I couldn't bear it."

I go over and sit next to her. I'm trembling, overwhelmed with emotion. "I wish you'd told me."

"Oh baby," she whispers, "I'm so sorry."

Tears pour down my face. I'm still a long way from true forgiveness. But for the first time in my life, I don't blame her, and I don't hate her.

I put my head on her lap like a child, and we sit there like that for ages, our faces wet, while she strokes my hair like a real mother.

*

Eventually, I fall asleep, worn out from all the emotion.

When I wake, I'm stretched out on the sofa, covered in a blanket, alone. I sit up, retrieve my clutch from the floor, and pull out my phone. I tap the screen—it's nearly eleven. I get up quietly and walk through to the bedroom. She's in bed, curled up facing away from me, asleep.

I go into the bathroom, close the door, then turn the light on and examine my face in the mirror. I clean up the smudged makeup as best as I can, and use a little of her face powder to cover any red blotches.

Then I sit on the toilet seat and look at my phone. I scroll through the messages—a couple from Gaby, saying she hopes everything's okay, and she's gone home to Dad's house with Aroha for the night. One from Alex telling me to call if I need anything.

Nothing from Damon.

He saw me leave with Mum, so I guess he must assume I'm up here. He's probably gone to bed now. I could go down to his room and knock on the door. He might hear me, and come and let me in. I long to feel his arms around me, to have him hold me tightly. But I'm a mess, and it's not fair to dump all this on him.

After turning off the light, I go out and into the living room. I slip on my shoes, collect my clutch, and let myself out of her room quietly. My feet practically silent on the carpet, I walk to the elevator, and descend to the ground floor.

The lobby is quiet. I can see that the restaurant is empty. I should catch an Uber, head home, and get a good night's sleep before the wedding tomorrow. It's not as if I'm a regular guest who can skulk in the shadows—I'm a bridesmaid, and I'm going to have plenty of eyes on me. I don't want to ruin it for Gaby.

But Dad and Sherry might still be up, and I'm not sure I'm ready to talk to them yet.

My feet take me across the lobby to the bar. I pause in the doorway. I wondered whether there might be wedding guests here, but once again it's nearly empty, everyone obviously deciding to get an early night so they're ready for the big day. An older, tired-looking businessman sits at a table nursing a whisky, studying his phone. A young Japanese couple talk quietly in the corner.

I go to the end of the bar by the wall and sit on one of the stools. The bartender is a striking young woman with short dark hair, wearing black trousers, a white shirt, and a black bow tie. She smiles at me. "Can I see some ID?" I take out my driver's license, and she runs her gaze over it, then nods. "What can I get you?"

"A G&T please."

"Gordon's or something else?"

"Gordon's is fine."

She makes the drink and brings it over. For a moment I think she's going to ask me what I'm doing here alone, but to my relief she returns to cleaning glasses, leaving me on my own.

Turning so my back is against the wall, I prop my feet on the bottom bar of the stool next to me and have a big mouthful of the G&T. The alcohol threads through me, and I exhale, releasing the tension in my shoulders and spine.

My insides are like a huge ball of knotted wool. My thoughts and emotions are tangled, and I can't unravel them and make sense of them. I feel angry and sad and resentful and hopeful and bitter, and they're all interwoven.

I'm furious that nobody has told me the truth: neither my parents, nor Alex or Gaby. And I can't even start to disentangle my thoughts about my father. He had an affair first? That revelation has shaken my foundations like an earthquake, and little aftershocks keep shooting through me, making me tremble. I want to go and find him, and scream at him for ruining their marriage.

But the thing is, I'm not twelve anymore. I'm a grown woman with several failed relationship behind her. Cole had a lot of issues, but I wasn't innocent in our breakup. I wasn't vocal or forceful enough—I should have made it much clearer what I did and didn't want both in and out of bed. I don't blame myself for that—I didn't know any better at the time—but Damon has shown me how important communication is in the bedroom, and I know it would have improved things between me and Cole.

So I understand that it takes two to tango. Mum obviously has to take some of the blame as to why Dad had an affair. He's a decent guy, and I don't think he would have slept with Sherry if he hadn't been driven to find affection elsewhere. Or would he? Maybe I'm being incredibly naïve. Once again, I think of Damon, and the way things have blown up between us over the past few days. I used to think it ridiculous when two people said they couldn't fight their attraction—I used to think it childish, because we're all in control of our actions. But when he's near me, I struggle to think straight. Can I really blame Dad if he felt the same way about Sherry?

I'm angry that Mum said she left because Dad asked her to. I'm upset that he blamed her for what happened. But he was just protecting me. Again, is he really at fault for that?

I remember something Alex said once when I was young, hurt, and frightened that my parents were separating. "Everyone's doing their best," he said. "Some people are just better at it than others." He was only eighteen, but it seems very profound to me now.

I've spent so long being hostile to my mother because she abandoned me. All these years, I've resented her, even hated her, for leaving me. But I've never thought about it from her point of view. *I met Tom, and I fell in love with him.* I can only think about the man with contempt and hatred. But she loved him. The events of that year must have torn her apart. She's had to live with that knowledge for nine years. She blames herself, and that's why she's kept her distance from me.

I finish off the G&T and beckon to the bartender. "Another, please," I tell her.

She pours it and brings it over. "Are you okay?" she asks kindly. "Can I call anyone for you?"

I shake my head. "I'm fine."

"Okay." She hesitates, then goes back to cleaning her glasses.

I drink the G&T slowly. Then I order another.

I've had several glasses of champagne tonight, and the G&T with Mum. So it's not long before things start to feel fuzzy.

I should go home. But instead I keep sitting there, staring into my glass.

After a while, I pull out my phone. Damon is probably asleep now. I was so close to going to bed with him tonight. I know he wanted me—I could feel his desire radiating from him. Have I fucked it up? My eyes prickle again. I want to text him, but I don't know what to say.

In the end, I just send him a red heart emoji, then order another drink.

The bartender slides it across to me, then leans on the bar and says, "I think we'll have to make this your last one, sweetie."

"I'm not drunk."

She just lifts an eyebrow. Then she glances at the clock on the wall. It's 11:45. "We close at midnight anyway."

"I'll go soon," I whisper. "I swear. I'll get an Uber home."

"All right. You wanna talk?"

"No. But thanks."

She nods and goes back to her glasses.

I look at my phone. Damon's sent a text. *Belle! Where are you?*

Me: *Having a drink.*

Damon: *With whom?*

Me: *On my own.*

Damon: *Are you okay?*

Me: *Yeah.*

I stare at the screen for a few seconds, then send another message.

Me: *Nah.*

Damon: *Belle, where are you?*

Me: *Just in a bar.*

Damon: *Which one?*

Me: *Don't worry, the bartender's cutting me off soon.*
Damon: *Please, tell me where you are.*
Me: *I miss you.*
Damon: *Which bar, Belle?*
Me: *We should have gone straight to your room.*
Damon: *Which bar, Belle?*
Me: *I was looking forward to all those orgasms.*
Damon: *BELLE, WHICH BAR?*

I put my head in my hands. I'm so fucking tired, but I know I'm not going to be able to sleep. I should go home, though. I put my feet down and almost slip off the barstool. Whoa. I've drunk more than I thought.

My phone buzzes.
Damon: *WHICH BAR*
Damon: *BELLE?*
Damon: *WHICH BAR*
Damon: *DON'T MAKE ME SEARCH THE WHOLE FUCKING CITY, BECAUSE I WILL*
Me: *Stop shouting. You're making my head hurt.*
Damon: *Where are you?*
Me: *I think I might have drunk a bit too much.*
Damon: *WHICH FUCKING BAR?????????*
Me: *Keep your boxers on, I'm downstairs.*
Damon: *In the hotel?*
Me: *Yeah. On my own. So I'm safe. Stop panicking. I'm going home now.*

I stare at the screen for thirty seconds, but he doesn't reply. I bet he's right pissed off with me. I slide my phone into my clutch, then put my head in my hands again. Jesus. I can do this. I'll get to the lobby, and then I'll call an Uber.

Ohhh… I'm not sure my legs will make it that far…

"Looks like someone's not happy you're here," the bartender tells me with amusement.

I look up to see Damon striding into the bar. I blink. He's clearly dressed in a hurry. He's wearing his shirt and suit trousers, but only half the buttons are done up on his white shirt, his hair is ruffled, and he's barefoot. Oh wow.

"Jesus," he says, stopping before me. Hands on his hips, he blows out a breath and glances at the bartender.

"She's all right," she says gently. "I was about to put her in an Uber."

I look up at him, my bottom lip trembling. He cups my face and looks into my eyes for a moment, his gingerbread-brown eyes searching mine as if he's in a forest at night, hunting for a rabbit with a flashlight.

Then he puts his arms around me and gives me a hug.

I bury my face in his shirt, inhaling his cologne, unable to fight the feeling that everything's going to be okay now he's here.

"Don't leave me," I mumble.

"I won't. It's all right. You're okay. Look, I can't drive you home because I've had a few drinks, but how about I call us an Uber, and I'll come with you, make sure you get home all right?"

"I don't want to go home," I whisper.

He strokes my back. "All right. What do you want to do?"

"I don't know." I nestle as close as I can to him. "I want to stay with you."

"Are you her boyfriend?" the bartender asks.

"No." He kisses the top of my head. "Not quite. She's my best mate's little sis and the bridesmaid at the wedding tomorrow—her name's Belle Winters, and she's obviously upset. I'm Damon—we're good friends and I've known her for, like, fifteen years. Put her bill on room forty-two, okay? I'm going to take her up to my room, put her to bed, and let her sleep it off. I'll sleep on the sofa. Are you all right with that?"

Part of me is incredibly touched that he's asking the bartender's permission. Of course he is. He'll always put the girl's safety first.

The bartender touches my arm. "Are you happy to go with him, honey?"

I nod.

"All right. Go on, then."

"Thanks." He slides an arm around my waist. "Come on, ma belle."

He helps me off the barstool and grabs my clutch with his left hand. With his right arm tight around me, he takes me out to the elevators and presses the button.

"I'm sorry." I nestle closer to him. He's warm, and he smells amazing.

"Shh. It's okay." He hugs me until the doors open, then guides me in. He touches his card to the panel and presses a button, and the elevator rises.

Chapter Seventeen

Damon

Belle sways a little against me, and then out of the blue her knees buckle. Luckily I have an arm around her waist, and I quickly tighten it and slide my other arm under her legs, scooping her up into my arms.

"Sorry," she says, resting her cheek on my shoulder.

"It's all right." I rest my lips on her hair. It smells of strawberries.

What on earth happened tonight? I saw her going off with her mother, and when I didn't hear from her, I assumed she'd either stayed there talking, or had decided to go home. I was disappointed, but pleased in a way that she'd finally taken the time to talk to her mother. Clearly, though, things haven't gone as well as I hoped.

The doors open, and I carry her along the corridor to my room. I fumble to get the card out of my pocket, touch it to the door, then open it and take her inside. I think she might already be asleep.

The door swings shut behind me. The room is nothing special, just one allocated to the wedding party. Sometimes when I'm in hotels I rent the penthouse or one of the suites, but this time I knew I wouldn't be spending much time here, so I was content that it just has a comfortable bed and a decent shower.

I take her over to the bed, bend and peel back the duvet, then lower her feet to the floor. She's very woozy, a combination, I think, of alcohol and exhaustion.

"Come with me." Grabbing one of my tees from my open case on the way, I lead her through to the bathroom and turn on the light. She looks at her reflection in the mirror, winces, and turns away.

"Change into this," I instruct, "and when you've finished in here, we'll get you to bed, and you can sleep it off."

She rests her forehead on my chest. "I don't think I can do it on my own." She lifts her arm behind her back to reach her zipper, then lets it fall again.

I blow out a silent breath. "All right, come here." I turn her around gently, find the tab of the zipper, and slide it down. Yeah, of course, she's not wearing a bra. I wince as I think what the bartender would say if she could see us now.

But Belle sways against me, and suddenly she's just a young woman who's upset and unwell and who needs help. "Come on," I say briskly, "let's get this tee on you."

Staying behind her, I help her get her arms out of the bodice of the dress, and it slips to the floor in a whisper of material. Keeping my eyes averted, I grab the tee, pull it over her head, and hold it so she can push her arms through. I then tug it down over her body, desperately trying not to look at her pale skin, or her curves in the huge mirror that insists on showing me everything.

Once it's on, she leans against me, trembling. "I think I'm going to be sick," she murmurs.

I sigh, lead her over to the toilet, and hold her hair back while she vomits. When she's done, I take her to the sink so she can rinse her mouth, then leave her for a moment to use the toilet.

When she's done, I lift her up into my arms, take her back to the bed, and lay her on the mattress. I retrieve a bottle of water from the fridge, bring it back, and remove the top.

"Drink as much as you can," I instruct, and I stand over her while she downs half the bottle. Then I pull the duvet over her. She's white-faced, and her eyes are huge.

"I'm so sorry," she whispers.

"It's all right."

But her bottom lip trembles, and tears leak from her eyes. "I've fucked everything up," she says.

"Aw, Belle…"

She starts crying for real.

I watch her for a moment. Then, after extracting another tee from my case, I unbutton my shirt and toss it onto the chair. I tug on the tee, then take off my trousers. Finally, I have a look in the wardrobe and find a spare blanket.

I come back to the bed. The sofa is only a two-seater anyway, so I wouldn't get any sleep on there.

Propped up on the pillows, I lie on top of the covers and drape the blanket over myself. Immediately, she moves up close to me and slides her arms around my waist.

Sighing, I wrap my arms around her and hold her close.

"I'm sorry," she says, sobbing. "I'm sorry."

"Shh." I rub her back over the duvet. "It's okay. Everything's going to be all right."

She cries for a bit, then slowly the sobs stop, and she gives a big sigh. "I shouldn't have drunk so much."

"Ah, it happens. Don't worry about it."

"Thank you for rescuing me."

"I didn't rescue you. I just helped a bit. Come on, don't cry. It's going to be okay. We'll sort it out." I grab a tissue from the box on my side of the bed and hand it to her.

She blows her nose, then looks up at me. Her eye makeup is smudged and her eyes are red, but she's still beautiful.

"Will you kiss me?" she whispers.

"Not while you're drunk."

She leans her temple on my shoulder, still looking up at me. "I love you."

I chuckle and kiss her nose. "I love you, too."

She closes her eyes.

In less than a minute, she's asleep.

I slide down the pillows a bit, turning to face her, and she snuggles right up to me.

We stay like that for the rest of the night.

*

Belle

When I next open my eyes, the sun is streaming through the open curtains, buttercup yellow.

I'm lying on my side, facing Damon. Even though I'm underneath the duvet and he's on top, we're entangled, my top knee between his, and our arms wrapped around each other. My nose is buried in his neck. He's wearing a tee, and smells of freshly washed cotton, along with the subtle scent of his cologne, all mixed in with warm male. Ohhh… if someone could bottle that smell, they'd make a fortune.

For a moment, I don't move, enjoying being so close to him. He's asleep, I think—his breathing is slow and even, his breath feathering across my forehead.

He was so sweet last night. I vaguely remember him coming into the bar and talking to the bartender. I seem to recall him picking me up at one point and carrying me in. I'm wearing a T-shirt, so I must have changed out of my dress—I don't remember doing that. I think I was sick, though. I have a recollection of him holding my hair back. Jeez.

He obviously refused to get into bed with me, but cuddled up just the same. Oh God, did I tell him I love him? I'm sure I remember him laughing and saying he loved me too. That's embarrassing.

His lips touch my forehead, light as a butterfly.

I move back and look up into his brown eyes. "Oh, good morning."

"Morning," he says, and smiles. "How are you feeling?"

"Okay. I think."

"You slept well."

"Better than I thought I would." Wow, he looks amazing. Better than I do, I'm sure. His hair is all ruffled. His jaw bears a light stubble. His eyes survey me sleepily. Mmm, imagine waking up like this after a night of lovemaking. Imagine knowing that he was yours.

I swallow and sit up. My makeup will be all smudged, and I have badger's breath. I can't imagine I've ever looked less attractive.

Leaning over to the bedside table, I retrieve my clutch—he must have left it there—and take out my phone. "It's seven thirty," I say with some surprise.

"Late for me," he says. "I'm normally up at six."

I have a few messages. Several are from Gaby, asking if I'm okay—one from last night, two from this morning.

"Gaby's wondering where I am," I tell him.

"Of course. Today's the big day."

I text her that I stayed at the hotel, and that I'll be home in a while. Damon watches me, head propped on a hand.

When I'm done, I lower the phone, and we study each other for a moment.

"I must look horrendous," I say.

"You're beautiful," he says simply. "Like a freshly plucked rose."

"Did you say plucked?"

We both give a short laugh.

"I'm so sorry," I say. "For all the inconvenience."

"Belle, come on. We've known each other long enough not to worry about stuff like that."

"Even so. You thought you were going to get your leg over, and instead you got to hold my hair while I threw up."

"I also got to hold you all night. I can't complain."

"I am sorry, though," I say sincerely. "I was looking forward to… you know. I'm incredibly disappointed to have ruined it."

"Who says you've ruined it?"

"Damon… I can't. I look awful, and I have to go and help Gaby."

He shrugs. "There's always tonight."

My eyes widen. "Are you serious?"

His lazy gaze studies my mouth for a moment, then lifts back to mine. He doesn't reply, but his lips curve up.

We study each other for a moment. The sunshine streaming through the window highlights motes of dust dancing in the air. They sparkle, as if someone's scattered fairy dust across us. It feels like a magical moment, as hope and excitement rise inside me, pushing down the negative emotions that overwhelmed me last night.

I'm conscious of badger breath, but even so, I can't resist leaning forward and pressing my lips to his. His mouth is firm and warm, and he slides a hand to the nape of my neck and holds me there for a few seconds before releasing me.

My face warms, so I know I'm blushing. "I'm going to get dressed," I whisper, "and then I'd better get going."

"All right."

I get out of bed, grab my clutch, and, conscious I'm not wearing any trousers, run across to the bathroom and go inside.

Blowing out a breath, I lean on the sink and look at my reflection. Oh Jesus, I look like a witch. My hair is all over the place, my eye makeup is all smudged, and my skin is blotchy.

There's no point in having a shower as I'll have a bath when I get home. I clean my face, though, removing my makeup with one of the hotel wipes, then take an elastic band out of the clutch and twist my hair up into a scruffy bun. I discover a toothbrush in a packet in the drawer, and steal a bit of his toothpaste to clean my teeth. My dress is hanging on the back of the door, so I take off Damon's tee reluctantly and pull on the dress. I can't do the zipper up myself, so I go back out into the bedroom.

He's got up, and he's sitting in one of the chairs in front of the window, looking at his phone, but he rises as I come out.

"Would you mind…?" I turn my back to him.

"Sure." He comes over, and I feel his fingers against my skin as he takes the tab of the zipper and slides it up carefully.

"Thanks." I turn to face him.

"You look amazing," he says, reaching out to tuck a strand of hair behind my ear.

"I've cleaned my teeth," I reply, then blush again as I realize what a clumsy statement that was.

He just smiles, though, cups my face in his hands, and moves up close to me. "Ma belle," he murmurs, and lowers his lips to mine.

This time, he brushes his tongue across my bottom lip. In response, I open my mouth, and he slides his tongue against mine, and we indulge in a long, leisurely kiss that soon has my heart racing.

He lifts his head and looks at me for a moment. Then he pulls me into his arms and gives me a hug.

I bury my face in his neck, clutching his tee in both hands. "Thank you," I whisper, "for last night."

"You're welcome. Will you tell me what happened?"

I swallow hard and move back a little to look up at him. "Mum told me that Dad was having an affair with Sherry before she slept with Tom. Dad cheated first. It really shocked me, that's all."

His eyebrows rise. "Shit. Yeah. I'm so sorry."

"I just couldn't face him last night."

"What are you going to do?"

"I don't want to spoil the wedding. I'll have to keep it to myself today and speak to him when Gaby's left for the honeymoon." I hesitate. "It's just… will you be honest with me? Have you ever cheated on a girl?"

"No," he says immediately. "Never."

We study each other for a long moment.

"I don't get it," I say eventually. "I don't understand why people cheat. I know that's incredibly naïve, but it's so fucking cruel. If they're not happy, why don't they end the relationship, then look elsewhere?"

He thinks about it. "I suppose people don't think about the repercussions of their actions. They get carried away in the heat of the moment."

"But he had an affair for six months before she found out. That's not a crime of passion, is it? That's cold and calculating."

"Sometimes I'm sure vengeance plays a part. But mostly I think it's about solace. Relationships can be tough, and when things are hard, people look elsewhere for comfort."

"I guess." I need to think about that.

"Okay," he says. "Well I guess I'll see you back here later, for the wedding?"

"Yeah. In my bridesmaid's dress."

"I can't wait to see it."

I smooth out his tee where I clutched at the cotton. "What are you wearing?"

"A navy three-piece suit."

"Mmm. I love waistcoats."

"You'll like this one, then. It cost me a fortune, but it fits like a dream."

I smile. "I'll see you later?"

"Yeah. You going to be okay?"

"I'll be fine." I blow him a kiss, slip on my sandals, grab my clutch, and head out of the room, letting the door close behind me.

Outside, in the corridor, I lean against the wall for a moment and blow out a shaky breath. Wow. I press a hand to my forehead. Talk about a whirlwind of emotions. I'm still upset about last night, but excited to think that maybe I haven't blown it with Damon. There's a lot to get through before this evening though.

I go down to the ground floor, pull out my phone, then hesitate as I bring up the Uber app. I should go straight home, but there's something else I want to do first. I type in Alex's address and order the Uber. It only takes minutes to arrive, and soon I'm heading the short distance to his house.

I text him to let him know I'm on the way. He comes back: *Everything okay?*

Me: *Yeah. Just need to talk to you about something.*

Alex: *Uh-oh.*

I don't reply. I'm hoping it'll make him nervous. I'm angry that he never told me about Dad. I understand that he wants to protect me, but I'm tired of being treated like a child.

Alex's house is one of six modern, bespoke homes on a private country estate not far from Hagley Park. I punch the code in on the gate, then walk the short distance to his house. He's waiting by the front door, leaning on the door jamb with his hands in his pockets, and he frowns as I walk up.

"You all right?" he asks. His gaze slips down me, taking in the fact that I'm still in the dress I wore yesterday. My face burns at what it implies, but he just says, "Did you stay with Mum last night?"

I clear my throat. Talk about a guilty complex. "Yeah."

"Okay. Come in."

I follow him into the house, and across the large living room to the spacious kitchen. It looks out onto a generous deck and a well-manicured lawn. Beyond it, the Avon is a curling ribbon. The house also has its own pool, which glitters a deep blue in the sunlight.

"I was just making a Spanish omelet," he says, taking the pan off the heat and sliding the omelet onto a plate. "You want one?"

It smells amazing, but I'm too anxious to eat. "No thanks. I need to ask you something."

Folding his arms, he leans against the counter. "Okay." His hair is sticking up, and he needs a shave. He's wearing a faded tee and a scruffy pair of track pants, and he's barefoot. He's a good-looking guy, though, smart and hardworking. If only he wasn't so grumpy, he might be able to find himself a girl who'll put up with him.

I take a deep breath. "Mum told me last night that Dad was having an affair with Sherry before she slept with Tom. Dad cheated first." Emotion rushes through me again. "Why didn't you tell me?"

Silence falls between us. Alex is staring at me.

"Oh my God," I whisper. "You didn't know."

"No," he says. "I didn't."

"Does Gaby?"

"I have no idea. Probably not. She's never mentioned it, anyway."

I wrap my arms around myself, biting my lip hard so I don't cry. "Mum said Dad blames her for what happened. And she blames herself too. That's why she left, Alex. He told her to go, and she thinks it was all her fault." I press my fingers to my lips as they tremble. Suddenly, I miss Damon with every bone in my body.

Alex sighs, then he comes over and puts his arms around me. "Jesus. I wish I'd known," he mumbles. "It explains a lot."

I turn my head and rest my cheek on his chest. We don't cuddle often. He's not as big as Damon, but he still smells nice. "I thought you would have heard them arguing about it," I whisper.

"I never heard either of them mention it. They always argued about her career."

"She said she hadn't slept with Dad for a year before, because of her depression. She said she drove him into Sherry's arms."

He sighs again. "They obviously only talked about that when they were alone."

"He cheated first, Alex. I don't know why, but I feel so shocked by that. I've spent all this time blaming her for their marriage ending. I'm so confused."

He rests his lips on the top of my head. "I guess nobody's innocent in a breakup."

"He let us blame her, though. For years and years."

"Yeah. He should have told us the truth. But I guess he was trying to protect us. Protect you, especially. He was angry, Belle. He still is. He's your father, and he wasn't able to keep you safe. Can you imagine how that makes him feel? How it makes *me* feel?"

We fall quiet. I listen to his heart, which is racing, even though he appears calm.

We've never really spoken about it, me, Alex, and Gaby. It fucked all of us up. We all went to therapy, and I'm sure the therapist told them the same as she told me—that we should talk about it, get all the anger and resentment out in the open, but we never did. Alex tried a few times, but I always backed away from the conversation. His words though, *How it makes me feel?* tell me that I'm sure he feels he abandoned me as well, because he stayed in Wellington to go to university.

"Incidentally," he says, "Damon told me that he had to throw Cole out of your house. Why didn't you tell me?"

I move back, and he lowers his arms. "I didn't want to worry you. It wasn't a big thing. Damon was great and very sweet, but I'd have handled it if he hadn't been there."

"I'm glad he was."

I just smile.

"You're sure you're okay?" he asks.

"I'm fine."

"Are you going to tell Gaby?"

I shake my head. "I'll talk to her when she gets back from her honeymoon."

"Are you going to speak to Dad?"

"Not today." I close my eyes for a moment and think of Damon. *There's always tonight.* My lips curve up, and I open my eyes. "Don't worry about it. It's all good. I'm going home now, and I'm going to help Gaby become the most beautiful bride in the world. Nothing's going to spoil her day."

"Belle," Alex says, "you know you can always talk to me, right?" His tone is firm.

It's a nice thing to say, but it's too late, and too much time has gone by. I don't want to talk about it, not to him, anyway.

"It's okay, I'll be fine. You have a great day, okay? I'm so sorry for coming over."

"Not at all," he says. "You're my sister. I'd do anything for you." He lifts a hand to touch my face in an uncharacteristic display of affection.

"I know," I say softly. "Thank you."

"You take care of yourself. You know where I am if you need me." I kiss his cheek. "You're very sweet."

He scowls. "Don't tell anyone. You'll ruin my reputation."

I smile. "I'll see you later. I'll let myself out."

I go outside and call for an Uber, then stand on the pavement and lift my face to the sunshine while I wait.

I think about Damon, and the way he kissed me, his tongue teasing mine. That's what I need to concentrate on. Not the past. Not all the old emotions, the hurt and the pain.

I haven't forgotten that he told me he wasn't offering a relationship. We might sleep together tonight, and then I might never see him again. But at this moment, I don't care. I want to go to bed with him. I want to make some memories that are positive and uplifting. And if it is only one night, so what? He's already taught me so much about myself and my sexual journey, I can't help but think that one whole night with him is going to blow my mind.

Who knows what the future will bring? I have the six seduction tips under my belt now. I'll just have to do my best to use them!

Chapter Eighteen

Damon

The wedding begins at three p.m. on the dot.

I have to admit that organizer Pam knows her stuff. The garden looks amazing, with everywhere bedecked in even more pink and white balloons and ribbons than the evening before. The hundred or so guests are all seated and ready with time to spare. The couple from the UK, Cillian and Tori, play a duet as Gaby walks down the aisle between the chairs with her father, the deep notes of Tori's cello striking a wonderful contrast to the high notes of Cillian's violin.

Gaby's wearing an elegant, plain satin wedding dress with lace sleeves stitched with pearls. The dress also has a long line of pearls down the middle of her back, and more pearls adorn her veil.

Belle walks behind Gaby with the other bridesmaids, and I catch my breath at the first sight of her. Bridesmaids' dresses can be flouncy and unflattering, but although the dresses of the two younger girls are like princesses' gowns, Belle and Aroha are wearing off-the-shoulder dresses in a slightly darker dusky pink than the balloons. It has what I think is called a mermaid tail, with a split to the thigh, and they're both wearing matching pink high-heeled sandals. Their hair is pinned up at the side and coils over one shoulder.

Her gaze slides across as she passes me, and our eyes meet for a moment. I wink at her, and she gives me a lovely smile before she walks by.

I find myself oddly touched by the ceremony, maybe because it marks the progression of yet another of us from youth into true adulthood. We're all heading toward thirty. We're homeowners, some of us have girlfriends, and soon most of us will get married and have families.

Will I?

I told Belle that I didn't think it was in the stars for me. I meant it when I said I was cursed where relationships were concerned. After what happened with Rachel, I've found it difficult to trust, which is why I've kept all my hookups short and sweet. I've thrown myself into my work and told myself I don't need commitment and forever. But as I watch Gaby approaching the altar, I find I'm filled with a wistfulness I hadn't expected.

It only increases when, just before she gets to the altar, Mason stops walking, and I realize the moment for our big surprise has arrived. James steps forward and gives everyone a big smile.

"We have a little surprise for you," he says to Gaby. Then he turns and looks at Tyson.

Juliette has been working tirelessly with Tyson, running him through a physio routine every day with MAX. Since I arrived, we've all spent a couple of hours each day practicing this moment. But even so, I feel a lump in my throat as Tyson braces his hands on the arms of the wheelchair, pushes up, and gets to his feet, without the aid of crutches.

Everyone in the crowd who isn't in the know gasps. Gaby's hand rises to her mouth.

"Hello, beautiful," Tyson says to his bride, walking a few steps forward. "I wanted to be able to stand at your side at the altar." He holds out a hand to her.

Unsurprisingly, Gaby bursts into tears.

"Aw!" Belle, who's also blinking away tears, runs up to her sister. "Don't cry, you'll smudge your makeup!"

It eases the tension, and everyone in the crowd laughs and delves into pockets and purses for tissues. Belle looks around, and I grab the square from my top pocket and wave it at her. She grins and comes to take it, and then lifts her sister's veil and dabs away the tears as Gaby composes herself.

"Go on," I see her whisper to Gaby. "He's waiting for you."

Gaby approaches the altar, and the crowd gives a wistful sigh as she takes Tyson's hand and they turn to face Susan, the celebrant.

The ceremony progresses, but Gaby has eyes for nobody but her husband-to-be. I can see she's concerned about him standing for so long, but we've timed it carefully to make sure he has a couple of breaks. They take a seat when Cillian and Tori play, and again when Henry and Alex do their set pieces.

I thought Henry was going to read a Māori poem, but he brings out his guitar and, to our surprise, performs a song he apparently wrote himself, *He ra ataahua tenei*—This is a beautiful day. He sings it first in Māori, then in English, the words talking about the natural beauty of the land and the ocean and comparing it to the love of the two people getting married. It earns him a huge round of applause, and yet more tears from the bride and her friends.

Next is Alex's reading. Once again, I assumed he was going to read out a famous poem, maybe one of Shakespeare's sonnets, or something like Rumi's 'In Your Light I Learn How to Love.' I wouldn't have put it past him to read something by Spike Milligan, either. Alex is rarely serious where matters of the heart are concerned, his natural cynicism making it hard for him to be romantic.

He walks behind the podium and says, "I know Gaby's worried about what I'm going to say." As everyone laughs, she pokes her tongue out at him. He gives her a rare smile and continues, "But today I'd like to read out to you a poem I wrote for this occasion."

My eyebrows rise. He used to write poetry when we were studying it at university, but we were both a lot more open-hearted in those days. I didn't know he still composed.

"Gaby gave me the inspiration for it," he continues, "when we were talking about her writing her own vows. I—ever the cynic—said it must be difficult to come up with something meaningful. She told me that all she had to do was remember all the beautiful things Tyson has told her over the years, all the compliments and endearments she's kept inside her like a box of jewels, and her vows practically wrote themselves. I thought that was a beautiful way to put it."

I look at Gaby's who's pressing her fingers to her lips, obviously emotional. Tyson looks touched, too.

"So here you go," Alex says. "It's called Vows."

He reads it from memory, and for a moment I see a family resemblance in the way his voice becomes low and mesmerizing, not unlike Belle's when she's doing her magic.

"She writes her vows in her private journal,
The one inside her, the color of blood, heart-red,
Its skin-thin pages are crammed with words,
The secrets you tell her that only she has heard.
Scrawled on her bones, etched into her head,

Swimming in her blood, so intimate, so personal.

She's overflowing with all your words, bursting
at the seams, like an overstuffed cushion.
Soft murmurs, gentle phrases, snippets of speech
Slip through and float round her, brush against her cheeks;
Slices of kisses and sighs, slivers of passion;
They clutch at her hair like cobwebs, entangling.

Like flowers that soak up the rain and the sun,
Vowels and consonants line themselves in rows,
Reach up to the light, spread themselves, unfurl.
She picks them, strings them together like pearls
to lay around her neck, sew them on her clothes,
Let you unbutton them, leave her undone.

Wedding vows are a solemn, binding promise,
A token of time, inscribed on the heart,
A brand, a seal, unique as a snowflake,
An oath that only you and she could make,
To bind you both forever, never to part,
Signed and sealed with a loving kiss."

He finishes and gives a boyish smile to the guests, who instantly break out into a round of applause. Belle watches him return to his seat, then glances at me, widening her eyes and giving me a 'I never guessed he'd do that' kind of look.

After this, Tyson and Gaby stand again, and it's time for them to take their vows. They turn and hold hands, while they read out the vows they have written themselves. Gaby talks about how much she loves him, and how she's excited to spend the rest of her life with him. I've known her as long as I've known Alex and Belle, obviously, and I find it incredibly touching to hear her honest declaration of love.

When Tyson talks, though, there's not a dry eye in the house. Still standing, holding her hands, he tells her how touched he is that she's stood by him all these years. How he can't believe she's done that when he knows he's been hard to live with. He says he's been working hard to get his mobility back, and that he's going to continue with his physio because he wants to be a good dad to all the children he's convinced they're going to have. And now Gaby's crying for real, and the ceremony has to stop for her to compose herself.

"Jesus," I mumble to Henry, who's sitting next to me. "I'm going to be bawling like a baby if they don't get a move on."

He chuckles. "It must be moving if it's got to you."

His comment doesn't surprise me, because, like Alex, I've cultivated a reputation of being cynical and scornful of love and marriage. I've had my heart broken too many times to be anything but. And yet today, watching the ceremony, and maybe because of what's been happening with Belle, I feel my heart swell.

Jeez, I'm getting old.

Gaby and Tyson are exchanging rings now, and for the first time in maybe ever, I wonder how it must feel to slide that gold band onto a girl's finger, so every other man who looks at it knows that she's yours, she belongs to you.

It means forever, I tell myself. Monogamy. Tying yourself to one woman for the rest of your life! How ridiculous is that?

And yet, right now, as Susan tells Tyson and Gaby that they are man and wife, and he can kiss the bride, the only emotion I feel is envy.

Belle looks over her shoulder, right at me, and something hits me in the chest as if someone's shot an air rifle at me.

Ahhh, no… I padlocked my heart up so this wouldn't happen again. I'm not going to let another girl fuck me over, rip up my heart, and stomp all over it. This is why I gave up dating to concentrate on my work.

But her lips curve up, just a little, and even though I'm scowling inside, I can't stop mine doing the same.

The service over, it's time for the photos. We hand Tyson a pair of crutches, and with care, he progresses down the aisle with Gaby, and over to the area in front of the trees, which provide a glorious backdrop.

There's no time to catch up with Belle, because the photographer puts us through our paces, and when I'm not in the photo, I'm helping James and the ushers to shepherd people around.

Eventually, though, the photographer is happy, and then it's time to form a line all the way to the restaurant.

I feel a presence at my side, and look down to see Belle slotting herself between me and James.

"Hello," she says, passing me a packet of confetti.

"Hey." I take the packet. "Thank you."

"Gaby and I made it ourselves," she says. "Shapes punched out of leaves and rose petals. It smells wonderful." She lifts it to her nose and inhales.

"You smell wonderful," I tell her, catching the scent of her perfume. It's not her usual light, flowery scent, but something deeper and more sensual. Much more grown up. Much more womanly.

She bumps shoulders with me. "So do you. You always do. I love your cologne."

We stand side by side, waiting for Gaby and Tyson to approach. I feel ultra-aware of her, from the pale skin of her shoulder and neck, to the flash of thigh I keep seeing through the split in her skirt.

"Lovely ceremony, wasn't it?" she says after a moment. Her voice sounds a tad breathless—she's not unaffected by my nearness.

"Very touching," I agree.

"I think Gaby's relieved she wore waterproof mascara." She looks up at me then. "You obviously knew about Tyson's plan."

"Yeah. He's been working hard with the guys and MAX for months."

"James said you were the one who worked out the timings of how long he could stand for the ceremony."

"Yeah. He's doing great, but it's exhausting for him, and we wanted him to be able to make it through as much as he could. We worked with Pam to make sure we knew how long all the sections were going to take and fitted the other bits around those to give him a break. He really, really wanted to be standing for the photographs, so we did our best to make that happen."

"Thank you," she says, her big blue eyes filled with warmth. "It meant the world to Gaby."

"I didn't do anything," I say awkwardly. "Tyson did all the hard work."

"Damon, I know how hard you've worked with Alex and the others to get MAX and now THOR working. Alex said he practically has to drag you out of the office whenever you visit. So you can act as modest as you like—I know the real you."

She looks away, delving a hand into the confetti as Gaby and Tyson approach, but her words send a shiver down my back—*I know the real you.*

We toss the confetti over the bride and groom, and then as they head for the terrace, we follow them. It's all decorated with the pale-pink and white color scheme, accentuated with potted palms and floral displays. Belle leaves me with Alex and some of the others, says she's going to make sure that Gaby doesn't need anything, and slips off.

I watch her go, wondering when I'll next get to talk to her.

"Did you have a good time last night?" Juliette murmurs beside me as waiters serve the guests cocktails.

"What do you mean?" I ask.

"Alex said that Belle stayed with her mum last night. But Kaitlyn told me she had breakfast on her own this morning. So I'm guessing Belle stayed somewhere else…?"

"It's not what you think. She was upset and had a bit too much to drink. She slept it off in my room."

"In your bed?"

I just give her a wry look.

"Amazing how orgasms can take your mind off things," she says.

I laugh. "There were no orgasms involved. Tonight, however…" I grin.

She chuckles and holds up her cocktail glass. "To multiple orgasms."

"I'll toast to that." We clink glasses.

"What are you two laughing about?" Alex asks, joining us.

"Rugby," Juliette says, at the same time that I say, "The election," and we both laugh.

"Secrets, eh?" Alex says. "Would this be anything to do with Henry?"

"What?" Juliette turns scarlet. "No!"

Alex smirks.

"I'm here with Cam," she snaps. "So you can keep those kinds of comments to yourself." She walks off.

"Oops," I say.

Alex pulls an *eek* face. "Think I touched a sore spot."

"She's been with Cam a long time. Probably best not to tease her about Henry."

"Mmm." He studies his glass, then finishes the cocktail in one gulp.

"I liked the poem," I tell him.

"Took me all of five minutes."

"Yeah, right. I've watched you write poetry. You take two hours just to decide whether to rhyme 'moon' with 'June' or 'spoon.'"

That makes him laugh. "Yeah, okay."

"I'm kidding, dude. It was a damn fine piece of work." I sip my cocktail and take my life in my hands by adding mischievously, "Something tells me you're going to be writing more romantic poetry in the near future."

The rather gloriously named Mistletoe Macbeth came into Kia Kaha yesterday to talk to Alex and James about her son, Finn, taking part in the trial with THOR. She was gorgeous, with big dark eyes and dark hair pinned up in a bun. James introduced her to me and Henry on the way to Alex's office. She's been through a lot, and I wouldn't have blamed her if she'd been the most miserable woman in existence, but she had the sunniest personality, a beautiful smile, and a gracious way of talking that made me like her immediately.

"She's a glass half full kind of person," he comments.

"Well, let's lock her up, quick, before she spreads that bad behavior to other people."

He meets my eyes, and his lips curve up, just a little.

"She must be something if she can bring a smile to your face," I tease.

He just gives me a wry look, and I chuckle as he walks off.

Belle eventually appears again with Gaby, who's freshened up her makeup after all her tears, but I don't get a chance to talk to her again because she stays by her sister's side, circulating through some of the guests.

It's only when James calls for everyone to move into the restaurant for dinner that Belle appears at my side.

"I suppose you're sitting next to Freddie again," I say, a little grumpily.

But she chuckles and slips her arm through mine. "Don't worry. Gaby let me play with the place settings."

Surprised, I let her lead me into the restaurant.

The room is full of circular tables that seat eight. Sparkling silver cutlery tops pristine white tablecloths, and each spotless white plate bears a pink serviette with a piece of silver fern, topped with a card bearing a guest's name.

Similar to the rehearsal dinner, Gaby and Tyson are sitting with Mason, Sherry, Tyson's parents, and James and his date, Cassie. The two young bridesmaids are with Freddie and the other young ushers, and Freddie's disgruntled expression at being sat with the kids makes me laugh.

But Belle's name is next to mine, at a table with Alex, Kaitlyn, Henry, Juliette, Cam, and Aroha. Touched that she wants to sit with me, and pleased because it doesn't look odd as Aroha's there, too, I hold Belle's chair for her, and then take my place beside her.

The next couple of hours prove to be great fun. Alex and Henry are on good form, and jokes and stories flow, keeping everyone entertained. I wondered whether Kaitlyn's presence might be a problem for Belle, but they talk pleasantly enough, and I'm sure Kaitlyn's probably relieved she doesn't have to make polite conversation with Mason and Sherry.

And Belle... Belle is delightful, glowing with energy despite her troublesome night, obviously thrilled that the day has gone so well. I have trouble taking my eyes off her. She's so competent and organized—I never realized. She works with James, Freddie, and the ushers to get everyone seated, and runs a few errands for Gaby, fetching her wrap when she obviously feels the cold a little. When there's a slight delay while we wait for one of the courses to be delivered, she gathers the kids up and does magic tricks with coins and cards she seems to always keep in her purse until the food is ready.

The food is exquisite but hearty, as both Gaby and Tyson liked the idea of comfort foods for the cooler autumn weather—mini grilled-cheese sandwiches with shot-size cups of tomato soup, bacon-wrapped dates, and cranberry chicken salad to start; pork chops with figs and grapes, cider-braised chicken with apples and kale, or butternut squash ravioli for mains; and for dessert, spiced churros with hot chocolate, apple butter donuts with a maple glaze, spiced carrot cake, and berry tarts with pumpkin spiced lattes.

After the meal are the speeches, and then it's time for Gaby and Tyson to cut the cake.

"Seems a shame as it's such a work of art," Tyson begins to say, and then he stops and glances around, eyes widening.

It takes a second for me to realize what's happening. The room is shaking, accompanied by the rattle of cutlery on plates, the clink of glasses and bottles, the exclamations of guests, and the peculiar groan of the building itself as it's shaken to its very foundations. It's a fucking earthquake.

Chapter Nineteen

Belle

I've experienced many earthquakes in my time, in both Christchurch and Wellington, as they're both on fault lines. Usually they're just like a loud bang, and most of the time we roll our eyes and carry on with what we're doing. This one goes on and on, though, the whole building trembling, and my heart rate doubles. I wasn't in the city for the devastating earthquake that hit in 2011, but I watched with the rest of the country as the cameras revealed the extent of the damage and the numbers of the dead, so I know it's no laughing matter.

"Jesus," Alex says, "we should get everyone under the tables." Around us, other people are obviously having the same thought, diving beneath the tablecloths. I see Tyson pull Gaby down, and opposite us Henry grabs Juliette and pulls her off her chair.

Damon and I stand, and he grabs my hand. I'm not sure he even realizes he's doing it. I'm just about to duck down, but at that moment the building stops shaking, and the tremors die away.

We freeze, looking at each other with wide eyes.

"Is that it, do you think?" I say.

We wait in case it starts again, but the room stays still, and as one, everyone exhales with relief. There's nervous laughter as people start getting to their feet, checking that everyone else is okay.

Alex is already Googling on his phone, and he says, "It was a 5.9, and only fifteen kilometers down, that's why it felt so strong."

"Holy shit." I look up at Damon.

He cups my face. "Are you okay?"

I nod, although I'm shaking a little. "That was so powerful."

He pulls me into his arms and wraps them around me. Alex looks at us, but to my surprise he just gives a small smile before turning away.

"Hey Gaby," he calls out. "Looks like Tyson's making the earth move for you and you haven't even got to the wedding night yet."

That breaks the tension, and everyone starts laughing. James beckons to the members of hotel staff who've come in to make sure we're all okay, and he instructs the waiters to top up everyone's glasses with champagne. When they've made the rounds, and everyone is starting to take their seats again, he calls for quiet.

"Reports are coming in from across the city," he says, "and it looks as if damage was minimal. I think we got away with it this time."

Everyone exchanges glances and blows out a breath.

"It's a sign that we should appreciate the loved ones in our lives," James says. "Please, turn to the person nearest to you and show them how you really feel. Don't hold back now."

I glance around. Tyson gives Gaby a long kiss. On our table, Alex looks at Mum, then pulls her into his arms for a big hug. Cam finds himself standing next to Aroha, and she obviously cracks a joke because he laughs and kisses her on the cheek. Henry and Juliette stare at each other, and then, without saying anything, he slides a hand to the nape of her neck and holds her there as he kisses her. When he releases her, she's turned scarlet, and she walks away without another word.

I look up at Damon. "Maybe a hug?" I whisper, knowing he won't want to kiss me in front of Alex.

To my surprise, though, he takes my face in his hands and bends his head to touch his lips to mine for the sweetest kiss I think I've ever had. When he eventually lifts his head, he looks into my eyes, then gives me a big hug.

"When the earthquake hit," he murmurs, "all I could think was that I wasn't going to get to take you to bed, and I felt devastated. Is that crazy?"

"No. I felt the same."

"Belle…" He moves back and hesitates.

I put a finger to his lips. I know what he's thinking. During the ceremony, when Gaby and Tyson were exchanging their vows, I looked across at him and saw the look of puzzlement and something approaching envy on his face. He glanced at me then, and something passed between us, so sharp it almost hurt—a recognition of the desire we feel for one another. The answering resentment that flickered across his expression didn't escape me. He doesn't want to have feelings for me. He doesn't want to get hurt again. I get that, and I'm not going to try to trap him into a relationship, like his ex apparently did.

Equally, I'm going to fight for him, because at the moment I want him more than I even want air to breathe.

"You don't have to say anything," I whisper. "We'll let our bodies do all the talking."

He meets my eyes and nods. We break apart then, and I go over to Gaby to check she's okay. But I feel as if, no matter how far apart I am from Damon, we remain connected by an invisible ribbon. I can feel him from across the room, and every time I glance at him and see him looking at me, a frisson passes through me, like someone walking across my grave, at the thought of what's going to happen later that night.

Soon it's time to go through to the ballroom. The guests all gasp as we enter. It's not a huge room, but Pam has bedecked it with fairy lights and more pink and white balloons, and it looks like a beautiful grotto, like something out of *A Midsummer Night's Dream*. The band begins playing *You To Me Are Everything* by The Real Thing, Gaby and Tyson's song, and once again the tears flow as he rises from his wheelchair, determined to dance this first song with her. Everyone cheers and claps as they turn in the center of the floor beneath the spotlights. Gaby's so ridiculously happy. Tyson has kept his new mobility very quiet, and although I know her well enough to guess she wished he'd told her earlier, she's also very touched that he wanted to make their wedding super-special.

People gradually start taking to the floor. Dad dances with Tyson's mum, and Tyson's dad leads Sherry onto the floor. I feel a lump form in my throat as Damon immediately goes over to my mum and offers her his hand. As much as I'd love to dance with him, it's such a wonderful thing to do for her so she doesn't feel left out that I adore him for it.

I get to dance with the inimitable Freddie, who steps on my toes at least twice, and has no sense of rhythm at all. But I don't care—the fairy lights cast us all in their magical glow, and after the danger of the earthquake, everyone seems in high spirits, determined to enjoy themselves.

When the song finishes, the band strikes up Aerosmith's *I Don't Want To Miss A Thing*, and even though Freddie is determined not to release his grip on my waist, he looks up as Damon walks up and huffs a sigh, moving back.

Damon smiles at him, then pulls me into his arms.

"Good evening," he says.

"Evening." I loop my arms around his neck, while he slides his arms around my waist. At some point, he ditched his jacket, and he looks gorgeous in his white shirt and navy waistcoat. The front is the same material as his suit, while the back is a light-blue satin. Mmm, it's wonderful to be so close to him. He smells amazing. I brush the short hair at the nape of his neck with my thumb, just enjoying touching him.

"How are your toes?" he asks. "Still in one piece?"

"Don't be mean," I scold. "He's very sweet."

"I don't like him touching you."

I look up into his eyes, and my heart races at the heat in them. "I know."

"You might dance with other people this evening, but you're mine tonight. Remember that."

I press my lips together and nod.

He bends his head and whispers into my ear, "I'm going to make you come so many times, you're going to forget your own name."

I shiver. "Damon…"

"I can't wait to taste you, Belle."

"Oh God." I feel a little faint.

We don't talk again, but, like I promised earlier, our bodies continue to communicate. I can feel him with every cell in my body. Up close, I notice all the little things: the curve of his Adam's apple, and the hollow at the base of his throat, almost hidden by the Windsor knot of his tie. The smoothness of his jaw, not yet darkened by stubble. His neat sideburns, and the curve of his ear that I long to trace with my tongue. The slight sweep of his lips. I want to kiss him. And I want him to kiss me, all over. I can't wait to go to bed with him. I'm so excited at the thought that I can barely breathe.

But first we have the evening to get through, and now we both know where we're heading, all my anxiety and stress disappears. The music changes to Fleetwood Mac's *Dreams*, and Damon's eyes sparkle.

"You can dance, right?" he says. "I know you used to go to all sorts of classes when you were a kid."

"Yeah…" I give him a doubtful look. "Don't tell me that you dance…" It's so rare for guys of his age to take to the dance floor. Normally they hover around the bar until a slow song comes along.

"Mum and Dad were champions," he says. "They taught all three of us." He takes my right hand in his left. "Come on, ma belle. Show us what you got!"

He spins me around, and I laugh and start dancing with him for real. Wow, the dude can move, and he knows how to lead, guiding me where he wants me with a touch of his hand, turning me and spinning me away before pulling me back into his arms.

Throughout the evening, I dance with loads of other guys, including James and Henry, who I've known as long as Damon, as well as Freddie, again, the other young ushers, and several others who don't mind taking to the floor. Damon dances with Juliette, Aroha, Mum again, Sherry, and then takes the time to ask any women who are sitting on their own to dance, which is so sweet I fall for him all over again. But he doesn't dance with them the way he dances with me.

I like that.

We dance together every few songs, and whenever I see him approaching, my pulse picks up, and I get to my feet hurriedly, eager to join him.

It's much later when my father finally comes up and holds out his hand. I take it and let him lead me onto the dance floor, tensing up inside. I've managed to avoid him most of the day, but this was always going to happen at some point.

"Enjoying yourself?" he asks, as we turn slowly to the music.

"It's been a great day," I reply. "Apart from the earthquake."

"Yeah, that could have gone a lot worse." He steers me out of the way of another couple, then says, "You've danced with Damon a lot tonight."

"He's light on his feet. It's nice to dance with a guy who isn't self-conscious on the floor."

"True." He smiles. He's trimmed his beard neatly, and he had his hair cut yesterday. He's a good-looking guy for his age.

"I know about you and Sherry," I blurt out.

His eyebrows rise. "What do you mean?"

"I know that you had an affair first. Before Mum did."

We stop dancing, and he stares at me. I wait for him to deny it, and to tell me that Mum's a liar.

But he doesn't. "That's true," he says.

My face flushes. "You should have told me. All these years, I've blamed Mum for breaking up your marriage."

He lowers his hands, gestures with his head, and I follow him off the floor, to one side. He slides his hands into his pockets, and studies the floor. Light beams from the stage sweep across us in rainbow colors. There's glitter in the air from the balloons held in a net above the floor that will be released later on. The music is loud, but we're near the back, and I can just hear him when he speaks.

"I've made a lot of mistakes in my life," he says. "Not being there for your mother when she needed me is one of the biggest ones. Living with someone who has depression is hard, Belle. It's a selfish condition, and it overwhelms everyone and everything around it. It's like living close to a black hole, and it's impossible not to get sucked in."

I'm breathing fast, shocked by the words it's taken him years to say.

"Your mum's career was taking off," he says. "She was hardly ever home, and when she was, she was exhausted. She had no time for me, and I was lonely and resentful. Was I the perfect husband? No, of course not. But I'm only human. Sherry and I fought our attraction, but she was there, and so loving, so easy, and your mum was so difficult, Belle. So difficult. I hated her back then, and I hate her now because she made me turn to someone else for affection. And that led to her going with that man, and he hurt my little girl, and I'll never, ever forgive her for that. I know it's ridiculous and unfair, but it's how I feel, and how I suspect I'll always feel. Does that make sense?"

I think about what Damon said: *Sometimes I'm sure vengeance plays a part. But mostly I think it's about solace.* Relationships can be tough, and when things are hard, people look elsewhere for comfort. And then I think about Alex's wise words: *Everyone's doing their best. Some people are just better at it than others.*

"I know she was difficult," I say. "She still is. And I know things weren't good between you at the time. But she was ill and struggling, and you hurt her, Dad. So, just like you did, she looked elsewhere for comfort, and she fell in love, and then the guy she chose let her down in the worst possible way. You could never hate her as much as she hates herself. So just think about that the next time you talk to her."

His brow creases. "Ah, Belle…"

"All this blame and guilt," I say, tears pricking my eyes. "If I can put it behind me, why can't you two?"

"Baby…" He moves up close and puts his arms around me.

I rest my cheek on his shoulder, squeezing my eyes shut, trying not to cry. I've had such a lovely day. I shouldn't have mentioned it to him, but it just came out.

I open my eyes, and even though he's on the other side of the dance floor, I see Damon immediately. He's standing on his own, a whisky glass in his hand, the other hand in his pocket, watching me. He doesn't smile—he's obviously guessed that I'm upset.

I move back from my father and look up at him. "Promise me you'll try," I say.

"I promise."

The song has ended, and now the band is playing *I Feel it Coming* by The Weeknd. I love this song, and I kiss Dad's cheek, then walk across the dance floor. Damon sees me coming and turns to place his glass on the nearest table.

Freddie steps in my way and says, "Wanna dance, Belle?"

I shake my head though and say, "Sorry, I'm taken," and I step around him and continue on to Damon.

He smiles as I approach and holds out his hand. I slide mine into his, feeling as if I'm coming home, and let him lead me onto the dance floor. Without talking, we start dancing, and my heart lifts as he turns me around, the two of us moving together effortlessly.

When the song changes, this time to Marvin Gaye's *Sexual Healing*, Damon doesn't release me. Instead, he pulls me close to him and slides his arms around my waist. I loop mine around his neck and look up into his eyes.

Thirty seconds later, someone releases the net above our heads, and pink and silver balloons float down onto the dancers, along with fluttering hearts and sparkling glitter. We both laugh, turning to the music, and then I look up again into his beautiful brown eyes, and suddenly I want him more than anything in the world.

I lower my arms and take his hand in mine. "Come on," I say. "Let's go upstairs."

His eyebrows rise. "You don't want to stay to the end?"

I shake my head. "Not as much as I want you."

His lips curve up. "Come on then," he says softly.

"I'll just get my purse." I go over to the table where I left it and pick it up. Gaby's sitting there taking a rare break from dancing, sipping a glass of champagne.

"You okay?" she says.

I nod. "I'm shooting off, hope you don't mind."

She glances at where Damon's waiting for me and grins. "The six-step plan worked?"

"Most definitely."

"Wonderful. Go have amazing sex."

"Thanks sis. You too."

She smiles. "Thank you for everything, Belle. It's been a wonderful day."

"It has, hasn't it?" I give her a big hug. "I love you."

"I love you, too."

"I'll see you when you get back from your honeymoon." I know I'm going to have to talk to her about Mum and Dad, but I push that to the back of my mind. "I hope you have an amazing time."

"Thanks, sweetie. See you soon."

Leaving her with a wave, I walk across to Damon, and we quietly slip out of the room.

We walk across the lobby to the elevators, and he presses the button to call the car. After a few seconds the doors open, we go inside, he taps his key card to the panel, and presses the button for his floor.

From a few feet away, I study him with a racing heart. He's wearing his jacket now, standing with his hands in the pockets of his trousers, casually sexy. He looks young, wealthy, and incredibly handsome. He's also looking at me as if he ordered me for dinner, and I've just arrived on his plate.

"How are you feeling?" he asks, gesturing at my tummy. "Are you better now?"

I realize he's referring to my period. "Yeah, it's practically over, so you don't have to worry."

"I wasn't worried. I told you, it doesn't bother me."

Oh. I forgot how earthy this guy was.

"Your eyes couldn't get any bigger," he says, looking a mixture of amused and concerned. "Are you sure you want to do this?"

I try to act sassy, meeting his eyes and moistening my lips with the tip of my tongue. "Yeah. I'm looking forward to screwing your brains out."

If I'd thought to surprise him, I'm to be disappointed. Instead, he looks interested. "How?" he asks.

"Ah… dunno. Hadn't thought that far ahead."

He chuckles, closing the distance between us. "You want to go to bed with me?" he murmurs. He lowers his lips until they're just above mine. "Do you wanna get naked with me, Belle?"

"I do," I whisper. "Oh God, so much."

He smirks, takes my face in his hands, and crushes his lips to mine.

I thought I was closer to the wall than I am, and as he presses himself against me, I stumble back and meet it with a jolt that makes me gasp. It doesn't stop him, though; he just takes advantage of my open mouth to plunge his tongue inside. I inhale deeply as my thermostat rises from zero to approximately a billion degrees in seconds.

Oh wow… the man kisses like a god. Or a demon. I'm not sure which. The devil emoji pops into my head, and I moan against his lips as he claims mine with such passion that I'm convinced he'll set me alight. It's going to turn us both to ashes, and when the doors open, they'll wonder what happened to the cute young couple who the receptionist saw going into the elevator on the ground floor.

I lift my arms around his neck, filled with joy, wanting nothing more from him at that moment than the pleasure of lovemaking—to share my body with him, and to enjoy his in return.

My brother once told me cynically that dreams never come true. Oh Alex, you silly, silly boy. You've got such a lot to learn.

Chapter Twenty

Damon

When the elevator pings and the doors open, I walk her backwards, still kissing her, out of the car and along the corridor.

"You can stop for a second," she says, laughing, as I continue to press kisses over her lips and face.

"Don't want to." I kiss around to her ear. "Ahhh… Belle… you smell so good." The sultry scent she's wearing tonight is driving me insane. Her perfume and her elegant dress lend her an exotic womanliness I find extremely attractive. In a few minutes we're going to ditch our clothes and be skin to skin. The thought makes my pulse pound.

I maneuver her to the door, touch my card to the panel, and then open it. Steering her in, I let the door swing closed behind us, still kissing her. Unfortunately I've forgotten about the small table in the entranceway, and we bump into it, sending half a dozen hotel fliers scattering to the floor.

"Oops." I don't stop to pick them up. Instead, I continue to walk her backward to the bed.

I flick open the buttons of my jacket. Belle pushes it off my shoulders, and I catch it in my hands, then toss it over a nearby chair. Her hands are immediately loosening my tie, and then that joins the jacket on the chair.

Jesus, I can't jump her the second she's in the door. "You want a drink first?" I ask, my voice husky with desire.

"Nuh-uh." She strokes her hands over my waistcoat. "I love this. You look so handsome in it, Damon. You wear a suit exceptionally well."

"Thank you." I can't help but be flattered by her compliment.

"I've watched you all evening," she says, undoing the waistcoat buttons. "Dancing and talking with other women. And I just kept thinking tonight he's mine. You have no idea how good that made me feel."

I find myself speechless as she opens the waistcoat and pushes that over my shoulders too. I'm the one who's supposed to have the praise kink, who enjoys making girls feel good. But her words, and the way she's looking at me as she begins to undo my shirt buttons, fills me with a glow I hadn't expected.

Incredibly happy, I slide my arms around her, turn my back to the bed, and fall onto the mattress with her on top of me. She laughs and props herself up on her hands to look down at me.

"You could have any woman at the wedding," she says. "Except for Gaby, probably. Why on earth have you chosen me?"

"You're kidding me?" I brush my hands down her back, confirming that she's not wearing a bra. "You were the most beautiful girl there by far."

"Aw. You're just saying that."

I frown at her. "I told you, I never lie. I've been watching you all evening, too. Talking to everyone. Helping Gaby. Dancing with all the guys, young and old, and none of them could keep their eyes off you. I was ready to go nuclear on any of them that touched you."

"You missed Freddie grabbing my arse, then?"

"Fuck, you're kidding me? That little shit."

She giggles. "I thought you were going to stride across the floor and smash his teeth down his throat."

"I would have, if I'd seen him. Fucking twat. Are you okay?"

She laughs. "I'm fine. I told him to stop wandering and moved his hand up to my waist. He didn't do it again."

I stroke my hands down her back again, following the sensual curve of her waist and the swell of her bottom, then tighten my fingers on the soft muscles there. I'm allowed to do it. Nobody else.

"Damon Chevalier is squeezing my butt," she says. "I still can't believe it."

I chuckle. "I don't know why it's so surprising. You have a fantastic butt."

"Yeah, but I've watched you from afar for years. You're like a movie star to me, Damon."

I smile. "You say the nicest things." Lifting a hand, I let the long curl that hangs over her shoulder slip through my fingers. "Would you let your hair down?"

Her eyebrows rise and she flushes, then says, "Sure." She pushes up to a sitting position and lifts her hands to take out the pins holding it up. I watch the way the dress clings to her breasts, enjoying the way they move as she raises her arms.

"You like my boobs?" she asks, leaning over to put the pins on the bedside table.

"Very much." I watch as her hair tumbles around her shoulders.

"It's a bit fluffy," she says, trying to smooth it down.

"Don't worry about it. I intend to muss it up real bad."

She gives an impish smile. "Naughty boy." She begins to undo the buttons of my shirt. "You're wearing too many clothes. I want to see you." When she reaches the bottom, she pushes the sides open to reveal my torso. "Oh…" Her eyes widen. She places both hands on my chest, then strokes them apart, across my ribs, her fingers brushing my nipples. I shiver at her gentle touch.

"Let's get the shirt off," she directs.

I sit up and say, "Wait," but she's already tugging it over my shoulders and down my back.

"I'm wearing cufflinks." I can't get the sleeves over my hands. I go to undo them, but she leans all her weight on me, pushing me back onto the mattress. Now I'm pinned there, unable to move my arms because I'm lying on the shirt.

"Oh…" she whispers, "now I have you at my mercy." She moves her hips, keeping her eyes on mine as obviously feels my growing erection. "You like that idea? Mmm." She taps her finger on her chin, pretending to ponder, lifts her right hand, and shows me her empty palm. Then she does one of her little magical flourishes and produces a condom in her fingers.

I laugh. "Neat trick."

"I think I'm going to ride you for a while," she murmurs, looking down into my eyes, "and then I might go down on you and suck you dry." Her eyes glitter in the low light. "What do you think?"

I absolutely adore this girl. "I think it's time you let me lead." I lift up and wrap one arm around her waist as I get to my feet, easily lifting her off the bed.

She squeals as she puts her feet to the floor and nearly falls over. "How did you do that?"

"Skill." I pop the cufflinks through the holes in my cuffs, toss them onto the bedside table, then get rid of the shirt. I divest myself of my trousers and socks, then, clad in only my black boxer-briefs, I take her by the shoulders and turn her away from me. "You asked me if I wanted to see you naked. The answer is yes, ma belle." I take the tab of the zipper in my fingers and, carefully so I don't damage the fabric of her dress, slide it all the way down to reveal her bare back. She catches it at her breasts, holding it to her.

Groaning at the sight of all that bare flesh, I scoop her hair over one shoulder, then place a finger at her nape and draw it down her spine, and she shivers.

I move close behind her and bend my head so I can nuzzle her ear. "You're so gorgeous," I murmur, sliding my arms under hers and wrapping them around her waist. My chest presses against the bare skin of her back. She sighs and leans against me, turning her head to look up at me, and I kiss her, slowly, taking my time. Now I have her here, I don't want to rush it.

Eventually, though, I can't resist any longer, and I slide my hands up her ribs and cup her breasts through the silky fabric. I sigh against her lips. "You have the most amazing breasts," I tell her. "They're so soft and high." I tease her nipples with my thumbs. "I've driven myself insane trying to imagine what color these are. Pink? Light brown? Darker? Will you let me see?"

She sucks her bottom lip, then gives a small nod and releases the bodice of her gown. It falls to the floor, leaving her standing there wearing only the tiniest pair of lace cream panties.

I cup her breasts, weighing them in my palms. Her nipples are a dusky pink, the tip a shade darker. Aaahhh… I want to touch them, suck them, and find out what pressure she likes, but I'm determined to take this slowly. I have a feeling her ex was rough with her, and I think she'll respond well to a gentler hand.

"You're so incredibly beautiful," I murmur, tracing my forefingers around the areolas before lightly teasing the tips. She moans, tips back her head, and arches her spine, pushing her breasts into my hands, so I increase the pressure a little, tugging lightly.

She sucks her bottom lip, holding her breath, then turns in my arms, throws hers around my neck, and crushes her lips to mine.

With a growl, I lift her, then climb onto the bed, lowering her onto her back, and lie on top of her. She wraps her legs around me, linking her ankles. I don't want to squash her, and support myself on my elbows, but she seems to like my weight.

"You're so big," she whispers, stroking up my chest and over my shoulders.

"You say all the right things."

"That, too." She rocks her hips against mine as a joke, then closes her eyes for a moment as her mound presses against the root of my erection. "Mmm."

"*Je te trouve belle.*" I kiss her.

"What does that mean?" she whispers.

"I think you're beautiful."

"You actually speak French?"

"A little."

"Say something else."

I start kissing her face—across her forehead, down her nose, and over her cheeks. "*Je pense à toi tout le temps.*" I kiss her lips. "I think of you all the time."

"Aw."

"*Je suis fou de toi.*" I brush my tongue over her lips. "I'm crazy about you."

"Mmm. Damon…"

"You just have to be careful with the word 'baiser'," I tell her. "The noun *un baiser* is a kiss. The verb means to fuck."

She giggles. "Which one do you mean?"

"*Je voudrais te baiser les lèvres.* I would like to kiss you on the lips. But also *je voudrais te baiser. Beaucoup.*"

"You're a naughty boy."

"I aim to please."

She laughs, but it turns into a sigh as I kiss her again, delving my tongue into her mouth. At the same time, I rock my hips, gently moving against her, and when she meets each movement with a small thrust of her own, I know I'm hitting the right spot.

"Mmm," she murmurs, closing her eyes. After a few minutes, she says, "Mmm, that feels… good…" A couple of minutes later, her breathing begins to deepen, and I lift my head to look at her, although I don't stop moving.

Her skin flushes, and her lips part as she focuses on the sensations I know are rising inside her like a wave.

"Damon…" she murmurs.

"I know, baby. Just go with it."

Her eyes open, and she looks at me hazily. "Now?"

"It's just a warm up. Relax and enjoy it."

She blinks a couple of times, her eyes widening, but I don't stop my gentle thrusts, and in the end she closes her eyes again and gives a beautiful frown, her lips parting once more as she breathes with deep gasps.

"Yeah, baby girl," I say, watching as her orgasm hits, and feeling her body jerk with each pulse. I feel an intense sense of satisfaction at the knowledge of how much pleasure she's feeling right now. God, I love making her come.

"Oh…" She finally stops, her chest heaving with deep breaths as she tries to draw air back into her lungs. I kiss her, delving my tongue into her mouth, and she sighs and loops her arms around my neck as she returns it.

When I lift my head, her eyes are filled with dreamy happiness. "Mmm, that was heavenly."

"Just the first of many, baby." I lift off her, then start kissing down her neck. "Now it's time for me to taste you."

"Oh! Oh my God, Damon."

I kiss between her breasts, then across to her left nipple. "What?" I ask before I trace my tongue around the edge.

"Ooh. Um… maybe I should… um… have a shower first?"

"That would kind of defeat the object."

"What do you mean?"

"I want to taste you, baby. All that sweet nectar. Kind of a waste if you wash it all away."

"Jeez, you're disgusting."

"And you love me for it, remember?"

She sinks her hand into my hair as I cover her nipple with my mouth and suck gently. "Mmm. What do you mean?"

I chuckle, kiss back up to her mouth, and then look at her. "You told me you loved me last night."

Her eyes widen. "Did I? Shit. I'm sorry."

"Don't worry about it. I said I loved you, too."

She blinks a few times. "As a friend."

"Yeah. Totally."

Her lips curve up. I press mine to them, then kiss back down to her breasts.

I pay both nipples some attention for a while, swapping from one to the other, until her breathing deepens and she's squirming beneath me. And then finally I kiss down her ribs, dip my tongue into her belly button, and continue over her tummy.

Moving between her legs, I tuck my fingers in the elastic of her underwear, pull them down over her feet, and drop them on the floor. Then I lower down between her legs and push up her knees.

"Oh my God," she says, and covers her face with her hands.

"Try to relax." I rest my hand on her mound and slide my thumb down into the heart of her. Oh, man, her folds are swollen and glistening, the button of her clit just begging to be kissed. I press my thumb down, collecting her moisture, then lift it to my mouth and suck it. "Fuck, you taste fantastic." Hungry for more, I slide my tongue inside her.

With a loud squeal, she nearly leaps straight off the bed.

"Whoa." I catch her. "You okay?"

"Oh my God!" She collapses back. "Damon!"

"I thought I was being gentle, I'm sorry."

"You were gentle, it's just... it's the first time for me, remember?"

"Aw." I stroke her thigh.

"It was so sensitive. Wow." She covers her face again. "My head nearly exploded."

"I'll go more slowly this time, all right? I'm just going to kiss you for a bit. No tongues."

"Okay."

Trying not to laugh, I kiss the soft skin of her inner thighs, gradually brushing my lips inward. She sighs, and I kiss down, until I've covered the whole of her mound and outer folds. Then I place my hands on either side and gently part her. Aaahhh... all that soft pink flesh...

"Get ready," I warn her. "I'm going to kiss down the middle, okay?"

She just huffs a sigh in response.

Chuckling, I kiss right at the top, then carefully press my lips down.

"Now I'm going to use my tongue," I tell her. "On the sides first, and then I'll move inward."

"Okay."

I kiss her inner thighs again, this time alternating each press of my lips with a brush of my tongue, and gradually move toward the middle. This time, when I kiss her inner folds, she just emits a long sigh. It turns into a moan as I slide my tongue into them.

"You taste divine," I murmur, parting her further so I can slowly slide my tongue down toward her entrance. I feel her hand in my hair, and then as I slip my tongue inside her, she tightens her fingers.

"Oh my God," she whispers.

"I haven't done the best bit yet." I kiss back up her core to the little button nestled in its hood at the top. It's already swollen, but I'm going to make it throb for her. "I'm about to kiss your clit, okay?"

"Oh jeez."

I press either side of it to expose it, then kiss it.

"Ahhh…"

I touch the tip of my tongue to it, then slowly lick it.

"Holy fuck, Damon…"

"Not nice?"

"I don't ever want you to stop doing that."

I grin and do it again.

She groans. "Oh my God, it feels so…"

I cover her clit with my mouth.

"Ah jeez," she says, "your tongue is like magic…"

I swirl my tongue over it, then gently suck.

"Oh fuck, Damon, I'm going to…" She clutches my hair and comes on my tongue, crying out, half laughing, and by the end, I can't help but laugh, either.

I lift up so I can look down at her. "You all right?"

"Holy fucking shit."

"Is that a yes?"

"I'm so sorry. How long did that take me? About twenty seconds?"

"Something like that."

"Christ." She covers her face with her hands.

I chuckle, lift her hand, and bend and kiss her.

She groans. "I can smell myself."

"You taste great, too." I slip my fingers into her, then bring them up and slide them into her mouth.

"Oh my God!" She slaps my hand away, but I just replace it with my lips, crushing them to hers. She moans and wraps her arms around my neck, and we kiss for ages, legs and arms tangled.

When I eventually lift my head, she sighs. "I'm so disappointed I was so quick."

I kiss her. "It was just an hors d'oeuvre, baby. Now we have the main course." I lift up and move back down between her legs.

"What? Again?"

"Oh yeah. And this time, I expect you to hang on a little longer."

"Oh but I…" She moans as I sink my tongue into her folds and falls back on the pillows. "You're trying to kill me, aren't you?"

I rub her thigh, too engulfed in kissing her to reply.

This time, I add my fingers to the mix, sliding them inside her and curving them up a little to massage her G-spot, while at the same time I lick and suck and arouse her clit with my tongue. This time, it takes all of five minutes before her breaths begin to come in deep gasps, and her thighs loosen, falling to the side as she tilts her hips up to meet me.

"Oh jeez," she whispers, sinking her hand into my hair again. "Oh that feels so… oh wow…"

"You taste so good," I tell her, replacing my tongue with my thumb, circling it over her now-swollen clit. "And you look so beautiful down here, baby. All swollen and glistening."

"Oh…"

"I just love making you come with my tongue. And this time, I want you to come with my fingers inside you, okay?"

She just moans as I press up on her G-spot.

I cover her clit with my mouth and suck. She jerks, clenches my hair, and moans again. I lift my head. "Harder, baby?"

"Ahhh… mmm… yeah…"

So I do it again, this time sucking a tiny bit harder.

"Day… mon… Ohhh…"

She clenches around my fingers, her thighs and stomach tightening, and then I feel her clit pulse in my mouth, again and again, four, five, six… oh, baby girl… seven, eight, nine… Finally spent, she collapses back, groaning so loudly I know next door will be able to hear her, if they're there.

Hoping they can, somewhat smug, I kiss up her body and lie next to her. Her face and neck are pink, her skin is glistening slightly, and when she opens her eyes, they're hazy and a tad unfocused.

"I told you," I say, leaning over to retrieve the condom she left there earlier, "I'm going to make you come so many times tonight that you're going to forget your own name."

She watches, looking a tad bewildered, as I slide my boxer-briefs off, then roll the condom on. "I thought it was a turn of phrase."

"Nope." I lie on my back and pull her on top of me. "Climb on, baby girl. Now you're going to ride me, and I'm going to watch you make yourself come. Go on. Make my day."

BEAUTY AND THE BILLIONAIRE BOSS

Chapter Twenty-One

Belle

Holy shit. This man. I can't even. My body is so hot I think he's actually turned my blood to lava. Only a few days ago, I'd never had an orgasm in my life, and I've just had three in the space of about fifteen minutes.

And apparently there's more to come, so to speak.

I'm not sure I can do what he's instructing, though. It was one thing to touch myself when I was on the phone with him, but to do it while he's watching? God, he's so kinky.

Is it kinky, though? He acts like it's normal. And maybe it is. How would I know?

I'm sitting astride him now, just below his erection, which—oh my God—is like an iron pole, so much longer and thicker than Cole's.

"You're huge," I tell him, eyes wide.

He gives a short laugh. "Well, thanks, but I'm really not. You'll be fine. You're very wet." He smirks, and I blush. "Aw." He cups my face and brings me down for a kiss. "You do it," he murmurs in a gentler tone, "as slow as you like."

Holding my breath, I guide the tip of his erection beneath me until it just enters me, then brace my hands on his chest as I push down.

Oooh... I close my eyes. He's lying—he is big. I only make an inch before I have to stop.

"Slowly, baby girl," he says. "You're nervous, that's all, and you're tense. Just relax. There's no rush."

I exhale slowly, doing my best to release the tension in my body, and push down a little more. Mmm. I lift up and try again. And again, each time sinking down a little more, impaling myself on him as I coat him with my moisture.

"Fuck," I say, groaning. "You're not going to fit." Oh jeez, I'm totally screwing this up. I look like such a noob.

But he just laughs and pulls me so I fall forward onto his chest. "Come here." He kisses me, delving his tongue into my mouth, and I sigh as he cups my breasts and tugs gently on my nipples. Mmm... that feels nice... He does that for a while, and then eventually slides his hands down my ribs and over my waist to my hips, holding me steady as he pushes up. This time, he slides right inside, filling me to the brim.

I open my eyes and look into his eyes. "Balls deep," he says, blinking in slow motion. "Jesus, that feels good."

It's the first time I've given him pleasure, and the thought thrills me. I love that he's so giving, but I want to drive him to the edge and watch him come, too.

And then I realize—the best way to do that is to show him how much I'm enjoying this. His pleasure is directly related to mine. I push myself up to a sitting position, tipping my head back as I adjust to the feeling of him being so deep inside me.

"Ahhh, yeah," he says, cupping my breasts. "You look fucking amazing."

I look down at him. "You want to watch me come again, handsome?"

His lips curve up. "Definitely."

Wow, am I really going to do this? Gathering my courage, I slide my hand down my body to between my legs. His eyes flare and he lowers his hands to my thighs so he can get a better view—oh, this really turns him on.

I close my eyes and sink my fingers into my folds.

It's the first time I've done this properly. He guided my hand there in the car, but I didn't do more than feel how wet and swollen I was. And when I was on my own, I used the bullet rather than touch myself.

It's crazy how much a simple sentence when you're young can rule the whole of your life. Girls shouldn't think about sex. The memory makes me feel a surge of anger and resentment. I don't believe that. Damon's so open, and his earthy attitude to sex makes me feel as if nothing that two consenting adults do in the privacy of their own room is wrong. It's natural, and it's beautiful, and I'm done with feeling as if it's somehow wrong.

I'm all swollen again, my folds coated with my slippery moisture. Wow, that's sexy. I know he's watching me, and my face flushes, but

I'm not going to stop. I lower my hand, sliding my fingers either side of his erection. Mmm, that's surprisingly erotic, feeling him inside me. Oh yeah, I like that.

Bringing my fingers back up, I explore myself for the first time, finding out where everything is, how it all fits. My clit feels bigger than before—I guess that's all the orgasms he's given me—and super sensitive. I brush it lightly, circling the pad of my finger over it. Ooh, that's nice. When I touch the tip of my tongue to my lips, it only adds to the feeling. Now I understand why erogenous zones work—every part of my body is connected.

Damon takes my left hand and lifts it to my breast.

I open my eyes. "You want me to do all the work?"

He stretches his arms above his head, giving me a sexy, lazy smile. "I want you to show me how you like to be touched."

"It turns you on to watch me?"

"Oh yeah." His gaze is setting me alight.

Shyly, I tug my left nipple while I circle my finger over my clit. I can't believe I'm doing this, but Damon's hot gaze encourages me. I rock my hips while I arouse myself, thinking how gorgeous he is, unable to believe I'm actually here, doing this with him. After a while, he lowers his hands to my thighs, lightly stroking them, and then he brushes his fingers up my sides and around to my back. Everywhere he touches me, I tingle.

Lowering down, I kiss him, still touching myself, and he plunges his tongue in my mouth and slips his hand into my hair to hold me there so he can deepen the kiss. Ooh, I'm firing him up. Excited, I rock harder, and when he releases me, I sit up and circle my finger faster over my clit. Mmm… I'm not far away. I'm beginning to recognize the signs, the way my focus turns inward, how my breaths come in uneven gasps, the tightening of my muscles in my tummy and thighs. It feels like a stone dropped into a lake but in reverse, the ripples beginning wide, then zooming into the center as the orgasm hits.

"Oh God," I say, without thinking, starting to lose the plot, "oh fuck…"

But before I get there, without warning, Damon holds me tightly around the waist and somehow lifts up and flips me onto my back.

I squeal in surprise, and he laughs, taking my hands in his and pinning them above my head. "Time to take the lead," he says, and starts thrusting.

Oh shit... He's been so gentle, letting me go at my own pace, that I hadn't thought about what he'd be like when he took over. Somewhat surprised that he didn't let me finish, I can't move, I can only lie there and watch him, so I give in, wrap my legs around his waist, and let him go for it.

It's only as he moves, though, that I realize he's grinding against me with each thrust. Ooh, he's hitting the spot, oh yeah, right there... Oh my God, I think I'm going to come with him inside me. I remember asking him if that was possible, and he said, *Sure, if you're in the right position.* This must be what he meant. I look up at him, mouth open, eyes wide, in shock, as pleasure builds inside me.

He bends and kisses me. "Going to come for me again, baby girl?"

"Looks like it," I say helplessly.

His lips curving, he lifts up so he can watch me, thrusting hard.

Oh my... unable to do anything but let him take me to the edge, I stare up at him, realizing at that moment that he's totally in control of my arousal. He's going to make me come, and I'm completely unable to stop him.

Not that I want to, of course.

I bite my bottom lip, my eyes closing of their own accord as tension begins deep inside me. "Damon..."

"Yeah, gorgeous girl, come on, let's fucking do it." He increases his pace, thrusting hard.

"Oh my God..." My toes curl and I dig my nails into his back as my orgasm hits, and it's unbelievable, every pulse heightened by the feeling of having him inside me. Ooh, it's fucking amazing. How have I gone so long without having this?

He's still thrusting, giving a sexy grunt with every movement of his hips, and oh I think he's going to come...

"Oh yeah," I whisper, "come on baby, I want to watch you fill me up..."

He slams into me, almost driving me up to the headboard, then shudders and stiffens as his climax hits. Ooh, man, he looks amazing, all his muscles tensing, his fierce frown showing the intensity of what he's feeling as his cock jerks inside me.

"Ah fuck," he says. He opens his eyes and looks right into mine, blazing hot, and his hands tighten on mine where they're still pinning me to the bed. "Fuck, fuck, fuck..."

Little aftershocks of pleasure shoot through me, and he obviously feels them because his lips curve up as I clench inside.

It seems to take forever for the paroxysm of bliss to release us, but eventually he exhales, and I relax back into the pillows, limp as a noodle. He unfurls his fingers and releases my hands. I flex mine and groan.

"Sorry," he says, still propped up on his hands looking down at me. "Did I hurt you?"

"No, not at all."

"You're sure?" He lowers down, still inside me, and kisses me, soft, light kisses on my mouth, my cheeks, my nose, my eyelids, then back to my lips. The intensity of our passion has dissipated, and now he kisses me tenderly, his tongue teasing mine, lazy and slow.

"Mmm." I sigh, enjoying the warmth of his big body on top of me, the feel of him still inside me. Cole used to roll over the moment he was done and look at his phone. I always felt abandoned, and it left me kind of cold. This is... mmm... very pleasant.

"My beautiful baby girl," Damon says, kissing the rest of my face again. "So incredibly sexy." He kisses around to my ear and nuzzles there, inhaling. "Jesus, you're a hundred percent woman, you know that? You smell and taste and feel amazing. You make me feel so good." He rocks his hips, still hard inside me. Ooh.

"That's a nice thing to say." I don't think I did anything, really, but I appreciate the compliment.

"You were made for sex," he assures me, his hips still moving. He brushes his lips against mine again. "I could make love to you all night. In fact, I think I might just do that."

A thrill passes through me like the shock of static. "You've just screwed me senseless, you horny devil. I've had three orgasms. I need five minutes to recover."

"Only three? Seems a shame to go down in the rollercoaster when you're up so high." He nips my bottom lip with his teeth.

I slide my hands down to his butt, feeling the muscles clenching as he rocks. "How are you still hard?"

"Skill."

That makes me laugh. "You're something else," I tell him, looking up into his gingerbread-brown eyes.

"Not sure if that's a compliment."

I kiss his nose. "It definitely is."

We study each other for a moment. I feel shy, suddenly conscious again that this is Damon Chevalier, nearly six years older than me, an incredibly hot and sexy guy who's very au fait with bedroom decorum.

He kisses me again, lifts up, carefully withdraws, and disposes of the condom. Then he rolls over and rises.

I sit up, missing the warmth of his body. Is he expecting me to leave right away? I'm not sure of the protocol with one-night stands. It doesn't seem right to stay the night. This is all about sex when it comes to it—I'm not stupid. Should I start getting dressed?

He's getting something out of the fridge, so I sit on the edge of the bed, find my underwear, and pull them on. I should have brought a change of clothes with me. Oh well, I'll have to put my dress back on. I pick it up and start gathering it in my hands, ready to slip it over my head.

He turns and comes back carrying a bottle of water and something else—chocolate?—and stops before me, surprised. "What are you doing?"

"Um, getting dressed? I... uh... wasn't sure of the etiquette, you know."

He studies me for a moment. Then he says softly, "Get back in bed."

I lay the dress over the chair and climb onto the bed, pulling the duvet over me. He unscrews the top of the bottle of water and hands it to me. I take it, and while I have a drink, he gets in beside me.

"A bit more," he says when I go to hand it back after a couple of mouthfuls. "It's good to stay hydrated."

Smiling, I drink some more, and then he takes it and has some. After screwing the lid back on, he leaves it on the bedside table. Next, he opens the bar of chocolate and breaks off a couple of chunks.

"Open," he says, holding one up to my lips.

Obediently, I open my mouth, and, looking amused, he slides the piece in. Popping a piece in his own mouth, he moves up close to me. Then, lying on his back, propped on the pillows, he pulls me into his arms and wraps them around me.

I'm half lying on him, snuggled up against him, and I feel a surge of happiness and contentment. "You're so warm," I murmur, sliding my arm around him. The chocolate is velvety smooth and adds to the feeling of luxurious satedness.

"Body heat is one thing I'm not short of." He lifts my chin and claims my lips again.

He kisses me for ages, while he brushes his hand down my back, my hip, and along the thigh that I hook over him, his fingers moving over my skin with long, lazy strokes. It's sensual but not sexual, almost reverent, and it makes me glow all the way through.

"My beautiful girl," he murmurs, stroking my face. "I can't believe I finally got you in my bed."

"Likewise." I kiss his chest. "All those years I've watched you from afar, and you're here, naked. Talk about a dream come true."

He chuckles and kisses my nose. "Do you think Alex would go supernova if he found out?"

"Maybe. I don't really care right now."

"Me neither," he admits.

"Hmm." I lean on his chest and rest my chin on the back of my hand. "I'm not sure you mean that. I know Alex's friendship means a lot to you."

He strokes my hair while he thinks about it. "That's true."

"Don't look so worried. He doesn't have to know. This is just between you and me, right?"

He slides a strand of my hair through his fingers. "I don't want you to think I'm putting his feelings above yours. That's not how it is."

"Hey, I know." I move up so I can kiss him. "Come on, I don't want to spoil this by getting caught up in what my brother thinks. This has nothing to do with him. It's separate from your working relationship, and even your friendship. You haven't seduced his little sis. If anything, I seduced his best mate. I'm sorry about that."

His lips curve up. "No, you're not."

"No, I'm not, that's true."

We both laugh.

He continues to play with my hair, clearly enjoying the feel of it sliding through his fingers.

"You're sure you don't want me to go?" I ask him. "I could use the stairs so I don't bump into anyone in the elevator."

He frowns at me. "If you think I'm letting you out of my bed before daylight, you need to think again."

"Oh." Every part of that statement surprises me. He wants me to stay the night?

"When are you going back to Wellington?" I ask.

"I'm driving back tomorrow. I have an important meeting with a couple of employees on Tuesday."

"Oh, okay." I feel a sweep of disappointment. So this is it, then. Ultimately, it's just been a one-night stand.

I shouldn't be surprised. He told me himself that he's not offering a relationship.

"When do you get back?" he asks.

"Not for a few weeks. I've got some kids' parties booked in Christchurch, and some studying to do. Uni starts up again on Monday the seventeenth of April. I'll probably fly up the Sunday before."

He nods, still playing with my hair.

"I'm going away in May," I tell him.

His eyebrows rise. "Where?"

"Australia, for eight weeks. I've got an internship at a law firm in Sydney."

"Oh. That'll be an adventure."

"Yeah, I guess. Mum knows one of the partners and got me a place. I thought it would be interesting. Now I'm half regretting it, but…" I shrug.

"It's a great opportunity," he says. "Would you consider working in Australia?"

"Dunno. Maybe. I haven't thought that far ahead."

We lie there for a while. He continues to stroke my back and play with my hair.

"Catie will probably have the twins soon," he says. "Apparently they're likely to be born early."

"Oh, you'll be an uncle!"

"Yeah." He takes a strand of my hair and curls it around his finger. "It'll be odd, Saxon having two babies. Things are changing, you know?"

"Yes, I know what you mean." I draw a finger through his chest hair. "Your birthday's on the nineteenth, isn't it?" I ask. He nods. "What are you up to?"

"Nothing exciting planned." He tugs the strand, then lets it slide through his fingers.

I bite my lip. I want to ask him if I can see him again, but I don't think I could cope with the rejection I'm certain I'd get. So I don't say anything, and neither does he.

He cups my face and kisses me. Then he rolls over and gets up. He collects his phone and taps something in. To my surprise, music starts playing. I don't know the song, but it's slow and sultry. The singer is saying that he and someone called Mrs. Jones have got a thing going on.

Damon turns to me and holds out a hand.

"You're kidding," I say. He shakes his head. Starting to smile, I accept his hand and he helps me up.

He collects the duvet from the bed and wraps it around us both, pulling me tightly against him. Keeping a hold of both ends with one hand, he slides his other around my waist, and we begin to dance.

"You old softie," I murmur, lifting my arms around his neck. Mmm. I'm now pressed up against his warm body. "You act like you're a bad boy rebel, but you're an old romantic deep down, aren't you?"

"Only with you," he says, kissing me.

He's told me he has a praise kink, so I know it's obviously his thing to give women compliments, and to want to make them feel wanted and adored. I mustn't think I'm anything special.

Despite it being a one-night stand, he does make me feel special, though. And for that, I'm immensely grateful.

Chapter Twenty-Two

Damon

We make love twice more before we finally fall asleep. I could probably have managed a couple more, but I don't want to make her sore, and after her number of orgasms reaches double figures, I let her rest.

She dozes off in my arms, exhausted. I'm tired too, but I lie awake for a while, listening to her breathing, and just enjoying holding her. It's always fun to make a woman feel good, but there's something different about Belle. I love the look in her eyes just before she comes—that complete surprise, as if the intensity of the pleasure shocks her every time. Will it ever fade? Maybe eventually she'll get used to it, but I've enjoyed being the source of her ecstasy.

Part of me is tempted to ask to see her again. But I don't. I tell myself it's because of Alex. Deep down, though, I know it's nothing to do with him. The truth is there's something about this girl that has the potential to infiltrate the barrier I've placed around my heart. Maybe it's her innocence, or perhaps it's that I feel comfortable with her because I've known her for so long. Or maybe it's just that she's beautiful and warm-hearted, and she seems to enjoy my company. But I know that seeing her in Wellington would be a mistake. I don't want to open myself up to being vulnerable again. Especially as she told me she's going to Australia for two months. She might meet a guy there and fall in love, and then decide she's not coming back. The last thing I need is to have my heart broken again.

No, best end it now. It's been great, wonderful even. But all good things come to an end.

I close my eyes, squashing my disappointment, and trying not to think about how I wish I could have her in my arms every night.

Eventually I fall asleep.

*

In the morning, we order breakfast from room service, and we sit up in bed, eating cereal and fruit, croissants with butter and jam, and drink piping hot lattes, while we talk about what we're up to in our lives.

For the first time, I tell her about my upcoming meeting with Lewis. I'm lying back on the pillows, legs stretched out, and she's sitting beside me, cross-legged, the white sheet draped around her.

"It's my first sexual harassment case at Kingpinz," I admit. "I've had some training, but I'm... confused."

"What about?"

I swirl the coffee in my cup. "Can I ask you a question?"

"Of course."

"What do you think would have happened if I hadn't stopped Cole the other day? Would he have taken it further?"

"Do you mean would he have raped me?"

I meet her eyes. "I suppose so." I don't want to upset her, but she considers the question thoughtfully.

"I don't think so. He was frustrated, and drunk. He thinks I still like him, and he was trying to make me admit it. I don't think he realized he frightened me."

I hold out my hand, and she slides hers into it. "I didn't realize how he made you feel at the time," I say softly. "I thought you were annoyed and frustrated, but Juliette explained how scary men can be when they use their strength to intimidate women. I am sorry about that."

"It's okay."

"The thing is, Helen, my head of HR, said she thinks Lewis might have just read the signs wrong—that he genuinely thought this girl liked him. Helen said she thinks the girl might have tried to laugh it off because she didn't know what to say. If that's true, how do I know I haven't intimidated women without knowing it? The thought horrifies me."

"Aw." She leans forward and kisses me. "The way you put women on a pedestal? That's never going to happen. Look, don't talk to him about signs and whether she was into him or not. That's irrelevant. The fact is that she didn't seek or want his attention. It's important that you listen to his side of things, but it's also your role to make it clear that sexual harassment is not tolerated at Kingpinz, that his behavior was unacceptable and must not happen again, and that Kingpinz's policy is to discourage workplace relationships because it exposes the company to this sort of complaint. Read out the company policy about what constitutes sexual harassment and tell him that he's a professional and he needs to keep his hands and comments to himself."

"I forget you're studying law," I say softly, impressed.

She shrugs. "I might not enjoy it, but I guess I've picked up some stuff along the way. I'd also advise that Helen explains to the girl that if she receives unwelcome attention, she needs to say the word 'no' loudly and clearly. Most men will stop when that happens. Cole didn't, but he was drunk, and I think if things had carried on, he would have if I'd repeated it. Am I glad you were there to stop him? Yes. Did he scare me? Also yes. Could things have gone south? Maybe. I like to think I'd have stopped him one way or another, though. I didn't need rescuing. That doesn't mean I didn't appreciate it or enjoy it." She smiles.

Thinking about what she said, I take the tray with our empty plates over to the table and come back to find her standing in front of the window. The sun pours across her from behind, surrounding her in a gold glow. She's holding the sheet at her breasts, and it hangs around her in folds. She looks like a Greek goddess.

She turns to look at me. "Don't move," I tell her hastily. I retrieve my phone. "Would you mind if I took a photo? Just say no if you'd rather I didn't."

"I don't mind," she murmurs, so I move back to fit her in the frame and take a couple of pictures.

When I'm done, I go up and slide my arms around her from behind, showing her the photos I've taken. "My muse," I tell her, kissing her shoulder.

"Oh yes, I've got a bone to pick with you," she says.

"A boner?"

"A bone," she scolds. "You never told me you were a painter."

"Who told you that?"

"Juliette. Why do you keep it a secret?"

I shrug. "It's just a hobby."

"Damon, I know you painted the big picture in Kia Kaha. I love that painting. It's amazing."

My lips curve up. "I'm glad you like it."

"I wish I could see some of your other work. Do you display it anywhere?"

"There are a couple of canvases in my office. The rest are in my house."

I want to ask her to come and see them. But I hesitate, and the moment passes.

She looks out of the window. "I should go."

I release her, disappointed, and a tad angry because I know I mustn't ask to see her again.

"I have to do the walk of shame," she admits as she takes off my shirt and starts putting on her underwear. "I'm hoping I can sneak in before Dad and Sherry see me."

"If they do, what will you say?"

"I'll tell them I crashed out with a friend at the hotel. Aroha or someone will cover for me."

"When's your mum going back to L.A.?"

She pauses in the act of lowering her dress over her head. "I'm not sure." She lowers the dress and turns her back for me to zip it up.

I rise, take the zipper in my fingers, and carefully slide it up, making sure my fingers brush her warm skin. She shivers. "Are you going to see her again?" I murmur, sliding my arms around her waist.

She turns in them to rest her hands on my bare chest. "I don't know. Maybe, just to say goodbye." She frowns and brushes a finger through my chest hair. "I don't know that I'll be able to forgive her fully, but I do have a lot more sympathy for her now. Relationships are so complicated."

We study each other for a moment. Afraid I'll blurt out that I want to see her again, I cup her face in my hands, lower my mouth to hers, and we exchange a long, sweet kiss.

"Drive carefully," she says when we eventually part. "And let me know how the meeting goes tomorrow."

"I will." I see her to the door, and we have one final kiss before she waves goodbye and runs down the corridor.

I watch her go, then let the door close.

I walk over to the window and look out at the autumnal day. It's going to rain, which will make my drive back slower than usual. And it'll be a lot less entertaining without Belle to brighten my day.

*

Monday

"Hey, bro!" It's Saxon, back from a stint in Auckland. He comes into my office, where I'm going through some folders spread out on a table, and we clasp hands and exchange a manly shoulder bump.

"Hey, dude. How's it going?" I ask.

"Yeah, not bad. Good to be back, though. I don't like being away from Catie at the moment."

I smile. The two of them had a rocky start, but he has adapted to married life and fatherhood with gusto. "How's she feeling?" I ask.

"She says she feels as if she's swallowed two bowling balls," he jokes. "She's quite uncomfortable now. But she still looks gorgeous." He grins. He certainly doesn't seem to find pregnancy a turnoff.

"I guess it could be anytime now, right?"

"Yeah. The longer the better, obviously, but the midwife has told us to be ready, so we've got the go-bag all prepared." He runs a hand through his hair, giving me a look that says he's looking forward to it but is also terrified.

"You'll be great," I tell him. "You're going to be a fabulous dad. Not as great as the uncle I'm going to be, but it'll be a close thing."

He chuckles. "I hear you've got a meeting with Lewis today?"

"Yeah, soon, actually."

"Good luck. You know what you're going to say?"

"I think so. I've had some good advice."

His eyebrows rise. "From whom?"

"Juliette and..." I nearly say her name and stop. "A... um... lawyer," I finish unconvincingly.

"Ooh," he says, "a mystery girl. Anyone I know?"

"Nope."

"That means yes."

"No it doesn't."

"Are you blushing?"

"No." Exasperated, I tug on my jacket. "I'm going to the meeting now."

He pats me on the back. "Good to hear you're back in the saddle."

"Jesus. I fucking hate having older brothers."

He laughs and heads out. "Good luck, bro."

Sighing, I collect my phone and head down to the board room.

Lewis is already in there, sitting in the chair nearest the one at the head of the table. "Hey, Lewis," I say, closing the door behind me and going over to the chair opposite him. "How are you doing?"

"Okay." He's the same age as me, an inch shorter, and quite a bit slimmer. His suit is off the peg, but it fits him well. He's exceptionally good looking, like a movie star. I'm not surprised he's popular with the women here.

"Thanks for coming in." I adopt a relaxed pose, one ankle resting on the opposite knee, hands loosely linked. "Do you know what this is about?"

"No idea," he says. He looks wary.

"I just want to have an informal chat at this point," I tell him. "Helen was talking to one of the office juniors, and she mentioned that sometimes you come on a little too strong to her, and it makes her feel uncomfortable."

His eyes widen. "You're kidding me."

"Unfortunately not. So I just wanted to talk to you about it."

"Who was it?"

"Jessica Chaplain."

He gives a short laugh. "Right."

You know we have a written policy here at Kingpinz about sexual harassment?"

"Jesus, seriously?"

"You're not being formally accused of anything at this point, and this isn't going on your record, but I do want to discuss with you what is and isn't acceptable in the workplace."

"I know what sexual harassment is. And I'm telling you, I didn't do anything."

I lean forward. "You might feel as if you didn't, but the fact is that you made this young woman feel uncomfortable."

"Because I told her she looked nice? And said I thought she was pretty? For fuck's sake. I didn't touch her."

"I appreciate that, but it doesn't have to involve physical contact to be harassment, Lewis. Look, I'm not saying I don't understand that many relationships begin in the workplace. It's natural for people who work long hours together to occasionally be attracted to one another. But it's our policy to discourage it. It can make for an unpleasant working environment if things go wrong, and even if they don't, it can make other employees feel uncomfortable or awkward."

"I didn't do anything." He's getting agitated. "Jesus, I've heard of this happening, but I never thought it would happen to me. Come on, you're a guy, you know how hard it is to talk to women nowadays. I got yelled at in a bar for trying to chat to a woman a few weeks ago. And on Monday I opened the door for a girl, and she said, 'Do I look as if I can't open doors myself?' I mean, Christ. I liked Jessica. All I did was talk to her."

"Lewis, please, calm down. I'm just saying that you need to keep your work and social life separate. In the office, please keep your conversations professional, and that way nothing you say can be misconstrued."

"This is fucking ridiculous." He gets to his feet. "That little bitch."

I stand as well, my hackles rising. "Please don't use language like that with me."

"Well, she is. Telling on me as if we're in year nine. She should have been doing a fucking dance to think I was interested in her."

"You're going the right way for a verbal warning, Lewis. Tone it down and remember who you're talking to."

"You're the same age as me," he snaps. "Just because you own the fucking company."

"You're right, I do, so watch your language."

He gives a short laugh. "Fuck off." He opens the door with enough force that it bangs on the wall and walks out.

I close my eyes for a moment. That could have gone better. Rising, I close my laptop, pick it up, and walk out of the office, straight into Jessica.

"Damon!" She's not as short as Belle, but she's a lot smaller than me, and she stumbles as I knock into her. I catch her arm, then release her as she gains her footing.

"Sorry," I tell her. "You okay?"

"Helen said you were talking to Lewis, and I just saw him storm out." Her brows draw together. "Why did you do that? I didn't want to make a formal complaint."

"He acted inappropriately," I tell her. "He needed to know what he did wrong."

"I could have handled him. I was sounding off to Helen, that's all. You've just made things worse. Now he'll know it was me, and he's going to be really unpleasant."

I feel a twinge of unease, knowing she's right. "If you have any further issues with him, come and see me or Helen."

"I won't," she says. "I didn't need rescuing. I wish you'd just kept your nose out of it." Turning, she walks off and disappears into the Ladies'.

"Fuck," I mumble. I walk to Saxon's office. The door's open. He's sitting in one of the armchairs, talking to Kip. I go in and close the door behind me.

"Hey," Saxon says, "how did it go?"

"I think I fucked up." I sit opposite them and flop back in the chair.

"Why?" Kip asks, concerned.

I tell them what happened. "Now she says I've made things worse, and she's probably right." I lean forward and sink my hands into my hair. "Fuck! I'm really angry with myself. But I don't know how else I could have handled it. Should I have left it? Let her sort it out herself?"

They both frown. "If he's been doing it to her, though, he might have been making other women feel uncomfortable too," Kip says. "He had to be told."

"You did the right thing by talking to him," Saxon assures me. "It's not your fault that he reacted badly."

"I dunno. Maybe I should have taken him out for a beer and a general chat about how difficult it is today to talk to women. Did you know Helen was sexually harassed in her first job?" They both look surprised. "A manager said he'd look after her, then told her to go down on him."

"Jesus Christ." Saxon massages his temples with a hand.

"Did she?" Kip asks.

"I think so."

"Ah, jeez."

"Don't say anything, obviously. But it shocked me. I know these things happened in the past, but even so… It's why I spoke to Lewis. I felt I should, you know? But I came on too heavy, and now I'm sure I've made things harder for Jessica."

"I'm sure he was shocked and embarrassed," Saxon says. "But hopefully he'll calm down when he's had time to think about it. Sometimes guys don't realize when they're coming on too strong. It's better that he knows and is more self-conscious about it."

I'm not so sure, but there's no point in talking about it.

"Damon," Kip warns, "don't obsess about this. You haven't done anything wrong."

"Yeah, right. I'm going back to work."

"Damon…"

But I walk out, leaving them to it. I'm angry with myself for screwing it up. I meant well, but that's not a good enough excuse.

I remember Belle telling me that she didn't need rescuing. She yelled no and stop, though. How would I have felt if I'd left her to it, assuming she didn't want my help, and then discovered that he'd raped her?

Angry and confused, I drop my laptop off in my office, then head out. I need a walk through the park to calm down. And then I'm going to lock myself in my office and lose myself in my work.

Chapter Twenty-Three

Damon

One p.m. on Thursday finds me walking into the café in our national museum, Te Papa. I stop and look around, and finally spot my cousin, Kennedy, sitting over by the window, with baby Eddie in a highchair, who's banging a spoon on the tray.

Grinning, I walk over to them. "Hey you two."

"Hey," she says, rising to give me a kiss. Eddie bangs enthusiastically, and she huffs a sigh and turns to take the spoon away from him with her fake hand. His face crumples. "Do you want it back?" she asks him. "Because you can only have it back if you stop banging." He pouts, then holds out his hand, and she gives it back to him. He pokes his tongue out at her, and I laugh.

"Don't encourage him," she scolds.

"You want anything?" I ask, gesturing at the table. She's already got a coffee.

"I've got a toasted sandwich coming. I'm good, thanks."

"Okay, I'll be back in a minute." I go over and order myself a toasted ham and cheese sandwich and a latte, pay for them, then take my number back to the table and sit opposite her.

"It's good to see you," she says, taking out a small plastic box and popping off the lid. It holds sticks of carrot, cheese, and small crackers. She puts it in front of Eddie, and he promptly helps himself. "It's been a while."

"Too long," I tell her, smiling. "My fault. I was down in Christchurch for Gaby and Tyson's wedding, and it's been busy at work."

"Kip said Saxon's only half there," Kennedy comments. "I've heard it said that each pregnancy destroys twenty-five percent of the mum's brain, but Kip said the same thing's happening to Saxon."

"He's stressed. He blew up in a Zoom call yesterday. Swore at Mack and told him to pull his effing finger out and get the effing program finished." Even though Eddie's not talking yet, I'm trying not to swear around him.

"Oh, shoot. What did Mack say?"

"Luckily he knows him well. He just said, 'You wanna take five, Sax?' We ended the call and sent everyone out. Saxon got a bit emotional. Said he was worried he's going to be a bad father. He doesn't want to let Catie down."

"Aw, he won't do that. He's going to be a great dad."

"Well, you know that and I know that… We sent him home. He said Catie sat him down and gave him a double whisky, made him eat a whole bowl of pasta and double portion of rice pudding, then put him to bed, and he slept eight hours straight. He's much better today."

"Oh, the joys of fatherhood."

"Yeah."

She smiles at me. "Something you're thinking of exploring soon?"

"I don't know why everyone's so keen on me becoming a parent. I'm twenty-six."

"Twenty-seven soon. Halfway to fifty-four."

That makes me laugh. "Cheers."

She grins. "Do you want kids?"

"Dunno. Haven't thought about it."

I lean back as the waitress comes over with my coffee and our sandwiches. Kennedy hands Eddie a sippy cup, then has a big bite of her sandwich.

I crunch into mine. I was at work by seven this morning and I haven't had time for a snack, so I'm ravenous.

She wipes some ketchup off her top lip, then says, "How was the wedding?"

"Good. Apart from the earthquake."

"Yeah, I heard about that. No damage, I take it?"

"Nah, but it was scary for a minute. If anything, though, I think it spiced things up a bit. Makes you appreciate what you've got, you know?"

She meets my eyes and nods slowly, and I think then about Christian, and how she once told me she thinks about him every day.

"I thought about him," I tell her softly. "When they were saying their vows. It made me sad to think he'll never fall in love, or get married, or have kids."

"Yeah," she says. "That's why we have to, so he can live vicariously." She has another bite of her sandwich. "He's watching us, you know."

I drop my gaze to my plate and pick up a few crumbs with my finger. Despite the tragedy her family experienced, they remain religious, and I know she finds solace in the thought that Christian is with her at all times. I don't agree, but I'd never try to pop someone else's bubble. We all take comfort where we can.

"I know you don't believe it," she says. "And that's okay. But he loved us, and I believe he watches over us. So you should go and do all the things he can't. He'd like that."

I dab the sandwich into the ketchup thoughtfully, wondering whether to confide in her. I love my brothers, but I'm closer to Kennedy than anyone, even my mother. Something happened in that sea cave that bound us together, and we've always had a special relationship.

"What's her name?" she asks.

I look up at her in surprise. "What do you mean?"

"Oh, come on," she scolds, "I know you well enough. You've got a girl on your mind. Who is she?"

I lean back in my seat. We study each other for a moment.

She lifts her eyebrows.

I sigh. "She's Alex's sister."

"Oh... not Gaby obviously... you mean Belle?"

"Yeah."

Her brow furrows. "Isn't she, like, fifteen?"

I give her a wry look. "She's twenty-one. She's taking a law degree here at Vic."

"An undergrad," she teases. "Naughty boy."

I give a short laugh. "I've always thought of her as Alex's kid sis. I mean, she was always a pretty little thing, but I would never have... you know..."

"Led her astray? Corrupted her?"

"Uh, yeah. When he asked me if I'd drive her down to Christchurch for the wedding, I was determined to keep my distance. But we spent eight hours together, and she was..." I think about how she did the

French kiss magic trick, and the way she somehow cast aside my view of her as a kid and turned into this sultry woman.

Then I think of the way I slid my hand into her underwear and made her come in the car and try not to blush.

"Oh…" Kennedy says, watching me struggle. "You really like her, don't you?"

"Yeah. We spent a bit of time together. And then on the night of the wedding we… ah…"

"Hooked up?"

"Yeah."

She grins. "You're a bad boy."

"I'd blame her, but yeah, it was all my fault." I huff a sigh. "Alex would kill me if he found out."

"Aw, come on, you're not fourteen anymore. What she does is her own business now."

"You don't know Alex."

"Look, all big brothers are protective of their younger sisters. Christian was, even at twelve. They just want to make sure their sisters are safe and respected. As long as you treat her right, I'm sure he'll be fine."

I drop my gaze back to the sandwich and pick at it moodily. We've exchanged a few texts since I came back to Wellington. Just fun and flirty messages, teasing each other about our night together, very lighthearted. Neither of us has mentioned meeting up again.

"Damon," she warns. "Are you treating her right?"

"It was just a one-night stand."

She leans back in her chair and surveys me. "Did she know that?"

"Yeah. I think. She's still in Christchurch. We haven't arranged to meet."

"Do you want to see her again?"

I meet her eyes. I sigh. "I really do."

"What's the problem?" she asks, amused. "If you got on well?"

"She's going to Australia for a couple of months soon as an intern at a law firm. She's so young, Ken. She might meet someone there. And then what? Another broken heart for me."

Her expression softens. "Yeah, that's tough for you. But what's to stop you flying over there to see her? You're not exactly short of cash."

"True. But I don't want her to think I'm stalking her, you know? She signed up to go, maybe she wants some freedom."

"Well, here's a tip—don't make her decisions for her. It's all about communication. Be open, tell her what you want, and let her do the same. You shouldn't second guess her. That's not fair on her."

"I guess. I keep thinking about a sexual harassment issue I had to deal with at Kingpinz."

"It's hardly the same, Damon. You've slept with Belle. That should give you a clue that she likes you."

"Yeah…"

She leans forward. "Sweetie, I know you've been hurt, more than once. Rachel did a real number on you. And unfortunately, there are no guarantees that it will work out next time. That really sucks. But you're very young to turn those experiences into a reason to stop dating. And before you say anything, I'm not talking about sex. I know you use Tinder and have one-night stands. There's nothing wrong with that, but it's just physical. It's hollow and unsatisfying. I know—I went through that stage after I broke up with Rich, before I met Jackson."

Her late teens were a tough time for her. She was angry and resentful, in pain a lot with her arm, and she missed Christian. She struggled with survivor's guilt, like we all did, and questioned her faith for a few years. But then she met Jackson, and everything seemed to come right for her.

"Not everyone's lucky enough to meet their soulmate," I tell her.

"I don't believe in soulmates," she says.

"Really?" That surprises me. I thought she was into all that.

"Not in the sense you mean. Or at least, there are different sorts. I think we're soulmates, of a kind." She smiles.

"Aw," I tease. "You're getting soppy in your old age."

"Maybe. Kids tend to do that to you. I cry at most movies now, especially if there are children or animals in them. But what I'm trying to say is, I don't think there's one perfect girl out there for you, Damon. Oddly, I think you've been looking for her, but I don't think she exists. Jackson and I don't have a perfect relationship. We bicker, and I think he's too untidy, and he hates the way I dither over things. But he's the best fit I've found. Sometimes people fit for a while. Emmi and Bridget and Rachel all fit for a time. You haven't had three failed relationships—you've had three successful relationships that came to an end."

"Glass half full, eh?"

"Kinda. I don't know what I'm trying to say here. Baby brain. Just… if you like this girl, I think you should tell her. Screw Alex, and screw anyone and anything else that stands in the way. If you like her, go and get her, Damon. Life's far too short for anything else."

She stops talking, and I can see her eyes shine. She's thinking about Christian again. Despite her words, she doesn't usually get emotional when she talks about him.

"If he was here, he'd tell you to," she adds. Then she leans forward and kisses Eddie on the forehead.

"All right," I say softly. I clear my throat. "You want some chocolate cake?"

"Oh my God, yes, more than anything in the world."

I laugh. "All right. I'll go and get us some."

I order some cake, and the two of us spend the rest of our hour together talking and playing with Eddie, bathed in the light of the autumn sun.

*

Later, after I finish work, I go home, order some Chinese food from Uber Eats, and take it out onto the deck to eat. My house is high on the hills surrounding Wellington, and it has a great view of the city and the harbor beyond. It has a large deck and its own pool, and to either side, trees hide me from prying eyes. The sun is close to setting now, and everything's painted with tangerine-colored light.

As I eat, I think about Kennedy, and her statement that Christian is still with us, watching over us, and I feel a deep yearning for the faith I lost as a child. Like Kennedy, I spent a lot of my teenage years furious at God and the world, but whereas she eventually accepted that Christian's death was part of God's plan, I could find no comfort in that thought. No God I wanted to worship would be so cruel as to take away a boy of twelve, who hadn't even started living. I told myself I didn't believe in God and turned my back on my faith.

So why does the thought of Christian watching over Kennedy and her baby fill me with such a warmth it brings tears to my eyes?

It's getting dark now. I rise from the chair, take my plate through to the kitchen, then continue walking through to my studio. I don't have a lot of spare time where I'm not doing anything. I work long hours, and when I am at home, I'm usually either working out, gaming, or watching TV. Painting is my only real hobby.

The big glass windows look out over the deck and the lawn, which are partially lit by the solar lamps half-hidden at the edges of the pathway. I walk slowly down the length of the room, looking at the two canvases already set up on easels that I'm working on. Both are progressing well, but I'm in the mood to start something new tonight.

First, I switch on my record player and put on a vinyl copy of Bowie's *Hunky Dory*. Once *Changes* fills the room, I'm ready to start.

Usually, I paint from photos of statues. I enjoy the process of turning them into real women, and breathing life into the cold, smooth marble. Tonight, though, I have a real-life subject to draw from.

I Bluetooth my phone to the projector, turn it on, bring up the photo of Belle standing in front of the window at the hotel, lit by the rising sun, and project it onto the plain white wall. The sight of her standing there, her hair tumbling around her shoulders, takes my breath away. I'm not sure I believe in angels, but if they do exist, they might look something like Belle.

I go over to the new canvases I had delivered a few weeks ago. I ordered a selection of sizes, including a couple of the biggest size the art store had. I take out one of them now—four feet by five—and carry it over to a free space. I bought an extra-large easel some time ago, and although the canvas is a little large for it, it does sit on the lower shelf, and the stand enables it to lean back at a slight angle, which makes it easier to draw on.

When I'm happy it feels secure, I choose a piece of willow charcoal and a rag, and take them over to the easel.

For a few minutes, I just stand there, looking at the photo of Belle on the wall, and thinking about how I could transpose it to the canvas. I want to make her into a Greek goddess, and turn the sheet draped around her into a diaphanous gown. I'll have a look at some pictures later, and think about colors and lighting, but for now I want to try and capture her shape and form.

In my head, I divide the photo up into nine large squares. Then I do the same on the canvas, placing light marks with the charcoal to indicate the grid. Only then do I start to sketch.

With the grid in place, it's easier to get the proportions right. Even so, I erase lines with the rag from time to time until I'm happy with them. I used to go to art classes in the evening, and my tutor there taught me how to look for shapes in figures—the horizontal line of the collar bone, the beautiful curve of the spine, the triangle of the hips, the vertical lines of the femurs and lower legs. So I begin with triangles, circles, and squares, then gradually add more detail once I'm content with the basic structure.

Slowly, she appears on the canvas. It's a magical process I never grow tired of. I guess it's the same as writing a novel, poem, or song. Saxon bought me a poster once that I hung above my drawing table, which states that creative people are touched by the divine because they can create something from nothing. When I'm painting, it's the only time I feel there's a slim chance that maybe God does exist. It's the only time I can believe that Christian is here, with me, even though I can't see him.

Feeling his presence, his bright spirit, standing with me, watching me work, I sketch for a couple of hours, until the sun has completely set, and stars are popping out on the night sky.

Finally satisfied, I walk backward and study the result. It's good. I had several tries at the natural curves of her figure, trying to capture the way she's twisting to look at me, and I think I've managed it. I've sketched the flowing folds of her gown, and the way her hair tumbles around her shoulders. I've caught the angles of her face, and the beauty of her wide blue eyes.

I stand there for a few minutes, looking at Belle. When we shared that night together, I honestly thought it would be a one-off, just an evening of fun, and we'd part the next day with a hug and a promise to exchange Christmas cards. I didn't expect to enjoy my time with her so much. And I didn't expect to miss her.

If you like her, go and get her, Damon. Life's far too short for anything else.

I huff a sigh. "All right," I scold Christian, hearing his voice in my ear agreeing with his sister. "I'll do it."

I go over to the sink and wash the charcoal off my hands, turn off the projector, then take my phone into the kitchen. After pouring myself a large whisky on ice, I go into the living room and collapse on the sofa.

I have a big mouthful of whisky. Then I send Belle a text.

Me: *Hey, you! How are you doing?*

Belle: *Oh, hi! I'm good, thanks. What are you up to?*

Me: *Just been in my studio. Hey, you up for a call?*

Belle: *Oh, sure!*

I press her number, and she answers after one ring.

"Hello!" She sounds as if she's smiling.

"Hey, you."

"Lovely to hear from you," she says. "So, you've been painting?"

"Sketching out a new project."

"Another goddess?" she asks.

I smile. "Yeah. Let's just say I had some inspiration..."

She laughs. "Me?"

"Yeah, you're my muse."

"Aw, that's a lovely thing to say!"

I have a sip of whisky and sigh. "I mean it. I miss you."

"Oh!" She sounds surprised. "I miss you too," she says softly.

"Belle, on Monday morning, I should have asked to see you again. I'm so sorry I didn't."

"I wasn't expecting you to. You did say you weren't offering a relationship. I knew what I was getting into."

I swirl the whisky over the ice. "I know what I said."

There's a moment of silence.

Then she says, in a teasing voice, "You wanna hook up again?"

That makes me laugh. "Of course I want to hook up again. You're *sexy as*. It's just..." I hesitate. I don't know what to say. She's still going away. And I still don't want to get hurt. But I miss her.

But she says, "I get it. Friends with benefits, right?"

I lie back, looking up at the ceiling, feeling my heart swell. "You're a special girl, you know that?"

"Aw, come on, we're both single, consenting adults, and we had a lot of fun. I'm not going to go and buy a wedding ring just because you want to have sex. I'm incredibly flattered, but I'm realistic. You're a busy guy, and you've been badly hurt, and you want to keep things light. I'm happy with that, Damon. I've got a lot on my plate, I've got my internship, and then my finals. I'm still recovering from a breakup. I don't need the hassle of a relationship right now. You want to have sex with me every now and again? Sounds great! Tell me where and when, and I'll be there. Possibly with some sexy underwear."

"Wow. Give me an hour and I'll fly down."

She laughs. "When are you free next?"

"What are you doing over the weekend?"

"Um... I have a kids' party on Friday until five-thirty, but apart from that, nothing at all."

"How about I fly down on Friday night, and you come and stay with me Friday and Saturday? I'll fly back Sunday."

"Sounds amazing," she says. "Oh my God, I'm so happy. You made my day."

I smile. "Likewise. I'll book us somewhere nice. But… ah… don't tell Alex I'm coming, okay? He'll wonder why I'm down there but not going to Kia Kaha."

"Hey, I'm not going to tell my brother that you're coming. That treat is for my eyes only."

I smirk. "Naughty girl. I'm going to bring you a special treat."

"Ooh! Now I'm excited."

"I'll let you think on that. See you Friday."

"See you."

I end the call. I feel a surge of pleasure at the thought that I'm going to see her again, especially as she understands the situation. Friends with benefits, yeah, that sounds great. No ties for either of us, no commitment. If we both keep that in mind, hopefully things will be fine.

Chapter Twenty-Four

Belle

I see my mum a couple more times before she eventually boards the plane back to L.A. I'm glad she's going, because she mixes up my emotions, although I am sad, too. Our relationship is better than it's ever been, and I promise to call her a bit more often and let her know how things go with Damon.

Then, on Friday afternoon, I pack a small bag for the weekend and take it with me when I go to the children's party.

Putting it in the corner and hoping desperately that none of them opens it and discovers the lacy underwear and bullet vibrator inside, I go through the next ninety minutes with a rising sense of excitement at the thought that I'll be seeing Damon very soon.

His phone call and the revelation that he wants to see me again came as a complete surprise. I honestly thought the next time I saw him would be in a few years, maybe at Alex's wedding or something, and we'd exchange a smile at the memory of the time we spent together and then move on with our lives.

I want more—of course I do. He's gorgeous and warm and funny and sexy, and he gave me so many amazing orgasms that my head is still spinning. I like him so much. But I refuse to be that girl who calls and begs him to see me. The thought that he misses me fills me with warmth and makes me almost tearful. But I'm determined not to get carried away. I said this was friends with benefits, and I mean it. We'll have a fun weekend, and then go our separate ways. And I'll just have to hope that the seed of something special that I can feel has been planted between us grows into something beautiful that he can't turn his back on.

I'll hope. But I'm not going to expect it.

The party goes well—the birthday boy is into pirates, so I tailor my routine to that. I wear an eye patch and have a fake parrot on my shoulder while I do my best Jack Sparrow impersonation, do magic with pieces of eight and skull-and-crossbones flags that the kids love, hand out pirate hats, and get them all playing games and hunting for bags of gold chocolate coins that I've hidden in the large garden.

When it's finally done, the mums present shake my hand and give me a large tip, and I gather my stuff and then check my phone, wondering if Damon has messaged me yet. He texted this morning to say he was taking the afternoon off and should be landing around five, and that he'd let me know which hotel he'd chosen so I could meet him there. To my disappointment, there's no message yet.

As I walk out of the house, I start typing a text to ask him, as I was hoping I could go straight there after the party. I look up to make sure I don't walk into the fence, and then my heart skips a beat as I see him sitting on the wall, waiting for me. He's wearing civvies—jeans and an All-Blacks rugby shirt, the kind that clings to a guy's body, the arms of it stretched tight across his biceps, the rest clinging to his muscular chest. Oh boy, he's gorgeous. He's had his hair cut, and it's real short up the back and in a stylish fade; he's shaved, too, bless him. No stubble-burned thighs tonight! I fill with heat at the thought.

He stands as I go through the gate and smiles.

"Damon!" Dropping my bags, I run up to him and jump up into his arms, wrapping my legs around his waist. He laughs and holds me tightly, and I crush my lips to his, filled with a wonderful joy at seeing him so unexpectedly.

A cheer from a couple of the girls who came to the party brings me to my senses, and I lower my legs and disengage from him while he chuckles.

"Is that your boyfriend, Belle?" one of the cheeky girls asks.

"Yes," I reply. "Sorry about that, I haven't seen him for a while."

They all giggle, and I grin and wave goodbye as he picks up my bags and takes them to the Uber waiting by the curb. We get in, and the driver heads off toward the city center.

"Sorry about that," I apologize to Damon. "Calling you my boyfriend, I mean. I didn't want to have to explain to a seven-year-old about one-night stands."

He chuckles. "I don't mind. Haven't been called a boyfriend in a long time."

A shiver runs down my spine at the lazy, sexy heat in his eyes. "I've missed you," I say, thinking there's no point in hiding it.

He cups my cheek with a hand, brushing his thumb across my skin, then leans forward and kisses me. This time, the kiss is slow and searching. He takes his time to press his lips across mine, and then eventually I feel his tongue touch my bottom lip. I open my mouth obediently, and he slides his tongue inside. We exchange a long, languid kiss that has my heart hammering, and the Uber driver glancing in his rearview mirror with raised eyebrows.

When Damon lifts his head, I'm seeing stars. "Wow," I whisper.

He kisses my forehead. "I've missed you too." He puts his arm around me, and I snuggle up to him.

"I'm so glad you came down," I say. "Where are we staying?"

"We have two nights in a boutique hotel called The Seven Sisters."

"Ooh, I've never been there. It's really swish."

He chuckles. "I've booked the Royal Skylight Room."

"The penthouse?"

"Kinda. It's right in the roof with all these windows, so it's really light. It has a huge bath." He waggles his eyebrows.

"I've died," I tell him, feeling faint at the thought of getting into all hot and soapy with him. "I've actually died and gone to heaven. Although that would make you an angel, and you're quite clearly not."

"Devil emoji." He nuzzles my ear and murmurs, "They have a great room-service menu, so we don't have to leave the room at all for two days if you don't want to."

"Oh my God." I sigh. "You're making it impossible for me to meet other men, you know. Nobody's ever going to live up to you." He goes quiet at that, just surveying me thoughtfully, and I feel a flicker of guilt. "Sorry, I shouldn't say things like that." I don't want him to think I'm falling for him, and that I'm trying to make him feel bad because I want more.

But he just says, "I'd rather you didn't talk about seeing other men."

Ooh. Part of me is irritated by that—he has no right to ask for exclusivity when he's made it clear this isn't serious. But I'm also thrilled by his possessiveness. I'm tempted to tease him for being jealous, but he's practically glowering at me.

Instead, I say softly, "All right. As long as it goes both ways." I don't want to hear about him with other women either.

He runs a strand of hair from my ponytail through his fingers and says, "No one could match up to you anyway."

I smile. This man makes me glow in about ten different ways.

It doesn't take us long to get to the hotel. It's on the northern edge of Hagley Park, close to the Museum, Art Gallery, and Botanic Gardens, with a great view across the park and the River Avon. The trees have all donned their autumn coats, and the park is a glorious blend of oranges, red, and browns. A couple of oaks stand outside the hotel, and we scrunch through their fallen leaves as we get out of the car, retrieve our bags, and walk into the building.

The hotel is an intriguing mix of past and present, built in the Gothic Revival style. It was badly damaged in the 2011 earthquake, but restoration work has finished now, and the hotel is busy and obviously thriving. The furniture is stylish and manages to maintain the Victorian atmosphere, even though the hotel provides all the mod cons, including a gym and a top-class restaurant.

I tend to feel intimidated by the smartly dressed staff and exquisite surroundings of posh hotels, especially in a five-star place like this, but Damon strides up to the reception desk and announces that we'd like to check in.

"Damon Chevalier," he says when the receptionist asks for his name.

I stand somewhat shyly beside him. Is the receptionist wondering what on earth someone like me is doing with a guy like him? I'm wearing tight jeans and a plain black tee, not unlike what he's wearing, but somehow, he manages to ooze power and wealth, and I feel like a scruffy waif he's pulled off the streets.

But the receptionist just smiles at me, and when he returns the sheet that she asked him to fill in, she just says, "Welcome to the Seven Sisters, Mr. Chevalier, and Ms. Winters. I hope you enjoy your stay. The Royal Skylight Room is our most premium room and it's located in the attic of the Alcyone building." She gestures to the elevators.

"Thank you." Damon takes the key card she offers. "Can I please book a table in the restaurant?"

"Of course. What time?"

He checks his watch—it's now 5:45 p.m. "Six thirty?"

"Of course, sir."

"Thanks." He smiles, takes my hand, and leads me over to the elevators.

"Forty-five minutes?" I tease as the doors open. "Doesn't give us long."

He leads me in, waits for the doors to close, presses for the top floor, then drops his bag and turns to take my face in his hands as the car rises. "I've missed you," he says simply. "I want you, Belle, but I want to spend time with you, too." He kisses me, just softly, on the lips. "I want to have dinner with you, and talk to you, and find out about the crazy party you've just done, and what magic tricks you've learned, and how your studies are going. And then I'm going to take you up to our room and spend hours kissing you and making love to you and making you come until you're so exhausted that you beg me to let you go to sleep."

"Oh…" I say faintly. "Okay."

He chuckles. "Your eyes are like saucers."

"I'm just puzzled," I tell him honestly.

"About what?"

"Why you like me."

His lips curve up. "Because you're beautiful in both body and mind and name. It's as if there's a star above you, Belle, and when I'm with you, it shines on me too, and it banishes all my shadows."

I don't reply because I'm actually speechless. He looks into my eyes for a moment, then drops his gaze to my mouth. Only then does he kiss me properly, sweeping his tongue inside, filling me with heat and longing.

The elevator pings, the doors open, and he moves back. I sigh. "Are you sure you want to have dinner now?"

He chuckles, picks up his bag, takes my hand, and leads me out. "It'll be worth the wait."

Grumbling, I follow him along the corridor to the room at the end. He touches his key card to the pad, opens the door, and moves back to let me go first.

I walk in, my jaw dropping at my first sight of the room. It's not enormous, but it's sumptuous. We enter a living room with a suite and a widescreen TV. Several skylights fill the room with the evening sunlight. To our right, through a door, is a white-tiled bathroom, and I can just see a large bath.

At the far end of the open-plan room is the bed, and it's a biggie— a four poster, bedecked with a dusky-pink duvet, white sheets, and lots of pink and white pillows.

Damon whoops, drops his bag, picks me up in his arms, and strides through to toss me onto the bed. I squeal and bounce, but before I can rise, he climbs on top of me and presses me into the mattress.

"I think we can spare fifteen minutes before we get ready for dinner," he says. "I've got the perfect starter." He kisses me fiercely, then leaves my lips to kiss down my body.

My mouth opens, but no words come out. Does he mean...? He unbuttons my jeans, and in seconds he's tugged off my Converses, peeled my jeans down my legs, and removed my underwear. I guess the answer's yes.

"Damon! I... oh..." I flop back with a groan as he pushes my knees apart, and without further ado, slides his tongue into my folds. "Oh fuck." The feeling is exquisite.

I've been thinking about him doing this all day, and so I'm not surprised when he lifts his head and teases, "Ready for me, already, Belle? I don't think this is going to take very long."

"Mmph," I reply, covering my face with my hands. It's embarrassing how turned on I am. His tongue contains more magic than any of the tricks I can do.

He flicks my clit with the tip, and then his fingers join in the fun, and slowly but surely, he teases me to the edge, as he slides his fingers inside me and presses firmly on what I've realized is my G-spot. I never thought they existed, but it doesn't surprise me that Damon's found mine.

Ooh, that feels good. It's been far less than his prescribed fifteen minutes, but I can already feel my tummy tightening. "Oh my God," I whisper, sinking a hand into his hair. He murmurs his approval, covers my clit with his mouth and sucks, and that's it—I come hard, clenching around his fingers with six or seven exquisite pulses.

When I'm done, I flop back, and he moves up the bed to lie beside me, propping his head on a hand.

"Hungry?" he asks when I eventually open my eyes.

"Famished."

We both laugh. He leans forward and kisses me. I complain as I taste myself on his lips, but I know it won't stop him, and sure enough he takes his time to slide his tongue against mine until I'm sighing, my body already stirring again.

"Are you sure you don't want me to return the compliment?" I ask, sliding a hand down to the bulge in his jeans. "It's not even six yet."

"This is about you, Belle. I want to make you feel like a million dollars, because that's how you make me feel."

I lift my hand to his face, then, and smile as I stroke his cheek. "You're very sweet, and so generous. But just like it makes *you* feel good to give *me* pleasure, it makes *me* feel good to do the same." I brush my thumb across his lips. "I want to taste you, too." I moisten my lips with the tip of my tongue, not missing that his gaze drops to them. "Won't you let me do this for you? For me?"

He hesitates, and it proves to be his undoing. Thrilled, I lift up and push him onto his back. He mumbles something, but I ignore him, and strip off my top and bra so I'm now naked. Then I straddle him and kiss down his chest to his groin. Carefully, I lower his zipper over the impressive bulge beneath the denim, and he sighs as I push down the elastic of his boxer briefs to reveal his erection. Ooh, this guy gets so hard, it's like an iron bar.

Once I knew I was going to see him tonight, for the first time in my life I ventured onto the internet to do some research. Specifically, I wanted to know more about oral sex. Even though he never said in so many words, I know that Cole thought my technique could do with some improvement. Well, it's not like you're given a manual when you come of age. How the hell do you find out what to do?

I was unsure about venturing onto a porn site, but I discovered a website, targeted at women, that talked about how to have better sex. It had sections on talking dirty, giving yourself and him better orgasms, sexual positions, and all sorts of other tips that I'm definitely going to read more about! But the bit I wanted to focus on was oral sex.

It was a real eye opener, and I read every page, especially the interviews with guys where they explained what they did and didn't like. And now it's time to put what I've learned into action!

One of the main things the guys talked about was how the girl's enthusiasm was a major turn on. I move back up him, shifting so the root of his erection is pressing into my wet folds, then, as I look down into his eyes, I rock my hips so I'm coating him with my moisture. His eyelids drop to half mast, and his lips curve up.

"I can't wait to taste you," I whisper, lowering my head so my lips brush his. "I've been thinking about this all week. You're so generous, Damon, so giving in bed, and I want to show you how much I appreciate it."

His pupils dilate—he likes me talking like that. I kiss him, delving my tongue into his mouth, then just as he's getting into it, I lift up and move back, kissing down his chest until I'm between his legs again.

His right hand is resting on the bed, and I slide my left hand into his and link our fingers, binding us together during this intimate act.

With my right hand, I give his erection a few firm strokes. The guide said the wetter a girl can make it, the better it is for the guy, so I gather some saliva in my mouth first, then begin to lick him.

"Ahhh…" His breath leaves him in a hiss. "Baby girl… that feels amazing…"

Encouraged, I make sure to go from root to tip lots of times, then spend a while licking around the head, making sure to add plenty of saliva, and to keep my teeth out of the way.

While I do this, I look up at him occasionally. He's pulled some pillows down and tucked his left arm beneath his head so he can watch me, and when our eyes meet, I feel his cock twitch in my mouth.

"You look so fucking hot," he whispers, his voice hoarse with desire. "That's so good. Jesus. It feels fantastic."

Pleased I'm turning him on, after a few minutes I close my mouth over the head, and he groans and drops his head back. While I continue to swirl my tongue over his sensitive skin, I stroke him, and soon I feel his fingers tighten on mine as he says, "Ah yeah, just like that…"

I didn't like the way Cole used to try and force himself deeper into my mouth, but Damon is gentler, letting me go at my own pace. Gradually I'm able to take him deeper, and even though he gives little movements of his hips, I can control how deep he goes, and enjoy it more.

Ohhh, this is hot; I can tell what he likes by his sighs and groans, and the way his fingers flex in mine. His breathing has sped up, and his body has begun to tense. I don't think he's far.

I remove my mouth, and instead just give him slow strokes, not touching the head, while I watch him.

His eyes open, and he blinks a few times, then sends me a wry look.

I run my tongue over my lips, smile as he gives a short laugh, then close my mouth over him again. Thrilled that it seems to be working, I slide my lips down the shaft, and suck gently. Once again, as he starts to tense, I lift my head and just stroke him.

"Belle…" He gives a long groan. "Have mercy…"

I stifle a laugh, wait until his breathing evens out, then say, "All right, honey, this time I'll take you all the way."

I suck him again, and this time when his body tenses, I don't stop. His left hand drops to my hair, and his fingers slide into the strands and tighten. "Ah fuck, I'm going to come," he warns, hardly able to get the words out.

Delighted, I take him as deep as I can and suck. He groans and twitches, and then I feel him fill my mouth with several jets of warm fluid. Without lifting my head, I swallow.

"Aaahhh…" His tense body relaxes. "Fuck," he says. "Belle…"

Releasing his hand, I lift up and look down at him. As he opens his eyes, I slowly lick my lips.

His eyes fill with a lazy, sultry heat. "Devil emoji," he murmurs, and I chuckle.

"That was a very nice starter," I tell him. "Kinda salty. I'm ready for my main course now."

Chapter Twenty-Five

Damon

Sometime later, we're sitting across a table from each other, tucking into dinner. Belle announced that she was in the mood for tapas, and we went for the chef's 'Feed Me' option. The waiter delivered a selection of amazing dishes for us to try: deep-fried potatoes with salsa, king prawns with chili and garlic, chorizo in hand-crafted cider, roasted pork and beef meatballs, ham croquettes in aioli, and lots more.

We decide to have a wine tasting, too, and the waiter brings us half a dozen glasses each in a rack, with a small sample of red, rosé, and white wines. Four samples in, we're relaxed and merry, thoroughly enjoying ourselves.

The restaurant is busy, but I slipped the waiter a fifty for a table by the window overlooking the gardens. While we eat, Belle talks about her studies and how well she's doing even though she doesn't really enjoy law, and then speaks with enthusiasm about her magic, and the parties she loves doing for kids' birthdays.

I watch her talking with enthusiasm about the pirate one she did today, and I feel a surge of affection and desire for her. She's now wearing a short black skirt and a thin, lilac-colored sweater with a V neck. She changed in the bathroom, so I'm intrigued by what she's wearing beneath her clothes. The way her breasts move suggests she's not wearing the underwired bra she wore last time, and I caught a glimpse of lace when she bent forward, so I'm thinking maybe a bodysuit or some kind of camisole top. Mmm.

I can't stop thinking about how she went down on me, either. Well, at least it's given me something else to think about, other than what's been bothering me for the past couple of days.

"Come on," Belle says, "spit it out. What's on your mind?"

Surprised, I say, "What do you mean?"

"You look haunted." She takes my hand. "Has something happened? You were going to tell me about the meeting you had on Monday with the guy accused of sexual harassment. How did it go?"

I blow out a long breath. "Badly."

"Oh no. What happened?"

I give her a rundown of my meeting with Lewis. "He was really upset," I add. "He didn't think he'd done anything wrong. But the worst thing is that I saw Jessica right afterward—the one who spoke to Helen. She was angry that I'd spoken to him. She said I'd made things worse, and that she could have handled him herself."

"Oh dear," Belle says.

I lean back, removing my hand from hers, and finish off one of the glasses of wine. "I feel so confused by all this."

"Of course you do." She smiles. "You're a paladin, Damon. A knight in shining armor. You rescue women. It's what you do. I know you're president of the Women's Refuge. Juliette told me. You want women to feel safe and secure. It's why you treat them like goddesses. And there's nothing wrong with that. It's a beautiful, sweet thing to do."

"But you said yourself that you didn't need rescuing. And yet you yelled 'no' and 'stop'. Should I have just stood back? With Jessica, should I have let her handle it herself, and waited until she made a formal complaint?"

She tips her head from side to side. "The fact is that, in the workplace, you can't really speak to the head of HR off the record. Helen can't ignore a possible case of sexual harassment. It's her job to protect the company, and I think you were right to have an informal talk to Lewis for the same reason. It's not your fault that both of them reacted badly. It's a shame you became the target of their frustration, but that's one of the drawbacks to being senior management, unfortunately."

It's a very adult conclusion to draw. Yet again, I'm reminded that she's a law student. "And what about you?" I ask softly. "Should I have left you to handle Cole on your own?"

"No, not at all. You heard a friend cry out, and you did absolutely the right thing. He won't come near me again, I know that. Could I have handled it on my own? Maybe. I like to think so. But there's no real way of telling. He's a guy—he's stronger than me. I'd rather you stepped in than I discovered I couldn't deal with him."

I fiddle with my fork. "I hate it when I hear stories of men abusing women, that's all."

"Of course you do." She reaches out and strokes my face. "You're such a sweetheart."

I lean my cheek into her hand for a moment, meeting her eyes. Once again, I'm reminded of the way she went down on me, setting me alight.

"So," I say, lifting the last glass of wine. "About what happened upstairs."

Her lips curve up and she gives a delightful girlish giggle. "I've been doing some research."

"Oh?"

"Did it work?" Her look turns hopeful.

"Couldn't you tell?" I ask, amused.

She shrugs and smiles.

My gaze settles on her lips. "I just hope you'll let me return the favor when we get back to our room."

"You've already given me one orgasm," she murmurs. "I was returning the favor."

"That's not how it works. Everything you do for me gets returned tenfold."

Her gaze caresses my face. "I love that you're so giving, but you don't have to do that."

"I do."

"Receiving pleasure is an important part of sex, Damon."

"I know."

"And it makes me feel good to make you feel good."

"I know. I'm not saying I'm so altruistic that I don't enjoy a good climax." I watch her lips curve up, and smile.

I glance out through the window to the view of Hagley Park. The sun has set, and the trees are shrouded in darkness. Solar lamps along the path in front of the hotel illuminate the dry leaves that are dancing across the grass, whipped up by the autumn breeze.

Should I say anything? It's a tough subject for me to talk about. But something tells me that if anyone is going to understand, it's Belle.

I return my gaze to my glass and swirl the wine around. "What happened today in the bedroom was… unusual, though." I clear my throat. "Sometimes I have difficulty… um… achieving an erection that quickly. It's why I like giving pleasure first."

I stop talking, studying my glass. Then, eventually, I lift my gaze to hers.

She doesn't look frustrated, angry, or exasperated. She just looks interested.

"So why didn't you have an issue today?" she asks.

"You took me by surprise." My gaze drops to her mouth. "You were very good at it." Her lips curve up.

We study each other for a while. Her gaze is gentle, thoughtful.

"On the night of the wedding…" she says eventually. "You didn't seem to have any issues then. When I lay on top of you, you had an erection."

"It's easier the first time with a girl. It's been more of a problem in my relationships."

"It was an issue with Rachel?"

I drop my gaze back to my glass. "Yeah." I scratch the back of my head. "She liked to have sex on the spur of the moment. You know, to sneak off into bathrooms and cupboards. Especially in public places. And I can't perform like that. She didn't understand and saw it as a sign that I was becoming less interested in her. We argued about it a lot. We were close to breaking up, and then she pulled the proposal stunt, because she was frightened about losing the money."

"Is that why you prefer one-night stands now? Because there are no expectations? You don't have to explain, and you can go at your own pace?"

"Yeah."

"So why did you ask to see me again?"

I lift my gaze back to hers. "Because I missed you." I say simply. "But I thought you should know, because I don't know if I can be fixed."

She reaches out and takes my hand. "You can't be fixed because you're not broken. You're not a robot, Damon. So you prefer a little warming up before you get into the action? That doesn't make you less than a man."

"Yeah, but men are supposed to be so horny that they're ready at the drop of a hat, right?"

"Maybe men who haven't been through what you've been through. You held Kennedy in that cave, when she was crying and hurt, and you couldn't stop her pain. That obviously affected you deeply. Have you had therapy?"

"Yeah, my parents took all three of us when we were young. I went a few years ago, too, when I was having trouble with Rachel."

"It didn't help?"

My brow furrows. "He seemed to think I have a repressed crush on Kennedy."

"You don't think that's the case?"

"She's my first cousin."

"That's not illegal in New Zealand."

"I didn't know that, actually."

"And it's not an answer, anyway." She tips her head to the side. "Are you sure you don't have feelings for her?"

"Not in that way. We'd drive each other nuts if we got involved romantically. She's far too ditzy and disorganized for me, and I'm too in my own head and analytical for her. We've never felt that way about each other."

"But you were close before the accident happened?"

"Yes, we saw each other all the time. Our dads are twins."

"Right. So you love her. Like a sister?"

"Yes."

"And you see her a lot. You like to keep an eye on her, make sure she's okay?"

"Yes."

She strokes the back of my hand with her thumb. "Do you feel guilty because Christian died, and for some reason you survived?"

I don't say anything. The room is busy, but over here by the window it feels as if we're in our own world. Out of the corner of my eye I see one of the waiters gesture to another to leave us alone, as if they're aware we're sharing an intimate moment.

She strokes my hand again. "Do you hate the fact that you're healthy and whole, but that Kennedy had to have operations and now has a fake arm?"

I inhale deeply, then blow a shaky breath out.

"Do you still dream about that day?" she asks.

"Yes."

She sighs. "Damon, you have PTSD, and survivor's guilt. What it means is that deep down you're terrified that if you don't look after the women in your life—all women, in fact—some harm will come to them. You feel you don't have the right to experience the joys of life—

and the pleasure of sex—unless you're doing your utmost to put the woman first."

I stare at her. How come I've been struggling with this my whole life, and she's figured me out in ten minutes?

She smiles. "All that's happened is that you haven't met the right girl, someone who understands that you have this basic need to protect and please. It's not a fault. It's a wonderful part of your psyche that needs cherishing and embracing. You think you're broken because you like to give women multiple orgasms before you let yourself come?"

"Well…" We both start laughing.

"Doesn't sound like a problem to me," she teases.

"It's just that Rachel—"

"I'm not Rachel," she says.

I close my mouth. Her eyes are very blue. "No," I say eventually. "Clearly not."

"And I know you think you're cursed, but you're not, Damon. Or at least, if you are, I know how to break it." She leans closer, lowering her voice. "Let me say right here, right now, that you can make me come as many times as you like. With your fingers, your mouth, your body, with toys, any way you want."

My eyebrows rise.

"You can take your time," she continues, "until you're ready to make love to me. There's no rush. Equally I don't expect multiple orgasms, so don't feel you have to give them. One is absolutely amazing! I have to tell you, though, I'm not interested in having sex in public places. And I'll never pressure you to have sex. But whenever we do have it, I can tell you, Damon Chevalier, it's going to be fucking amazing, because you're gorgeous, and hot, and I'm just crazy about you."

She stops talking at the sight of the waiter approaching, and we both lean back as he removes our plates and gives us the dessert menu. When he retreats, she studies her menu for a moment, then slowly, without moving her head, lifts her gaze to mine.

She chuckles. "It's your turn to have eyes like saucers."

"Can you blame me?"

She smiles and holds out her hand again, and I slide mine into hers.

"I want to paint you now more than ever," I tell her.

"I'd like to see it." She brushes the back of my hand with her thumb. "Juliette told me that you said your studio is the only place God exists for you now."

"Yeah."

"You lost your faith?"

"Yeah. Mum used to take us to church, but after the accident, Saxon, Kip, and I stopped believing."

"But in the studio, you let yourself believe in Him?"

I hesitate. "I suppose it's the one place I let myself hope."

She continues to stroke my hand. "Maybe it's not that you don't believe, but that you're furious at Him for allowing suffering?"

I look into her eyes, shocked by her insightful words. "Are you religious?"

"No. I don't believe in Santa either, but that doesn't mean I don't think Christmas is wonderful, and that there's a magic to that time of year, because we give gifts, eat together, and give to charity. For me, God exists in the form of doing good deeds—showing warmth and compassion and love to our fellow humans. In that sense, you are a very godly man, Damon Chevalier, and I have nothing but admiration for you."

Oh jeez, this girl.

Emotion washes over me, and for a few moments my throat tightens, and I can't speak. She continues to stroke my hand, though, her gaze gentle, a small smile curving her lips.

"I don't want dessert," she says when I'm eventually able to finish off my wine with a big gulp. "Let's go up to our room. I want to kiss you so badly."

"Okay." I don't need to be told twice.

We pay, leave the restaurant, and go up in the elevators. Another couple travels with us, so we stand quietly, holding hands, until they get out. Then, while we rise the last few floors, I turn to her and look into her eyes while I brush my thumb across her bottom lip.

"I'm crazy about you, too," I tell her honestly.

She responds with a beautiful smile that lights her up like a beacon.

"I have a present for you," I murmur.

"Ooh." She chuckles. "A 'special' present?"

"Yeah."

"Let me guess. Does it buzz?"

I laugh. "Yeah."

Her eyes flare. "You're so naughty."

"You have no idea."

The doors ping and open, and I take her hand and lead her down to our room.

As soon as we're inside, I start kissing her. She chuckles, grabs a handful of my shirt, and pulls me across to the bed. We fall onto it, both laughing, then move up so we're on the pillows. I lie on top of her, looking down into her blue eyes as I smooth strands of hair from her face.

"Thank you," I say to her. "For being understanding."

She looks up at me, her eyes filled with affection. "I have no expectations of you, Damon. I just like being with you."

I rest my forehead against hers for a moment. Then I kiss her.

I press my lips to hers, giving small butterfly kisses across her mouth, her cheeks, her eyelids, and down her nose back to her lips. Then I touch my tongue to her bottom lip, and she parts them to let me slide my tongue inside.

She tastes sweet, of the wine we had at dinner, and she smells of her sensual perfume, warmed by her skin so it rises to ensnare me. She makes no move to take off my clothes or speed things up. She seems happy just lying there kissing me, and so I let myself enjoy the moment, taking my time, while we slowly tease each other's bodies to wakefulness.

Eventually, as it grows warm in the room, I slide a hand beneath her sweater, and I'm thrilled to discover she's wearing a champagne-colored camisole top and a pair of gorgeous French knickers.

"You said you liked lace," she says shyly when I slide her sweater up to get a good look.

"Oh yeah." I make her sit up and pull the sweater over her head, then remove her skirt. Next I shed my shirt and jeans, and return to the bed, bringing the duvet over us. I pull her into my arms, rolling onto my back so she's on top of me, and slide my hands down from her shoulders to her bottom.

"You're so incredibly sexy," I murmur, turned on by the feel of her soft body pressed against mine, encased in the slippery satin and lace. She moves her hips a little, smiling as she obviously feels that I have an erection, but she doesn't say anything, and instead just presses her lips to mine.

We kiss for ages, exploring each other's bodies with our hands, just stroking, and her words at the dinner table drift into my head: *I know you think you are, but you're not cursed, Damon. Or at least, even if you are, I know how to break it.* She might be right. There's something about her that makes me feel... free.

I want to thank her for being so patient and understanding. Holding her around the waist, I turn so she's on her back, then spend a while brushing my lips over her breasts on top of the silky fabric before I lift it so I can take them in my mouth. She sighs and arches her back, and I tease her for a while, licking and sucking, before I finally slide my hand beneath the elastic of her underwear, down into the heart of her. She's wet and swollen, more than ready.

I roll over and collect the box I slid under the bed earlier. Bringing it back, I place it on the mattress between us.

Her lips curve up. She takes the box, looking at the object through the cellophane front. "Wow."

The box claims it's a rabbit vibrator. It has two 'arms'—one thicker and longer, curving up slightly, and another shorter one that bends toward it.

"This one can go inside you if you want it to," I tell her, tapping the longer arm. "And this shorter bit stimulates all the areas on top."

While she takes it out of the packaging, I retrieve my phone. "This is the best part," I say, bringing up the app. "I can control it."

Her eyes widen. "Seriously?"

"Yep."

She takes it out and puts the packaging on the bedside table, then comes back with the vibrator. "It's quite big."

"No bigger than me." I kiss her, sensing her hesitancy. "You can just use it on the top if you like—you don't have to insert it. And you don't have to use it at all if you don't want to. I won't be upset. I just want to make you feel good."

"No, it's okay, I'd like to. How do I turn it on?"

"Here." I hold down the button, and it leaps into life. Then I show her how, using the app, I can speed it up or slow it down. "It also has a button that warms it up." I turn it on for her. "Apparently that's supposed to feel good."

"I thought the bullet was amazing," she whispers. "I can't imagine what this is going to feel like."

"Let's start with it on the slowest speed. Take these off." I tug her French knickers. She slides them off, removes her top, and lies on her back.

Pulling the duvet over us so she feels safe and secure, and sliding one arm beneath her so I can hold her, I tuck the phone behind me for now. "You use it," I tell her, handing her the vibrator. "Just get used to the shape and feel of it first."

She turns the vibrator in her hands, exploring the smooth plastic and the strange shape. I brush a thumb across her bottom lip, looking into her eyes. Then I lower my head and kiss her.

She sighs, opening her mouth, and our tongues tangle as she finally slides the vibrator down her belly. Murmuring her approval, she pushes the tip through her folds, stroking it slowly up and down as she gets used to the feel of it.

I kiss her for ages while she plays, and then she says, "Mmm, it's getting warm now."

"Does that feel good?"

"Yeah."

"You use it as long as you want, baby. Wherever you want it. Whatever makes you feel good. You don't have to do anything you don't want to do."

"I'll try it inside," she says shyly.

Pleased, I slide a hand down to her thigh and pull it across mine, opening her up, and she moves her hand down and eases the vibrator inside her.

Her lips part under mine, and she gives a low moan.

"Is that nice?" I murmur.

"Yeah…" She moves it in and out a little, coating it with her moisture. Then she slides it deeper, until it's all the way inside. I lower my hand on top of hers, feeling her angle it so the smaller arm rests on her clit. "Ooh," she says.

Carefully, I close her legs so the vibrator is trapped inside her. "Now you just need to let it work its magic," I tell her.

Reaching behind me, I pick up my phone. Then I slide the button on the app up, just a little. "That's the main part," I tell her. "And this is the top bit."

Her eyes widen. "Oh. Wow."

"Okay?"

"Mmm. Yeah." She nods, her cheeks flushing. "Ooh. That feels good."

I lower my phone, chuckling, and kiss her. "You're so beautiful," I murmur, kissing across her mouth and cheeks. "I want to make you feel good, Belle."

"You do," she whispers.

"I want to make you come over and over again. It's so fucking hot when you come. It turns me on so much."

She looks up at me, her eyes filled with wonder. "I don't deserve you."

"We deserve each other. So come on, baby girl. Close your eyes and let me take you all the way to heaven and back as many times as we can bear it."

Chapter Twenty-Six

Belle

When I was reading on the sex website, one thing it mentioned was something called subspace, which is apparently not a Star Trek term but a state a person can enter in BDSM. It's like an out-of-body experience, which combines intense feelings brought on by an influx of adrenaline and endorphins.

This isn't BDSM and I'm not really a sub, so I know it's not the same thing, but I do feel as if I'm entering something akin to a subspace at times like this, when Damon is controlling my pleasure, and I'm starting to lose all sense of reality.

I was nervous about using the vibrator at first, mainly because they're obviously designed to be inserted, and I wasn't sure how it was going to feel. But he's so patient and understanding, and I want to please him, to turn him on too. So I decided to try it... and oh my God, the feeling is amazing. It's more comfortable than I thought it would be inside, and the top bit is hitting the spot in just the right place...

Damon's body is warm against mine as he holds me, and I feel safe in his arms. How does he know that this is just what I need? To be able to explore my sexuality in a secure environment, where he's patient and kind, but also so damn sexy that I'm turned on before I even start?

"Ahhh..." he murmurs as I stir and sigh, "look at you, all flushed here." He brushes his hand down my neck to my breasts and circles a thumb over my nipple before tugging it lightly. I close my eyes, the sigh turning to a moan, and he gives a throaty growl and lowers his mouth.

As he sucks, I squirm a little, conscious of the inexorable approach of an orgasm, as the warm, buzzing vibrator teases me toward the edge.

"Oh God," I whisper, the feeling intensifying as I clench my thighs. I think he's turned it up a bit.

He lifts his head and touches his lips to mine. "Come for me, baby girl."

I have no choice but to do as he bids. The buzzing on my clit and the vibrations deep inside me take me there, and then it hits—my muscles tightening deep inside, the pulses making me catch my breath with their intensity, while he watches me, his lips brushing mine as if he's drinking in my pleasure.

As my climax releases me, the vibrator inside me is suddenly too intense—ooh! I slide it out with a squeal. He laughs, takes it from me, turns it off, and puts it on the bedside table. "That was fucking hot," he says, and then he starts kissing down my neck to my breasts.

I blow out a breath, my heart thundering, while he places light kisses on my skin, avoiding my nipples for now, as my body seems to burn with the beautiful afterglow of pleasure. It's not long though before he continues to kiss down over my tummy, and then he moves between my legs beneath the duvet and lowers down. I feel his lips on my inner thighs, gently kissing, and then eventually his tongue sliding into my folds.

Oh my God, this man… I can't believe he sees it as a flaw that he likes to give his partner multiple orgasms before he enters her. Most women would think he was a god.

But even though it sounds incredible to me, I know it stems from a place of insecurity for him. He feels guilty for taking his enjoyment before he's pleasured his partner repeatedly. It might be a positive thing for me, but it makes me incredibly sad. He was embarrassed and ashamed to admit that this guilt means it takes him time to get aroused. We expect guys to get instant erections and call them pussies if they need romancing.

I don't mind at all if he needs to make me come first. I decide then and there to make it my life's work to show him that he's as entitled to pleasure as I am, and that we deserve it equally.

I like doing the praising, although I'm not averse to a compliment or two, he told me on the ferry. I want to make him feel good, and to show him how much I like doing this with him. On the website, a lot of the men who were interviewed said they liked it when their girls were vocal—when they said what they were enjoying, and especially if they talked dirty. I've always been self-conscious of sounding silly in the past by giving theatrical moans, but this feels so great that I don't have to fake it.

Gathering my courage, I slide my hand beneath the duvet, slip my fingers into his hair, and caress it. "That feels amazing," I whisper, closing my eyes as he licks me slowly. "Oh my God, Damon, how do you know exactly what to do to drive me crazy?"

He murmurs something, then circles the tip of his tongue over my clit. I give a long, heartfelt moan, and I feel his fingers tighten on my thigh. Oh... he likes that.

So for a while, as he licks and sucks, and I descend into my own version of subspace, I throw off my self-consciousness and let myself express just how much he's driving me crazy.

"Oh Jesus, that's fantastic..." I tell him, unable to stop my hips rocking to meet each thrust of his fingers as he adds them to the mix. "You make me feel incredible... Mmm... Ah, I'm so sensitive there... It's going to feel amazing when you're inside me... Oh Damon that's so fucking good... Oh yeah, fuck me with your fingers, just like that..."

With another sexy growl, he suddenly rears up, making me jump. Leaning over to the bedside table, he collects a condom and rips off the packaging.

"You're driving me crazy," he says, his voice hoarse. "I want you to come while I'm inside you." He tugs off his underwear, releasing an impressive erection.

Thrilled, I watch him roll the condom on, then position himself between my legs and insert the tip of his erection inside me. "Ready, baby girl?" he whispers. When I nod, he pushes forward and slowly slides inside me.

I groan and stretch out under him, reveling in the sensation. "Ah, Jesus, yeah..." I purr like a cat. "You fill me to the brim. Ah that's so sexy..." I slide my hands up his chest and around to his back, dig my nails in just a little, and score them down. His breath hisses through his teeth. "You like that, baby?" I murmur, and do it again. "You feel so good inside me. Oh yeah... come on... fuck me properly..."

Beginning to thrust, he lowers down to kiss me, and when he talks, his tone is amused. "Have you been taking lessons in how to drive your man mad with lust?"

My man? His words thrill me, but I don't react. "Is that a complaint?" I tease.

"Nope." He slides his tongue into my mouth, and we kiss long and leisurely while he moves inside me.

"Mmm…" I slide my hands down to his butt. "You have a magnificent body," I murmur, feeling his muscles flexing as his hips move. "You're so gorgeous, Damon."

He kisses me again. "And you're so fucking beautiful."

"Does it feel good to be inside me, baby?"

"Yeah… You're so soft, so wet…"

"That's all you, baby. That's what you do to me. You turn me on so much."

He continues to kiss me, and our breaths mingle as we both sigh.

Mmm… this is amazing, but I want to fire him up, and it makes me think of something he said in the car on the way to Christchurch: *having sex from behind is awesome—it makes the guy more dominant, which I like*. I told him I wasn't keen on it, so I'm sure he's going to be hesitant to suggest anything I'm not sure of, but I want to turn him on.

"Damon," I murmur.

"Mmm?"

"Can I ask you something?"

He lifts his head, surprised. "Sure."

"Will you take me from behind? You said you liked it, and I want to try it."

His lips curve up. He kisses my nose. "Are you sure?"

"Yeah."

He kisses my lips. "Okay." He withdraws carefully, holding the condom, and moves to the side. "Turn over," he says softly.

I lift up onto all fours, but to my surprise, he says, "No, lie down on your front."

"Oh. I thought—"

"Let's start this way."

"Okay." I lie on my front. He moves between my legs, then gently pushes up my left knee. Finally he slides the tip of his erection down through my folds and presses it inside me.

"It feels deeper this way," he murmurs, bending to kiss my shoulder. "So we'll go slow, okay?"

I nod. He eases in carefully, withdrawing and then going a little deeper each time. In between, he kisses my shoulder, my neck, my face, and my lips when I turn my head. He takes his time, but eventually he's all the way in, and he pauses, pushing forward and burying himself deep inside me.

"Oh my God…" I pull a pillow toward me and bury my face in it. This is so different from anything I've experienced before. His body is warm on top of mine, and he's tucked one arm beneath me, so he's holding me tightly.

"Ah baby girl," he murmurs, moving inside me as he kisses my neck, "you feel so good. I love being deep inside you like this."

"Mmm… Damon…"

He moves slowly, and while he rocks his hips, he slides his other hand down beneath me, his fingers finding my clit. He circles the pad of his middle finger over it, and I moan.

"Does that feel good?" he whispers.

"Yeah…" My hands curl into fists on the pillow. He's right—there's something feral about this position, and it fires me up. "It feels… amazing…" I like the feeling of him commanding my passion, and here, like this, I'm totally in his hands, and he's completely in charge of me. I'm entering that strange mindspace again, feeling as if I'm floating, as if all there is in the world is Damon and his warm body and his strong hands guiding me…

For the first time, I understand why people enjoy the animal side of passion. Before, with Cole, I found it cold and unromantic, and I felt as if he was using me—as if I might as well just be a sex doll lying there. But I know Damon will never take his pleasure from me without a thought to mine. His fingers are unrelenting, stroking and teasing my clit, and I know he won't let himself come until I have. The thought turns me on more than anything else he could ever do or say.

I want him to take me, I want to come like this, with him inside me. But he's thrusting so slowly, and every now and again he stops touching me, making me wait.

"Oh God…" I whisper, "please…"

He kisses my cheek, and down my neck. "Please what, baby girl?"

"I want…"

"Tell me what you want."

"I want to come. Ahhh… Damon… This is like torture…"

"Tell me what to do."

"Ahhh… please… just… take me there."

"How, baby?"

"Please…" I widen my thighs, trying to push back against him.

"You want me to go faster?"

"Yes…"

"Harder?"

"Oh God, yes…"

He turns my face and gives me a hard kiss. "Whatever you want, gorgeous girl." He lifts up then onto his hands. This time, when he thrusts, he's plunging down into me, and I groan at how deep it feels.

"Is this what you want?" he says, his voice harsh with his ragged breaths.

"Oh my God, yes…" I bury my face in the pillow.

"Get ready, sweetheart, I'm going to make you come now."

I love how confident he is, how sure. He moves inside me with deep, hard thrusts, and I know he's not going to stop until my orgasm hits. How he holds his own pleasure in, I don't know, but he doesn't stop, he keeps going, and sure enough, my tummy begins to tighten, and the exquisite tension begins deep inside me, and then *ooohhh…* the wonderful, exquisite pulses start, and I squeeze around him, making him grunt as he continues to thrust me through it. Oh wow, I'll never get tired of this, orgasms are just fucking amazing, the best thing in the world, better than ice cream and chocolate and coffee and wine combined, and that's saying something!

"Ah baby," he says, "you feel so good…" And then he gives a couple more thrusts and stiffens. "Fuck," he adds, and I feel his hips jerk and his cock twitch inside me as he comes. Oh, I love his throaty groans, the feel of his warm skin sticking to mine, the sensation of having given him such pleasure.

"Oh my God I love sex," I say, collapsing onto the pillow.

He buries his face in my neck. "Ah jeez… Don't make me laugh."

"I mean sex with you," I elaborate, feeling as if all my bones have been removed, and loving the feeling of him finishing inside me. "It's just something else. Mmm. Fill me up, big boy. Wow. That feels so good."

He does laugh this time, then gives me a kiss on the shoulder before he finally withdraws. I lie there, watching him as he disposes of the condom, rises to get a bottle of water, brings it back and drinks half of it, then gets back into bed and passes it to me. I finish it off, and then he puts it to one side and pulls me into his arms.

"Are you all right, sweetheart?" he asks, brushing my hair away from my face before kissing me.

"Mmm. Superb." I smile, cuddling up to him. "Wow. That was just amazing."

He cups my cheek. He has a puzzled look on his face.

"What?" I ask.

But he just shakes his head, slides down the pillows a bit, then gives me a long, luxurious kiss.

I rest my head on his shoulder, allowing myself a small private smile. I'll let him think about what just happened, and maybe we can talk about it tomorrow, once he's had time to muse on it.

*

The next morning, although we're tempted to stay in bed all day, we agree it would be fun to go for a walk around the park and get some fresh air, and maybe visit the Botanic Gardens or the Museum. I wondered whether he might be reluctant to go out in case Alex or someone else he knows sees us together, but he doesn't seem bothered.

We walk through the park, enjoying the cool breeze and the smell of the autumn leaves, then stop and have breakfast at a café in the Gardens. Both ravenous, we tuck into eggs, bacon, and toast with piping hot coffee, while we talk about everything under the sun, just enjoying being in each other's company.

Damon is happy to talk, but several times I look over to find him lost in thought. I'm not sure whether he's reflecting on what happened last night. If he was any other guy, I'd say he was thinking about the rugby, but when he was talking about Kennedy he said, *I'm too in my own head and analytical for her*, so I know he's more reflective than most guys.

I don't push him to talk, though, and I just enjoy his company as we stroll along the Avon, ducking under the willows and watching the tourists on the punts that sail up and downstream.

As a shell goes by, the rowers pulling hard at the oars, he tells me how he's been a member of the Wellington Rowing Club since uni, and how he used to row as part of a coxed four with Alex, James, and Henry.

"Do you miss not seeing them all as much?" I ask. I know that after they graduated, Alex put forward the suggestion that they all move to Christchurch to open up Kia Kaha. James, Henry, and Tyson agreed as they had family here, but Damon, who was Alex's closest friend, made the choice to stay in Wellington. It was a tough decision for Alex, but I know part of it was because he wanted to be closer to me once Gaby left for uni. If he'd known I'd end up at uni in Wellington, he might have made a different decision, but it was nice to have him close by for a few years.

"Sometimes," he admits. "Obviously I've got Kip and Saxon, and I'd miss them if I moved away. But they've always got each other, being twins."

"Do you feel like the odd one out?"

"They've always been great older brothers and included me in everything," he says. "They've never shut me out, even down to wanting me as a director of Kingpinz."

But I can sense the words he doesn't want to say—that twins have a special connection, and he's always been on the outside of that.

I curl my fingers around his hand where he's holding mine. "Do you ever wish you'd gone to art school rather than doing your degree in computing?"

"Sometimes. But all I would've been able to do is paint pretty pictures. With my software skills I can design things that can help people in their everyday lives."

"That's a pretty poor view of artists you have there. You don't think that creating art—painting, music, writing—improves people's lives? Helps them escape? Gives them hope?"

"I guess. At the time that I was making the choice, painting felt indulgent. It still does. I only paint at the end of the day, if I've worked hard and feel I've earned it."

"Oh, Damon."

"What?"

"Are you trying to make me cry?"

He laughs and puts his arm around my shoulders. "Come on, let's go and look at the Museum."

We spend a couple of hours browsing through the dinosaur exhibition with its T. rex skeleton and examining the historic objects from the Antarctic and Early Settlers galleries. Afterward, still full from our big breakfast, we stop for a light lunch—a cake and a coffee—in town, then browse the shops together, hand in hand, enjoying each other's company. We spend a while in a large toy shop so I can go through the magic tricks and props, and I treat myself to a wallet made out of recycled playing cards with slots for cards and coins.

When we're done, we cross into Hagley Park and follow the Avon back to the hotel. It's in sight when he stops me and produces a small box with the logo of the magic shop.

"I wanted to say thank you," he says, handing it to me.

"For what? The orgasm?"

"Yeah," he says. "For the orgasm."

I chuckle and open it. "Oh, Damon…" It's a tiny pair of earrings, each in the shape of a rabbit coming out of a hat.

"They're just for fun," he says awkwardly.

"I love them." I take one out and study the smiling rabbit. "Nobody's ever bought me anything to do with my magic before," I say in a husky voice. "Everyone always thinks it's a joke."

"I don't."

I look up into his gingerbread-brown eyes.

"I think you're amazing," he states. Then he slips a hand to the back of my neck, moves closer, and kisses me.

They're just earrings, and I don't even think they're silver or anything. It's hardly an engagement ring. It's nothing to get excited about, I tell myself.

But the feel of the box in my hand warms me all the way through. He's trying to tell me that he appreciates the things I've said and done. And I think he's trying to tell me has feelings for me.

I don't know what the future's going to hold yet. But for the first time, I'm filled with hope that maybe the magic I've always loved will spill over into my real life.

Chapter Twenty-Seven

Damon

Even though my body is already longing for her, part of me doesn't want the day to end. We sit on a bench for a while, watching the ducks sailing by, enjoying the peace and quiet, while she cuddles up to me, her arms around my waist and her head on my shoulder. The sky has clouded over and it's going to rain soon, but for now a burst of sunshine turns the river into a dazzling sheet of gold.

It seems important to just *be*, to let myself process this time alone with her. I'm prone to overthinking, to dwelling on the past and worrying about the future, but I do my best to quieten my mind and concentrate on my senses, on the here and now. It's not an onerous task. It's a beautiful autumn afternoon, and the earthy smell of the leaves and the freshness of the river mix with Belle's light and flowery daytime scent. She produces a bar of chocolate, breaks off a couple of pieces, and pops one in my mouth, and I let it melt on my tongue. Her curves are rounded where she's pressed up against me—she doesn't seem to have any angles. Her hair smells of mint.

Sliding a finger beneath her chin, I lift her face so I can kiss her, and enjoy the softness of her lips, the whisper of her breath across mine as she sighs with contentment.

"I love your mouth," I murmur. "So soft."

"Mmm. And I love your tongue. That knows how to do real magic." She parts her lips and lets me slide it against hers, and we indulge in a long, luxurious kiss that sends my pulse racing.

"We should go back," I whisper. "Or we might get arrested for being lewd."

"I would love to get arrested for being lewd. What a thing to have on your CV."

I chuckle, get up, and pull her to her feet. "Come on, gorgeous. If I'm not naked and on my knees with my tongue inside you in five minutes, I think I might explode."

Her eyes light up, and the two of us practically run back to the hotel. We're halfway there when it starts raining, and by the time we enter the lobby, we're soaked through, and laughing as we drip all over the carpet.

We take the elevator up, and we're already kissing before we get there. I sink my hands into her wet hair and hold her as our tongues tangle. She slips her hands beneath the hem of my wet tee and skates them over my ribs and around to my back. I growl and push her up against the wall of the car, pressing my body against hers, heat rushing through me. I love that she's eager for me, but also willing to follow my lead. That she'll wait for me, but that she doesn't expect anything. I hadn't realized I needed a girl like this in my life, but now I have her, I don't want to let her go.

When the elevator dings, I move her out of it backward, still kissing her, and she laughs against my lips. "Someone will see!"

"Don't care." I walk her all the way to our room, swipe the card, and open the door, letting it close behind us.

It's raining hard now, pounding on the skylight windows, and filling the room with a silvery light. We left the heat pump on though, and the room is pleasantly warm, so I don't feel guilty when I start unbuttoning her jeans and help her remove them.

"Ooohhh…" I slide my hands around to her butt as I discover she's wearing some kind of silky bodysuit. "Another treat."

"Just for you." She smiles and takes off her tee, and I see then that it's made of silky black material to just beneath the bust, and the top part is stretchy lace.

"Wow." I cup her breasts and brush my thumbs over her nipples. They're soft at the moment, but as I tease them, they tighten to little buttons, and she tips back her head and sighs.

"You're so beautiful," I murmur, lowering my lips to hers. She lifts her arms around my neck, and we kiss as I continue to walk her backward to the bed.

She bumps into the post, but instead of moving her to the mattress, I drop to my knees in front of her. She slides her hands into my hair as I study the way the silky material has stretched across her tummy, and I trace the two strips of lace that direct me down between her thighs.

I lift one of her legs over my shoulder, pull aside the stretchy fabric, and kiss her soft mound. Smiling, I kiss down, then slide my tongue into her folds.

She gives a long moan, tilting her hips up, and I sigh and slip my fingers down so I can tease her entrance while I swirl my tongue over her clit. She's already a little swollen, and it's not long before I slide my fingers inside her and withdraw them coated in her sweet, salty nectar. I suck it from my fingers, and she groans.

"You're so filthy," she tells me. "Naughty boy."

"I told you, you taste good," I murmur, licking as far inside her as I can.

"Oh God, Damon…"

I move my fingers inside her and set up a slow rhythm while I continue to arouse her with my tongue. I don't care how long it takes her to come—I'd do this for hours if I had to. But it's literally only about five minutes before her breathing turns erratic, and she begins to tremble.

I fasten my mouth on her clit and suck gently, and she clenches my hair as she says, "Oh jeez…"

I continue to suck, the fingers of my other hand tightening on her bottom as I sense her orgasm approaching. She says, "Oh, oh, oh," her body tenses, and then she clamps around my fingers with a squeal, threatening to pull my hair out by the roots where she's gripping it. I don't care though, because I feel a flood of oxytocin or dopamine or whatever chemical it is that makes a man feel good when he makes his girl come, loving the way she shudders and cries out my name.

When she's done, her knees give way, and I rise to catch her, laughing as I transport her onto the bed.

I roll, bringing her on top of me, and she looks down at me with eyes full of an emotion I can't quite decipher—affection? Tenderness? I love the way she looks at me.

I kiss her for a long time, moving to the side so I can stroke her at the same time. I sigh as I slide my fingers down into her, enjoying the feel of her moist, swollen skin, and I arouse her until she's sighing against my lips again, and squirming beneath my touch.

In the past, I'd have felt the need to make her come again, and maybe a third time before I felt I finally deserved my own climax, but she lowers a hand to stroke me, smiling up at me with no pressure and no expectations, and suddenly all I want to do is make love to her.

I catch myself mid-thought. Make love to her? Not have sex with her? Not fuck her?

Well, shit. I might need to think about that later.

For now, though, I rise, roll on a condom, and slide into her in one smooth thrust. We both exclaim. It's like sliding into hot, wet velvet.

"Jesus," I say, "you feel fantastic."

"I can feel you all the way up," she whispers.

I pull almost out, then thrust all the way in again. "Your body drives me crazy," I tell her as I kiss her, our tongues tangling.

"Likewise," she says. "Just look at you. You're magnificent." She runs her hands up my biceps and over my shoulders, admiration in her eyes.

It's a nice thing to say, and I admit I glow a little as I begin to move with purpose. I don't want to rush this—I want to drive us both to the edge and leave us teetering there, dangling by our fingertips, our hearts racing, as long as I can.

So just as her breathing grows ragged, or I feel pleasure building deep inside me, I switch position, the break giving enough of a pause to halt any climax in its tracks. We try a couple we haven't tried before, including lying side by side, and something she calls 'the chairman' she's read about, which involves me sitting on the edge of the bed and her on my lap, facing away, her legs drawn up and feet resting either side of me. We both like that one, her because she says she likes me being able to put my arms around her, and me because it allows for deeper penetration, as well as the fact that I can arouse her with my fingers while I'm inside her.

This time I don't stop as she begins to tremble, and I manage to hold on just long enough to enjoy her orgasm before my own climax sweeps over me. I fasten my mouth on where her neck meets her shoulder and suck as I come, fighting the urge to sink my teeth into her like some kind of feral dog. Time and again I pulse inside her, and she groans, shuddering.

Eventually it releases me, and I lift her off me, and we both collapse back on the bed.

"You'll be the death of me," I tell her. "Your pelvic floor is incredibly strong. I'm sure you're going to squeeze me to death."

She giggles. "God bless the Kegel exercises."

"Man, yeah." I blow out a breath. Then I roll onto my side to look at her. "Would you like a bath?"

"With you?"

"If you like."

"I'd love one," she says, smiling.

So I get up and turn on the taps in the big bath, and let them run for a while, adding some of the foam from the bottle the hotel supplies, filling it with bubbles.

When it's ready, we both slide into the hot water with a groan. Luckily the taps are in the middle, so we're able to have an end each.

I rest my arms on the edge of the bath, observing her as she sinks up to her chin, then emerges, her shoulders glistening.

"Mm," she says, "this feels so good."

"I'll wash you in a minute," I tell her.

She wrinkles her nose. "You're so good at this. I'm glad I found an expert."

I chuckle, stroking a foot up her thigh, sending the water swirling around us. "Hardly."

"You are. If you hadn't done what you did in the car, I'd still be clueless. You've given me confidence to explore, Damon. To communicate what I like with a guy rather than just lie there and hope for the best."

I frown. I know she means it as a compliment, but I can't suppress a niggling feeling that she's going to take what I've taught her and apply it to other men.

"Did I say something wrong?" she asks.

I think about what went through my head as I slid inside her. There's no point in ignoring it. I have feelings for this girl. I might as well be honest about it.

"I don't want you to see other men," I tell her.

She blinks and stares at me. Then, slowly, her lips curve up, just a little. "Okay."

My eyebrows rise. "Aren't you going to argue with me?"

She shakes her head.

"I have no right to ask you," I point out.

She tips her head to the side. "Are you going to see other women?"

"No."

"Good." Her eyes flare.

We both study each other. Then, slowly, we both give a small smile.

"You're going to Australia soon, though," I point out.

"True."

"You might meet some young Aussie surf dude there and fall in love with him."

She pokes me with her toe. "Why would I do that when I have you here?"

The rain is still falling on the skylight, and the light behind it sends the reflection of the rain across us. Her eyes are full of amusement and pleasure. She likes that I'm being possessive. She wants to be with me, but she wasn't going to say so first. She was happy to let me come to that conclusion myself.

I'm not sure what this all means. I'm busy with work. She's got to finish her degree, and I have no idea what she wants to do after that. And I'm still wary of giving my heart away. I like her. But there's so much up in the air right now.

She reaches for the sponge, pours some gel onto it, moves forward, and starts washing my chest. "We can still be friends with benefits," she suggests. "Just exclusive ones. Right?"

God, I adore this girl. "Okay," I murmur.

"Why don't we talk about it again when I get back from Australia?"

I nod. "Yeah. What date do you go?"

"First of May."

"And you're back in Wellington in a couple of weeks?"

"Yeah."

"I don't know if I'll have time to come down before then. Catie will have the babies any day, and Saxon will be taking a few weeks off, so I'll have to cover for him. And I'll probably have to go to Auckland for a week."

"That's okay. I wondered whether you'd like to do something on your birthday? I have an idea for a special present." She winks at me.

"Does it buzz?"

She laughs. "Actually, no. But I promise you'll enjoy it."

"Then the answer's definitely yes."

Smiling, she picks up her phone where she left it resting on the tiles. She brings up Spotify and puts on Kiwi musician Bic Runga's *Beautiful Collision* album because she knows I like it, and *Listening for the Weather* starts playing.

Feeling happy, I turn her around and pull her back against me. Then I take the sponge and begin to wash her, while the rain patters on the skylight above our heads.

*

The next morning, we check out, then carry our bags outside and both call an Uber—Belle to her father's house, me to the airport.

"I hope all goes well with Saxon and Catie," she says with a smile. "Let me know when the twins are born."

I cup her face. "I'll be texting you as soon as I get to the airport."

She flushes with pleasure. "I'll miss you," she whispers.

"I'll miss you, too." We had a great evening yesterday, ordering dinner to our room, and talking, listening to music, and making love all night.

I kiss her, taking my time, wishing she was coming with me. But I mustn't get carried away. I'll be seeing her soon, and I'm going to be super-busy until then.

Her Uber draws up, so I give her a final kiss, lift her bag into the back, and she waves goodbye and gets in. A minute later, it's heading into the traffic, and she's gone.

It's raining again. I wait inside for my Uber, then run out when it comes and get in. Soon I'm on the way to the airport, looking out through the window at the rainy day.

*

As always happens, as soon as we're apart, self-doubt sets in. She's younger than me, and still at university; she's surrounded by young guys, and I know I have plenty of flaws. Surely she'll meet someone else better than me?

But she sends me a text before I even arrive at the airport, saying what a great weekend it's been, and she can't wait to see me again. I message her back to say ditto and my next birthday is going to be the best ever. She comes back on Snapchat with a selfie of her wearing her new earrings. And that's it. From then on, over the next week, we message constantly, sending each other photos, memes, songs, and texts. We keep it light, mostly, although occasionally it turns steamy, especially once we're both home during the evening. I call her, then, and several times we have phone sex, which is a new thing for me. Hearing her innocent little gasps on the phone is enough to fire me up, and then the way she whispers dirty nothings in my ear soon has me taking myself in hand for some DIY. I know she's found a website that she's been reading, and I'm thrilled that she's trying things out, especially as I'm the recipient of her experiments.

The fear that she might meet someone else still lingers, but I don't have much time to worry about it because I'm flat out at work. Then on Friday, I get a phone call from Saxon late in the evening to say that Catie's finally gone into labor. He insists there's nothing I can do, so I wish him luck and tell him to call as soon as he has any news, go to bed, then phone Belle to tell her.

"You'll be Uncle Damon soon," she teases. "I might have to start calling you that. Or would you prefer Daddy?"

"Someone's been reading again," I say wryly. "And no, I told you, I'm not into the Daddy Dom thing."

"You do call me baby girl, though."

"True."

"So it doesn't turn you on when I say 'would you like me to go down on you, Daddy?'" She says it in a soft, breathy voice, and a shiver runs all the way down my spine.

"Every naughty thing you say turns me on," I admit, and I sigh and lie back as she proceeds to tell me all the wicked things she's going to do to me next time she sees me.

But afterward, when we end the call and I lie there, my body sated, and my mind tired, her words continue to flutter around my head like butterflies. I know she was being playful when she called me daddy, but I guess, with the imminent arrival of Saxon's babies, I feel all mixed up.

I thought I was cursed. Doomed to a life alone because of my failed relationships because I felt unlovable. But Belle's done something to me. It's as if she's shone a flashlight into my eyes and illuminated the attic of my brain, showing me that although I thought it was filled with scary dark corners, nothing is hiding there except a few dusty cobwebs. There are no monsters. Maybe a few ghosts flitting about, but they don't mean me ill.

Anxious for Saxon and worried about Catie, I doze fitfully, but it's Belle I dream about. I'm at the beach, the one where I saw her in her bikini, and I'm looking for her. Eventually I see her standing looking at the sea, but she's not fourteen—she's the age she is now. She turns as I approach, and I see she has a big bump, and she's resting her hand on it.

"Is it mine?" I ask her, heart racing.

"I waited," she says, "but you never came."

I jerk awake with a start. My phone's buzzing beneath my pillow. The crack in the curtains reveals the sun is just coming up. I take the phone out and see that it's Saxon.

I sit up, heart racing, and answer it. "Hello?"

"It's me," he says. He sounds elated. "The babies are here!"

"How are they? How's Catie?"

"Everyone's fine. Two beautiful healthy boys. And my wife is wonderful! Just amazing. I can't believe she did it! It was so fantastic. She took my breath away. She's so… you know. I can't find the words. And the boys are amazing—I have two sons! Jesus. I don't know whether to laugh or cry."

I chuckle. "You sound happy."

"I feel on top of the world! Knackered, but happy. I can't believe it. You'll come over, right? Come and see them?"

"Dude, I'll be there as soon as I get some clothes on." I hesitate. "Not every guy would have reacted the way you did if a woman turned up on their doorstep four months pregnant. You've been there through thick and thin for that girl. I'm so proud of you, man."

He doesn't say anything for a moment, and then I hear him snuffle and say, "Ah, fuck, are you trying to make me cry? I'm full of baby hormones, remember?"

I smile. "I thought that was the mum."

"Nope, definitely the dad too. Or it could just be lack of sleep. But thanks. That means a lot."

"I'll see you soon," I tell him gruffly.

"Yeah. It'll be good to see you," he says, and ends the call.

I get up and shower, then call Kip while I make myself a coffee to go. "You heading over there?" I ask when he answers.

"Yeah. You want me to pick you up on the way?" he asks.

"Yeah, sure."

"Will do." He pauses. "Weird, isn't it?"

"Just a bit." I turn and lean on the kitchen counter. "Are you okay?"

"What do you mean?"

"It must be weird, your twin having kids."

He doesn't say anything for a moment. Then he replies, "Yeah, a bit."

"How's Alice?"

"She's good."

"Everything's going okay with her?" I know that her mother has M.S., and Alice looks after her full time, which means it makes it difficult for her to see Kip, unless he flies up there.

"Yeah. I'm still not sure how we're going to work things out," he admits. "But I can't let her go, you know?"

I think about Belle. "Do you think you and she will... you know... get married and stuff? Have kids?"

"I'd like to. I just need to work out the technical issues."

"How did you know? That she was the one?"

He pauses again. "I guess you don't, really. Love doesn't come with a guarantee. But I don't like being apart from her. I think about her all the time. I'm not sure what the definition of love is, if it isn't that?"

"Yeah." I clear my throat. "Okay, see you soon?"

"I'm leaving now, I'll only be five to ten minutes."

I end the call, pull on my socks and Converses, and go out the front of my house to wait for him. It's a beautiful, sunny day, just right to celebrate the birth of the babies.

Sitting on the low wall out the front, I text Belle that Saxon's boys have been born, and I'm going to see them. She comes back, *Oh, that's amazing news! I'm so thrilled for you all. Have a cuddle with the babies and tell me all about it later!*

I will, I reply, ending with a smiley face and a heart.

Kip's right that love doesn't come with a guarantee. I guess sometimes you just need to take a chance.

Chapter Twenty-Eight

Belle

Although I miss Damon, the days speed by. In the week I set myself to studying, and I catch up with some old schoolfriends. I have a lot of kids' parties, mainly at the weekends, and when I'm free, I wander around the city doing magic tricks just for the hell of it.

When Gaby comes back from her honeymoon, I pay her a visit to tell her what I found out about Dad cheating on Mum before she had her affair.

After I've finished talking, she quietly says, "I know, Belle."

I stare at her in shock. "What do you mean? Alex didn't know."

"I overheard Dad on the phone once. He was down in the shed, and he didn't realize I was outside. He was talking to someone—Sherry, I realized later—about Mum, saying how hard life was with her. He said to the person on the phone that he really missed them… and he said a few more intimate things, before I got embarrassed and ran off. But I knew then that he was seeing someone."

"Why didn't you tell me?"

"Honestly, Belle, I didn't know how to. It all happened fast, and it was so horrible. We were all so upset."

"But I've blamed her for years," I say, my voice hoarse.

"And you were right to do so." Her voice is hard. "It was her fault."

"She had depression, Gaby. And she was under a lot of pressure."

"Then she should have quit acting and come home to look after her family. She broke up their marriage, Belle, not him. She's the one who left, and the one who shacked up with that vile man. I'll never forgive her."

I hug her then, because I don't want to make her unhappy so soon after her wedding, and say, "I'm sorry."

"It's not your fault, sweetheart." She squeezes me before releasing me. "Now, I want you to tell me all about Damon! Juliette told me that something happened on the night of the wedding…"

"We're kind of seeing each other," I say bashfully, and she squeals. "But it's really early days," I add, "and I don't want to scare him off, so don't tell Alex, okay? I want to wait until I get back from Australia, and then I'll see where things are. If Damon is still interested in seeing me, I'll tell Alex then."

She agrees to keep it to herself, although I know she'll tell Tyson, because she tells him everything. I have no doubt that Alex will find out eventually. I'll just have to deal with him when he does. He's so protective of me. I hope he takes it easy on Damon. I am a bit concerned that if Alex makes too much of a fuss, Damon will want to put his friendship and business relationship first, and he'll back off and change his mind.

He's been calling and messaging a lot, so I've tried not to worry too much about it. After Catie's babies are born, though, he has to go to Auckland, and he's super busy, so I don't hear from him quite so much. He does call every night, though, telling me about his day.

I knew he was a director of Kingpinz, of course, and that he helps Alex out at Kia Kaha, but it's only when he talks about his time in Auckland that I realize how important his work is. He's very offhand about it, but in Saxon's absence he's working at Titus's AI company, holding daily meetings with Mack Hart, who built the supercomputer that's processing all the data from the IVF trials, and Elizabeth Huxley, who's the chemist in charge of the trials. It's clear that Damon's not an empty suit who's there in name only, but that they respect his expertise with programming.

It's a bit daunting, and I can't help but wonder what on earth he sees in me. But I try not to dwell on it too deeply. He tells me he's looking forward to his birthday, and the items have arrived that I sent off for, so I'm excited about it as well.

And then, late on Easter Sunday, when I'm asleep in bed, my phone buzzes beneath my pillow, waking me up. I pull it out and look at it blearily—it's nearly one a.m., and it's Damon. I sit up and answer it with a racing heart. "Hello?"

"It's me," he says softly. "Were you asleep?"

"Yes, but it's okay. Is everything all right?"

"Ahh… not really. I'm at Kip's place."

"What's happened?"

"Kip and Saxon had a fight."

"What?"

"Yeah. Kip and Alice broke up."

"Oh no."

"We were at Mum and Dad's place, celebrating the birth of the twins. Kip was drunk and in a foul mood, being obnoxious. Eventually Saxon snapped and provoked him. So Kip hit him and broke Saxon's nose."

"Oh shit, really?"

"Yeah, there was blood everywhere. I took Kip home and put him to bed. He's vomited a few times, but now he's crashed. I think he'll be out until morning now."

"Oh Damon," I say, "I'm so sorry. Are you okay?"

"Yeah. It's just… It upset me, you know? I hate seeing them fighting. Always have."

"Of course. They'll make up though, right?"

"Yeah, I'm sure tomorrow it'll all be forgotten. Kip was so sad, though. He really loves her."

"What happened between them? Did she break it off or did he?"

"She did. I think she's convinced they won't be able to make it work, and she wanted to end it sooner rather than later." He goes quiet.

I sit back on the pillows. "And that's made you think?" He doesn't reply. "Is there something you want to say to me?" I ask softly, my heart racing. "Are you calling me to end it?"

"No. I don't want that. I wondered if you thought we should."

"Because I'm going to Australia?"

"Not necessarily. I just wondered why you want to be with me? I'm fucked up, Belle. You deserve better."

I let out a breath slowly. He doesn't want to break up with me. He's just feeling insecure, that's all.

"You're not fucked up," I tell him. "And you're not cursed, whatever you think. You're a kind, generous man who's been hurt badly. And you deserve love the same as any other human being. Kip's a pretty determined guy, right? He's rich and resourceful. He'll figure it out and win her back. If a love between two people is strong enough, it'll work out."

"You think?"

"I do."

We both fall quiet for a moment. We haven't said we love each other yet. It's too early for that. But I know he's wondering whether what we have—whatever it is—is strong enough to last.

"Get some sleep," I tell him. "And I'll be seeing you very soon. I have your present all ready and wrapped up!"

"Do I get any hints?" he asks, amused.

"Let's just say it'll help you express your natural talents."

He chuckles. Then he says, "I'm close to finishing my painting of you, by the way. It'll be ready by the time I see you."

"Oh…" I've never had anyone paint a picture of me before. "That's exciting. I can't wait to see it."

"I hope you like it."

"I'm sure I will, Damon. You're an amazing artist."

He sighs. "You always know what to say to make me feel better."

"That's what I'm here for." I smile. "Sleep well, honey."

"And you, baby girl."

I shiver, sigh, and end the call.

*

Sure enough, Damon messages me the next day to say that Kip and Saxon have made up, and that Kip's heading up to Alice's house in Gisborne to try and patch things up. A few days later, he lets me know that Kip proposed, Alice said yes, and she's going to move down to Wellington with her mum to live with him.

I'm thrilled, both for them and for Damon, because seeing both his brothers settled and happy can only have a positive impact on him.

The next week is super busy for both of us. He's back in Auckland, and I start packing up my things ready to go back to Wellington for the start of the next university term. On Saturday, we have a big family dinner, so I get to say goodbye to Dad, Sherry, Gaby, Tyson, and Alex, and then on Sunday I fly back up to Wellington.

The next few months are going to be interesting. I'm heading off to Australia in a fortnight, and that's going to be a very different eight weeks for me. I'm nervous about it, but determined to enjoy it. First, though, I have two weeks in Wellington, and of course, Damon's birthday.

He calls me the night before to let me know he's back from Auckland. "How were your first two days at uni?" he asks.

I'm back in the house I share with Jo and two other girls, currently in my room, sitting on my bed. I glance over at the door, where Damon burst through only five weeks ago to rescue me from my ex's clutches. My lips curve up.

"Intense and rather dull," I reply, "but not bad. You still on for tomorrow?"

"Definitely." I can tell he's smiling. "You want me to come and pick you up?"

"No, it's okay, I'll come over to yours if you like?"

"Sure. I'll text you the address. Unfortunately, I've got an afternoon meeting that I can't miss, but I'll be home just after five."

"No worries, I'll see you then."

In the end, the next day my Uber pulls up outside his home at nearly 5:15. The drive is empty, but I assume his F-Type is in the double garage. I thank the driver and get out, and he drives away, leaving me surrounded by trees, the only sound the occasional twitter of birds and the rustling of the leaves.

Jesus, I'd forgotten how rich he is. The house is built high on one of the many hills surrounding Wellington, and in the distance I can see the city, and the glittering water of the harbor beyond it. It's a magnificent view. The house itself is on several levels, and as I enter the gates I realize it has a pool and a generous deck that runs around the side and front of the house. The walls are mostly glass, and just down the steps must be his studio, because I can see several canvases on easels. It looks huge. Wow.

Shouldering my bag, I walk down to his front door. It opens before I reach it, and there he is, barefoot, wearing black trackpants and a gray tee, looking oh-my-God gorgeous, and smiling.

"Damon!" I drop my bag, run up to him, and throw my arms around his neck. "Oh, happy birthday!"

He laughs and hugs me, his strong arms squeezing and making me gasp. Then he lowers me down, takes my face in his hands, and kisses me. Mmm... this man sure knows how to kiss. His lips move across mine with slow, deliberate kisses, and then he slides his tongue into my mouth, and everything turns sultry and sexy, making my head spin.

"Ooohhh..." I sigh when he finally releases me. "What a welcome."

He chuckles and picks up my bag. "I've missed you, can you tell? Come on in."

I take the hand he offers and let him lead me inside. "Oh Damon, this place is amazing."

"I'm so glad you like it. I fell in love with it when I first saw it."

"It's very you." It's spacious, open plan, and filled with light. The furniture is minimalist—chrome, glass, and cream leather. The kitchen is large and clean. There's a dining table that seats eight and an outside table too, and a covered area on the deck with an outdoor suite, lamps, and a deck heater—I'm guessing he spends a lot of time out there.

He takes me through to the other end of the house, showing me the small gym, the several spare rooms, and the impressive master bedroom. The huge bed faces the window, with all the wardrobes behind it, so there's nothing to mar the incredible view.

The only thing more impressive than the bed is the bathroom. It's all white marble, and at the far end is a square area with a couple of steps up, and a ginormous white sunken bath.

"Wow," I say. "That's amazing."

"Looking forward to getting in it with you," he says, smirking. I grin, because my birthday present for him will definitely mean we'll need a good wash afterwards, so I'm very happy with that!

Lastly, he takes me into his studio. It's clear that it was once a dance studio because of the mirrors on one wall, but it also makes a great artist's studio. The setting sun glints off the mirrors, filling the room with a golden light. It feels peaceful and positive—he's happy when he's in here.

He takes me up to a sheet-covered canvas on an easel and gives me a mischievous look.

"It's finished," he says. "Want to see?"

Suddenly I'm nervous. I'm determined to pretend I like it, even if I don't, but I'm anxious as to what it's going to look like.

"Okay," I whisper.

He lifts the sheet from the corners of the canvas and lets it drop.

I stare at it. He's painted a Greek goddess, dressed in a diaphanous white gown. She has dark hair curled to hang over one shoulder, and the strands are decorated with small white flowers. Her golden armband is studded with jewels. She looks like Aphrodite. But it's quite clearly me.

"It's called *Limerence*," he says softly.

I blink and look at him.

"It means obsession, or all-consuming passion," he adds.

SERENITY WOODS

My jaw dropping, I look back at the painting. "I thought it was just going to be a portrait of me," I whisper. "You've made me into a goddess."

"I haven't made you into anything. This is how I see you."

I give a short laugh. "Talk about putting a girl on a pedestal. Damon, if you see me like this, you're going to be sorely disappointed. I'm about as far from being a goddess as it's possible to be."

He moves behind me, slides his arms around my waist, and kisses my shoulder. "You're kind, gentle, funny, elegant, and warm. You make me feel whole again, Belle. Ma belle. My beautiful girl." He turns me in his arms to face him.

Then he kisses me again.

I'm so overcome, I can't say anything. I try to blink the tears away, but they trickle out anyway, and soon my cheeks are damp with them. He lifts his head and looks at me, puzzled, brushing them away with his thumbs. "Don't cry."

"I'm sorry. It's just… nobody's ever seen me like this before."

He looks at my mouth. "I've seen you like this ever since that day on the beach. I'm crazy about you." He hesitates. "When I asked Kip how he knew that Alice was the one, he said he didn't like being apart from her, and that he thought about her all the time. He said if that's not the definition of love, then what is? So… I think I'm in love with you, Belle."

I glance at the painting, then back at him. "I think I'm in love with you, too." How can I not be, when this guy looks at me and sees this?

We study each other for a moment.

"Didn't expect to say that," he says, looking surprised.

"Me neither." I smile and sniff.

He grins and moves closer to me, holding my hands. Then he looks around the studio. "I've never had sex in here," he says. He looks back and gives an impish smile. "There's a first time for everything."

I hold up a finger. "First of all, I have to give you your birthday present."

He chuckles. "Okay."

I look around. There's a sofa, but I was hoping for some cushions. "Hold on. I have to get something."

I run out of the room, grab the duvet from his bed, bring it back in, and lie it on the floor, in front of the windows. I get the sheet that was covering the painting and put it over the top. Then I retrieve my bag

290

and take out the present I bought for him. It's in a medium-sized box. He watches me do all this with amusement.

"Here you go." I hand it to him.

Giving me a puzzled look, he tears off the wrapping. It's a tub of body paints in all the basic colors plus a few metallic and sparkly ones, complete with a black eyeliner for detailed work, and sponge applicators.

His eyebrows rise, and he stares at me.

I toe off my shoes and take off my socks. Then I peel off my T-shirt. I'm not wearing a bra, and his eyes widen. My jeans follow, and now I'm just wearing a pair of black lacy knickers I bought especially.

"Thought you might like to paint me," I tell him, my heart racing. "Then you can take some photos, if you like. And after that, maybe we could have a bath. They wash off with water." I lift my hair, which had been down, and pin it up with a butterfly clip I had in my bag.

A smile spreads slowly across his face. "That's the best birthday present I've ever had."

I grin. "Why don't you go and get us a drink? Then you can get painting."

He pauses though, pulls me into his arms, and gives me a long, slow kiss, before he leaves me to pour us both a drink.

Blowing out a breath, I sit on the sheet-covered duvet and wait for him to come back. He returns with two tall glasses of G&T. Putting them on the polished floorboards, he brings over a low table and transfers the drinks and the paints onto them. He adds a roll of kitchen paper, some rags, a jar of water, brushes, and a few other items. He also collects his phone and puts on a playlist of some folksy blues.

Then he stands in front of me and starts unbuttoning his jeans with a sexy smile, keeping his gaze fixed on me.

"The plan was for you to paint first," I say, a bit faintly.

"Thought you might enjoy having a go, too," he says. He slides the jeans down his legs and steps out of them, grabs a handful of his tee at the back of his neck, and tugs it off. Now he's just wearing his black boxer-briefs.

I feel a swell of happiness as he lowers onto the duvet opposite me, and we sit cross-legged in front of each other. He passes me my drink, and we clink glasses and have a few mouthfuls.

He leans forward, slides a hand to the back of my neck, and brings me close so he can kiss me. When he finally releases me, I look across again at the painting he calls *Limerence*, still stunned by how beautiful he's made me look.

"I wonder how many of your women you've made into goddesses," I tease. Juliette told me he has several canvases hanging in his office at Kingpinz.

"Just you," he says. "None of my other paintings were inspired by real women."

"Seriously?"

"I never lie."

"Oh yeah," I say softly. "I forgot."

He smiles and turns to the box of paints. He gets out the pots and opens them up, so the colors are all ready to dip into. Then he passes me a brush and takes one for himself.

"I'm not great at painting," I say doubtfully.

He laughs. "Just cover me in rainbows if you like. I don't care. Go on. You can start."

I sit and study him for a moment. What kind of design should I do? I think of the painting he did of Rangi and Papatūānuku. In Māori legend, their son is called Rehua. He's also known as the Lord of Kindness.

Smiling, I dip the brush into the yellow paint and draw it across his chest.

Chapter Twenty-Nine

Damon

Belle paints for a while, as the sun goes down, and the light turns from gold to orange to purple. Normally at night I put on the overhead lights, but I don't want to ruin the sensual nature of this activity, so when it's too dark to see, I turn on a couple of lamps instead, moving them to cast us in a warm glow. Even though it's a large room, I also make sure the heat pump is on high so Belle doesn't get cold.

At one point, we take a break so I can refill our glasses, and then it's time for me to pick up my brush and start my masterpiece.

I start by turning her around so I can do her back first. I use the white and gold paint mostly, and she shivers when I first draw the brush across her skin.

I have to fight not to keep stopping to kiss her while I paint, because I want to finish it tonight. But it's impossible not to lean forward occasionally and press my lips to her neck or shoulder.

Her thoughtful present delighted me, as did the way she reacted to me saying I was in love with her. It would have been so easy for her to laugh it off, but the way she repeated it immediately filled me with incredible joy. I want to return that gift, and the only way I know how is to give her pleasure. But first, I want to finish the painting.

I paint across her shoulders and along her arms, and continue the design down her spine. When I'm done, I turn around so she can do my back, then return so I can work on her front.

I lose myself in it for a while, loving the notion of using the colors to follow the dips and curves of her body. I spend a long time on her breasts, enjoying drawing the brush over each swell, and painting around her nipples.

When we're finally happy with each other's bodies, we move a little closer and begin painting each other's faces.

Now it's impossible not to kiss her, and she seems to find it as hard to stay apart as I do. We kiss, and paint, and kiss, and paint, and the kisses grow longer, and the brush marks become shorter, until eventually we drop our brushes and I sink my hands into her hair and kiss her hard, delving my tongue into her mouth, turned on by hours of touching and yet not touching her. She moans, holding her hands out, not knowing where to touch me, and it's with some reluctance that I eventually move back and say, "Okay, maybe we should admire our handiwork now."

Breathless, she nods, and we get to our feet and go and stand in front of the mirrored wall.

"I've turned you into Rehua," she tells me. "The star god with the power to heal." She gestures to the big star on my chest. I rotate slowly, seeing that she's transformed me into the night sky, covering my back and arms with golden stars.

"Wow." I'm genuinely impressed.

"He's a heavenly guardian," she whispers, kissing my shoulder. "Just like you are mine. You saved me, Damon. I don't want to come on all heavy, but even in the short time we've spent together, you've healed me, and shown me what it's like to feel loved. Whatever happens now, I'm thankful for that." She slides her arms around me from behind and kisses the back of my neck.

Touched by her words, I stand there for a moment, resting my arms on hers. Then I bring her around to stand her before me. I've had some fun painting her front, and I've filled her skin with a sixties-style paisley pattern of teardrop shapes in psychedelic colors. She spends a while admiring my work, telling me, "I love it, Damon." But it's only when I turn her around and show her the reflection of her back that her eyes widen.

I lift her arms so they're outstretched, which reveals the painting in all its glory. I've drawn a pair of wings on her back, arms, and shoulders, outlined in black and filled in with glorious silver and gold.

"My angel," I tell her.

She doesn't answer. It's only now that she can see that hidden between all the feathers is a word, emblazoned across her shoulder blades in reverse so she can see it in the reflection.

Her eyes meet mine. "You've written your name."

"I'm branding you," I tell her. "Even when you wash it off, it'll stay there. So you don't forget me."

"Forget you?"

I shrug. "When you meet all those young Aussie dudes."

Her expression turns wry, and she turns to lift her arms around my neck. "Yeah, because I'm totally going there for the sex."

I narrow my eyes at her. "Don't mock me. I might end up handcuffing you to the bed and refusing to let you go."

"Promises, promises," she whispers, lifting up to kiss me.

I sigh, and we kiss for a long time, moving a little to the music that's still playing. Gradually, though, it gets harder not to press myself against her, and finally I say, "Maybe we should get in the bath now?"

"Aw." She sighs. "Yeah, I guess. Photos first though, right?"

"Are you sure?"

"I trust you," she says.

Oddly, that means more to me than anything else she could have said. I cup her face, looking into her eyes, then give her a quick kiss before I grab our phones, and we take a few pictures of each other.

Only then do we head for the bathroom, and I start filling the deep, sunken bath with hot water, adding a generous amount of bubble bath. I've already placed half a dozen candles around it, and I light them now, filling the room with a warm glow.

We get ourselves another drink, and then when the bath's half full, we strip off our underwear, then lower ourselves down into the soapy water.

"Ooh, that's nice." She waits for me to get in, then moves up close to me, turning so her back is to my chest. I slide my arms around her, and we both sigh, relaxing and sliding down until the bubbles are up to our necks. "I absolutely adore this bath," she says. "The view is amazing."

"It's one reason I loved the house." You can see right over the city from here, and we're not overlooked either, so there's no need for curtains or blinds.

I kiss her neck, moving my hands over her body beneath the hot water. "Thank you so much for my birthday present. I loved it."

"I'm so glad." She turns a little to look up at me. "And thank you for your gorgeous painting of me."

"You're welcome." I kiss her. Then I pour some shower gel onto a sponge. "I'll do your back first."

Slowly, I wash the wings off her back, and I turn in the bath so she can do mine. Next she cleans my front, and lastly I bring her so her back is against my chest again, and wash her shoulders and breasts.

By this point, we're both aroused and kissing between every stroke of the sponge. Her skin glows from the heat of the bath and where we've scrubbed to get the paint off, and now she's rosy all over, strands of her hair curling at the nape of her neck.

"I want to tell you something," she whispers, sitting astride me and moving up close, her arms looped behind my head.

"Okay."

"I... um... had a Mirena IUD fitted last week. And I'm clean. So... if you didn't want to use a condom... you don't have to." She kisses my nose. "It's up to you. If you'd rather use one, that's fine too."

"I've never had sex without one," I tell her honestly. "Are you sure?" She nods, and I swallow hard. "Okay then." I clear my throat, once again touched that she trusts me. "Before that, though... I have a present for you," I reveal.

Her lips curve up. "It's not my birthday."

"I know. But it's a present for me, too." I lean across to the item that's sitting just behind the candles and bring it forward.

"Oh!" Her eyes widen. "I thought it was a candle."

I pass it to her, and she takes it. It's in the shape of a large rosebud that nestles comfortably in her hand. On the top, in the middle, is a hole not much bigger than the end of a pencil.

She investigates the smooth silicone surface, her face flushing. "What does it do?"

"It's a clitoral suction vibrator," I murmur. "You might have seen it on TikTok. Apparently it's supposed to give very intense orgasms."

I show her how to turn it on by holding down the button on the front. It leaps into life with a low hum. She places it on her palm, her eyebrows rising as she obviously feels the light suction on her skin.

"Turn around," I whisper.

Her eyes meet mine, and her pupils are as big as saucers. She turns in the water, leaning back against me, and I scoop all the bubbles toward us and wrap my arms around her so she feels all safe and secure.

"Try it on here," I tell her, cupping her breasts beneath the water.

"It's waterproof?"

"Yeah."

"Oh." She slips the rose beneath the surface of the water, and I slide my hands up her arms so I can feel when she places the end over her nipple. She gives a slight jump. "Ooh!"

I chuckle. "How does it feel?"

"Mmm. Quite nice, actually." She passes her other hand through the water, making it swirl over our skin. Her body is tense, and I think she's nervous.

"Try to relax," I tell her, kissing her neck. "It's supposed to be quite intense, especially if you're sensitive down there. So do whatever you feel comfortable with." I kiss her neck, her throat, and up to her ear. "I just want to make you feel good."

She sighs and lifts her face so I can kiss her. "You're so good to me," she whispers against my lips.

"It's only what you deserve, baby girl."

She moves her bottom against my erection, and I murmur my approval. I've been fired up at the thought of this all day, and although I want her to concentrate on herself, I want her badly.

Beneath the water, I slide a hand up her thigh to between her legs and slip my fingers into her folds. She's swollen and slippery, more than ready for me.

"Would you like me inside you while you use it?" I ask her.

She looks up at me, and gives me a beautiful smile. "You're sure?"

I nod. "I've been thinking about you doing this for days. But... if you'd rather I wait, that's fine."

"No, I'm ready."

Lifting her a little so she's on my lap, I slide a hand under each thigh and move her legs so they're either side of mine. When I feel the tip of my erection part her folds, I release her so she sinks down onto me.

"Jesus," she says, closing her eyes.

"Ahhh…" I ease my way into her, making it all the way inside after a few careful thrusts. The sensation of being inside her without a barrier is incredible. "You feel amazing…"

She leans back against me, and now, impaled on me, she's open wide, with plenty of room to use the toy.

Taking it in her right hand, she moves it down between her legs. I place my hand on hers so I can follow her movements.

"As slow as you like," I whisper.

She guides it up her thighs and nestles it in her folds.

Then she jumps, says, "Ooh!" and laughs.

I chuckle. "I told you it was intense."

"Oh my God." She leans back and does it again. "Oh wow."

"Move it around and try different angles."

She turns her hand, directing it, her body jerking as it obviously hits the spot. "Oh! Mmm... ooh! Wow."

I try not to laugh. "How does it feel?"

"Ee-ow! Powerful. Oh my God, Damon. Ooh!"

I kiss her neck and bring my hands up to cup her breasts. "Too much?"

"No, no... ooh! It's just... so... intense!" After a few moments, relaxes back. "Mmm... oh yeah... that's better..."

"Found the right place?"

"Mmm..."

I tug her nipples lightly. "Tell me how it feels."

"Mmm... pretty amazing... ooh! Mmm..." She sucks her bottom lip. "Ooh yeah..."

She continues like that for a couple of minutes, her body giving sexy little jerks every now and again, while she continues to suck her bottom lip and emit tiny moans that have me fighting not to hold her and thrust up into her.

When she begins to rock her hips, driving me in and out of her, it sends me nearly insane.

"Oh man, that feels good..." she says.

"You feel terrific," I say, my voice husky with desire.

"Oh, I... mmm... oh! Mmm..." She opens her eyes and looks up at me. "Ah..."

"What?"

"I..." She looks amused. "I don't think this is going to take very long."

"Really?" I'm thrilled.

"No. It's very... mmm... strong and... fierce... oh fuck..." She closes her eyes again. "Oh jeez..."

"Tell me how it feels," I demand.

"Oh God... I can't... speak... so... intense..." She stiffens and holds her breath, her lips parting, then her brow creases, and she says, "Oh, oh, oh my God! Ohhhh!" She squeals, and then she clamps around me, her body contracting in numerous strong pulses that seem to go on forever. I try to hold back, but I'd have to be superhuman not to come, and I've forgotten my cape and tights. It feels so sensitive without a condom, and there's no hope of me waiting. Without any effort at all, I erupt inside her, and the two of us lock together, as she clenches and exclaims, and I groan, for what feels like an eternity.

When she finally lifts the rose and turns it off, I let my head drop back on the edge of the bath, completely spent.

"Holy shit," she says, panting. She looks around at me then. "Did you just… come?"

I start laughing. "There was no way I was going to survive that."

"Oh my God."

"I'm so sorry."

She joins in laughing, though, and in the end I withdraw from her and turn her so I can give her a hug.

"I'm sorry that was so quick," I say.

"I'm flattered." She kisses my chest, then rests her forehead on it. "Jesus, Damon."

I stroke her hair and chuckle. "Did that feel good?"

"You have no idea."

"Come on, you've got to explain it to me."

She lifts her head, looking totally bewildered. "I've been practicing a bit," she admits. "So I'm sort of getting used to the feeling. But that was completely different."

"In what way?"

"I dunno… it started with this really intense contraction across the bottom of my tummy, and I mean really intense, almost painful, and then the pulses were…" She mimes her head exploding. "And it went on forever. It was incredible."

"So it worked, then?"

She gives me a wild look. "Like you wouldn't believe."

I pick up the rose and kiss it. "You can take it to Australia with you and practice while you're there."

"Oh my God, what if Customs see it?"

"It just looks like a candle. I'm sure they've seen far worse, anyway."

She giggles, turning it in her fingers. Then she puts it down and leans on my chest, looking at me. "Was it good for you, too?"

"Best. Birthday. Ever."

She chuckles. Then she leans forward, and we exchange a long, luxurious kiss.

"We should get out," she says eventually. "I'm turning into a prune, plus this water is disgusting."

I laugh. "You want a quick shower?"

"Might not be the worst idea."

So while the bath drains, we get under the shower and rinse off the last of the paint. Afterward, we dry ourselves on the big fluffy towels, and I pull on my track pants, while she tugs on a pair of pjs from her bag, and then we head off to the kitchen. We're both hungry, so we make ourselves a platter of cold meat, cheeses, pickles, and thickly buttered bread, and take it into the living room to eat. We sit on the sofa together, she chooses a movie to watch, and we dip into the platter, stretch out together, and just enjoy being in each other's company.

When the movie finishes, we tidy up and take everything to the kitchen, I lock up, and then make our way to the bedroom. We clean our teeth together, then climb in bed and cuddle up.

I've left the curtains open, and it's clear tonight, so we can see the stars twinkling on the night sky. I realize how happy I am.

I wish she wasn't going away. I want her by my side permanently.

The realization hits me hard enough to take my breath away.

We've already admitted we're in love. But it's too soon for declarations like that, surely? I know that even though it would make my brothers laugh hysterically to hear it, deep down, I'm a romantic. Maybe I just want this to work. I'm hoping it will work. But how do you know if any girl is 'the one'?

I need to wait. Her being away will be a good test of our feelings for one another. Maybe when she's gone, the magic will fade, and I'll wonder why everything felt so intense.

And if it doesn't, that'll be the time to declare how I'm feeling.

She kisses my chest, then my jaw, then my mouth. "How are you feeling?" she whispers.

My lips curve up beneath hers. "If I was to say horny, would that be too forward?"

She giggles. "I wondered whether I wore you out earlier."

"Nowhere near, baby girl. You're not sore?" I could tell how intense the sensations the rose aroused in her were.

But she shakes her head. "I want you," she murmurs, moving up the bed a little so she can kiss me properly. "So much. Plus, it is your birthday. You deserve a treat."

"I do," I agree. "You have to do what I say, right? Isn't that the law?"

"Oh, absolutely."

I lift up and roll her onto her back. "Then lie down, open your legs, and let me have my wicked way with you as many times as I can manage it."

Her eyes flare. I wonder whether she's going to say again that she doesn't expect multiple orgasms, but she doesn't. Does she understand that I feel guilty for not pleasuring her more in the bath? Sure, the orgasm she had seemed intense, but I'd rather it had been the culmination of a lovemaking session. I want to make love to her, but I need to make it last this time.

She lifts her arms around my neck, slides her hands into my hair, and pulls my head down so she can kiss me. "You can do whatever you want to me," she whispers. "As many times as you like, Damon. You're amazing, and I'll never say no to such a generous offer."

My throat tightens. Unable to speak, I just kiss her, savoring the softness of her lips. Then I kiss slowly down her throat, over her collar bone, and down to her breasts.

I kiss her nipples for ages, licking and sucking until she's squirming beneath me, then finally move between her legs, lower down, and slide my tongue into her folds. Ohhh... she's swollen and wet, and she tastes heavenly.

I tease her to the edge, then stop and kiss her thighs, and repeat that a few times, until her breaths are coming in deep gasps, and she's begging me to let her come. Only then do I take her all the way, her cries of satisfaction filling me with a satisfied glow.

I'm not done yet, though. I move up and kiss her while I arouse her again with my fingers. Then, after she comes again, I roll so she's on top of me and kiss her for ages, until she takes my hands, pins them above my head, and begs me to let her take me inside her. Finally satisfied that I've done enough, I let her climb and sink down on top of me, and it's a short journey then to the end, as I watch her ride me, her beautiful face creased with pleasure as she teeters on the edge and then topples over.

When she's done, she leans over me, still moving, and covers my mouth with hers. "Sweet boy," she whispers, "come for me, baby."

So I let her take me all the way, until I cry out with the sheer intensity of it, erupting inside her with a deep groan.

She lies on my chest and nuzzles my neck while my heart returns to something approaching its normal pace.

"I love you," she says.

I kiss her hair. "I love you too."

"Happy birthday."

I smile, running my hands down her back, and give a long, content sigh.

Chapter Thirty

Damon

We see each other as many times as we can over the next two weeks, which is better than nothing, although it's not as much as I'd like. She's busy at uni, and I'm flat out at work, plus I have to go to Auckland for a few days, so our meetings consist of snatched visits late at night, frantic lovemaking, and then curling up in bed, not wanting to be apart, until the sun rises the next morning.

The first of May approaches all too soon, though, and then it's time for us to say goodbye, as she departs New Zealand for her eight-week internship in Sydney. I take her to the airport, and we hug for ages in the flight lounge before she finally kisses me goodbye with tears in her eyes and heads for the gate.

It's only three-and-a-half hours to Sydney, but the Tasman Sea— what Kiwis nickname The Ditch—divides us, and the fact that she's in another country depresses me. I mope around for the first week, missing her at night, trying to tell myself to man up and that I don't need a woman to make me complete, then spending ages either messaging her or calling her when she eventually gets back to the apartment she's sharing with another girl from the law firm where she's working.

By the end of the second week, I'm missing her so much that I tentatively suggest I fly over and see her. I keep the suggestion as lighthearted as possible—no worries if you're busy, please say if you'd rather I didn't—but Belle is thrilled and says she'd love to see me. So I hop on a plane to Sydney for the weekend and I treat her to a couple of nights in one of the city's most luxurious hotels. We spend most of the weekend in bed or in the sumptuous restaurant, only leaving the hotel for a quick stretch of our legs. I take a selfie of the two of us in front of the Opera House, and that becomes my screensaver for the next few weeks.

After that, I fly out to see her every weekend. Well, what's the point in being a billionaire if you can't treat yourself?

The days slowly slip by. I spend a week in Auckland, then a week in Christchurch, helping Alex at Kia Kaha. I'm also starting work on a new project with Kip, working on an innovative facial prosthetic, and that's taking up a lot of my time. May turns into June, and Belle announces she's halfway through, which delights us both.

It's now officially winter Down Under. We're heading toward the solstice, which is going to be extra special this year. Saxon and Catie married back in January while they were away in the Bay of Islands, Saxon deliberately keeping the event quiet because he wanted to surprise her but wasn't sure how she'd react. It worked, but it did mean none of his close friends and family were able to be there, so now that the babies are born and Catie has settled down a lot, they've decided to renew their vows on the twenty-first and invite everyone to our parents' large home for a big party.

I have mixed feelings about it. I'm thrilled for Saxon and Catie, and it'll be fun to see friends and family that I haven't seen for a while. They're also having a baby naming ceremony, and I'm going to be one of the Guide Parents and promise to keep an eye on the babies as they grow up. I'm looking forward to that.

But I'm also feeling oddly restless, and deep down, although I'd never admit it to them, I'm jealous that both my brothers have their happy endings all sewn up. Seeing Belle at weekends isn't enough for me. When we're not together, I feel edgy and irritable. When she says she's only interested in me, and that she's not going out with other men, it's not that I don't trust her, but I can't believe she's not being surrounded by a flock of interested guys who are all clamoring for her attention. The thought makes me want to put my fist through the wall.

I realize it's one situation that's completely out of my control, and I'm not used to that. When you're rich, it's rare to be out of control. If you throw enough money at a problem, it usually makes it go away. But this won't vanish by flashing dollars around. I just have to accept that Belle will be back soon, and until then I need to wait.

I'm not great at waiting and accepting, and it's not doing my blood pressure any good.

I spend the evenings in the studio, working somewhat feverishly, sketching and painting goddesses and angels that all somehow seem to look like her.

The end of June creeps ever closer. She's coming back to New Zealand on Saturday the twenty-fourth, and now I can start counting the days. I have an important meeting with Kip and some American visitors the Saturday before she gets here so for once I can't go to Sydney, but I've been counting the days and I'm down to single figures now, so it makes the waiting a little easier.

Nine days. Eight. Seven…

The Sunday before she's due to come home, I spend the morning working at home, finishing off a report for Kip, then give myself the afternoon off. I work out for an hour, take a shower, then decide I'm going to spend a while Googling places to take Belle when she gets back. I want some kind of luxury lodge in the middle of nowhere, with a great view from the bedroom over a lake or the sea, as I don't plan on letting her out of bed for days…

I've just opened my laptop when the doorbell rings.

It startles me, because I rarely get visitors without warning. If Saxon or Kip are going to call in, they usually text me first.

I'm only in a tee and track pants, but I'm presentable enough. Running a hand through my hair, I go up to the front door and open it.

It's Alex.

I stare at him in surprise. "Hey, dude! What are you doing here?"

He's leaning against the post that holds up the porch roof but pushes off as I stand back. "Coming to see you," he says, walking into the house past me.

"I meant what are you doing in Wellington?" I close the door behind him.

"I told you, coming to see you." He goes into the living room, then turns and waits for me.

I frown, because he usually only comes to Wellington on business, maybe once a month, and we usually meet either at my office or at his hotel in the city. He's never actually been to my house. He's wearing jeans and an All-Blacks shirt, not a suit, so he's obviously not here on business.

"Something up?" I ask, concerned.

He slides his hands into his pockets, and his gaze drifts past me. I turn and follow it, and realize he's looking at *Limerence* where I've hung it on the wall. It's quite clearly Belle in the flowing robes.

I look back at Alex. He doesn't seem surprised. Oh… he knows about us. That's why he's here.

I go completely cold. Belle and I have joked about how to tell Alex about us, making teasing comments about how he's going to go thermonuclear when he finds out, but the truth is that she's his baby sister, and he's very protective of her. The reason I haven't told him is because I don't want to jeopardize our friendship or our business relationship.

We study each other for about thirty seconds. His gaze is steady, calm. My heart races, and my mouth has gone dry.

I can't think what to say. This guy is my best friend. He told me years ago to stay away from her, and I know I've betrayed our friendship by seeing Belle. I can't talk my way out of this. And I don't want to. I surprise myself by feeling a surge of resentfulness. I'm crazy about Belle. Of all the people that could be dating his sister, surely I'm one of the better options?

I realize he's waiting for me to explain myself. I clear my throat. "Are you going to hit me?"

He rarely smiles, but for the first time the corners of his mouth curve up. "Do I need to?"

I blow out a breath. "Did you Uber here?" He nods. "You want a whisky?"

"Yeah, sure."

I lead the way into the kitchen, retrieve two crystal whisky glasses, and toss in some ice cubes. I take out a bottle of forty-two-year-old Bunnahabhain Islay malt and, hoping he can't see the way my hand is shaking, pour a splash in each glass, then pass him one. He takes it, and when I gesture at the living room, he goes in.

I look at the bottle of malt, pick it up, and take it in with me. I think I might need it before the night is out.

He sits in one of the armchairs and leans back, one ankle on the opposite knee. "I could totally take you, you know," he says, having a mouthful of the whisky.

I give a short laugh. He's lighter than me, and although we haven't wrestled in many years, I'm pretty sure I'd win any physical battle. "You and whose army?"

"I'd cut you down with my witty sarcasm."

"That I can believe."

He runs his tongue across his teeth and swirls the whisky over the ice in his glass. "When were you going to tell me?"

"Soon," I say. "How did you find out?"

"Juliette let it slip. She's very upset about it."

"Did you yell at her?"

"A little bit. It came out of left field."

"I'm sorry. I should have told you before now, but I wanted to make sure there was something to tell, you know?" I realize that might sound as if I expected my fling with his sister to be a short-lived sex-fest, and almost blush. "I mean… Christ. You know how much I value your friendship. I would never jeopardize that…" Except I have, haven't I? I swallow hard and stare into my whisky glass.

"Bro," he says softly, "I'm not mad at you."

I stare at him. "What?"

"Dude, she's twenty-one. She can date whoever she likes. And I can hardly be outraged if she chooses you. You're smart, dependable, loyal, and loaded. You're my best mate. I'd rather her be with you than anyone else in the world. It's not her I'm worried about."

I blink. "Huh?"

He has another mouthful of whisky. "You've been through some shit, that's all. I know you have issues after what happened with Christian and Kennedy."

I've never told him the more intimate details, but I guess he's picked up through the years that Christian's death had a profound effect on me.

"The thing is," he continues, "Belle is…" He hesitates. "She's complicated. And I'm worried about the pressure it might put on you."

We study each other quietly. I'm both touched and flabbergasted that it's me he seems to be worried about. And now I'm concerned at what he's insinuating.

"What do you mean, complicated?" I ask eventually.

"I don't think you know everything."

"We don't have secrets from one another," I reply, but I'm not feeling so certain now.

"You know that Kaitlyn pays her university fees," he says.

"Yeah."

"It was she who organized the internship in Sydney."

"Yeah, I know."

"She's friends with one of the partners. And they're going to offer Belle a full-time job when she graduates."

I have a mouthful of whisky, even though it's suddenly hard to swallow. "You know she hates law, right?"

His eyebrows rise. He didn't know.

"And you know how much she loves her kids' parties?" I continue. "She wants to do it full time."

"Seriously?"

"Yeah."

"So you'd let her throw away four years of study?" he asks.

"It's not about me 'letting' her do anything," I say sharply. "If she wants to do it, I'd support her, financially and emotionally."

He purses his lips. You can't always tell what Alex is thinking, but I'm pretty sure that comment impressed him.

He stares into his glass for a moment. Then he says, "What do you know about Tom?"

It's my turn to lift my eyebrows. "Kaitlyn's partner?"

"Yeah."

"Uh… she left your dad to be with him. She was with him for about a year, and then they broke up. I don't know much more. I asked you at the time what happened, but you wouldn't talk about it."

"You know that Belle and Gaby used to stay with them on weekends in Wellington."

"Yeah, and live with your dad and Sherry in Christchurch during the week."

He finishes off his whisky and puts the glass on the table. "Tom sexually abused Belle during that year, until she finally told Kaitlyn. That's why she broke up with him."

My jaw drops. Oh Jesus.

"Belle was twelve," Alex continues. "To be fair to Kait, as soon as Belle told her, she took the girls and walked out. She went straight to Dad, and he went thermonuclear. He phoned the police immediately, and Tom was put away."

"Fuck."

"He used to work at the local sports center, and it turned out he'd also abused several other girls."

"What about Gaby? Did he…"

"No. He must have thought she'd tell on him. She was fifteen, and she's always been more outspoken. Belle was an easier target, I guess— younger, gentler, more timid."

I wonder whether Belle ever resented Gaby because Tom left her alone? I know Belle loves her, but equally they're not as close as some sisters I've seen. I wonder also how it affected Gaby. Is it one reason why she's stood by Tyson? Because she felt she couldn't help her sister? Who knows. It's clear that it's obviously screwed over the whole family.

Oh, Belle. I think of her at the age of twelve, quiet and unsure, shy and yet already beautiful, and white-hot anger boils in my stomach at the thought of what happened to her.

"Anyway," Alex continues, "Tom got life, and had to serve ten years before he was eligible for parole. But he's out next year."

"Does she know?"

"No. I haven't mentioned it. She refuses to talk about it. I'm guessing she hasn't told you?"

I give an abrupt shake of my head.

"I don't know if he'll live in Wellington," he says. "I'll do my best to find out. I have contacts. But it's possible she might see him around. And I thought you should understand what she's been through, and what an effect it all might have on her." He doesn't add *in case it makes you change your mind about her*, but I know he's thinking it.

We sit quietly for a while.

Eventually, I say, my voice little more than a squeak, "What did the abuse involve?" Even as I say it, though, I know it doesn't really matter. She was twelve, and whatever he did would have had a profound effect on her.

"I don't know exactly what happened," he replies. "She's never spoken about it to me or Gaby. And Kaitlyn won't discuss it with me either. I only found out because I was still living with Dad when it all blew up, and when the police came around." His brow darkens. "Our family doesn't talk about stuff. It completely fucked us all up. Dad blames Kait, and she blames herself, too, enough so that she didn't tell us that Dad was the one who cheated first. I blame myself for staying in Wellington when I should have gone back to Christchurch to be there for her."

"Ah," I say, finally realizing why he's the way he is—withdrawn, quiet, and grumpy most of the time. "It's not your fault."

"Yeah, well, I was eighteen and frustrated as hell because nobody would talk about it. I couldn't deal with it, and I just wanted to get away from it all. But I felt bad about it, and I've always tried to look out for Belle ever since."

It explains why he's been so protective of her. I would have been too, if I'd been in his shoes.

"Look," he says, "I know she'll be angry with me for telling you, but you're my best mate, and I didn't want you to go into the relationship blind. I thought you should know. She'd hate me for saying it, but she needs protecting."

I nod. "Thanks." His brows draw together—he can obviously see how upset I am. "I mean it," I tell him with more feeling. "I'm glad I know."

Kaitlyn's comment to Belle that girls shouldn't think about sex makes more sense now. She must have been terrified about the effect Tom had had on her daughter, and she was trying to keep her safe. Unfortunately, all it did was make things worse. Now I realize why Belle was so confused about sex, and why she felt that enjoying it was wrong.

Ah, God. I put my head in my hands as I think about what I've done. Talking to her on the ferry and in the car about the most intimate things. Shoving my hands down the front of her jeans without a touch of romance, and making her come—me, an almost-stranger. I bought her a vibrator and made her use it while she told me in detail what she was doing—on the phone, for Christ's sake. She actually told me a couple of weeks ago when we were in Sydney that I've turned her into a nymphomaniac. She was joking, I know—she just meant that we've been having a lot of sex, and she's been looking forward to it. But even so...

"Oh holy shit," I mutter, pressing the heel of my hands into my eyes. "What have I done?"

"What do you mean?" Alex asks.

"Ah... jeez..."

"Damon..."

"I'm such a fucking idiot."

"Do you want to break up with her?"

I lower my hands and stare at him in surprise. "No, of course not. I love her, man."

He stares back. Then, out of the blue, he smiles. It's so unusual that it lights up his whole face. "Okay, then."

"It's just... I wish I'd known. I wouldn't have... I mean I'd have been more..."

"Juliette told me some of it," he says. He meets my eyes with a kind of exasperated amusement. I wince, thinking about that night in the Jag. "I'm still Belle's brother," he adds wryly, "so let's not discuss the details. But I think you've helped her, not hindered her. She's like a different girl now. Juliette said Belle's crazy about you. I knew that, obviously. She's always liked you. And I think you're good for her. So I guess the reason I came today was because I want the two of you to work out. And I don't believe in secrets in a relationship. I didn't think Belle would tell you, and I thought you should know. I hope I haven't done the wrong thing. She's going to be mad at me." He gives me a look that says *Women... what can you do?*

I feel warm all the way through. He wants the two of us to work out. He doesn't mind that I'm with her.

It doesn't assuage my guilt. I need to talk to her about it. But it does make me more hopeful about the outcome.

"So you're not going to walk away?" he asks.

"Of course not." I finish off the whisky in my glass. "I do need to discuss it with her, though. And I guess where we go from there depends on her reaction."

"Don't be surprised if she doesn't want to talk."

"I don't expect her to give me details. But we talk about everything else. And something like that... it's important to me that she feels she can talk to me."

He nods.

We sit in silence for a moment. My mind is whirling. I hadn't realized until now how worried I was that he would react badly to finding out about us. But he doesn't mind. I don't have to sacrifice my friendship or my business relationship to be with Belle.

It should fill me with joy, but the news overrides any pleasure I might feel. It physically hurts to think of what the beautiful, gentle Belle has been through, both with Tom and Cole. I wish she were here. But I can't talk to her about it on the phone. She'll be back at the weekend, and I'll have to bring it up then.

"Sorry," Alex says. "I can only imagine how hard it is for you to hear that."

"It makes me feel sick," I admit. "Fucking bastard."

"Get in line. I've wanted to take a flamethrower to him for years." He stares moodily into his empty glass.

"You in any hurry to leave?" I ask. When he shakes his head, I pick up the bottle. He leans forward, offering his glass, and I pour both of us a generous measure.

He stretches out his legs, puts his feet on the coffee table, and slides down so his head is resting on the back of the armchair. I do the same, making myself comfortable.

He lifts his glass. "To wives and mistresses."

"May they never meet."

It's a toast we used to give while we were at university. We thought it was hilarious back then. Now, we can barely raise a smile.

"To the women we know and love," I offer instead.

"I'll drink to that."

We lift our glasses, and drink.

I cough, then say, "I've got an idea."

"Oh?"

"Yeah. Tell me if you think I'm being an idiot."

"You're being an idiot."

I give him a wry look, then proceed to tell him my plan.

Chapter Thirty-One

Belle

My plane lands in Wellington mid-afternoon, and I disembark with a spring in my step, thrilled to finally be home.

It's not been a terrible eight weeks at all. The law firm I was working for was close to the harbor, and big enough to be impressive, but small enough to make me feel like a valued member of the team. I learned a lot about practicing law, which, like most professions I guess, is vastly different from studying it in books, and I met a lot of people and made plenty of contacts.

The biggest thing to come out of it, though, was that just yesterday, Margaret Bellingham, one of the senior partners, offered me a full-time job when I graduate. I know she's a friend of Mum's, and that Mum no doubt had a hand in that, but even so, I'm hopeful that I made a good enough impression so that it was an easy decision for Margaret to make.

Whether I take it… well, that's a whole other question. I asked her for a few days to think about it, and she said yes.

As I walk through the airport to the exit, my stomach flutters. Damon has come to pick me up. It's only been a week since we were together, but I can't wait to see him again. When I first went away, I thought maybe he'd realize while we were apart that his feelings for me weren't as strong as he thought they were, but he's come to see me most weekends in Sydney, and our relationship has gone from great to amazing over the past eight weeks. I don't know whether we'll talk about it tonight, but I know there's a conversation coming about our future together. I can't yet call how it's going to go, but bubbles of excitement and nerves rise inside me as I think about it.

I go through the turnstile, and I see him immediately, leaning against one of the posts not far away. He's hard to miss—tall, broad-shouldered, and incredibly good-looking, enough to draw the glances of most of the women and even some of the men passing nearby. He has a cocky insouciance I adore, as if he doesn't give a hoot what anyone else thinks of him. And he always looks a million dollars, with his sharp haircut and expensive clothes. Today he's wearing tight dark jeans and, as it's cold, a dark-gray sweater over a white shirt. Oh man. I could put him on a cracker and crunch him up.

He's already seen me, and he smiles as I run up to him, then laughs as I jump up into his arms.

"Ma belle," he says, swinging me around before lowering me to the ground and kissing me.

"Damon." I hug him tightly. "Oh my God, I've missed you."

"I've missed you too, baby girl." His deep voice murmurs in my ear, sending a shiver through me. He smells amazing. Oh, this man… please, God, tell me he's all mine for the rest of eternity!

"Let's get your case," he says, "and then we'll head off." He takes my hand and leads me over to baggage claim.

I chat away while we wait for my case to appear, telling him about the flight. He listens with a smile, but he's quiet, and he seems thoughtful and a tad… reserved? Maybe I'm imagining it. I'm on overdrive, and I can feel myself gabbling a bit, especially now I've got it in my head that he has something on his mind.

"You okay?" I ask as we go out of the airport.

He nods and puts his arm around me, pulling my case for me. "Yeah, fine. Look, I know you said you wanted me to drop you off at your house so you can unpack, but I wondered whether you'd come to my place first?"

"Can't wait to get your hands on me?" I tease.

He smiles. "Obviously." It doesn't reach his eyes, though.

Puzzled, I don't say anything as we cross to the F-type in the car park. He puts the case in the back, we slide inside and buckle ourselves in, and he heads out into the traffic.

"So come on," he says, "tell me how you've been. How did your last day go?" My new friends held a party for me last night, so we didn't get a chance to chat.

As he heads through the city to the suburb of Brooklyn, where he lives, I tell him about the party, and chat away for a while about the work I've been doing. He listens, asking questions occasionally, but he's definitely quieter than usual. He gave me a huge hug and kiss at

BEAUTY AND THE BILLIONAIRE BOSS

the airport, so I don't think he's about to break up with me or anything. But something's bothering him.

And then it occurs to me. Mum would have told Alex, and I bet he's let it slip.

As we pass the Prince of Wales Park and turn onto his road, I say, "You know about the job offer, don't you?"

He doesn't reply. He slows the car, navigating a roundabout, takes the turning left, and heads toward his house. After opening the garage door, he slots the Jag inside and turns off the engine.

He glances across at me. "Yeah," he says.

"Alex?"

"Yeah."

I roll my eyes, feeling a surge of frustration. My brother can be such a knob sometimes.

Damon unbuckles his seatbelt and gets out. I do the same, then stop. My brain can't catch up. I watch him unlock the door and go into the house, and scramble to get out and follow him.

"Hey," I say, closing the door behind me and following him into the kitchen. "When did you speak to Alex?"

"Last weekend." He opens the fridge. "Would you like a drink of anything?"

"No, thank you. How did I come up in the conversation? Were you calling him about work?"

He closes the fridge door. Then he leans back against the counter and folds his arms. "No. He turned up here on Sunday afternoon."

"At the house?"

"Yeah."

"Why?" I whisper. But I can guess. "He knows about us, doesn't he?"

Damon nods.

My mouth has gone dry. "What did he say?"

To my shock, Damon's lips curve up a little. "He pretty much gave us his blessing," he says softly.

My jaw drops. "Seriously?"

"Yeah."

"Jesus. I thought you were going to say he gave you an ultimatum—me or him."

He lifts one eyebrow. "I think he understands that if he did that, he'd be losing a friend and a business partner."

315

"Yeah, but I…" My voice trails off. "Wait, what?" I can't have heard that right. There's no way Damon would choose being with me over his friendship and working relationship with his best mate.

"There's no competition, Belle. I love Alex like a brother, but I love you more." He smiles.

Now I'm speechless.

We study each other for a good thirty seconds. I thought he'd be thrilled that Alex doesn't mind us dating, but he's not exactly swinging me around in his arms. Something's still bothering him.

"Are you worried about the job offer?" I say softly. "Because you needn't be. I'm not planning to take it. Sydney was fun, but I don't want to leave New Zealand."

He blows out a long breath, then studies his feet. Eventually, he looks up, walks over to me, and takes my hand. "Come with me."

He leads me into the living room, and gestures for me to sit on the sofa. Then he sits beside me.

"What's going on?" I say, starting to get nervous.

"Alex told me," he says. "About Tom."

I go completely cold.

"He had no right to do that," I whisper. I drop my gaze to where my hands are twisting in my lap.

When Damon speaks, his voice is very gentle. "He knows you're going to be angry with him. But he said he didn't think you'd tell me, and he wanted me to know so that I can support you, if you need me to. He told me because he wants us to work out, Belle."

Bile rises in my throat. "I didn't want you to know."

"Why?"

"Because I don't want to talk about it. And I didn't want you to look at me differently."

"Well, I'm afraid I do see you differently now."

My bottom lip trembles. My body is rigid, as I fight to hold in my emotion. Inside, I'm screaming, no, no, no!

He reaches out a hand, tucks a finger beneath my chin, and lifts it so I'm looking into his eyes. To my shock, they're full of kindness.

"I've always admired you," he says. "I thought you were clever and quirky and fun. But knowing what I know now… Belle, I'm absolutely astounded. You experienced something terrible, at such a young age, but you haven't let it define you. You've grown into a beautiful, bubbly, strong, confident woman, who could be, I'm sure, a fantastic lawyer, and yet you also have this inner magic, the Marilyn Monroe effect, that gives you this gift with children, and that spills over into all your relationships. I've watched you interacting with your friends and family, and you radiate warmth and generosity. You have a beautiful soul, Belle. You're special, and I love you so much for being so strong."

I'm so stunned, I can only stare at him.

"You don't have to talk to me about it," he clarifies. "It's in the past, and I'm not your therapist. We never have to mention it again, if you don't want to. But I need you to know that I'm here for you. If ever you want to talk, or if you just want a hug, you don't have to explain, but I'll be there. Because I love you."

"I thought that if you found out, you'd see me as tainted somehow," I tell him. "And I thought you'd force me to go through what happened. I didn't want to do that ten years ago, and I don't want to do it now. It's not that I want to pretend it didn't happen. But you're right, I don't want it to define me. I don't want to rake over the coals every week with a therapist, and I don't want to talk about it with my friends and family. I don't want them, or you, to see me as the abused girl. Does that make sense?"

He nods. "I went to therapy after Christian died, and a couple of times since. Sometimes it helps to talk. Mainly when I want someone to say yeah, you've had it tough, and it's okay to feel what you're feeling, to be angry or resentful or whatever. But I don't think it's the answer to everything. For some people it is, and that's great. But as you say, constantly going over it isn't right for everyone. Once you've accepted what's happened, I think it's okay to want to move on, and to find a way to heal."

My eyes sting at the realization that he understands. He's the first person who hasn't told me that talking will only make it better.

He clears his throat then. "I do want to say, though, that I'm so sorry for how things happened between us. For what I said on the ferry and what I did in the car, without thinking. If I'd known, I'd have been much gentler and more considerate."

"No," I say quickly, taking his hand as I fight against my rising emotion, "please don't say that. Don't regret what you did. You were so open and matter of fact—it was exactly what I needed. You've taught me that sex isn't something to be ashamed about. That it's okay to enjoy your body, both alone and with someone else. I can't explain what a revelation that's been to me."

He blows out a breath. "I thought maybe I'd done more harm than good."

"No. No, no, no. You released me from my cage, Damon. Don't ever think you've been anything but liberating for me."

I feel a lightness in my heart that I haven't felt before. I didn't want him to know, but now that he does, and after his sweet words telling me I have a beautiful soul, I finally feel the old wound closing over, to be replaced by something that's new, clean, and bright.

"Okay," he says, in a determined tone. "All right."

He gets to his feet. He slides his right hand into the pocket of his jeans and extracts it. A black velvet box sits on his palm. He passes his left hand over it, and does an acceptable sleight of hand, distracting my gaze. I can't help but give a short laugh when he opens his left hand to reveal the box has vanished. When I look back at where he'd actually kept the box in his right hand, it sits open, revealing an enormous diamond solitaire.

"I've been practicing that all week," he says. He gets down on one knee. "Michelle Winters, will you marry me and make me the happiest man in the world?" His gingerbread-brown eyes are wide, kind, and hopeful. "If you want to live and work in Sydney, I'll come with you. Or if you want to stay here and do magic on the streets or your wonderful children's parties, I'll do everything I can to support you. I want to marry you and have children with you. I want you by my side more than anything in the world."

I stare at him for a good ten seconds.

Then my face crumples, and I burst into tears.

"Oh crap," he says, and sighs. "I didn't mean to have this effect. Come here." He sits next to me again, pulls me into his arms, and leans back, taking me with him.

I curl up beside him and sob my heart out into his sweater. It takes a good ten minutes for me to calm down, and by that stage the wool is sodden, and partly covered with mascara. He doesn't complain, though; he just waits for me to stop, then gets up so he can retrieve some tissues and comes back to press them into my hand.

"I'm going to get us a G&T," he says. "I think we both need one. If you still want to go home later, I'll call you an Uber."

I nod, and he kisses the top of my head and goes off to the kitchen.

I get up, peer into the mirror hanging over the fireplace, and hurriedly try to clean up my face. My heart is racing, but I can't get my brain to focus enough to concentrate on the things he's just said to me.

With most of the smudged mascara removed, I turn and glance at the coffee table. He's left the velvet box there, open. The ring glitters in the late-afternoon sunshine. Oh my God. The diamond is enormous. It must be five or six carats at least. It would have cost him an absolute fortune.

Is this real? Does he really want to marry me?

He comes back in, without his sweater and carrying two glasses, and I let him lead me back to the sofa, where we sit, holding hands as we have a large swallow of the G&T.

"Oh, that's good," I say thankfully, and he chuckles.

He puts down his glass then, and cups my face. "How are you doing?"

"I'm okay."

"I'm sorry I made you cry."

I shake my head. "Don't apologize. It wasn't you. It was me. I just can't believe it, that's all."

"Can't believe what? That I'd want to spend the rest of my life with the girl who dispelled my curse?"

"Whatever you think, Damon, you're not a beast. You weren't cursed. You just hadn't met the right girl."

"Maybe. But you've been so patient with me. So understanding. You haven't pushed me, either. You've just let me be myself. And I can't tell you how much I appreciate that. It's the least I can do to reciprocate."

My eyes sting again, and I sniff to stop them falling. "Did you mean what you said about supporting me if I didn't go into law?"

"Of course. I told Alex that you didn't want to be a lawyer. He asked me if I'd let you throw away your years of training, and I said it wasn't about not letting you do anything. Whatever you want to do— if you decide you want to practice law because you've worked so hard at it, or if you want to follow your passion instead, I'll support you financially and emotionally. I just want you to be happy."

"I didn't think I had a choice," I say honestly. "I thought everyone would think I was an idiot if I didn't go into law."

"Education is never wasted." He hesitates. "Actually, I wanted to ask you something."

"Okay…"

"You know I'm president of the Women's Refuge here in Wellington?"

"Yes."

"Even if you decide not to practice full-time, I thought maybe you might like to give free legal advice to the women about restraining orders, custody battles, and divorce. They're desperate for help, but often they don't know where to start."

My jaw drops. "I'd love to do that," I whisper. "So… I could do that, and still do the children's parties?"

"That was my thought."

Emotion swells inside me. It's the perfect answer. How does he always know exactly what to say to me?

He picks up the box from the coffee table, takes out the ring, and holds it out to me.

I put down my drink and stare at it. "It's so beautiful," I whisper.

"Alex helped me choose it. The jeweler thought we were gay."

"I can imagine Alex's face."

"Actually, he went along with it. He put his arm around me and said, 'He's every man's dream.'"

That makes me giggle. I can't continue to be mad with my brother. Not when he obviously wants us to work out.

"You still haven't answered me," Damon says softly.

"Oh honey. The answer's yes. Yes, yes, yes." I lean forward and kiss him. Then, gently, I take the ring from him and slide it onto my fourth finger. It fits perfectly. "I've never seen anything like it in real life," I whisper. "Thank you so much."

"It's only what you deserve." He watches me observe the way it sparkles in the sunlight. Then he leans forward, puts his arms around me, pulls me toward him, and lies back so I fall on top of him. I laugh, kiss his nose, his cheeks, his eyelids, and then his lips. Mmm…

"You're the best kisser in the world," I tell him when I eventually lift my head.

He chuckles. "That's a nice thing to say."

"I'm so lucky."

"Me, too. Not every story has a happy ending like this one."

"Are you thinking about Christian?"

"Yeah. And your mum. And even Lewis."

He told me a week ago that Lewis quit his job at Kingpinz. I guess he couldn't get over what had happened, especially when in his eyes his manner didn't constitute harassment. I know Damon's upset over it, although he hasn't said much.

Leaning on his chest, I hold up my hand and look at the ring again. "Do you really want to marry me?"

"I do." He smiles.

"Where would you like to get married?"

"I don't know. I thought... maybe... in church?"

My eyebrows rise. "Really? Have you found your faith again?"

He links his fingers with mine, so the diamond glitters in the middle. "I feel... hopeful. When I was younger, I had blind faith. Now I feel as if I'm coming at it from an adult point of view. I know it has its flaws, and I have lots of questions, the same ones everyone does, like why does God let bad things happen? But I'm beginning to realize that those questions can coexist with a belief in a creator. I'm just kinda letting it happen, you know?"

I nod, a lump in my throat at his words.

"And anyway," he adds, "I like the idea of the big wedding. You in a beautiful gown. Me standing there waiting for you. The light from the stained-glass windows on the floor."

"You're just an old romantic."

He doesn't argue. "I think... maybe I feel that Christian will be there, if we have it in a church."

"It surprises me that you always paint women," I say. "Maybe you should paint Christian as an angel?"

His eyebrows rise. "I've never thought about that. Perhaps I will."

I smile and touch my lips to his. I'm about to move back, but he slides his hand into my hair to hold me there, and it turns into a long, sensuous smooch.

"You're so good for me," he murmurs when he eventually lets me go.

"I think we've healed each other," I tell him honestly.

"How many kids do you want?" he asks.

I laugh. "Plural?"

"I want a multitude."

"Of angels?"

"Yeah, but I'll settle for four."

I laugh. "Why?"

"I don't know. Obviously, we don't have to start until you're ready. But I like the idea of trying to get you pregnant." His eyelids fall to half-mast as he gives me a sultry look.

"We don't have to try for a baby to do that," I tease.

"Yeah, but the thought of coming inside you and making a baby…" He slides his hands to my butt and rocks his hips against mine. "It gets me all riled up."

"I think you're permanently riled up."

"That's true, when you're around."

Humbled by how much he wants me, I kiss him. "I love you," I whisper.

"I love you, too." He gives me a lovely smile.

So I kiss him again, as the late-afternoon sun slants across us both, making the diamond on my finger glitter.

Epilogue

Damon

Eight weeks later

"I love it," Kennedy says. Then she bursts into tears.

"Jesus." I roll my eyes and put my arms around her, looking up at the painting of Christian that I've just revealed to her. "I don't know why I have this effect on women."

It's August, and Belle and I are having an official engagement party for friends and family. Kennedy and I have left most of the guests in the living room to come into the studio so I can show her the painting, but I didn't expect this reaction from her.

Jackson, her husband, chuckles as he walks up carrying baby Eddie. "It's not you," he says. "She's a bit hormonal at the moment, aren't you, sweetheart?" He smiles.

My eyes widen, and I look down at her as she moves back. "Are you...?"

She smiles and nods. "Twelve weeks."

"Oh Ken, I'm so happy for you." I give her a big hug again, and she laughs as she tries to wipe her eyes.

"It really is amazing," she tells me, looking up at the painting. "I know you've made him into an angel, but you've really captured that mischievous look he used to have."

"I'd like you to have it," I tell her softly. "If you want it."

"Oh Damon, really?"

"Yeah. I think he'd much rather watch over you and your children than me."

"I'd love it," she whispers. "Thank you."

"Does she like it?" Belle asks, joining us in front of the painting.

"It's wonderful," she whispers.

"It was Belle's idea," I reply, putting my arm around my fiancée. I kiss her temple, and she turns her head so I can kiss her lips.

"I'm thrilled you're engaged," Kennedy says. "And I'm so excited about the wedding! December isn't long to plan everything!"

"I know," I reply, "but neither of us wanted to wait until next year."

"It's well doable," Belle says, "with plenty of planning. It's going to be huge!" She grins.

"I didn't think you were the sort who'd want all the fanfare," Jackson says to me, amused.

"I want it all," I tell them. "Several hundred guests, a big church do, and Belle's going to wear a gown fit for a princess. And we're going to the northern hemisphere for a honeymoon."

"We're traveling from London right across Europe by train," Belle says enthusiastically, as we all start walking back to the living room. "It'll be amazing."

"You'll have to take millions of photos," Kennedy says.

"Oh God, yes. Everyone's going to be so bored with my Insta account." Belle giggles, and Kennedy links her false arm through Belle's as the two of them walk off, talking about dresses.

"That'll keep them occupied for a few months," Jackson says with a grin. He hefts Eddie in his arms. "Let's get you a drink, little fella." He wanders off to the kitchen, and I hear my mother asking Eddie whether he'd like some juice.

Smiling, I walk over to where Alex is standing looking out at the view of Wellington, sipping a whisky.

"Is that the Balvenie?" I ask him, nodding at his glass. I bought the forty-year-old sweet, honey-filled whisky for the occasion. I knew he'd appreciate it.

"Yeah," he says. "It's great. Want me to get you a glass?"

"In a minute. I've got something to ask you first."

"Oh?" He lifts an eyebrow.

"Yeah. You're going to be my best man, right?"

He looks genuinely taken aback. "Really?"

"You must have guessed I'd be asking," I say, amused. "I thought we had an unspoken agreement."

"That was years ago. I assumed you'd have Saxon or Kip, or maybe both of them."

"Nah. They're cool, but you're my best mate." Like most guys, we rarely talk about our emotions, but I'm feeling unusually warmhearted today, and I want to spread my good cheer. "You've always been there for me," I tell him, "right from the early days."

He gives me that rare gift—an Alex smile. "I should have guessed you'd end up with Belle. I can still remember you singing *Michelle* to her when I introduced you. She was only six, but she lit up like a Christmas tree when you told her it meant beautiful."

I look over at where she's standing talking to Kennedy, Alice, and Catie, laughing at something that Kennedy's said. "She's the best thing that ever happened to me." I look back at her brother. "So, you'll do it?"

"Of course," he replies, and he gives me an uncharacteristic bearhug.

"Aw," James says, coming up behind us with Henry and Juliette. "That's really touching. Brings a tear to my eye."

Alex moves back and gives him the finger, and we all laugh.

"I meant it," James protests.

"Yeah," Juliette agrees, "Alex, honey, you're so sarcastic and grumpy, and it makes a change to see you showing some emotion."

I give a short laugh at the look on his face. "She has a point."

He has a mouthful of whisky. "Happiness is overrated."

"Ha!" She grins. "We'll see. I've noticed you spending a surprising amount of time in the physio room when someone's mum is around."

"Are you talking about Mistletoe?" I ask, amused.

"Yeah, Finn started his therapy in May. It's funny how often Alex is around when Missie comes in to pick him up." She flares her eyes at Alex.

He scowls. "Don't start."

"She's single."

"Juliette…"

"And you're single…"

"I'm warning you."

"I know you like her," she states. "Your face does that thing when you see her."

"My face does not do a thing, and I'd appreciate it if you contain your fantasies to your own love life."

"Remember," she says, "pineapple is a great safe word."

"What?" Belle walks up just in time to catch the last sentence. "Wow, I totally have to be a part of this conversation."

We all laugh, while Alex glowers.

"We're teasing him about a client," Juliette says. I think she's had quite a few glasses of wine, because she doesn't normally provoke him as much as this. "Her name's Mistletoe Macbeth."

"Oh what a great name," Belle says.

"It's a ridiculous name," Alex replies. "She sounds like a stripper."

"I wouldn't say that to her face," Juliette points out. "It's not a great way to start a relationship."

"We're not having a relationship."

"Yet."

"Juliette!" He yells her name.

She jumps. "All right, keep your hair on."

"Stop interfering. I don't need any help with my love life."

"You're single and have been for over a year. It looks to me as if you need all the help you can get."

"Yes, I'm single, and I'm quite happy being that way. So for God's sake, stop bothering me. I'm going to get another whisky." He strides off to the kitchen.

Juliette looks at us and pulls an 'eek' face. "Think I touched a nerve."

"He likes her," I reply, "and you know he gets embarrassed. Stop pushing him. If he wants to ask her out, he will."

"But he's so dour," she says with exasperation. "She'll assume he doesn't like her."

"Well, then he'll have to work extra hard to make it obvious," James tells her. "Should be fun."

"I'll get the popcorn," Henry says, and we all chuckle.

Belle turns to me and puts her arms around my neck. "I hope he settles down soon. If he ends up half as happy as I am right now, he'll be a lucky man."

"Bleugh." Juliette rolls her eyes. "I need another glass of wine."

I chuckle. "Don't listen to her." I kiss Belle. "Not long now, and I'll be able to call you my wife."

"Mrs. Chevalier," she murmurs back. "I can't wait."

Smiling, I kiss her again, while our family and friends give a big cheer that fills me with happiness.

Newsletter

If you'd like to be informed when my next book is available,
you can sign up for my mailing list on my website,
http://www.serenitywoodsromance.com

About the Author

USA Today bestselling author Serenity Woods writes sexy contemporary romances, most of which are set in the sub-tropical Northland of New Zealand, where she lives with her wonderful husband.

Website: http://www.serenitywoodsromance.com
Facebook: http://www.facebook.com/serenitywoodsromance

Printed in Great Britain
by Amazon

29441555R00185